## "YOU DON'T WANT TO HOLD ME?"
## ARLISS ASKED GIDEON.

She needed to lose herself within his warmth and his strength.

"I am holding you," he said. He tightened his arms around her.

"And to have me? Don't you want that, too?" Beneath her she felt the stirrings of his desire.

He didn't bother denying it, though from his groan as he eased her back onto the bed, she knew he wished he didn't want her so badly.

Well, she wished she didn't want him either.

He was slow with her, deliberate. Each touch was singular, and yet melted into the next one. . . .

He kissed her eyelids shut, kissed her in places where there had been clothes and now there were none. . . .

Outside it glowed bright, the moon lighting every flake of snow and filling the air with winter candles. Inside, deep within Arliss, something glowed and burned so brightly as to put the moon to shame. . . .

## SWEETER THAN WINE

## THE MARRIAGE BED

# A Kiss To Dream On

## Stephanie Mittman

A Dell Book

Published by
Dell Publishing
a division of
Bantam Doubleday Dell Publishing Group, Inc.
1540 Broadway
New York, New York 10036

ISBN: 0-440-22554-X

Printed in the United States of America

Published simultaneously in Canada

November 1998

10  9  8  7  6  5  4  3  2  1

OPM

This book is dedicated to:

—my husband, Alan, who listened to every word and made suggestions while cheering me on;

—my friend Bernardine, who read each successive draft and said it got better and better;

—my friend and critique partner, Sherry, who despite "stuff" in her own life always had time to kick ideas around;

—my former editor, Laura, who could have seduced and abandoned me and didn't quite;

—my new editor, Christine, who valued my opinions of her suggestions;

—my agent, Irene, who held my hand, patted my back, and told me it was time to play with the big guys;

—my daughter, Arika, who said she is proud of me;

—my son, Asa, who was a whiz of a Web master even when he had papers of his own due;

—and to every single reader who has ever liked my work, especially those of you who have taken the time to let me know.

I appreciate you all more than
I could ever put into words.

# Chapter One

⤂⤃

**G**IDEON FORBES RECOGNIZED THE LOOK IN SLEVIN Waynick's eyes. Heck, he'd seen it a million times before—that sudden knowledge that the limb he'd climbed out on was cracking beneath him. And same as always, he was expecting Gideon to catch him before he hit the ground.

"What do you mean, you just can't go through with it?" Gideon asked, wincing at the racket Slevin was making. "Slick," as he was better known to everyone but his mama, was rushing about the room yanking open drawers and throwing whatever he could find toward the open valise on the bed. Every slammed drawer, every squeal of the floorboards, pierced Gideon's aching head. Served himself right, he supposed, for spending half the night trying to drink himself into oblivion.

"It means I ain't packing this bag so as I can head on over to the church," Slick said with a sigh, as if Gideon was the one being difficult.

"Don't your word mean nothing no more?" Gideon demanded, grabbing the razor he had lent Slick out of his friend's hand before it was packed in with the other belongings. He'd be lucky if Slick didn't walk off with the rifle he'd left in the corner.

Slick shrugged, flashing Gideon that stupid grin that had been getting him out of trouble ever since they were little. He carefully slid several folded dollar bills into his pocket and then raised his hands in mock surrender. "Go ahead and shoot me, Gid, but I just can't do it. I just can't stay here in this town and be piss-pot poor all my life. Look at it this way—what have I got to offer a girl like Arliss?"

"It sure as hell beats me," Gideon said. "But money's the last thing she's after. God help her, she'd be content with just a hand to hold, now and then. Or a shoulder to lean on . . . I don't know. What do you think a girl like Arliss wants, anyways?" As far as Gideon could see, Lissie didn't long for fancy things. He'd never heard her ask Slick for anything more than a smile when he was touching the bottom of the well.

"Maybe it ain't so much what *she* wants, as what I want to give her," Slick hedged.

"Maybe it ain't got nothing to do with her, and it's what *you* want that we're talking about. Elsewise you wouldn't be willing to embarrass her in front of half the town. Not with the way people talk around here."

Slick ignored him, placing a new black Stetson on his head and studying himself in the mirror. He angled the brim down far enough so that Gideon couldn't see his eyes, but Gideon knew that bigger plans than marrying Arliss were dancing in his head.

"You ain't really thinking of just up and leaving that girl, are you? I've seen you do a mountain of stupid stuff, but I ain't never seen you be outright mean before," Gideon said. Then again, maybe he just hadn't been looking. Maybe he'd been closing his eyes all this time. Maybe the truth was that being friends with Slick had meant being around Lissie—talking to her when he could muster up the courage, watching out for her, keeping her safe.

Not that it had ever been his place. And not that he ever thought she wanted him protecting her heart. But damn it all, he'd rather give up a slice of his own hide than see her hurt.

"Don't do it."

The words came from so deep inside his soul that he couldn't have silenced them without a lead bullet in his gut. His head ached in the silence, throbbing mercilessly while he waited for Slick to see reason.

"Gotta," Slick said, running his tongue across the scar that split his lip and saved him from looking too perfect, too girly. Gideon had given him the fat lip and the scar when they were both boys, long before he'd learned to control his temper and to use words to get what his fists were after. "It ain't like I'll be gone forever. I'll be back."

Gideon figured he would be, when the money in his pocket was gone. With Slick it was always the money. And that was precisely why Gideon had to let him go. Because what Slick wanted most, more than Arliss even, was money. And if Gideon told him what he suspected about Lissie's prospects, then it'd be the money, and not Lissie that Slick was staying for. Arliss would be just a bonus, not the prize.

"I never meant for it to go this far. Honest I didn't," Slick said, sitting on the bed with his head in his hands. "You know I ain't ready to be halter-wise. In a way I'm doing her a favor, Gid. Really I am."

"Some favor—leaving her at the church. If someone did a favor like that for Berris, I'd break both his legs and carry him down the aisle before I'd tell my sister she was getting left at the altar."

Slick fastened his traveling valise and hefted it to check the weight. With a callous shrug, he said, "Guess I'm lucky Arliss ain't your sister then, 'cause I'm getting on that ten o'clock train and there's nothing short of them two broken legs that'll stop me. But you tell her I'll make it up to her. You tell her that I'll—"

"What do you mean, 'you tell her'?" The pain in Gideon's head was sinking into the pit of his stomach where it knotted tightly. "Don't go expecting me to do your dirty work for you. I ain't telling her a damn thing. I don't even want to be on the same side of Granite when *you* tell her." Gideon could just imagine the tears streaking down that freckled face of hers.

"You're just gonna leave her waiting at the church?" Slick asked with eyes that looked at Gideon as if he were the one doing Lissie wrong.

For a moment, Gideon felt that way, too. When it came to Lissie, his senses just got all knotted up like a horse's tail. But of one thing he was sure. He'd lay down in front of a stampeding herd before he hurt her. "You're the one leaving her," he corrected. "So if you're bent on going, you best get." Maybe it would turn out better for them all if Slick left, though he was sure Lissie wouldn't see it that way at first. Maybe she never would.

"I'm going," Slick said. "But I just can't believe you ain't gonna go over to the church and tell Arliss. It'd surely be easier coming from you, her knowing how much you like her and all."

The back of Gideon's throat itched just thinking about how he'd find the words to tell her. He hoped that Slick was wrong about Lissie knowing how he felt. It was the embarrassment of his life that he carried a torch for a woman who only gave him leftover smiles. "Why're you doing this?" he asked. Lissie was prettier than a mountain stream glistening on a July afternoon. She had a ready smile, an easy laugh, and legs that went on further than a man had a right to look—even if it was by accident that he'd caught her with her skirts hiked up that day at the creek.

Slick pointed at his reflection in the mirror. "That man don't deserve a woman as fine as Arliss Mallard. Not yet, anyways."

And then it dawned on Gideon like morning over the mountains. One minute it was dark, the next the sun was blinding. "You gotta game, don't you? In Butte? Helena? You gotta game on your wedding day and for a deck of cards you're leavin' that little girl who's countin' on your name and a nice bitty house somewheres to cook your meals and raise your babies. You got a winning hand here and you're gonna cash in your chips and move on, ain't ya?"

Slick pushed the rickety pine dresser away from the wall and reached behind it to pull a small velvet bag from its hiding place. "And what if I don't want them babies, Gideon?"

The pouch, clutched tightly in Slick's hand, turned Gideon's stomach and set his resolve in stone. Slick was right. He didn't deserve to be Lissie's husband, didn't deserve to lie down next to her at night and wake up beside her in the morning. Even if that was what Lissie thought she wanted.

"What if what she wants and what I want ain't the same?" Slick continued. "All she wants is for me to spend my life in some two-bit close-collared town that thinks a dance hall with a few felt tables upstairs is some Sodom and Gomorrah, and a visit with the girls on Lilac Row every now and then is sure to buy me a one-way ticket to hell."

"Lissie ain't like that and you know it. But this ain't

about Lissie. I can see that." He held out his hand, palm up, for the pouch. "You're right about Granite, though. It might be a close-collared town, all right, but you'd be hard-pressed to find any town that abides stealing these days."

"You playing deputy with me, Gid?" Slick asked.

He tapped the star on his chest. "It ain't play no more. Guess I know what's in the pouch, don't I?"

"Jeez that hurts, Gid. It really hurts. I'd never doubt *your* honor." He reached for his valise, but Gideon took a step closer, and it was all Slick could do to keep his balance and not fall down on the bed in Gideon's wake.

"I'll ask you one more time what's in the pouch," he repeated. How many times had the two of them faced off like this in the past few months? And how many times had Gideon backed down for Arliss's sake and because he wanted to believe that Slick wasn't rolling downhill so fast that the man's elbows and knees ought to be scraped to the bone?

"I didn't steal 'em, if that's what you're thinking," Slick said. "Everyone knows she was careless and lost them. And after she said they meant so much to her, too."

"She *thought* she lost 'em," Gideon corrected. Lord, Gideon had turned the damn town upside down searching for them little garnet earbobs Slick had given Lissie for their engagement.

"Oh no," Slick said with a shake of his head. "She lost 'em all right, and I found 'em. I'd never take 'em back, and if I did, I'd do it honest and open-like. But you know how careless Arliss can be. It's just the way she is. About everything. And you can't go blaming that on me. Strictly speaking, none of this is my fault."

"Give 'em here," Gideon said, his hand still out-stretched and waiting. "And then you'd best catch your train."

"They cost me ten bucks," Slick complained.

Gideon pressed the tips of his fingers against Slick's ribs and shoved him so hard that Slick had to grab at the dresser for balance. "I thought they were your grandma's," he said with more than a hint of sarcasm. "I remember quite distinctly Lissie showing them off and bragging on how they was family heirlooms."

Slick tried the lopsided grin again. Gideon wasn't having any. "Give me the damn earbobs, or I'll run you in for theft."

"I don't know what you're so mad about," Slick said, reaching into his pocket for the pouch. "They ain't even real gold."

Gideon chewed at the inside of his cheek and waited, his hand out. At least he'd have something to give Lissie to soften the blow. Maybe he could tell her that Slick sent the earrings for her and promised he'd be back. And maybe by the time he did come back, *if* he did come back, it wouldn't matter anymore.

Slick dropped the small dark blue velvet sack into Gideon's waiting hand. The bag was about as heavy as a bird's under feather, and Gideon guessed the earrings were worth about as much. Except of course, to Lissie.

Now all he had to do was figure out what to tell her. And untie his tongue long enough to get the words out.

"You know there ain't nothing better out there than you got right here," Gideon reminded him. "And you ain't got much time to come to your senses." All he could think about was sweet Lissie, her dancing eyes overflowing with tears, and how he could stop Slick in his tracks if he really wanted.

"Can't stay in this town another minute," Slick said. "There's a world out there waiting on a man like me. I got a way about me that's gonna make me a fortune before I hit twenty-five."

Gideon caught sight of their shadows on the wall. The truth of Slick's words was painted by the sun on the whitewashed plaster. Where Slick had had the sense to stop growing before he had to duck through doorways, Gideon had passed him and nearly everyone else in town. Only he and Lissie's pa could light the candles in the church without a ladder. Where Slick could buy one of them ready-made suits down at the dry goods store and have it look like it was handstitched for him right down to the black-on-black embroidered vest, Gideon had to order his clothes from the special catalog at Hughes' Mercantile that gave him a choice of light or dark brown trousers, and shirts in white or blue.

It wasn't easy to admit that Slick was right. Where Gideon was plain, Slick was a sight to behold. And it wasn't just the man's size or that smile of his—there was something special about him. Something that had kept all of Granite making allowances for him over the years, cutting him the slack they'd never allow the average man. Something that convinced the old men to indulge him, fancying themselves like him in their youths. Something that had the young men envying him and, like Gideon's fifteen-year-old brother Cluny, imitating his every move.

Something that had been wearing mighty thin of late, but it didn't seem to Gideon that the other men had noticed.

Not that Slick's appeal was reserved only for the men. There wasn't a woman in Granite that didn't blush and titter when Slick flattered her, no matter how outrageous his lies. Well, Berris didn't bite, of course, but then she'd developed some sort of immunity to Slick's charms over the years. The others bit. Lissie bit the hardest.

So, if Granite was any measure, Slick was surely right about his effect on men and women. Especially women.

Yup, a woman could lose her heart when a man like Slevin Waynick, all big blue eyes and wavy black hair, hugged her. Should Gideon, a giant whose messy brown hair matched his worn calf boots, try holding her tight, she could lose her ability to breathe.

"But it's Lissie," he said finally, when there was nothing else to say, no way for him to understand Slick's callousness. "How could you do this to Lissie?"

Slick bit at his lip, worrying the scar, as if for a moment he might actually change his mind. Then he shrugged. "Look Gid. If Arliss is so all-fired great, why don't you just go on and marry her? You ain't got bigger plans than that anyhow. For me, when it's all said and done, she just ain't worth it."

Gideon was a slow man to anger. Some folks praised him for that, while others found fault. He'd learned early in life that a man could do a lot of damage before he got his temper under control. And the likelihood was that he'd regret what he'd done when he'd cooled down. Slick's lip was only one reminder. But there were limits to every man, and Slick had pushed Gideon to his limit and beyond. He heard the bells and whistles in his head, warning him that he was losing control, but the rush of anger that came barreling up from his gut felt too good, called too loudly, and it drowned out all warnings.

In one swift movement, Gideon had Slick pinned to the wall with one hand, feet dangling like a marionette waiting for the show to begin. His free fist struck deeply into the man's belly, knocking the air from his chest in a rush. Slick raised one eyebrow at him, as if to ask if

Gideon's anger was spent and whether he might be set back on the ground.

Like everything else about Slevin Waynick lately, it grated on Gideon's nerves. He punched the wall beside Slick's pretty face, hoping the pain that raced up his arm would register in his head. Maybe it was all the booze he'd consumed, maybe it was all the years of standing in a smaller man's shadow, maybe it was that stupid half-smile just begging to be wiped away.

He couldn't help himself. While ashamed, he also felt a deep satisfaction when he heard the crunch of bone and saw the blood gush down Slick's face and onto the man's fancy gambling suit. Shocked at his callousness, he let Slick down to puddle at his feet, the starched white shirt turning red below the string tie. While the body before him crumbled, he slammed his fist against the wall where he had already punched the real thing.

At his feet, Slick heaved, both hands clutching his nose. "She sure as hell ain't worth this!" he said spitting blood with the words.

He'd have liked to break him then, just pick him up from the floor and snap him like some twig. But then Lissie would take pity on what was left of him, and Gideon wasn't prepared for that.

"Get up," he said instead, throwing a towel in Slick's direction. "I wouldn't want you missing your train."

Slick rolled to his knees carefully, wincing with each movement. The blood had made Gideon forget about the first punch he'd thrown. Slick would probably be sore for a week. Lissie would be hurting for a much longer time.

"You'll be sorry you did that," Slick said as he made a fist with one hand while holding the towel to his nose with the other. Gideon waited, sure the man wasn't stu-

pid enough to try fighting back. One thing Slick possessed was a strong sense of self-preservation. "When I
come back for Arliss and—"

"You don't want to miss that train," Gideon re-
peated, reaching for his rifle. He wasn't as foolish as
Lissie. He knew nothing would bring Slick back to
Granite while there were bigger fish to fry.

Slick climbed up, using Gideon as a ladder, hand
over hand until he was on his feet. "I think you mighta
broke a rib."

"Then you better see a doctor in Helena," Gideon
said. "You'll want that nose looked at, for sure."

"You goin' to the church?" Slick asked. For a minute
Gideon was fool enough to think that Slick was asking
to walk along with him, do right by Lissie, see the thing
through. But then Slick, one hand pressing against his
nose, reached for his valise, and Gideon turned on his
heel and headed for the door without looking back.

Outside he put his collar up against the first fall
winds as he headed north. In the distance he could see
the spire of the Granite Methodist Church set against
the smoke rising from the refinery. The smell made him
sick to his stomach.

"Tell her I'm sorry," Slick shouted from behind him.
He sounded like he had a real bad cold. "And I'll be
back."

Gideon didn't bother acknowledging that he'd heard.
The last thing he wanted to tell Arliss Mallard was that
Slevin Waynick would be back. No, that was the next to
the last thing. The last thing he wanted to tell her was
that the man she was waiting to marry was gone.

# Chapter Two

A RLISS LEANED AGAINST THE SIDE OF THE CHURCH trying to calm her breathing down, trying to stop the spinning in her head. The sight of Gideon Forbes in the distance momentarily comforted her, the way it had so many times in a past that was just laced with disasters. But when there was no sight of her groom, when it was clear that Gideon was walking up the path alone, her breakfast came barrelling up her throat and . . . well, at least she'd been careful enough to miss her new pale kid boots.

"Where is he?" she asked after she'd reluctantly accepted Gideon's clean white hankie and wiped her face. "It's after ten o'clock."

"You're sick," he said, touching the corner of her mouth with his sleeve. His eyebrows seemed to frown along with his lips. Gideon always looked as sad as Slick looked happy.

"Where's Slick?" she repeated, carefully controlling her breath so that she wouldn't appear as frantic as she felt. There was no sense in jumping to conclusions, even ones as obvious as this. She had to be mistaken. After all, Slick had promised. He'd sworn.

Gideon ignored her question. He put a big hand under her arm and with a surprisingly gentle tug tried to pull her from the wall. "I'll take you home."

"I'm not going home," she said to him, as if by will alone she could make Slick appear. "I'm getting married, today. Now."

The sad way he looked at her was worse than anything he could have said.

Still, she asked again. "Where is he?" Slick had told her long ago that Gideon made it a rule never to play poker. Now she saw why, as his eyes darted in the direction of the train whistle and then fell to the ground.

Instead of confirming what she supposed she already knew about Slick, what she'd always known in her heart, he told her again, "You're sick. I'll take you home." Two whole sentences. For Gideon Forbes this was a long conversation, more than he usually said to her in an entire afternoon.

"He isn't on that train, Gideon, is he?" she demanded, her breath coming in hard little puffs as she fought against dry heaves and the truth. "Tell me you didn't let him get on that train."

"I'll just go tell them inside that you're sick." It was as though he refused to hear her as he gently let go of her arm and took a step back to make sure she was steady enough on her own two feet.

"Botheration, Gideon! I'm not sick," she said, heaving and sobbing and sliding down bumpily against the church siding. "I'm . . . I've a . . . that is, I'm practicing lullabies, Gideon. I'm . . . in the family way." As an afterthought she mumbled, "But it seems I've got no family."

Even through her tears she could see it shook him. He spread his feet slightly, as if he could withstand the blow more easily that way, and tipped back his hat to swipe at his brow. "Did he know that?" he asked real softly, quietly, as if it would be their secret.

She couldn't look at him. A man like Gideon Forbes couldn't possibly understand. For sure he'd never wanted something so badly that he'd let himself be fooled into believing the unbelievable. He'd never been so strongly tempted that he'd allow himself to do something he knew he shouldn't do.

"Did he?" His voice was stronger this time, harder, before he softened it with her name. "Lissie? Did he know?"

She nodded. Why else did Gideon suppose Slick ever agreed to marry her? And why else would he have run?

"I could wire the sheriff in Helena," he offered. "After I take you home."

She shook her head. She could get on the next train and follow him, but if he didn't want her here in Granite, he wasn't any more likely to want her in Helena, where there were women and gaming tables and . . . "My money!"

She'd given him all her savings to make arrangements for a suite of rooms in Mrs. Bailey's boarding house. No wonder the woman hadn't seemed to know what she was talking about this morning. Arliss had let herself believe that Slick had made Verna Bailey think the rooms were a surprise.

Just like she'd convinced herself that Slick would be there this morning. Just like she'd convinced herself that he'd be there when she swelled like a watermelon and presented him with an extra mouth to feed. Just like . . .

"What money?" Gideon asked, his voice drifting down from way above her.

Any woman could fall in love with the wrong man

and get carried away by passion—but to turn over all she had, even when all she had was eleven dollars and eighteen cents! It was too embarrassing to admit. She opened her mouth to speak, but no excuse came out. Gideon Forbes surely thought badly enough of her without knowing the extent of her stupidity. Lord knew she'd given him enough reasons over the years.

And every time he'd caught her, he'd just shaken his head at her, a soft half-smile forgiving her stupidity again and again.

Except of course, that time she'd fallen out of a tree Slick had dared her to climb. She'd lain on the ground laughing afterward, and Gideon had actually growled at her like some papa bear sick to death of his cub's shenanigans. *You coulda got hurt,* he'd hollered at her, and Slick had told him he was scaring her—standing over her like some giant and making noises.

But she hadn't been scared. Not of Gideon. Maybe his hugeness seemed like a threat to Slick, but to her it had been a comfort, always.

And Lord, she needed comfort now.

Someone knocked on the stained glass panel above her head, signaling that it was time for the bride to get herself to the front hall of the church.

"Oh dear God!" she whispered. "All those people in there waiting."

"I'll take you home," Gideon said for the millionth time. "Or do you want me to get your pa?"

"My pa? No, don't get him, poor thing. He's arranging all his flowers in there like the right arrangement's gonna make up for the wrong groom. He thinks I'm just having an attack of nerves out here. What'll I tell him?"

"He'll understand," Gideon said, leaning his rifle against the church and crouching down beside her. Even so, his head was far above hers. One hand hung limply between his knees, the knuckles bruised. Slick had said Gideon had a gift for stopping a fight with words, and if that failed, just one of his punches could put an end to a riot. She supposed there was some hungover cowboy or miner waiting in the church and wearing one of Gideon's shiners like it was a medal. "Everyone'll understand."

"No." She said it so calmly she actually surprised herself. "My papa won't. There isn't a person in there that will. And I can't say as I blame them. Decent women are gonna cross the street to avoid me. Every man will think he can have his way with me. Remember Rose Perkins? How everyone turned their backs on her? How no one even came to the funeral when her baby died? Papa had to provide those flowers for nothing so that at least that baby would go out of this world right and proper."

She looked up at Gideon and sniffed. Someone banged again on the window and she heard the church doors open. Her father called her name—once, twice, a third time.

"Do you have any money on you? Enough for a train ticket somewheres? I could leave town before anyone knows, and you could tell them Slick and I just ran off and eloped. That would work. And I could get a job somewheres and—"

Pulling his cuff down over the heel of his hand, Gideon brushed at her tears and dried her face. He pushed the hair out of her eyes and dusted at her cheek, looking every bit as sad as she felt, then shook his head at her. "I don't think so," he said, dropping his eyes to her belly shyly as if she needed any reminding.

"I don't have any choice," she admitted with a ragged sigh. "There's a whole church full of people just waiting to say 'I told you so' about Marcus Mallard's *wild child*. It would kill my pa."

Gideon frowned at her as if she were some child talking gibberish. Slowly, tentatively, he reached out and petted her, his hand tracing her back so lightly he was almost not even touching her. It was truly amazing that a man so big could manage to be so gentle. It was all she could do not to lean into him, get lost in him. "There's another choice," he said, followed by so long a pause she was sure he was just trying to come up with something, anything, to keep her calm. " 'Fore you say no outta hand, promise me you'll think about it."

"Oh, Gideon," she sighed. "I don't want to have Slick arrested." You couldn't order someone to love you and put him behind bars because he didn't. It would be nice, but still you couldn't do it.

"I'll marry you, Lissie," he said. At least, that was what it sounded like. But she was weak, and tired, and the church bells kept ringing above them, and clearly she hadn't heard right.

Okay, it was probably true that Gideon did have a soft spot for her, like Slick was always saying. But still, a man, any man, would want to know the woman for whom he was giving up his freedom loved him. Gideon certainly couldn't believe that. Why, this was the first time she'd ever looked close enough to see that his brown eyes were flecked with gold.

And a man would want to be first with his wife, even if he didn't wait for the Lord's blessing before they went ahead and cleaved. And Lissie wasn't just ruined. For the love of God, she was carrying Slick's seed in her womb! Gideon couldn't want her. She was just so crazy with shame she was hearing things.

Gideon backed up from her a step or two. "If you don't want to . . . "

"Want to?" she asked, this time studying his lips intently as he spoke, so that there'd be no mistake.

"Lissie?" her father called. He was closer, probably not more than a few feet away, but Gideon's bulk hid her from him. "Slevin? You out here? Everyone's waiting."

Gideon looked over his shoulder and back down at her. His eyes locked with hers. "Marry me."

Slick had gotten down on one knee in the snow. He'd kissed her hand—the palm, not the back—and promised her a ring, and flowers that would put her father's to shame, and given her his grandmother's garnet earrings. And in exchange he'd taken her innocence.

No. That wasn't fair. She'd given him that—her gift to him for finally asking.

Then, of course, being Slick, he'd hemmed and hawed about a date until a few weeks ago when she'd told him she was carrying. But he had vowed he loved her and would stand by her, and went straight away to the minister to set the date. And then that night, in the dark, what she'd let him do . . .

And even after that, he'd run out on her and her baby. Lord, but she was dumb. Loving a man who was only interested in planting his seed in her, and then leaving her to face the town alone.

And did he care? She'd been an idiot, one of those pathetic morons born with only half a brain, falling for a man like Slick.

Gideon stood towering over her like an oak tree in the rain, sheltering her just by being there. He rubbed his hands on his pant legs, watching her. He even managed to look hopeful instead of trapped. Well, wouldn't it serve Slevin Waynick right if she did marry Gideon

Forbes? Wouldn't that be something when he came back for her and she was the wife of Deputy Forbes?

"Gideon? You seen Lissie?" her father asked, and she watched as he shook his head. "I'll try the other side. I don't know where that girl . . . " His voice drifted away.

"Why would you want to do this?" She kept her voice down, not wanting her father to hear her and return. Again she brushed at the hair in her eyes and smoothed the front of her dress in a hopeless attempt to make herself presentable.

He shrugged and raised an eyebrow at her as though she ought to know the answer to her own question. It brought to mind each and every time he'd rescued her from some mess Slick had suckered her into. The time she'd worn the beautiful dress Slick had presented her with for the Miner's Ball, only to learn that he'd stolen it off Hattie Agrin's clothesline. Lord, how Gideon had blushed when he'd told her she'd have to return it and she'd fingered the buttons as if she meant to take the dress off right there in the Grange Hall!

And then there was the time she'd gotten drunk on Slick's special fruit punch and taken off her stockings and climbed into the horse trough on Elm Street. She'd been more slippery than an eel when Gideon, his breath ragged and his heart pounding against her own, had finally fished her out.

And then there was the time she'd gotten lost in the blowing snow on the way to meet Slick, and Gideon had managed to find her. Oh, but he'd been mad at her then!

Still, he'd covered for her, over and over—each time making up some excuse for the foolish things she'd done.

"Habit?" she suggested to him.

"Something like that," he agreed. "You know what they say about a friend in need—"

"Arliss Mallard, where are you?" her father demanded, his quavering voice at odds with his angry words.

"Over here, Marcus," he called over his shoulder, then stepped aside so that her father could see her plainly standing within his shadow.

It took a minute for the crowd to figure out what was going on. Gideon didn't blame them, he was not too clear on what had happened himself. No doubt they all supposed he was just some overanxious best man, waiting at the front of the aisle for the bride and groom to show up. But he was the only one waiting there when Marcus walked down the aisle with Lissie, and he was the one that stayed there with her after her father kissed her gently and took his seat.

The Reverend Lambert leaned forward and inquired in a whisper as to Slevin's whereabouts.

"There's been a slight change in plans," Gideon said. Beside him, poor Lissie looked a little unsteady, and though he hesitated at first, he decided it would probably be best if he put his arm around her waist. It felt like heaven, that tiny little waist of hers finally in his hand. He didn't even care when the people behind them gasped and began whispering.

"Gideon!" Berris's gasp was ripe with the shock of the entire congregation. He didn't bother to turn, not even when he heard his father order his sister in hushed tones to sit back down.

He could hear Slick's name bouncing off the arched ceiling, and he bent slightly at the knees and the waist until he could whisper near Lissie's ear.

"You're sure?" He certainly didn't want to force her into anything.

"If you are," she answered, looking wholly miserable.

He wasn't the least bit sure, but he nodded at the reverend anyway and reluctantly let go of Lissie's waist.

It was a blur leading up to the moment when Reverend Lambert asked him for the ring. At first he just stood there, gawking at the reverend's request, staring at the man's waiting hand. And then he remembered his duty as best man had been to hold the ring for Slick. He reached into his jacket pocket and produced the copper band of flowers Lissie had pointed out to Slick at Hughes' Mercantile months ago.

The reverend instructed him to place it on her finger, and Gideon took her tiny hand into his huge one. Clumsily he slipped the thin band onto her wedding finger. He heard the catch in her throat and kept his eyes focused on the coppery band, wishing he'd convinced Slick to get her a gold one. He studied the tiny fingernails, clean and shiny, the cuffs of her sleeves—he looked anywhere but at the eyes he knew damn well would be shining just a little too bright.

"You may kiss the bride," Reverend Lambert said softly, finally. And Gideon leaned down, never more aware of how small she was, how fragile and delicate, and kissed her very gently on her lips, barely brushing them with his own.

And it was done.

No shouts, no cheering, no egging them on to *do it again!*, to *do it longer!*, to *put more feeling into it!* the way it usually was at a Granite Methodist Church wedding.

Just "I now pronounce you man and wife," and a shocked silence that wasn't his alone.

The day he had dreamed of since Lissie's thirteenth

birthday party, when she'd scandalized all the other girls by allowing each boy to kiss her once on the cheek, had arrived.

It wasn't exactly all that he'd been anticipating over the years.

But then it wasn't what she'd been wishing for either, he supposed. He wasn't suave like Slick, wasn't handsome or smooth, or even just plain fun. When he said anything at all to a woman, it wasn't ever the right thing. He was big and awkward, and probably downright scary to a little bit of a thing like Lissie.

And not only was she not in love with him, she was in love with someone else. And within her, growing, was a child to remind her of what she'd had, and lost.

The reverend wished them health and happiness and fulfillment, which Gideon figured they sorely needed, and he thankfully left out all wishes for being fruitful and multiplying, which Gideon knew they did not.

They turned away from the altar and Gideon hoped that Lissie had found a smile to paste on her face. His own was a little shaky as he faced the crowd.

"Never thought I'd see the day," his father said, shaking his head in the same bewilderment Gideon supposed everyone was feeling. Gideon certainly felt it.

"Where did Berris go?" Gideon asked, watching Cluny shake hands awkwardly with Lissie as if he hadn't known the girl his whole life.

His oldest sister, Juliana, stood off to the side with Jeannie clinging to her skirts. She whispered to her husband and beamed like a lighthouse. The little family inched their way toward him and Lissie.

"Home," his father said, settling his hat back on his head. "To prepare. Arrange. You know."

He didn't know. Hadn't any idea.

"You leave your room clean, son?" His father's eyes

studied Lissie intently, as if he, too, had never seen her before.

And then it hit Gideon like two sticks of dynamite tied to a boulder. Lissie was coming home with him. She'd be living with Pa and Cluny and Berris.

And sleeping with him.

Berris looked around her brother's room as if there was a hope of setting it to rights. And as if she had even the smallest inclination to do so. Despite the opinion of more than one of her acquaintances—especially after she'd refused to go to the last ice cream social with Johnny Phelps—Berris was nobody's fool. Her father might think that Arliss Mallard had suddenly come to her senses. Her baby brother might think that the bigger the man, the more a woman would want him. Her sister might think that love won out. But Berris knew better.

She pulled the covers down off Gideon's bed and reached for his sheets.

For years—oh, heck and hightops, *forever*—Arliss had looked through Gideon like he was some mist rising off the Columbia River and if she waited long enough he'd just disappear.

And usually he did, Berris thought, as she dragged the linens to the doorway and shook her head.

Everyone knew that the only reason Arliss even tolerated her sweet bear of a brother was because he was usually attached to that idiot Slick Waynick's side.

And now they were supposed to be in love? Oh, yes, certainly. And the fields would plow themselves and the mines would belch up their copper and Carson Maddigan would ask her to marry him and . . . well, maybe the last would happen, if she were really, really lucky, but the rest? She thought not.

Berris stared at the bare mattress and tried to picture her brother sharing it with anyone. Even Marmalade, the cat, didn't fit in there with Gid.

Knowing her brother, he'd offer to sleep on the floor and let Arliss roll around in comfort. The man was too sweet for his own good and as usual it fell to her to protect him.

Well, there was only one thing to do. With a quick hand, she scooped everything off Gideon's dresser and marched down the hall to her room. Gideon and Arliss would have to have their father's bed, which could be put into the bigger room that she and Juliana had shared. Berris would have to move into Gideon's.

Barely married an hour and Arliss Mallard was already turning their world upside down.

Just wait until Samantha heard about the new Mrs. Forbes. Didn't it just serve her right for skipping the wedding! Berris sat down on her bed and allowed herself one quick minute of self-pity at the injustice of a woman like Arliss winding up with the sweetest man in all of Granite, Montana. Heck and huckleberries, Gideon was probably the sweetest man in the whole state.

And Berris had always harbored this little tiny hope deep in her heart that her best friend Samantha and her brother . . .

And now that awful girl, who looked more like some wanton from Lilac Row with her hair always tangled from the wind and her clothes mussed . . .

Throwing down Gideon's brush and comb and collars onto her bed, she assessed her room with the eyes of her new sister-in-law. The title stuck in her throat. Arliss Mallard was related to her. For life.

Maybe Berris was the only one who hated her. Maybe there wasn't another person in Granite who thought that Arliss Mallard was a stuck-up girl who was too self-centered to see beyond her own turned-up and very freckled nose.

But then maybe the rest of them hadn't seen Gideon watching her and wishing. No wonder Arliss's father was positively beaming when he gave the girl away.

She'd have been happy to give Arliss away, too.

Ecstatic.

If it had been to anyone but Gid.

After the reception where everyone stood around looking at the ceiling or the floor and talking too loudly about what wasn't important and too quietly about what was, Gideon walked his new wife and his father-in-law back to the clapboard house they lived in and tried to come to terms with what he had done. His *wife*. His *father-in-law*. The words didn't seem to have the meaning that they should. They seemed to have no meaning at all.

"You go on up and get your things together, honey," Marcus said to his daughter. "Gideon and I will just wait down here on the porch for you."

Her eyes only went as far up as Gideon's neck before she nodded and hurried into the house. He wanted to help her, but the thought of touching her things—her clothing, her hairbrushes, the bottles and sacks and boxes that women had their private things in—made his hands shake. He shoved them into his pockets and stood on the porch rocking on his heels and looking over what was left of Marcus's garden.

"Cut everything that was blooming for the church," Marcus said, standing close enough for Gideon to recognize that the brand of bay rum Marcus wore was the same as his own. He bet Slick wouldn't have smelled like Lissie's father when he'd kissed her in front of God and most of Granite.

He bet Slick would have done something scandalous, like used his tongue for the kiss. And Lissie would have taken a tiny little bite and he'd have screamed and she'd have laughed and . . .

"So how do you expect to play this out, son?" Marcus asked him.

"Sir?"

"Everyone in that church came to see my daughter marry Slevin Waynick. Which isn't to say that there weren't those of us thinking God had to be watching over us to make things come out the way they did. . . . Still, people are going to wonder. People are going to ask."

"Think so?" Gideon fiddled with a loose nail on the porch railing, stalling for time. He liked Marcus, liked being able to talk to someone without being self-conscious about his size. Did Marcus know about Lissie's condition?

"Well, *I'm* asking," the man said. He was older than Gideon remembered. His skin was paper thin and hung in folds down his face like a lady's fine handkerchief that had been in the bottom of her pocket too long.

"Don't suppose we could call it a miracle and leave it at that, huh?" Gideon asked as casually as he could. Lissie was his wife. If that wasn't a miracle, what was?

"My guess is Slick ran out on her," Marcus said evenly. "You wanna tell me why?"

"He found out about us." The words just popped out of his mouth, unbidden, unplanned. They hung in the air, drifted down to the garden and took root as Marcus nodded.

"Thought maybe I'd scared him off when I told him the rumors about Lissie's grandpa being wealthy weren't gonna put food on his table or scotch in his gullet." He looked hard at Gideon, sizing him up, wondering what Gideon's own expectations were, no doubt. As if it would take money for Gideon to want to marry Lissie. As if whatever amount her grandfather did or didn't leave her would make any more difference to him than it had to Marcus all those years ago when he'd run off with Honora Mallard. Gideon had always seen it as a measure of their affection that neither had ever appeared to regret the decision. "Wouldn't have minded if I had scared him off," Marcus added. "Especially the way things turned out."

Gideon nodded, taking the compliment for what it was. He'd always suspected Marcus wasn't fond of Slick. And Marcus hadn't even known that Slick had said more than once that he'd marry for money in a minute. And that Honora Mallard had been a fool to give it up. Well, Gideon supposed that he, too, was a fool because if a man had a woman like Lissie, he just couldn't see needing anything more. And he aimed to stand as proof of that.

He remembered with a bitter taste in his mouth Slick speculating about whether or not Arliss could make her grandfather's heart melt. Gideon expected Lissie could make any man's heart melt and had been foolish enough to say so. But that had been years ago, long before Mrs. Mallard had passed on and her pa hadn't so much as sent flowers to the funeral. Not that there hadn't been a million of them everywhere, all hand-raised and picked and cut by the man who had taken her from all that she knew and given her all he had to offer—love and flowers. It was as happy an end as Gideon looked forward to, and then some.

"I hear there's trouble up at Belmont's Columbia Mine again," Marcus said, staring at Gideon's hands where they were splayed on the railings.

"Every town's got its troubles," Gideon said, jamming his hands into his back pockets. "If it ain't a mine owner, it's one of them cattle barons. And if it ain't some miners blowing off steam on a Saturday night, it's a bunch of rowdy cowboys. From what I see crossing my desk, we got it better than most towns west of the Mississippi."

Maybe he was simplifying things a little bit for Marcus, playing down the growing discontent in order to give the man a little peace of mind. Or maybe Gideon's father was right, and Gideon was making more out of it than necessary. He hoped so, at any rate.

"I worry for Lissie's sake, you know," Marcus said. "She's awfully fond of those miners up in Coppertown, and life can change so fast. Seems the ground can shift in a minute and leave you standing in quicksand where just a moment before you had rich soil oozing up between your toes."

Marcus spoke like that a lot, saying one thing, meaning another. Sometimes Gideon had no inkling what the man really meant. But he knew what the man was hoping to hear and was glad to be the one to say it. "Lissie's my wife, Marcus. I'll take good care of her."

Marcus nodded. "I know you will," he said. "You're a good man, Gideon Forbes. A compassionate man. The kind of man who'd take the hurt upon himself before he'd let someone he loves come to any harm."

Gideon had rarely heard his praises sung and wasn't real comfortable with the tune. He wondered if Lissie was packing every stitch she owned and wished she would hurry.

Finally she came out of the house. She was struggling with a suitcase and Gideon grabbed it before the screen door slammed behind her.

"So you'll be living with your pa, then?" Marcus asked.

"Just for now," he said quickly, realizing how much Lissie was probably dreading it. Not that he blamed her after the way Cluny had stared at her and Berris had left without even wishing them well. Berris had hated Arliss since that November years ago when Gideon had finally gotten up the nerve to ask her to dance at one of those ridiculous Miner's Balls. Arliss had told him she was hoping Slick would ask her. Dutifully, he'd trotted over to Slick and paid him a nickel to dance with the girl Gideon was already dreaming about.

He could still remember the smile on Lissie's face when Slick had bowed at the waist and held out his hand to her. She'd been thirteen, just like Berris, but her curves had begun and they'd left Gideon weak at just the thought of them pressed against his own chest the way they were plastered to Slick's.

It was the last time he'd confided any disappointment to his sister regarding Lissie, but the damage had already been done. Berris wasn't one to forgive and forget.

"It won't be so bad," he said as he gingerly put his hand under her elbow to help her down the porch stairs.

"Your ma would be real happy," Marcus said, and the big man's voice caught in his throat. "She used to say how mallards—the ducks, you know—mated for life, and that we did, too. Think I'll go out to the cemetery and have a little chat with her. About time I brought her some good news."

"Good-bye, Pa," she said, staring at the house she'd grown up in as if she'd never see it again, as if she were moving clear to the Klondike instead of just to the other side of town. "I'm glad you're happy."

Gideon was glad, too. *Hell,* he thought. *Someone* ought to be happy on his wedding day.

They left Marcus at the corner of Main and Church, turning their separate ways, and walked the next block in silence.

"Are you sorry?" she asked him, so softly he had to bend to catch her words.

"No," he said honestly. He had his doubts, that was for damn sure, but he wasn't sorry.

There was only silence as they walked on. He didn't dare ask her the question in return.

On the 10:30 train to Helena, Slick sat with his head back, one hand pressed against his nose. The other fiddled with the coins in his pocket, keeping time to the clanking of the big steel wheels and the steady rhythm of the rocking train. Man, but he ached.

He still couldn't believe that Gideon had turned on him like that. Sure, it had been a rotten thing to do, leaving Arliss at the church, but it wasn't like he'd be gone forever. Just long enough to make some real money. There were only Milquetoast tables over at Dawson's place—penny ante stakes for henpecked husbands. The merchants didn't bet and the miners made so little at the Columbia Copper Mine that there was little to risk on cards or dice. A man couldn't get rich in a town like Granite.

In Helena there was bound to be some real action.

He winced as he fingered the garnet earbobs he'd lifted back out of the good deputy's pocket when he'd climbed back up from the floor. His nose was surely broke, and he thought there was a good chance his rib was, too. Still, he was on his way to bigger and better things while Gideon was still stuck in Granite. The man, for all his size and strength, was a fool—always playing by the rules, living by some code of honor only he could understand, never letting loose or having any fun.

And it sure did grate on him that Arliss had taken lately to praising the good deputy. Why only a few weeks ago she'd even thrown Gideon up to him when he'd suggested bending the law just a little bit and borrowing Doc Agrin's rig for a ride in the moonlight. Sometimes he even got the feeling that Arliss was sweet on Gideon.

But sometimes he just didn't have much sense.

Maybe when he was flush he'd tell her how sorry he was by getting her a nice necklace to match those earbobs, and maybe even a dress for when he took her out on the town.

Pressed against the back of the seat, his head bobbed as the train lurched and he bit at his lip to keep from calling out. Gideon was the one that ought to be sorry. When Slick got back from Helena, he'd make him pay. Just a month in Helena—two at the tops—and he'd go back for Arliss. And he'd tell Gideon how he'd made more in a night than Gideon made in a month. Slick had heard that even Nathaniel Hill himself sometimes sat in for a few hands. He'd show Gideon and everyone else what he could do given a fair deal and half a chance.

Sure, he might have to go as far as Anaconda. Everyone knew that since the mother lode came in there the miners fought each other to get to the tables and lose their money. But it would be worth it.

And there was always Virginia City if Anaconda didn't pan out. The copper barons all hung their hats in Virginia City. Men who'd made their fortunes in silver and gold and precious gems sat at the tables with anyone who had enough to see the stakes. Men like Arliss's grandfather. And he had a few choice words for him as well.

If that didn't work, Montana was a big state. If worse

came to worst, he could always go east to where the cattle barons were all settled.

And jeez, there was always Butte. He sure wouldn't mind getting a firsthand look at Butte. Not that everything they said about the women there could be true, but he wouldn't mind finding out for himself.

First thing, though, he'd get his nose seen to and his rib set. Then he'd look for some tender loving care while he did a little recuperating.

And then there was a fortune to be made. A table never called to him that he didn't hear and answer. And there was a table in Helena that was singing his name.

Wherever he needed to go. Whatever it took. And then he'd surely be back for Arliss before she really needed him.

# Chapter Three

ARLISS WENT AROUND TO THE BACK DOOR WITH GIDeon, same as always, but this time felt funny to her. She tried to convince herself that it was because Slick wasn't there with them. Maybe it was, because Gideon seemed to sense it, too, his hand stopping before he reached for the knob.

"The front?" he asked. Or maybe it was more of an offer, like he was willing to treat her as a guest or something.

"No need," she said, not really wanting to change the way things were between them—which was just plain ridiculous considering she was Gideon's wife now. Good glory! Gideon's wife!

"Maybe I oughta—" he began, staring at the screen door while she busied herself with noticing how tidy even the back porch was. Noticing too, that while there was a garden ripe with the foliage of early fall, row upon row of cabbage stumps and spent squash blossoms, trellises heavy from a successful season of peas and beans, there wasn't a flower to be seen.

"Aren't you going to carry her over the threshold?" Berris's voice came from beyond the screen door and

Arliss could just make out her form, arms crossed and foot tapping.

Gideon looked at her, then back at the screen door, and put the suitcase down.

"Want me to?" he asked, so ready and willing to make this the day she'd been hoping for. Kind as it was of him, pretending wasn't gonna make a clear stream out of a mud puddle, especially the one she'd jumped into with her eyes wide open. She shook her head and pulled open the screen door.

"Kind of old-fangled," she explained to Berris, who looked her over from messy head to soiled toe and clearly wished her anywhere else. Arliss figured Berris had some choice locations in mind—a collapsed shaft at the Columbia Mine, the rapids at the Flint Creek, Hornet's Pass . . .

"I see," Berris said, nodding as if she were Gideon's mother instead of his sister. "Well, is it old-fashioned to keep company before showing up at the altar? Is it *old-fangled* to marry the man you're engaged to? Because I certainly wouldn't want you doing anything old-fangled, Arliss."

"Don't start," Gideon warned his sister, but apparently that wasn't enough to stop her.

"Oh no," Berris agreed, changing her tone but not her meaning as she waived a hand about in the air. "We want you doing just as you please, your own sweet way. Just whatever you want," she added, trailing off.

Gideon grimaced at his sister, his jaw clenching.

Berris, for her part, grimaced, too. And then she shrugged her shoulders as if there simply wasn't anything to be done about the situation. Arliss didn't believe for a second that Berris was done with her, not even when she gave Arliss a quick hug and waved them into the room. "Well, come on in then, you two. Imagine you loving my brother in secret all this time. Why, I can hardly believe it!"

Well, Arliss was sure that made three of them.

Gideon was still standing there with her suitcase in hand, as if he wasn't certain she was staying. He seemed like one of those old men who had been through the great war and never quite recovered from the horror of it. He stood silent, not saying anything to his sister, not saying anything to her. Above them, all the louder for their silence, heavy feet moved slowly with much thudding and thumping.

"Dad and Cluny are moving around some furniture," Berris explained with a smile as phony as any of Slick's promises. "You might want to help them get the double bed for you and your bride." She said it like a challenge, a dare, and kept her eyes locked with Gideon's.

He nodded, put down her valise to take off for the bedrooms, seemed to realize that that was where the case had to go, came back for it, and lifted it again. Had he uttered one word to her since they'd left her father's house? Even when he'd bent to pick the one flower her father had overlooked and given it to her, he hadn't said a word.

Slick would have told her how pretty she looked, even though it wasn't so. He'd have taken that last rose of summer and threaded it into her hair and told her that it paled in comparison to her beauty. He'd have told her where they were going and assured her of the plans he had for the day, and the night, and the next five years. Even if none of it had been true.

Gideon had handed her the flower and pointed with his chin in the direction of his house.

And now, after a sharp word of warning to Berris to "watch her tongue and let Lissie be," he'd gone off and left her alone with his sister, who was pouring them each a cup of tea. Arliss watched her like a hawk, waiting for her to slip in some poison, more than willing to drink it.

"So all this time behind Slick's back," Berris said, shaking her head like she'd just seen a hummingbird in winter. "And he never knew. None of us did. Why I'd swear even Gideon didn't know! You are a wonder, Arliss Mallard."

"Arliss *Forbes*," Lissie corrected through gritted teeth. God damn Slevin Waynick for putting her in this position, leaving her to Gideon as if she was just one more of his messes. But if Berris had any plans to box her into a corner, she'd better be prepared for Lissie to fight back. Of course, Berris had better ammunition than Lissie, who was standing on a steep ridge in a stiff wind, wild Bannocks coming up behind her.

She couldn't exactly deny what Berris said about her loving Gideon in secret because then her new sister-in-law would think, and rightly so, that she'd simply taken advantage of Gideon's good nature and would have yet another good reason to hate her. On the other hand, if she said Berris was right, then she was a two-timer and a cheat, and Berris would have every right to hate her for that.

So she said the only safe thing she could think of. "This is a very nice kitchen." She said it as if she'd never been in it before.

"I'm so glad you like it," Berris said, all cheery, as if they were now the best of friends. "Because you'll be in it a lot. A full man is a happy man, you know. And it takes quite a bit of cooking to fill Gideon's big body."

"I've been cooking for my father since my mama passed on," she answered, raising her chin a bit. Just a look at her pa and anyone could tell he was no spring sapling bound to bend in the wind. "If I could keep him fed and full, I suppose I can keep Gideon satisfied."

Berris raised an eyebrow and looked her over slowly. Really slowly. With only Lissie's spoken words hanging in the air between them.

Like some rodent cornered by a rattler, Arliss kept her eyes fixed on Berris, returning dry grin for dry grin while her mind raced upstairs and into Gideon's bedroom. What had she been thinking when she had agreed to marry that mountain of a man? A man about whom she knew so little despite knowing him so long? Of course she would be expected to satisfy Gideon. In every way. Why else would he have married her? Why else did a man ever marry a woman? Her mother's admonitions had been branded on her brain, but when she had been alone with Slick down by the river, with the moon full, and the little kisses behind her ear, and . . .

Well, that was behind her, and she was prepared to see her duty through with Gideon. In fact, contrary to what they all thought, she intended to make Gideon the best wife in all of Montana.

It was the least she could do after what Gideon had done for her.

Not to mention how sorry Slick would be then.

"I'll satisfy your brother," she repeated, blowing on the hot tea and then taking a sip. "I'm a very good cook."

Slick had told her she was good at the other part, too. That he'd been with enough women to know, and that she was just a rung or two below the best. And, having no desire to be as "good" as the women on Lilac Row—having been warned against those "desires" from the day her skirts reached the floor—she'd been more than happy with the compliment.

Actually, she really didn't know what she was doing that was so right, lying there in the dark with her legs spread and letting him do what a man needed to do. But it was a comfort to know that at least she hadn't done anything wrong.

Just thinking about it was embarrassing. No wonder they called them private parts and it was only done after the sun went down. At least that way no one saw anything they shouldn't be seeing.

She thought about lying in the dark with Gideon beside her. She and Slick would talk for hours after— him telling her about how rich they'd be and how happy; her decorating their house in her mind and making him choose the colors for the walls and the pattern for the sofa.

"And then there's Lester Pincus down at the jail," Berris went on. Arliss wasn't certain she'd ever actually stopped talking, or if she'd even taken a breath. Berris probably could talk the paint right off the walls. "And any other prisoners that might be warming the bunks. Since mama passed on, I've been responsible for the breakfasts and dinners, and Juliana's been seeing to the suppers. Now that you'll be the woman of the house, I guess you'll want to be seeing to all that."

"I guess," Arliss said. She'd never cooked for anyone but her father, who had always praised her cooking like she was that famous cookbook author, Mrs. Beeton herself. She surely did have a soft spot in her heart for Lester Pincus, and it was the least she could do to contribute to the household anyway. It wasn't like she was looking for a free ride from Gideon and his family, most of whom were clomping around upstairs and shouting things like "Turn it!" and "Tip it!" and "Watch your back, Gideon!"

She figured it was a little late for that last warning.

"You can start with breakfast in the morning, if that's all right. That way I can stop off at Verinda Ruth Tenbrink's for a trim before I go over to Samantha's for the day."

"Samantha Maddigan's? I heard her brother Carson is home from Virginia City," Arliss said in a sing-song voice, getting in a little jab with her own needle. Berris's dislike for Arliss was like the sun on Echo Lake at sunset. It came right back with blinding force. "Is that why you're dropping in at Verinda Ruth's?"

"Carson's home?" Berris asked, looking for all the world like she didn't give a swirling pollywog about Samantha's brother. Not that Arliss understood the attraction. Carson Maddigan scared the daylights out of her and everyone else in town, walking around with a loaded pistol on each hip and a twitching trigger finger on each hand to match—as if the town wasn't any more civilized than Last Chance Gulch.

As far as Arliss knew, Berris was the only one with nerve enough to be friends with Samantha Maddigan. Arliss was willing to bet, though, that for all her bravado, her new sister-in-law wasn't brave enough to talk to Samantha's brother directly.

"Slick saw him yesterday down at the train station," Arliss said. Now why hadn't she thought to ask Slick what he was doing down there, anyway? Why had she let him distract her with stories about Carson and the two saddlebags he was carrying which Slick reckoned were full of reward money?

"Really?" Berris asked, that eyebrow of hers flying again. "I suppose you were telling him good-bye yesterday? I mean so that you could marry my brother today?"

o     o     o

Gideon allowed how supper could have been worse. His head could have split open at the dinner table instead of just throbbing like some grizzly was sitting atop his shoulders.

Or Cluny could have made some of the bawdy comments in front of Arliss that he'd made while they were moving beds. As it was, the boy stared at her like he was memorizing her so he could watch for what would be different in the morning.

And then, just when he thought things might be all right, what with everyone making a fuss over Lissie's melt-in-your-mouth biscuits, Juliana had to show up with Jeannie like that, without Ezra, saying she wanted to have a little heart to heart with Lissie since she didn't have no mama. That must have gone great. Still, if his niece hadn't been content to ride on his shoulders and touch the ceiling, she might have started to cry and Lissie would have found out how little he knew about children.

That would have been worse.

Or worse would have been Berris coming right out and saying she'd be checking the sheets for stains in the morning instead of just mentioning, ever so casually, that they weren't to worry about the brass headboard being right up against her wall because she was a very heavy sleeper.

And while he was supposing the worst, he guessed his father could have come right out and said he was glad to see that all Gideon's dreams had finally come true, as surprising as that was, instead of just sitting there beaming like a gosh darn campfire on the desert. Of course, Thaddeus could have been that happy just because he figured Arliss's cooking had to be better than anything Berris made.

After dinner Gideon had rushed Lissie away from his

family and they'd sat on the porch swing until the house had gone all quiet. The crickets were crazy with the first flush of fall in the air. And in his head words began to accompany their tune. *What were you thinking?* they asked. *When you asked her to marry you, what were you thinking?*

He'd wanted to shout that he wasn't thinking or he'd have never asked Lissie to be his. It was what he got for all the drinking he'd done the night before. The woman was curled so close to the far end of the swing that she was nearly falling off it all in an effort to avoid him.

"Are you cold?" he asked, using the question as an excuse to touch her face, trace the line of her little nose to its end. "I could get you a shawl."

"Oh, I like the fresh air," she said, backing away still more so that he was afraid she'd go right over the arm of the swing and wind up on the porch floor.

And then they fell silent again, at least as silent as the crickets allowed.

"I suppose you think you're doing the right thing, keeping poor Lester Pincus in jail," she said after a while.

"The man did shoot four horses," Gideon said, wondering what choice she thought he had. "For looking at him the wrong way, at that."

In the moonlight he could see her shaking her head sadly as if the man deserved her sympathy. She made little noises that sounded an awful lot like she thought Gideon didn't understand, which, to be truthful, he didn't.

"It's not like you to be mean, Gideon," she said, almost as if she were surprised that he'd lock up someone as dangerous as Lester Pincus.

He wanted to ask her if she expected him to let a man who went around shooting other people's horses

roam the streets? A man who was a danger to himself
and everyone around him. A man who'd clearly lost his
marbles and could do real harm—*had* done real harm.

Not that he actually said anything like that. No, he
just sat there with his tongue tied around his molars,
and answered "fish" when she asked what Lester liked
for breakfast, and "fish" when she asked what he preferred for lunch. "Fish," he said again if she was making
him supper. "Any ways," was his answer when she
asked him how Lester liked his fish.

Later, when they were creeping up the stairs quietly
to the bedroom, he thought that it might have been
funny to have answered "fine," but it was too late.

He opened the door to their new bedroom for her,
glad to see that his sister had gussied the place up some.
Despite how she felt about Lissie, Berris still had put
on their ma's old pillowcases with the lace edging and
the embroidered hearts and flowers on the fronts, and
the wedding ring quilt at the foot of the bed. He and his
father had brought Berris's dresser into his old room
and carried his into this room, along with his ma's highboy for Lissie's things.

And now here they stood in his sister's room, he and
his wife, staring at the fancy brass bed his parents had
slept in, and the window that looked out on a nearly full
moon, and the flowered walls his sisters had once
fought over. Anywhere but at each other.

All day he'd wondered about it, but now his heart
pounded wildly in his chest when he thought of crawling into the bed beside her, of pulling her into his arms,
of covering her body with his own. In just minutes he
would be feeling the softness of her skin, tasting the
sweetness of her lips, smelling the flower scent that
lingered around her hair. For years he had drifted off to
sleep imagining Lissie beside him. And now, the mo-

ment finally at hand, he could do little more than swallow and blink and stare while she ran her hand over the quilt his mother had always treasured.

"I'll just go down the hall and wash up," he said finally, then reconsidered. Well, he'd finally gotten a thought out and it wasn't the right one. It'd be better to let her go first. Then she could get into her night things later, while he was out of the room. A woman would probably like a little privacy in the beginning. Soon enough he'd see in real life what he'd only glimpsed in dreams. "Maybe you should go first and then I'll . . ." his voice trailed off as he opened the door and pointed down toward the doorway beyond Cluny's room.

She pulled some things out of the suitcase he'd set on the chair. Swallowing hard, she pulled a long white gown from the leather bag and shook it out before laying it across the bottom of the bed.

And then she was gone and he was standing alone looking down at the most beautiful nightdress he'd ever seen. Not that he'd seen anything beyond the no-nonsense ones his sisters and his mother had worn, and then only the necks of those, sticking up out of their robes or wrappers.

This one had lace around the top edge, which wouldn't even come close to Lissie's long neck. It had little flowers sewn in white thread in stitches he had never seen—little balls, ones that looked like daisy petals, even one that was wide and flat like a ribbon. Mrs. Mallard, who'd been tutored as a girl and raised to be a lady, had wound up a seamstress, sewing fine dresses for the wealthier women in Granite to wear to the Miner's Ball each year. He remembered that Lissie would complain about helping her finish in time and how exacting her mother was about doing the job perfectly.

Berris could sew on a button so that it would never come off again. And Juliana could hem a cuff and mend a tear. But this was like a painting—white on white—a drawing in the snow.

He was fingering it when she slipped back into the room.

"It took me nearly four months to make it," she said, her face shiny from the cold water she'd rinsed with.

Four months. She was telling him this nightgown wasn't made for him to see, but for Slick.

"Nice," he muttered as he grabbed up his toothbrush and powder and left the room, kicking himself all the way down the hall for not telling her how beautiful it was, how he couldn't wait to see her in it, how maybe she'd meant it for Slick, but he was the one who'd be seeing it. It just didn't seem right to remind her of that, to make it sound like he was expecting what Slick would expect.

The light peeked out from beneath the door to his old room. He knocked softly and Berris opened it as if she'd been standing against it. Her face was streaked with tears and she wiped at them with the sleeve of her gown.

"The room looks real good," he said, staring at her bare feet. "Thanks."

"How did she get you to marry her, Gid?" Berris asked him, more wonder than reproof. "I know you've always had a soft spot for her, but—"

He put his finger on his sister's lips. In all the years, he'd found only this simple gesture ever stopped the flow of words she always threatened to let loose. "Things aren't always how they seem, Ber. I got *her* to marry *me*, not the other way around."

"Well, she might not be the brightest apple in the orchard, but she's no fool," Berris said, smiling through her tears. "Anybody would marry you, Gideon. Anybody lucky enough to be asked."

His mama used to tell him and his sisters that home was where they had to love you, and Berris seemed proof of that to Gideon. "Go to sleep, Ber," he said, rubbing her arm gently and giving her a wink. "You'll want to look your best tomorrow, I'm sure."

"I always want to look my best," Berris said, touching all the little rags she had fastened around her hair to make it curl the way Samantha Maddigan's did. "Everyone knows a man thinks with his eyes instead of his head."

Gideon smiled to himself as he walked down the hall to get washed up. So that was what women imagined men thought with. He let loose a small quiet whistle of relief and opened the bathroom door before his heart fell into his stomach.

He had no pajamas.

Back in his sister's bedroom, Lissie would be waiting in her fancy nightdress for him. Since the last growth spurt of his youth had left him too big for all but specially-made clothes, he had taken to spending cold nights in his long johns and warm nights in the altogether. The covers would have been enough for tonight, under other circumstances.

He walked back in his day's clothing and found Lissie waiting by the window. She was tall for a woman, probably about five and a half feet, which was still a good foot shorter than him. He remembered her fat little mama calling her *gangly* at one point. Legs too long and thin, like a colt, Mrs. Mallard had complained, and his ma had assured the woman that Lissie would grow into them. *Gawky,* Mrs. Mallard had decreed.

*Someday she'll be elegant,* his ma, a little bit of a thing herself, had promised.

Someday had surely come for Lissie, as she stood in her flowing white nightdress with the low-necked front that showed the top of two breasts that were fuller than he'd ever imagined them. She stood still, expectant, while he drank in the sight of her. She was as smooth as the finest brandy, and she burned his innards just as much.

Beautiful. Glorious. The right words were all stuck on his tongue. But he knew that if he so much as opened his mouth, it would be other words that would escape his lips. Three words in particular that he'd wanted to say since years ago when he'd fished her out of Winnow Creek where the icy mountain runoff had turned her pale skin nearly blue. He'd been ready to tell her then, but there'd been Slick to rescue along with their canoe—of course, it hadn't been *their* boat, but another of Slick's appropriations—drifting further downstream.

And dutifully Gideon had plunged into the freezing waters after his friend and pulled him out, too. And watched as Lissie gratefully clung to the man who had almost managed to get her drowned.

But Slick wasn't here, wasn't about to crawl into bed with Lissie and touch her silky skin and taste the sweat he raised on her body.

Carefully she turned back the blankets and crawled beneath them, leaving one side turned back for Gideon. She fussed under the covers for a moment, apparently fighting with her nightgown, and then lay still and stoic, her eyes closed, while he got ready for bed.

As he always did first, he emptied his pockets. He discovered that the velvet pouch with Lissie's earrings was gone. Oh, he'd stood there in Slick's room while the man had all but climbed him, hanging onto his pockets, pulling at his clothes, moaning in pain, until he'd gotten to his feet.

Lord Almighty, how could he blame Lissie for her mistakes when he, too, was easy prey?

He slipped out of his work pants and toyed with the idea of leaving on his lisle drawers, but then decided against it. Best to get off to the right start. There'd been no mention of a marriage in name only and he'd no intention of allowing it—couldn't even if he'd wanted to. Lying next to Lissie every night and not touching her was unthinkable. Unbearable.

He shucked his clothes quickly and hurried under the covers.

She didn't turn into him the way she always had in his imagination. She didn't fit herself to him, one leg slipping over his, one arm on his chest the way he'd seen her lay with Slick by the banks of the Columbia. She didn't nuzzle her head on his chest and tickle his nose with her hair.

She lay like a log, her breathing shallow, waiting.

"What are we going to do, Gideon?" she asked softly in the darkness.

He didn't suppose she wanted an explanation of a woman's wedding night, and so, after sighing, he said, "We're gonna make it through. Do the best we can."

"What are we gonna tell people? This baby ain't gonna wait for June to come rolling around."

"Babies come early all the time," he answered.

"People got fingers to count on," she said. "Sometimes I think that's what God gave them to old biddies for."

"Don't make yourself sick with worrying," he said. "The baby'll be mine when it gets here, and nobody's gonna dare say otherwise."

"And you don't want to change your mind? Now

would be the time, Gideon. I could go now, and you could say that I was damaged goods, and—"

"You wanna go?" he asked. And then he lay there still, his breath held as he recited silent prayers and made silent promises.

He felt the pillow beside his head rock and hoped she was shaking her head.

"Do you?" he asked, knowing that what this night would bring would bind them to each other for life. At least that was how he felt about it.

"No."

It wasn't a rousing, confident *no*. It wasn't a joyous pronouncement of love. But it would have to be enough.

With the matter settled, he turned on his side and let his hand rest on her midriff. At least he thought it was her midriff beneath the covers. He inched up slowly until he was cupping one breast through enough blankets to make it feel kind of like a good sized melon. Amazingly, it still excited him.

He peeled back the blanket so that only the top sheet and her nightgown covered her and replaced his hand. Through the layers of fabric he could feel the firmness of her breast, the pebble of her nipple, and it was all he could do to hold his groan silent.

He pushed at the top sheet until it was out of his way and stared at the swell of her breasts in the moonlight. In his whole life nothing had ever been as perfect as this moment. He lowered his head and placed a kiss on her collarbone.

He should have kissed her lips, looked into her eyes, touched her cheek. He should have whispered something into her ear. But what if she didn't kiss him back? What if her eyes didn't reflect the love in his own? What if he whispered that he loved her, had always loved her, and there was only the resounding silence of what she couldn't say in return?

And so he let his lips drift down to the rise of her chest and kissed her through the incredibly soft fabric of her gown.

And his hand tugged gently at where the cotton covered her belly, gathering her nightdress in small bunches until it refused to move any further up her body without her help.

"Lissie? Is this all right?" he asked when she didn't raise her hips to let the nightgown pass.

"Yes," she said, lifting herself for him while he could clearly hear the tears clogging her throat. "Of course. I'm your wife, Gideon. You can do whatever you want."

He raised his head and studied what he could see of her face in the moonlight. It was every bit as beautiful on the pillow beside him as he'd always imagined.

Except for the tears falling silently down the side of her cheek, breaking his heart in two.

"Turn over," he said softly, backing away from her to give her room.

Her eyes widened but obediently she turned, not just onto her side, but all the way onto her stomach. He watched, chills playing with his neck, his bare shoulders, his chest in the cool air, as she clutched a handful of pillow and spread her legs slightly.

All day his stomach had been unsettled, his brain fuzzy. Now he found it difficult to breathe. If he ever saw Slevin Waynick again, he'd probably kill him.

"No, Lissie," he said softly, not trusting his voice. "On your side. Turn on your side and go to sleep."

"But—" she started, then hesitated, as if she didn't know quite what to say.

She smelled like all the flowers that always surrounded her house. He tucked the quilt up around her and wasn't sure where the satin binding ended and she began. He'd seen the swell of her breasts and now he resigned himself to watching the rise and fall of her back throughout the night. He leaned over her and kissed her gently on her forehead—*a kiss to dream on,* his mother had called it when he was a boy—then backed up all he could so that their bodies were no longer touching.

"It's your right, Gideon. I owe you that much, at least. Don't you want to—"

"No," he answered, punching the pillow and then rocking the bed several times to satisfy his sister's curiosity. "I don't." And then he pushed the headboard against the wall a few times for good measure.

He pulled at the covers and tried to settle himself down. "Go to sleep now," he said, as much to himself as to Lissie.

He waited, hoping to hear the relief in her sigh, but there was none. Just some ragged breaths and a stifled sob and before long the soft breathing of a woman asleep.

He closed his eyes and inhaled deeply, hoping for sleep.

In his dreams, same as always, he'd hold her tight.

# Chapter Four

## ↷⋐ℬ

*H*E WAS STARING AT HER WHEN SHE WOKE UP FOR
the first time as Mrs. Gideon Forbes. She felt
his eyes on her even before she opened her
own. Somehow in the night she had turned and moved
into him, or maybe he'd moved toward her, and now
she felt his breath on her face, felt the warmth rise off
his body and envelope hers, felt his fingers tangled in
her hair.

Her nightdress was twisted up and bunched beneath
her uncomfortably, and she was pretty certain her bare
leg was resting against that of a boy she'd known all her
life who was now a man she hardly knew at all. She
tried to pull her weight back and forced herself to open
her eyes.

Her hand rested on his chest, the fingertips lost in
curls of soft black hair. Beneath her head she felt the
muscles in his upper arm twitch and she raised her eyes
to his.

Dear God—she was married to Gideon Forbes!

And she was right, of course. He'd been watching
her sleep, probably waiting for her to wake up so that
he could retrieve his arm and get out of his bed. How
sorry was he that he'd married her—a woman who

cringed at his touch, cried when he'd tried tenderly to assert his rights? She'd felt him pull his body back from hers, heard his sad sigh, before she'd drifted off to sleep. And now he lay beside her, silent and still, no doubt wondering what he'd done and whether he could get out of it.

Not that she blamed him. This whole mess was Slick's fault. Well, maybe not *entirely* his fault. She'd been warned. How many times had she heard that a man wouldn't buy the cow if he could get the milk for free? Or that a man didn't care who owned the mine so long as he could get his hands on the ore? She knew the rules and she'd chosen not to play by them.

And now she was paying. It didn't seem fair, though, that Gideon Forbes was, as well.

She lifted her head and let him pull his arm out. He flexed his hand a few times while she moved far enough away on the bed for him to place it down between them without touching her. The familiar nausea hit her hard and she swallowed against it.

"You all right?" he asked, his voice croaking as he sat up. He pulled yesterday's shirt from the floor and shoved his arms into it. "Need anything?"

She shook her head. The motion made things worse, and she covered her mouth with her hand. If she threw up in the poor man's wedding bed, on his dead mother's quilt, she would just kill herself. Of course, she'd probably die of shame before she actually had the chance to do herself in.

He backed off the bed gingerly, one hand attempting to stop the mattress from rocking, the other quickly grabbing at his pants, which he balled in front of him. "Hold on," he told her, hurrying to the dresser and grabbing the wash basin. He came back to her, his legs bare, his privates hidden behind his clothing, and held out the bowl.

It wasn't a moment too soon, it turned out. She grabbed for the china bowl with the delicate yellow flowers on it, and heaved the contents of her stomach into it. When she found the courage to look up, Gideon's pants were on, his blue shirt tucked in neatly. "Done?" he asked, reaching tentatively for the bowl.

"I'll see to it," she said, a little stronger now that the worst of the morning was over. If he wasn't going to enjoy the benefits of marriage, she didn't see why he should have to deal with the difficulties.

He didn't say anything, but he didn't let go of the bowl, either, and she didn't have the strength to fight him.

"I'll just get dressed then," she said as he took the basin and headed for the door.

He nodded, setting the bowl on the dresser while he stuffed his feet into his socks and boots.

"I'll be down in a few minutes to fix your breakfast," she said quickly before he shut the door behind himself. "Fast as I can," she added as she slipped from beneath the covers.

From the hallway, Berris's voice sailed beneath the door. "Well, the newlyweds are up," she said.

If Gideon answered her, Arliss didn't hear him.

"Why should I be quiet? Isn't she up yet?" Berris boomed. Apparently Gideon had suggested she keep her voice down. Again she couldn't hear his answer.

"A headache? Oh my Lord, Gideon! Did you drink yourself sick last night?" There was a pause, and then, "You did?"

"I had a lot to celebrate," she heard Gideon say. "And I'm paying for it this morning."

"Oh Gid! How romantic! Throwing up on your wedding night. I guess marriage to Arliss doesn't quite agree with you, huh?"

Arliss clutched her dressing gown closer around her and fought against what her mama used to call "truth tears"—the ones she'd cried so often as a child when she was forced to face the reality of something awful she'd done.

"Gideon, I'm sorry!" she heard Berris call out while Gideon's feet hit the stairs heavily. "It was just a joke, Gid. Where's your sense of humor? I didn't mean . . . "

Two thuds hit the bedroom door. Arliss guessed it was Berris's foot, rather than her hand.

"Arliss? You awake? I left fish down in the kitchen for you to gut and fry for Lester," she called through the door. "And Gideon takes four eggs and half a slab of bacon. Cluny and my father will split the other half and have a couple of eggs each. And they'll all want potatoes and onions and strong coffee."

Arliss dry heaved twice.

"And they're waiting."

Arliss wiped at her mouth and opened the door a crack. In the hall, her sister-in-law stood waiting in a pale blue dress that made her look better than Arliss ever remembered feeling. "Maybe you'd like to stay, Berris," she said as sweetly as she could feign without increasing her own nausea. "I could show you how to cook the eggs so that they don't turn brown, and slice the bacon so that it cooks all the way through."

"And you know there's nothing I'd rather do than spend the day here picking up pointers from you," Berris said with a smile that threatened to break her face in two. "Maybe tomorrow you could show me how to stuff my corset cover the way you do. Well, maybe a little less obviously. You do know how people talk."

Arliss rounded her shoulders. How long would it be before her belly stuck out further than her breasts, despite how fast they were growing? "Some people talk, others listen," she said. "And some just repeat what everyone else says. I guess you'd better get over to Verinda Ruth's before you miss anything."

"Well, here's something original," Berris said. "Something I've never said to anyone else, and I'm not gonna say twice." She leaned in close to Arliss and raised one finger in warning. "You better make my brother happy," she said with quiet determination. "Or I'll make you sorry."

Arliss said nothing, as if Gideon's reticence was suddenly contagious. And then, after all, there really wasn't anything to say in response to Berris's threat. She was already very, very sorry.

Coming into the sheriff's office with the day's mail, Gideon handed his father three new wanted posters and put the inquiries from Anaconda and Butte on his own desk.

"Well, I'm glad to see no one offered you a drink on the way to the mercantile," Thaddeus said as he leafed through the stack and cast yet another amused glance at his son.

"A man's entitled to drink on his wedding night," Gideon said, sick by now of the man's teasing about what hadn't even happened.

"And to puke the next morning?" his father asked with a bit of a smirk as he tacked up the new wanted posters on the wall beside the locked rifle case. "It musta been real nice for your bride. Why if I'd done that to your mother . . . You know, Gid, if you're gonna drink it, you really ought to be able to hold it," he said.

"I'll try to remember that," Gideon said, watching out the window for any sign of Arliss. Soon she'd be by with Lester's lunch, and he'd get to see her in the middle of his day. *Every* day. He felt the smile creep up on him and tried to stop it. If he wasn't careful he'd start thinking of her as his wife and imagine there was more to it than there was—imagine that she felt something for him. Something beyond gratitude, anyway.

It hadn't been easy at breakfast, with his pa and Cluny around, but still she'd managed to thank him for covering for her just as he was leaving the house. He wondered when they'd have to own up to her being with child, and how they'd convince anyone the baby was simply early. He hadn't even thought to ask her when to expect the baby. Hadn't asked anything, hadn't thought beyond declaring to God what he could never find the nerve to declare to her—that he loved her more than life and would for as long as he lived.

"Well, look who's here," his pa said as she struggled in, juggling the basket Berris had left out for her.

Gideon jumped up and took it from her, wondering if she was supposed to be carrying anything beyond what was in her belly. Oh, he knew that women did it all the time—worked beside their husbands in the fields, held babies in their arms while another grew beneath their hearts, did their laundry and their chores and such—but Arliss seemed so frail to him, so delicate in spirit and body now, that he wanted to spare her any burden he could.

He wondered about how a man could put a woman in such a delicate condition, and do it over and over again. He wondered, not for the first time, how his father had put his mother through the pains and risks of childbirth five times when she was such a tiny, fragile thing.

"Raised right," his father said, clearing the desk so that Gideon could set the basket down. "Always come to a lady's rescue," he said.

Gideon watched a slow blush crawl up Lissie's cheeks, hiding her freckles and turning his insides to mush. Just looking at her made his stomach do flips. Taking her arm, accidently brushing against her . . . Lord, it was all he could do to breathe with her around!

"That my lunch?" Lester called out through the door that set off the three jail cells from the sheriff's office. "Bring it on back here!"

Lissie opened the basket and brought out several tins of food, lifting lids until she had it all sorted out. Twice she licked her fingers and Gideon found himself gripping the edge of his desk for dear life. She talked to herself while she worked, or at least Gideon supposed she was talking to herself, since she didn't seem to require any answers. Not that he was capable of any, what with his mind stuck on how he'd woken up that morning to find her laying across him, her bare leg slipped between his, her breasts pressed against his side and nearly bursting from her gown.

"This is his," she said, holding out Lester's plate to him and gesturing toward the door with the grated window in it. "Should I just . . . " she asked when Gideon didn't reach out and take it.

"No," he said, wishing his mind would get out of their bedroom and his tongue would find the words his brain refused to produce. "I'll take it."

He took the plate, heaped with vegetables and potatoes and a small piece of fried fish, and opened the door to the cells. He could feel Lissie behind him, right on his heels, and wished she wouldn't come in with him. You could never tell what Lester might do or say.

"You don't need to," he said over his shoulder, but

she was still behind him when he slid the plate through the space in the bars and waited for Lester to take it.

"Arliss Mallard?" Lester asked, squinting at Gideon's new wife as he grabbed for his plate. "That you? Where the hell's that Berris girl?"

"Hello, Mr. Pincus," Lissie said softly. "How are you doing today?" She wrapped her fingers around the bars as she spoke, and Gideon, fearing that Lester couldn't be trusted as far as the man could spit, gently took her hand and pulled it from the iron bar. He held it longer than necessary, but hardly as long as he wished.

"This is my wife, Lester," he said. "So I'd appreciate you watching your mouth around her."

"Your wife?" Lester asked, scratching at the scabs on his head that were forever bleeding. He took a bite of the fish, pushing the vegetables and potatoes to the side. "Slick know she's your wife?"

Gideon supposed that Slick didn't know and didn't care. As far as he was concerned, Slick didn't have a right to care. If Lissie and the baby had meant anything to him, he'd still be around.

"Good fish," Lester told Lissie. "Your mama's recipe. I remember when I'd bring over a string of fish and your ma would cook 'em up for me. You remember that?"

"I remember you in the kitchen nearly as much as any of us Mallards," Lissie said, her eyes too bright.

" 'Course, that was before the horses started talking to me." Lester studied the fried trout on his plate and poked at it once or twice. "You can count on fish to keep their traps shut. And if they don't, they pay for it with their lives, don't they?"

"Enjoy your meal," Gideon said, taking Lissie's arm and leading her out of the narrow hall and into the office. His father had set out three plates and three chairs and sat waiting for them to join him. Gideon had wanted to talk to Lissie, needed to talk to her, but it would have to wait until they were alone.

"Good chicken," his father grunted, coming to the same half-stand that he used to do when Gideon's mother came to the table. "Real good."

Gideon supposed he'd inherited his silver tongue from his father. He held out the chair for Lissie and then sat himself. It was awkward, the three of them around the desk. There was no room for Lissie's knees, but she didn't seem to mind, not even when they wound up pressed against Gideon's thigh. He wished his father would make his rounds, but Thaddeus Forbes was a creature of habit, and habit dictated that he ate first and checked on the town as he walked off his lunch at two. And then there'd be Gideon's whole family again at dinner, and before he knew it, it would be time to hang off the edge of his bed again.

"Think I'll build us a house of our own," he said as if that settled the whole thing and he could now enjoy Lissie's mouthwatering chicken. "Good," he said and wanted to kick himself. He was sounding more like his father every day.

"Build a house?" his father asked. "Why?" He didn't seem to think it was a great idea, but Gideon could tell just from the way Lissie's breathing changed that she liked it fine, and that settled it.

"Something small," he said. "Private."

"I'd like that," Lissie said, staring at her empty plate. "I'd like that a lot."

He wondered just how much privacy she was hoping for, and where he fit into her hopes.

"He sent his ma a telegram," Berris told Samantha Maddigan as they went through her friend's closet.

"Verinda Ruth saw it in her husband's office and told me that Slick said he was on a streak and would be back to set things to rights before too long."

"What about this one?" Samantha asked, holding up a green satin dress that took Berris's breath away. "Set what things to rights? Lord, is it possible he doesn't know about Gideon marrying Arliss? I thought that was why he left."

"Try it on," Berris suggested, wondering what she would wear to the Miner's Ball. She glanced at herself in the mirror and wondered if Verinda Ruth hadn't cut just a little too much off the left side of her curls. She'd tried to get more out of Verinda Ruth, but at the rate she was going, Berris would be bald for the Ball. "You don't really believe that Arliss loves Gideon, do you? Even if he does wish it more than anything—my mama used to say that if wishes were bullets there wouldn't be a man left standing."

"Forgive me, Berris, but your mother never did have a way with words."

"Oh, I don't mind—I don't take after her at all. It's Gideon that takes after her, not me. Anyway, I don't buy the whole idea."

"Wouldn't it be just awful for Gideon if Slick did come back?" Sam asked, taking off the pink dress she wore. "I don't know why I'm even going to this ridiculous ball. I only got far enough at Miss Emily's Finishing School to learn how little I know. Just enough to feel totally inadequate in every situation except when it comes to shooting. And fat lot of good that'll do when I'm looking for a husband."

"Maybe you could get him to the altar at gunpoint," Berris suggested. "It's been done before. Besides, when the boys see you in that dress—"

"As you may recall, Berris dear, Gideon was the only

one brave enough to ask me to dance last year, and this year he'll be busy with his bride."

Berris held the green dress up for Sam to slip into and made a very unfeminine noise. "Don't call her that, please," she begged. "And I'm sure Gideon will still dance with you. You know he's really so fond of—"

"Berris! Your brother is married, whether you like it or not. And Arliss is a very nice . . . " She hedged. "Okay, so she's not your favorite person. And maybe she's been a little wild. But she only did what we were all wishing we could do." Samantha took a deep breath and tried to fill out the bodice of her dress by shifting her breasts upward. When that didn't help, she pointed toward her bureau. "Get me a stocking out of that top drawer to stick in here."

Berris pulled out a pair of lisle stockings and threw them toward her friend. "Carson will kill you! And I never wanted to do any of the things that girl did. Not one!" Except, she thought, to go out on the river in the moonlight with a man and be given one red rose. Of course the man wouldn't be Slick Waynick. "Where is Carson? I heard he was home."

Samantha took a good look at herself in the mirror. Her breasts rose over the top of her gown, the dark circles flirting with the bodice at her every breath.

"Carson would have your head!" Berris said, imagining how Samantha's big brother would react if she ever tried to leave the house in that condition.

It didn't take a whole lot of energy for Berris to conjure up Carson Maddigan. He was always there on the edges of her thoughts. The same daydreams that had her setting Samantha next to Gideon in church had Berris there on Carson's arm, the Reverend Lambert smiling down at the two couples as he joined the families neatly.

*Do you take her brother? Do you take his sister?* Not that her family would be any too happy about the match what with their feelings about how bounty hunters took the law into their own hands. Berris wouldn't let that stop her if Carson ever asked.

Samantha twisted this way and that, studying her obviously enhanced figure in the mirror. Maybe Berris really ought to ask Arliss what she used in her bodices to make the buttons strain. It certainly looked convincing. "Oh, Carson'll probably be away, anyway," she said.

Berris flopped down on Samantha's bed and rested her chin in her hands. Nothing was going the way it was supposed to. If Carson wasn't going to be there, what difference did it make what she wore to the dance?

"What in the hell . . . ?" Carson Maddigan's voice boomed, and his body filled the doorway to Sam's room. "What have you got in that bodice?" he demanded.

Berris covered her mouth to hide her laugh and sat up quickly. No doubt she looked a mess, but Carson wasn't looking at her. He was staring at his sister's chest like no man ought to. Especially no brother.

"Carson!" Samantha whined, covering her chest. "I was just trying on some dresses for the Miner's Ball. Haven't you ever heard of knocking?"

"Trying on dresses . . . or breasts?" he asked, crossing his big arms over his chest and staring down at his little sister as if she were still eight years old and he was still raising her. "You looking to be locked in your room the night of that stupid dance?" he asked.

*That stupid dance.* Berris had been thinking about the dance for months, pumping Samantha for Carson's favorite color, dieting until the cat's collar could practically fit around her waist, and what did he call the Miner's Ball? That stupid dance.

"Are you going to be around for the ball?" Berris

heard herself ask. At least she managed to make the question sound casual, as if she were only asking for Samantha's sake.

"Don't I wish," Carson said, finally noticing her. "If only to watch out for this reckless child." He shook his head at Sam and handed her the dresser scarf, indicating she ought to cover herself up.

"I'll keep an eye on her," Berris offered. "I know which men are after what, and I can—"

"The blind leading the blind," Carson said with a laugh before looking at her intently. Oh, when Carson looked at her intently . . . well, she was lucky she remembered to breathe, though sometimes she didn't bother. "What's this I heard about your brother up and marrying that sweet Arliss Mallard? Bet the poor man thinks he died and went to heaven. Guess *fortunate* really covers it in this case. Still, seems kinda sudden, don't it?"

"You could say that," Berris said, trying her best to seem worldly and grown up. "Certain men just don't know what they want. And certain women, like Arliss Mallard, have a gift for confusing them."

Carson laughed again and tipped up Berris's chin with the same finger that had squeezed a trigger over most of Montana to keep it safer than her father and brother ever could—though they'd never admit it. Lawmen just didn't like bounty hunters, and vice versa. "Sounding a little jealous there, Berris honey. Maybe now that she's your sister-in-law, Arliss could give you a few pointers."

And then he turned, and with a shake of his head at Sam which clearly said that she wasn't wearing the green dress to the ball, he left the room, shutting the door behind him.

*"That sweet Arliss Mallard. Bet he thinks he died*

*and went to heaven!* What is it about that woman that men find so irresistible?" Berris asked, unfastening the back buttons for her friend. "Jealous! Hmph! And you should have heard Cluny this morning. You'd think he'd never eaten an egg before. The way he went on about her cooking, you'd have thought she laid the things herself!"

Arliss stood in the bedroom, the chicken liver clutched in her hand. *Better wash the sheets,* Gideon had whispered to her when he'd handed her the basket on the sidewalk and sent her back to the sheriff's house. *Stain them,* was what he meant, to save her reputation, and his own.

She should have told him she was nearly three months along, should have told him no one was ever gonna believe that her baby was just in a hurry to get himself born.

Holding the liver out over the bed she splayed her fingers until the dark brown liquid ran between them to the sheet below. Tears stung at her eyes, blurring her vision, but she blinked them away. At least she wasn't trying to fool Gideon. There was a certain solace in that. And maybe life wasn't all that perfect for her, but neither was it perfect for him. Still, he managed to smile at her. She didn't know where he got the strength, but no matter how hard it was, she was going to find the means to smile back.

When she was finished she went quietly downstairs and cut up the evidence for Berris's cat, Marmalade, to devour, then set some water on the stove to heat so that she could wash her soiled sheets and not cause her husband any further embarrassment.

At least not for now.

She was searching for the washtub when Cluny came up behind her and offered to help.

"I just need to wash a few things," she told him, her cheeks burning with the lie.

The boy's eyes widened with understanding. She'd heard Berris say that men were a gullible lot and she supposed it was true. But then she was surely proof that so were women. Maybe everyone just believed what they wanted to hear. "My brother sure is a lucky man," he said as he took the washtub from her hands and carried it into the kitchen for her.

She busied herself with pouring the water into the basin and let the steam hide her tears. "I'm quite sure I'm the lucky one," she told Cluny.

"Oh, Gid's a nice enough guy," Cluny agreed, "but I'd say he pulled to an inside straight." His eyebrows came down slightly as if making sure he'd said the right thing. "Yeah, that's it, right?"

"I don't know. I'm not one for gambling," she admitted, though Slick had tried to teach her more than once. Oh, he was a big one for taking risks and betting on the future. But then, not being a woman, he could always just pick up his chips and catch some outbound train. And leave her behind. "It's too easy to lose."

"Well, I still say that Gid sure cleaned up," Cluny said.

She answered with a shrug and excused herself to go up for the laundry. Behind her she could hear Cluny talking to the fat orange cat.

"Whatcha got there, dustmop? Gizzards?"

# Chapter Five

*IT HAD BEEN A LOUSY ENOUGH DAY AT THE OFFICE,* what with his royal highness Mr. Belmont coming down from the mountain to complain about sabotage at the Columbia Mine. Then, Miss Kelly stopped by to report a bottle of her best Indian Sandalwood aftershave missing from Hughes' Mercantile just so she could spend half the afternoon flirting with his father, who didn't even seem to notice.

The last thing Gideon needed was to see his bed-sheets flapping on the line behind the house. And surely he didn't need to see, just a little to the left of center, the remnants of a stain winking at him, mocking him for not taking what was rightfully his.

Beyond the damn clothesline was a mess of over-grown brambles and tall shade trees laden with vines. It would be a heck of a job clearing the land, but he and Lissie just had too many secrets to fit in one small room in his father's house. There were things that needed to be said, things that needed to be done. Things that *ached* to be done.

Oh, but she was some picture in that sleeping gown of hers! He'd kept his hands from her throughout the long night, but he had no intention of making that a permanent part of the arrangement.

They might have lied to the rest of the town, but he and Lissie knew the truth, and for whatever reason, they were now man and wife. And he meant to make it as right and as real as it could be, considering the facts. After all, lots of women didn't love their husbands when they started out their lives together. But by the time they were burying their men, something had grown between them that Gideon had a hunch had its roots in the bedroom.

If only his tongue could tell Lissie what he felt in his heart.

She was setting the finest smelling dinner down onto the counter when he peered in through the screen door. He watched her arch her back as if it pained her, swipe at her forehead, tuck a curl behind her ear.

"You gonna just stand there all night?" Cluny asked, coming up behind him with some wild mountain gentian clutched in his hand and smelling like he'd had a run in with some dandy and lost. Before Gideon could react, Cluny went around him, pulled open the door, and burst into the kitchen with a very loud "Mmm . . . that smells like heaven, Arliss honey!" and thrust the bouquet at Lissie.

"Oh, flowers!" Gideon watched *Arliss honey* exclaim, watched as pure joy came over her face at the sickly looking weeds, watched as she smiled warmly at his brother, despite his forwardness. It looked like Cluny had learned well from Slick. Lissie was putty in both their hands. "Do you suppose there's a vase . . . " Her voice trailed off as Gideon came through the door.

The broad smile vanished in a flash, replaced by a tentative, nervous one. She fussed at her hair and tried to straighten her apron while holding Cluny's paltry sprigs in her hand.

"Hello," he said stiffly, cursing his gruff tone and his hulking frame as he stood slightly hunched in the low-ceilinged kitchen. Words like *honey* and *heaven* would never roll off his tongue. No wonder he set her nerves on edge.

"Dinner's ready," she said. "I hope it's as good as what you're used to. I couldn't find where Berris kept the good spices, so I had to make do. And I wasn't sure if you liked . . . "

She had to be kidding about how good Berris's cooking was, but the sweet smile on her face was wide and innocent as she waved the flowers around the kitchen.

"I think Berris keeps the vases in here." Cluny opened one cabinet door after another, obviously having no idea where a vase was. As far as Gideon knew, they didn't own one, so he reached for the chipped pitcher in the corner cupboard and held it out to his wife.

"Ma always used this," he said, trying to remember when it was she had received flowers. When Cluny was born, maybe. From a neighbor. His ma's eyes had had the same light in them then that he'd seen in Lissie's when his baby brother had surprised her.

The light was gone now, as she took the milk glass pitcher to the sink and pumped at the handle, going onto her toes for a better angle.

"Here," he said, reaching over her and giving the pump just one good swift prime to get it going. She smelled sharp, like some flavor he could almost taste on his tongue, and the saliva pooled in his mouth with want.

"I'll put them on the table for you," Cluny offered, reaching for the pitcher. All three of them were crowded around the sink when the screen door slammed behind them.

"Stew?" Berris said with disapproval. "I didn't mean for you to *stew* that lamb. We always have it roasted. Is something wrong with the sink? Or is this one of those jokes about how many besotted fools it takes to prime a pump?"

"What's the matter, Ber? Wasn't the great and dangerous Carson Maddigan happy to see you?" Cluny teased. "Or are you just jealous of how good this smells?" He picked at a corner of the meat and popped a small piece in his mouth. He closed his eyes and sighed deeply.

Gideon knew he should have been the one to defend his wife and her cooking, but Cluny hadn't given him the chance. He was still smarting over being called a besotted fool. The truth sure did sting.

"Why does everyone keep saying that?" Berris barked. "You think I'd want those pathetic weeds? And she's your *sister* now, Clu. You can't just—"

"Yours, too," Juliana said, her voice startling all of them as they whirled around together to see their sister standing on the porch with a basket in her hands. She came into the kitchen with her hand raised to stop the conversation around her, just the way their ma used to do when they were all growing up. She sounded just like their ma, too. "Behave yourself, Berris, and watch that tongue of yours. Someday your words are going to come back and choke you. Cluny, set the table and give your brother and his new wife some room, for heaven's sake." She sniffed in Cluny's direction. "And I suggest you make a trip to the pump and wash off some of that scent before we all get drunk on it."

Cluny skulked out of the kitchen. He kept one eye on Gideon trying to read whether his brother might suspect what he'd been doing down at the mercantile, which of course, Gideon had known with his first whiff of the boy. Berris checked over the stove and sink, as if Lissie might have damaged something while preparing dinner. Gideon just stood there like some sort of jackass next to Lissie, shifting his weight, swatting at flies no one else could see, and trying to find something clever, or important, or even fitting, to say.

"I was just bringing over Lester's dinner and thought I'd check on how you were settling in," his sister said, reaching out to take Lissie's hands in her own. Gideon's hands ached to do just that, and he curled his fingers into his palms until he could feel his ragged nails carving arcs in the heel of his hand. "Are you finding everything all right?" she went on. "My but your hands are cold! Didn't anyone show you how to close the window? There's sort of a trick to it. And to opening it, too."

He hadn't really had time to take her around the house and show her all the little quirks about it. He'd been too worried about his own little quirks, and Lissie's as well, to think about the kitchen window. Before he could show her, Cluny smacked the side of the window frame, jumped back, and nodded as the window slid down into place. "To open it," he started, but Gideon had had enough.

"I'll show her," Gideon said, gesturing with his head for her to come to the window with him. He pointed at the smudges on the sash and the black line nearly hidden by them. "Put your hand on the black mark," he said.

Lissie wiped her hands on her apron and reached for the sash, the counter pressing deeply against her belly.

"The trick is to ask someone," Gideon said, reaching over her and raising the sash easily.

Juliana tried to hide her smirk, but failed. "She won't

break, Gid," she said softly with a little shake of her head.

He remembered when Juliana was carrying. Ezra had been a wreck of a man, always helping his wife walk from the door to the first chair in the kitchen. He knew how Julie missed the attention now, even as she'd made fun of Ezra at the time. He didn't know much about women, but it didn't take a Don Juan to realize that a woman carrying a baby ought to be babied a little herself.

"Don't fool with the window," he told her, wishing his whole family wasn't breathing down his neck with every word he spoke. It was hard enough talking to Lissie at all, talking with an audience was impossible. And sooner or later he and Lissie were going to have to tell them about Lissie being in the family way. He could just imagine what Berris would think of her then.

He cleared his throat, but instead of the truth, out came, "The new house'll have windows that work proper." It was amazing the things that had begun to pop out of his mouth since he'd married Lissie.

It was all they could talk about through dinner—Cluny asking if he could help build it, Berris asking about all the details he hadn't given any thought to. How big? How soon? And finally, how many rooms?

"A lotta rooms," Gideon told her and took hold of Lissie's hand, right out there in the open across the table for his siblings to gawk at. "For all our kids."

She didn't squeeze his hand the way he'd hoped. She didn't blush red as a ripe strawberry in June. She didn't send him a secret smile charged with meaning.

She just blanched slightly and stared at her plate.

She'd never seen people gobble up a stew so fast. With Gideon's three helpings, Cluny's two, and Berris's second helping when she thought that Arliss wasn't looking, there was just enough left for a meager plate for Sheriff Forbes. She left the dish covered for him on the stove top and set about cleaning the kitchen, intent on making it shine.

Cluny had offered to wash the dishes. Berris had said she'd clean, no doubt supposing Lissie didn't know the proper way to scrub a pot. And she was almost tired enough to take Berris up on her offer. But Arliss was sure that a good wife cooked and cleaned at the very, very least. Besides, cleaning was miles better than sitting next to Gideon on the porch swing, trying to imagine what he was thinking while he uttered one word every few minutes in answer to her questions.

Probably he was trying to figure out where he'd taken a wrong turn and wound up married to the likes of her.

She reached for the pump, but his hand was already there, doing for her what she ought to do for herself. He'd done enough—taking her in, saving her pride, offering her child a name.

And now the promise of a home of her own. She knew she didn't deserve the reprieve he'd given her, didn't deserve the consideration he'd shown her in their bed and with his family, didn't deserve the acceptance they'd each, in their own way, all shown her.

Botheration, but she hoped Slick was losing every cent he'd left with, even if the money had been hers. She hoped that he was down on his luck and tired and scared, just like she was. She hated him almost as much as she wanted him to come back for her, and the knowledge that she still wanted him, after he'd run out and left her to Gideon, sickened her.

Gideon, dear, sweet, ever-silent Gideon, who she

was so very certain she could never love, gave the pump another jerk.

"Thank you," she said, as the water flowed freely and she worked at rinsing dishes that were already clean from bits of bread mopping up any remains of gravy to be found.

Gideon shrugged. In his place, she imagined Slick sidling up behind her, fondling her while she tried to get her work done, teasing her with talk of what they would do later, in their bedroom, in their bed.

As if he could read her thoughts, Gideon hovered, frowning. She tried to think better thoughts—like how she really hated Slick and was determined to make a life with Gideon, be a good wife—but his frown deteriorated to a scowl despite her best efforts to control her heart.

Maybe she wasn't getting things clean enough. Gideon was a simple man. It could be as simple as that. She scrubbed harder, cleaning years of soot from the bottom of the pot. Her arms tired with the effort while he looked around the kitchen as if he'd never seen it before.

"This kitchen ain't set up right for you," he said at last, opening the cabinets and pulling down the glasses, dishes, and bowls, setting them on the counter. "No reaching up," he told her.

Old Mrs. Clovis had told her the same thing when she'd confirmed Arliss's worst fears. *Do you want the baby strangling on the cord?* she'd asked Arliss accusingly. *What would have happened if your mother had gotten rid of you like that?* Arliss had ignored the silly question but not the advice, and she'd walked around with her arms glued to her sides for two days. Then she'd seen Ida Rose Hoffer, ripe with baby number four, hanging out her clothes on the line.

"I'll be fine," she told Gideon, who looked at her as if she were some incorrigible child practicing handstands on the rails of the Willow Creek bridge. He continued putting the kitchenware on the bottom shelf where it would be well within her reach.

"You need anything above this shelf, you wait till someone's home to get it," he said. "Understand?"

She nodded. Whatever Gideon wanted, she would do. He'd saved her, after all. So what if he wasn't the man of her dreams? Where had dreaming gotten her, after all?

She'd made her choice—been lucky to have had one. And if she was maybe a little bit sorry, it didn't compare to how Gideon was surely feeling. It had been a rash and foolish thing for him to do.

No doubt he was thinking the same thing as he grimaced and glowered at her while she scraped at the bottom of the stewing pot.

She sighed and wiped her forehead with the back of her hand, dripping water from the dishrag onto her dress.

"Sit down, Lissie." He came up behind her and took the last pot out of her hands. Spreading his stance in front of the sink, he reached for the scrub brush. "I'll finish up."

"I can do it," she insisted, while his cuffs soaked up the greasy water from the pan.

"You're falling on your feet," he said, nodding toward the chair. "Sit."

"I told Berris I'd get the bread started," she said, but she let herself sink into the chair and lean back heavily. In her life she had never been as tired as this. Except maybe last night. And the night before that. She gave up the fight to keep her eyelids open.

"She'll do it," he said.

Oh fine. Yet another reason for Berris to resent her, she thought, fighting sleep unsuccessfully.

"But it won't be as good as yours," she heard him say. The voice seemed to come from somewhere far away, where water was ebbing and flowing like the tide, where she lay stretched out in the sunshine listening to Slick reading her poems from Harper's Monthly.

Slick had once said her body was pure perfection and seeing it in the sunlight was a very exciting thing for a man. To be seen naked was a very embarrassing thing for a woman, and she'd been grateful it had taken so little time for him to be satisfied.

It was nicer this time. As she drifted off, she felt the sun baking her face and his voice off in the distance, soothing, comforting. His head was heavier in her lap, his eyes browner, his chest bigger, and his arms stronger than she remembered. And the warmth was warmer, and the closeness felt so good.

Her arms were limp at her sides and her head was lolling by the time Slick's arms came around her and pulled her against him. She nuzzled against his chest and sighed his name into the wind.

Gideon stiffened at the sound of Slick's name.

He'd finally gotten out three of four full sentences to Lissie only to have turned and found her sound asleep in her chair, with Marmalade curled contentedly in her lap. He'd then taken a minute to simply stare at his wife under the harsh glare of the bright oil lamp that hung over the kitchen table.

She'd seemed pale, with a crescent moon of darkness under each of her eyes that was more than the shadow of her long lashes. Still she was beautiful, his Lissie, though he'd have loved her even if she had two heads and green hair. Her mouth, which he longed to kiss, to touch, to explore with his tongue, was hanging open slightly. Pale freckles were sprinkled over her nose and cheeks. Her chest rose and fell invitingly with each deep breath she took.

It hurt like a nail to his soul to hear her whisper Slick's name when he lifted her and she snuggled against him. Still, he held her to him and stole the warmth that was meant for someone else.

Carrying Lissie, he walked into the parlor softly. Berris was there and Gideon glared at his sister, daring her to say a word. She opened her mouth and closed it again, saying nothing. Instead, she watched in silence, hugging her knees to her chest as he went by and started up the stairs.

"Good night," he heard her whisper softly from her spot on the sofa.

Looking back at her, he tried to smile. He wished he was half as tired as Lissie. For him, it was bound to be another long, long night.

# Chapter Six

FOR NEARLY TWO WEEKS THINGS WENT ON IN THE same way. While Lissie seemed to sleepwalk through her days, Gideon found himself lying awake beside her through his nights. On the following Monday—Mondays being the quietest days in town and consequently the ones he usually took off—he awoke to the familiar sound of Lissie's retching into a basin beside their bed. He could see the top of her head as she crouched on the floor and heaved the meager contents of her stomach into the porcelain bowl.

Thirteen days of marriage and nothing had changed. Except that the burning in his privates no longer subsided with the sounds of his poor wife's discomfort, which he tried to remember outweighed his own.

After it had become clear that her sickness in the morning was not going to be a singular event but more a sort of continuing saga, Lissie had brought up to the bedroom what Gideon supposed was the largest book she could find, the world atlas. She used it each morning to cover her basin until she was alone in the house and could dispose of its contents.

While it saved him from making explanations to his family, it left the room with a ripe smell which should have pushed away the thought of ever taking Lissie into his arms.

Well, if he were being perfectly honest and truthful, he'd actually taken her into his arms already. More than once. He'd even cupped her breast while she lay in a sleep so deep he was tempted to further test its limits. Heaven help him, he'd gone as far as to lay his hand on her stomach and wonder about the child growing inside her.

But that was as far as he'd taken it. He was, he reminded himself, a decent man. At least he'd always thought so before, had prided himself on the strength of his character, had taken solace in his moral fiber. Now the only solace he was seeking lay beneath a wrinkled nightdress that did little to hide what he was trying desperately to rise above.

His opinion of himself plummeted several notches farther when he found himself wishing desperately for a flash of breast or a streak of thigh as she climbed back into the bed and tucked herself beneath the covers.

Perhaps it was just as well he saw nothing, he thought. He closed his eyes and listened to the sound of her gently scratching at the stretching skin on her belly and sighing the ragged breath that signaled she was about to start her day. An inch more flesh bared and he'd have lost control.

He'd been selfish enough in marrying her, thinking only of his own dream and letting Slick slip through her fingers in the process. If there was to be more between them, Lissie would have to give it. After all, love wasn't something that could be taken, and much as he wanted her body, he didn't want it without some feeling on her part beyond tolerance. For a few bucks a toss, Millie down on Lilac Row had given him tolerance for close to three years. What he wanted was as far from Millie as

Slick was from Granite. And however long it took Lissie to come around, he'd wait—impatiently, painfully, and with great difficulty—but he'd wait.

Beside him, Lissie started the search for her slippers, which always seemed to walk away during the night. "Told Julie to see to Lester today," he said. "And I told Berris to see to this house."

She kept her back to him as she spoke, her feet still seeking out her scuffs. "I wish you hadn't," she said softly.

He didn't understand her. As tired as she was, wasn't she grateful for a little time off? "Why?" he asked. He hadn't meant to say the word aloud. Heck, she didn't owe him any explanations, didn't owe him anything at all.

"Because you've done enough." She said it as if it was all over and finished, like he'd married her because it was what she needed, but now there'd be no more to it than that. "And they're beginning to wonder. Berris even asked me how come we're always so proper with each other, why we aren't just like two frogs on some lilypad, I think she put it. Now if I go shirking my responsibilities, too, how will your family ever forgive me when they find out the truth about what I've gotten you into?"

Her back shuddered and he patted it gently, awkwardly. It was heaven to touch her, even like this. "I asked *you*, remember? Don't go worrying about no one else." She hardly needed to win over his father or Cluny—his father salivated at the thought of her meals, and his brother, well, he just salivated at the thought of her. And if he had to show Lissie a little affection in front of Berris, well, he supposed he could manage that just fine.

She turned around to face him, those big green eyes

of hers so bright they burned his heart. "Have I said thank you, Gideon?" she asked softly, reaching out to him and then letting her hand drop so that her fingertips almost touched his. "I don't know what I would have done otherwise. I just didn't have any other choice, or I'd have never accepted your proposal."

Not, perhaps, what a man dreams of hearing his wife say. "Yeah, well, lucky for me, huh?" he asked, trying to sound offhanded as he threw back the covers and sat up in his summer underwear. He hated sleeping in the underwear, but he'd decided it would at least hide his desire somewhat, even if it couldn't cool it any.

He'd just made it to his feet when he heard the sob. Well, it was for damn sure she didn't feel lucky. Not with her face pressed into the pillow where his head had been resting and her body thrown across his bed in abject misery. He sat down next to her on the bed at a loss for what to say, what to do. This was, without a doubt, the last time he married a woman to get her to stop crying. Obviously it didn't work.

"Lissie? I'll start clearing the land for the house today if you stop crying," he offered.

She sobbed harder. How the heck was he supposed to know what she wanted? To turn back the clock? To take back their vows? He dared not ask. He held out a carrot, instead.

"You want the house, don't you?" he asked.

Her head bobbed up and down against the pillow. He was afraid she couldn't breathe with her face lost in the billowy white folds, but a noisy sob assured him otherwise.

"So then I should start clearing? There's a mess of thicket out there and the trees that need felling must be fifty feet tall."

She rolled slowly onto her back, her face swollen and

scarred by a crease from the folds of the pillow. He imagined kissing away her tears, pressing his lips to her cheeks, working his way to her trembling mouth, sending the world spinning for both of them. Before he could even bend his head, she sniffed loudly and asked, "Can I help?"

He rolled his eyes and shook his head at the wonder that was his wife. What was he supposed to do with her? She hardly ate, she cooked and cleaned and washed and was half-asleep on her feet. And now she wanted to rip out thicket? Didn't she know she was in a family way? Didn't she know what could happen?

"Please?" she begged, her voice breaking along with his heart.

"It ain't fun," he told her. "It ain't canoeing down the fork or riding in a buggy. It's hard work and it's man's work, Lissie."

"I ain't looking for fun," she told him, eyes all ablaze like he'd called her mama an easy woman. "I'm looking to carry my share."

"You're carryin' more than enough already," he said. Why couldn't she let him do the man's work and stick to sewing and cooking like a woman was supposed to do?

Hurt flashed in her eyes before she lowered them to study the wrinkles in his sheets. Lord, but he was a master of saying the wrong thing. Were they supposed to be pretending she wasn't pregnant now? He wished there was a list of rules somewhere he could check before he opened his mouth and stuck his size fourteen foot in it. It was a hard thing to get a foot that big back out.

"I've helped my father clear and plant," she said. "I'm stronger than you think, Gideon."

Uh huh. And that was why her lower lip was trembling, he supposed. Because she was so strong.

"Please?"

Damn. If she asked him to cut the dumb trees down with a butter knife he'd probably go on and do it. Damn, and damn all over again. "All right. But you'll follow instructions and stop when I tell you to or I'll—"

There was a tiny, tremulous smile. Somehow it lit up the whole damn room.

"Go do your business and get dressed before I start without you," he said, trying to pretend he was annoyed. Really, when he thought about it, he was more than happy she'd be spending the day with him. He'd have to watch out for her, of course—the woman obviously didn't know her limits—but yes, he was more than glad to have her beside him clearing the land.

He was eager.

By noon the mountain who'd married her had felled three trees and cleared the area she had in mind for the baby's room. Arliss had pulled out an equal number of weeds and been ordered to rest after each one. Granted the weeds were nearly as big as she was, and the roots went deep. Still, she was determined to be a true helpmate to her husband. It wasn't as if she were some precious little china doll—as she had pointed out to him several times—and she was uncomfortable when he treated her like one. No wonder Berris was a spoiled brat. The Forbes men obviously didn't like their women to so much as tie their own bootlaces without a man's help.

Now, Slick had had a healthy respect for her abilities. He'd let her help carry boats, hitch up horses. He'd let her fetch Pansy off the roof when she was fifteen. The stupid cat had taken off after a bird and had gotten herself stuck in the gutter. Arliss was lucky she'd only broken her forearm in the fall. And it hardly pained her at all anymore, except when a good storm was about to hit Granite.

It pained her now, as she pulled at the base of a vine, and she wondered just how much her stubbornness had cost her. Maybe if she'd taken a good hard look at Slick early on, instead of just fighting against her mother's advice, maybe if she'd opened her eyes and just looked, she'd have seen all of this coming. And maybe she could have prepared.

She and Gideon worked in silence, not the way she and her pa had cleared land. Marcus would stop every few minutes to show her something wonderful—a bird's nest, a flower that had survived beneath a rotting log, a salamander who hadn't time to change his color before they saw him. When Gideon had helped her pa in the garden, she'd shared things like that with him, but somehow now everything she found seemed silly and childish and she held her tongue.

Every now and then he looked over at her. Sometimes he called out to her to rest, and sometimes he simply shook his head and swung the ax so hard she could feel it in the ground beneath her feet. She knew the shock of marrying her had worn off and he was sorry. He couldn't even bear to touch her when they crawled into bed at night. He lowered the lights before she even returned from the bathroom so that he wouldn't have to look at her and turned his back to her as soon as she was settled in the bed.

Well, what had she expected? That he'd just forget that Slick had been there first? He was no more likely to forget it than she was. They were both stuck.

Berris called them for lunch, and Gideon put down his ax in the middle of a swing to come and help her up. He had the biggest hands, and they were hot from his work when he reached down for her. She didn't know why she hadn't just gotten up herself. Maybe because she was in no rush to face her sister-in-law. Or her sister-in-law's cooking, which was worse than before because Arliss had started changing the labels on all the spices. This way she'd be sure to outshine her new sister-in-law in the kitchen. It was petty revenge, but still it was sweet.

"It's on the table," Berris said, tying on a straw bonnet with green roses that went perfectly with her dress. "I've got to get to Verinda Ruth's by one or she'll be off to give old Mrs. Miller a wash and set in her bed."

"Berris, as long as you're going over that way, do you think you could drop the extra biscuits from breakfast off for Lester?" Arliss asked. "Juliana only makes them for his supper and I know he likes them."

"I think Juliana must be eating them herself. No wonder her old dresses aren't fitting anymore," Berris said. "I didn't expect that there'd be any leftovers from breakfast. Didn't you like them?"

Breakfast was the hardest meal for her to eat. Whatever went down didn't feel as if it would stay there long, and so she'd taken to just pretending to eat while she spread things about on her plate.

Gideon cleared his throat. "I wasn't hungry," he said. "So I only ate a couple."

Berris looked at Gideon, at her, and back at Gideon as if she clearly knew this was not the truth. "Oh, I see," she said, a bit of hurt glinting in her eyes. "If Arliss made them I suppose you two would have found your appetites?"

Maybe they would have. Surely Gideon would have eaten more if she hadn't switched the baking soda and power labels. Berris's already heavy biscuits sat like lead in everyone's stomachs, while hers were light as air in their memories. At least she was giving Gideon one reason to be glad she was his wife. And she didn't think Lester would mind all that much. A heavy biscuit was better than none.

"You don't want to be late, Berris," Gideon warned. There was something cold in his tone that cut his sister off. Maybe it was the way he used her whole name instead of just *Ber*. Whatever it was, the conversation was over and Berris was hurrying out the door.

"The biscuits!" Arliss called after her, but Gideon blocked the doorway.

"Go on, you've still got an inch of hair left," Gideon told his sister and watched after her. Then he went to the bread box and removed the biscuits she'd passed on at breakfast and set them on a plate in front of her.

She moved the plate to the center of the table and lifted the pitcher of lemonade.

Gideon moved the plate back in front of her. "Eat 'em, Lis," he said and reached for the platter of fish his sister had left for them.

She filled Gideon's glass and then her own, put down the pitcher, and placed the biscuits in the center of the table once again.

"I said 'eat 'em,' " he repeated, sliding them in front of her and folding his hands across his chest, waiting.

"You know Lester didn't know what he was doing," she said as patiently as she could, as if Gideon were a small child and couldn't understand that Lester's mind had snapped. "He's sick, Gideon, not bad. You know, really, he shouldn't even be in jail."

"Law says he's gotta be locked up until the end of the month when the district judge shows up and puts him on trial. It ain't my job to decide if he's crazy or not. The man shot four horses, for Pete's sake! You want me to wait until he shoots four men?"

She pushed the awful biscuits clear across the table. The Forbes were all so used to Berris's cooking she wasn't even sure they'd noticed that the biscuits were worse than usual. "So you want to starve him? Is that it?"

His look said he wouldn't bother answering her question. Not that she blamed him. Gideon couldn't intentionally hurt anyone, and she knew it. "If you won't eat the biscuits, then what *will* you eat?" He pushed the platter of fish toward her. Just the smell of the fried meal made her gag.

"I'm not hungry," she said. "But Lester—"

"You gotta get it through that sweet head of yours that Lester's a dangerous criminal. He doesn't deserve biscuits with every meal. And he sure as heck hasn't done anything to deserve cooking as good as yours." He pounded the table and pushed the platter under her nose before she could even appreciate the compliment. Pulling her head back, she held her breath. "I know Berris ain't exactly Isabella Beeton, or whoever it was that wrote that cookbook her nose is always buried in, but it's food and I want to see you eat it."

She fought to swallow and shook her head. "I can't." While she struggled for a breath, the room took on a funny yellow hue, and started to spin.

In a second the food was gone, her chair was turned away from the table, and her head was low across her knees. "Breathe deep," Gideon was saying, his hand on the back of her neck. "Lord almighty, Lissie, don't faint on me. Please."

She nodded against his hand, rough, but exerting only the slightest pressure. Somehow, without taking his hand from her, he reached the door and opened and closed it rapidly to create a breeze.

"You gotta eat," he begged, gently massaging her neck.

"I can't," she said, stilling his hand with her own and raising her head to take in the fresh air. "Don't you think I would if I could? I wanna give this baby everything it needs. Don't you know how hard I'm trying?"

"All right. Not fish. Not biscuits," he agreed. "What could you manage?"

"A banana." She studied her dress, wishing she could just eat the biscuits and not ask anything more of Gideon.

"A banana?" His voice came out a croak of disbelief. "Where the heck am I supposed to get—"

"A banana," she said again, thinking about the sweet taste, the smooth feel of it pressed against the roof of her mouth, the wonderful warm smell of a faraway place. She was certain she could get a banana to stay down. "Mashed, like my papa used to give me when I was sick."

"You'll be all right here by yourself if I go out for a while?" he asked.

"But you haven't eaten," she said, looking around until she saw the platter of fish pitched at an angle in the sink. "And you were making such headway with the clearing."

"After you eat," he said, rising and grabbing the biscuits off the table as he did, offering them to her one last time. "Sure you can't eat 'em?"

She shook her head. She couldn't have gotten them down even if they'd been her own. "You're never going to find a banana," she said, signaling him to forget she'd ever asked for one. "I'm sure I'll be able to eat supper."

He grabbed his hat from the peg by the door and buckled on his gun belt. "Go lie down," he said as he shoved open the screen door with his foot. "I'll be back."

Bananas.

Lord, it would have been easier finding her diamonds on the hillside or snow in July.

The ladies in town signed a list at Hughes' to claim the darn things before they were even unloaded from the Southern Railroad cars—bananas and oranges and half a dozen other delicacies that year-round warmth and the railroad could deliver.

And he'd paid dearly for them, too, when he'd finally tracked down the last two bananas in Granite at Mrs. Eula Mae Hurley's where they were about to become bread. *Gotta have 'em,* he'd told her. *Sheriff's business.*

Now what the heck kind of sheriff's business required two old brown bananas, she'd wanted to know. And he'd stood there like a damn fool and just pulled a silver dollar from his pocket and held it out to her.

*Monkey business!* she'd said under her breath as she'd taken the money in exchange for the fruit.

A dollar and an afternoon's work gone for two of the lousiest-looking bananas he'd ever seen.

He put them behind his back as he came up the street and saw Berris waving from the other direction.

"What a day I had!" Berris said as soon as they were close enough to hear each other. Maybe, knowing Berris, she'd been talking the whole way down and he hadn't heard her. He was sure he hadn't missed anything of importance. Across her forehead were short little wisps of hair that stuck out rather than curled about her face. "Verna Bailey and Ida Rose Hoffer and old lady Giovanni all came in to Verinda Ruth's while I was there, ranting about how you were going around town demanding their bananas."

They headed toward the back porch together, Gideon stewing about women and their inability to keep their mouths shut, Berris prattling on.

"Mrs. Clovis was visiting with Mrs. Hoffer, who just might be carrying number six, and she—" she stopped, interrupting herself and looking at the clearing. "What's Arliss doing back there?"

Gideon shoved the bananas at Berris and took off like his tail was on fire, shouting all the way for Lissie to stop pulling on the vine. He could see that it was ready to give, and another yank and she'd be—

It was more a gasp than a scream as she went peddling backward into the brambles, the vine folding down on top of her and trapping her in the thorny mire.

"Lissie!" Her name was ripped from his chest as her knees buckled under her and she tried to cover her face with her arms.

He'd told her to lie down, to take it easy. He'd told her to follow instructions and not to reach, and she hadn't heard a word he'd said. It was no wonder he talked to women so little. They never listened. "Lissie!" he screamed again when he got to where she lay buried under yards of wild vine and overgrown brush.

"Gideon?"

He saw movement in the thicket and his heart took to beating again, this time wildly.

"Don't move," he said firmly. "I mean it, Arliss. Move a muscle and I'll walk away and leave you here."

"There are thorns everywhere," she whimpered, while he tried to pick up the vine in one piece. Instead he had to drag it away from her, all the while hearing her yelling out that it hurt.

Beside him, Berris showed up with shears, his double-handled saw, a scythe—things she found in the tool shed that would cut through the branches and twigs that trapped Lissie.

"Keep your eyes shut," Berris told her. She ran off toward the house yelling over her shoulder that she'd get a blanket.

"Maybe she doesn't hate me as much as I thought," Lissie said, sniffing and making tight little sounds.

"Does it hurt you inside anywheres?" Gideon asked. "Do you think you broke anything or—" He wasn't sure how to put it.

"It hurts when I breathe. In my chest." It sounded as if she were testing.

"Don't breathe!" he warned. "I mean, don't breathe deep. Take shallow little breaths, Lissie." He demonstrated with little bitty puffs of air.

The leaves rustled over her.

"Better?" he asked, gently lifting broken branches. He wished he could just fling them out of the way and get to her, but he was fearful that he would injure her more if he did. "What about your arms and legs? Do they hurt?"

"No." She answered him slowly, as if taking stock. He watched her move one foot just a hair, and then the other. "Ouch!"

"Don't move! Is it broken?" He'd gotten the better part of the vine off and was now carefully cutting away each branch that held her captive.

"No," she said again. He could hear the terror rising in her voice when she added, "But I think I might be bleeding."

He stopped cutting.

He wasn't sure, but it could have been that he stopped breathing, as well.

"What?"

"Can you see my legs? Am I bleeding?"

He looked between the mass of leaves that nearly concealed her completely. He pulled several back with his bare hands while she took in sharp breaths with each move. There were tiny little red spots on the part of her leg that was exposed. He could see a good dozen thorns still imbedded and the trails others had made on her pure white skin. They were already beginning to welt up.

He moved more branches until he could see most of her apron. "I don't know," he answered, wondering how much blood he should expect, wondering if she would want to stay married to him if her reason was gone, wondering how she would get over losing both Slick and his baby.

"It feels like they're bleeding," she said, fighting the tears he could hear in her voice. "And my arms, too."

*"They're?* Were you asking if your *legs* are bleeding?" he asked, crazy with relief. "Hell yes, they're bleeding. What did you think you were doing out here by yourself? You think you're Davy Crockett out there in the wilds? You think you can do whatever you want, like you used to do? You think you can still just run loose like your pa let you? Like Slick let you? You think nothing's changed and that I'm gonna let you—"

"Gideon! Take your gloves!" Berris stood next to him, holding out his work gloves. For once she wasn't talking a blue streak. He was the only one ranting and raving, and when he stopped, all they could hear was Arliss's little panting breaths from beneath the thorny hedge.

"Well, I guess he found his tongue," Lissie said to Berris, raising a smile on his sister's lips.

"Fine time," Berris answered, kneeling beside him,

her gardening gloves donned. Gently she pulled the
thicket back while she spoke softly to Lissie, telling her
it would take a minute or two to get her out without any
more scratches. "Did the vine hit your head when it
came down?" she asked.

"No, my arms, mostly. And my chest," Lissie answered.

Meticulously Gideon cut the branches that covered
her arms and face and saw the marks where the vine
had come down on her forearms. That perfect skin of
hers would be black and blue come morning. And that
would be the least of it. He and Berris exchanged helpless looks before he reached into the nest of thorns and
tried to pluck her out. The branches fought him tooth
and nail, unwilling to let her go. They held onto her
clothing, her hair, and tried to trip Gideon as he rose
with her in his arms.

After Berris managed to wrap the blanket around
her, Gideon tightened his grip slightly and carried her
toward the house. Berris ran around him and opened
the door while Arliss whimpered in his arms.

"See if you can find Doc Agrin and tell him to come
by here soon as he can," Gideon told his sister, just as
Cluny came running in with a hundred questions.

"Is Lissie all right?" he demanded, one hand on Gideon's arm. Gideon didn't know the answer, and so he
just cradled Lissie all the tighter as if he could make
it so.

"Go for the doc, Ber," Gideon said again. "Tell him
to get over here now."

"Why don't we just get her upstairs first and see how
bad she's scraped up?" Berris asked, ignoring his order.
God in his merciful heaven, was there a woman who
ever, ever, did what she was told?

"I said get the doc," Gideon repeated, looking down at Arliss and watching her lip disappear between her teeth. "What hurts you?" he whispered to her.

"Gideon," Berris whined at him, "I know you're worried, but I can get out the splinters and we can clean out the cuts in a good bath. We don't need to bother Doc Agrin. Old man Pielman fell off his roof and the doc had to run out there and—"

Gideon turned on the steps and glared at his sister. Through gritted teeth he spoke simply and plainly. "Get him, Berris. Now."

Berris rolled her eyes.

Lissie moaned softly and shifted in his arms.

"Tell him to hurry. She might have broken a rib and God knows what that might mean." He caught himself. "I want to be sure she's all right."

"Gid . . . "

"Cluny," he ordered, looking beyond Berris at his younger brother. "See if you can find Doc Agrin. He may still be out at the Pielman place." Lord almighty, but Lissie didn't weigh so much as a sack of feathers in his arms.

"Gid . . . " Berris whined again.

"Open the door to our room and stay out of the way," he told her, watching as welts seemed to pop out on Lissie's forehead in the time it took for Berris to open the door. "Do you think you're—you know—all right?" he asked as he laid her on the bed and unwrapped the blanket they'd bundled her in.

"I think so." She answered him cautiously, her hand drifting down her belly as if she could feel something through her skirts.

"Of course you are," Berris said over his shoulder. So much for *stay out of the way*. "Why wouldn't you be?"

"Because she's carrying, Berris. That's why."

"Carrying what?" Berris asked before gasping and covering her open mouth with a shaking hand.

"Carrying my child," he answered with surprising ease. Lissie moaned and threw her arm over her eyes.

"Your child? But you've only been married two weeks. That's hardly time enough—how could you know she's carrying your child?" Berris demanded. Not that it was any of her business, but he supposed that now she wouldn't be the only one asking.

"I got carried away a month or two ago," he said, wondering how far along Lissie was. Her stomach was still nearly flat, so he didn't think she could be more than a month or two gone. But then, what did he know about such things? "I'd had too much to drink and forgot myself for a moment."

"You 'forgot' yourself?" Berris demanded. "What does that mean, 'you forgot yourself'?"

"We got carried away," Lissie said, putting her hand on Gideon's arm.

"Carried away?" Berris repeated, as if she still couldn't figure out what they meant, as if the idea was all too much for her.

"We were out by the creek," Lissie said softly, begging Berris to understand.

"And there was this silver moon," Gideon added, as if saying it could make it so.

"And I got cold," Lissie tacked on. "And Gideon—"

Berris put her hands up to her ears. "I don't want the sordid details," she all but shrieked. "I might believe it of you, Arliss, but Gideon, you'd never—"

"—lie," he said firmly. "And I'd never tolerate you speaking to my wife that way, Berris."

He waited for her to apologize.

"Gideon, you couldn't—" she started.

"You can think what you want, Berris," he said turning his back on her to tend to Lissie. "But you'll have to keep those thoughts to yourself when you address my wife."

"I'm sorry," Berris said, "but this is so . . . so . . . I mean you couldn't—"

"—help myself," he said, completing Berris's thought once again. If he and Lissie were to survive this, this was the only way. Claim the baby—and Lissie—as his own.

"Neither of us could," Lissie chimed in, as if there was a chance in hell Berris would believe that Lissie couldn't resist his charms.

"And Arliss wound up pregnant?" she finally asked, softly, sadly.

"Do you suppose she was likely to marry me otherwise?" he asked honestly. "If she wasn't carrying?"

"And that's why Slick left?" she asked, looking at Lissie lying there in the bed, a mass of cuts and bruises. "Because you're pregnant?"

"Yeah," Gideon said, not leaving it to Lissie to admit. "He left 'cause she's carrying." He supposed that part was true enough.

"You mean a silver moon and a soft breeze could make you forget right and wrong?" Berris asked.

"I told you no one would understand," Lissie said, still trying to control her breathing. Her face was swelling with stings and scratches. Thorns all but ringed her throat. He couldn't tell which marks were freckles and which were pricks in her creamy skin.

"She don't gotta understand," Gideon said. "Nobody's gotta understand."

He tried to get his big hands around a slender thorn near Lissie's collarbone.

"I'll see to her," Berris offered, taking a few steps closer. "No wonder Mrs. Clovis wasn't surprised by the bananas. She already knew Lissie was carrying, didn't she?"

"Bananas?" Lissie asked, looking up at him with teary eyes that were swelling shut. "You found me bananas?" Lord, if he looked at her right, he could almost imagine that the gratitude in her eyes was love.

"You best just stop talking and keep breathing real soft-like." He watched her chest rise and fall ever so slightly with every breath. "And Berris, go get me some hot water if you want to make yourself useful."

There were prickles sticking out of the neckline of Lissie's dress, and he shook his head and studied the ceiling wondering how he'd ever remove even one. There wasn't going to be enough ice in the cellar to keep him from wanting her once he started touching places in the light of day.

But wanting her and doing anything about it were as far apart as the east and west horizons on a clear day. Especially if she'd actually broken her rib. He touched her gently above the band of her apron, his fingers running the length of one rib.

"Does this hurt?" he asked.

She shook her head. "This side," she said, and her left hand, scratched and swelling, pointed at her right side just beneath her breast.

Berris came back into the room, each step shaking the floor, and uttered a deep, disappointed sigh like his mama used to do when one of her children had crossed the line. Water sloshed over the sides of the basin she held and she slammed it down beside them on the nightstand. "Cluny's going for Doc Agrin," she said, thrusting a wet rag over his shoulder. "In the meantime, let me just draw this real fine. You're telling me that you and Arliss . . . ?"

"Things happen, Berris," Gideon said, patting the scratches on Lissie's brow.

"But she was in love with Slick, Gideon. How could you let this happen to her when you knew how much she wanted to marry him?"

"Sometimes," Gideon said as he dabbed at the tear sliding down Lissie's cheek, "people don't get what they want, and they just have to settle for what they've got."

For a while no one said anything and the only sounds were Lissie's sharp intakes of breath as he poked and prodded at her.

"It must have been some moon," Berris said finally as she stood by the window and glanced out at the big Montana sky.

"It was," Gideon said, pulling a splinter from Lissie's arm.

"And you could smell the honeysuckle clear across the river," Lissie said dreamily, her eyes closed.

"Venus was up," he added.

"I recall you showing me that," Lissie whispered. He wondered if she was actually remembering that time he'd seen her safely home from the church social because Slick had wanted to make a poker game on Lilac Row.

Fancy her remembering that he'd shown her a star or two.

He heard Berris quietly shut the door behind her, but he didn't point that out to Lissie. Instead he added, "There wasn't a cloud in the sky."

"No," she agreed, her eyes closed. "It was a pretty perfect night."

"Close to perfect," he agreed, remembering how

he'd almost kissed her. And how she'd really, really, almost let him.

There was the hint of a smile on Lissie's lips, but it faded as he yanked another thorn from her side.

# Chapter Seven

D OC AGRIN DIDN'T EVEN RAISE AN EYEBROW WHEN Lissie admitted there was a chance she was carrying.

"Now don't you go looking like you've robbed the Granite National or murdered your pa, Arliss honey. Why, if I had two bits for every nine-pound premie I've delivered, I'd be living in a house as big as Belmont's," he said with a wink. He ran his hands gently over her belly and studied her silhouette. "And I'd say it was more than a chance now, girl, wouldn't you?"

With more little tsks and noises than Arliss knew a body could make, he checked out the cuts and bruises on her arms and legs like he was fileting a prize fish. Finally he declared that removing all the splinters would take him longer than he had left on this earth and that he felt sure Gideon or Berris could do just as good a job.

It was her rib that concerned him. He reassured her when she began to cry that even if the rib was actually broken—and he wasn't sure it was—she and her baby would both be fine. And crying, he warned her, would do more harm than good.

And then he tweaked her toes and left her alone to

fight off her tears while she listened to the shouting going on downstairs. She could hear the boom of Sheriff Forbes's voice, the staccato of Berris's outrage, the even, heavy tone of Gideon's response. And all of it punctuated by shouts at Cluny to stay up in his room, followed by a lowering of voices—voices that rose again to shake the house as they tore apart her husband's family.

"Arliss?" Cluny's voice followed a soft rap on her door. "You awake?"

She wanted him to go away. She wanted them all to go away and let her fade to nothing in an empty room. "Yes, Cluny," she said anyway. "You can come in."

Cluny's eyes were wide as he tiptoed into the room and stared at her. She was covered with moist cloths that had gone cold while the argument downstairs heated up. Beneath the covers her midriff was wrapped so tightly she could hardly draw breath.

"Can I get you anything?" he asked from across the room, his hands first in his pockets, then behind his back, then flailing in the air. "Is it true, Arliss—what Gideon said? Are you really having a baby?"

"Yes, she's having a baby," Gideon roared from behind Cluny like an angry bear. "And she needs her rest. Out, Cluny. And go warm up some water for me to bathe her and bring up that damn banana while you're at it."

"Gideon, I can't—" Arlis began, only to have him cut her off.

"You'll eat the banana or you'll eat something else, if I have to force it down that little neck of yours," Gideon ordered.

She'd known Gideon all her life, seen him frustrated, seen him peeved, but never had she seen him truly angry. He took several deep breaths, balled and unballed his fists, and then finally, as if he was as mad at himself as he was with her, he asked, "Is there something else you'd prefer? You almost got yourself killed while I was out looking for bananas, so you better answer careful-like."

"Gideon, I want to tell your family—" she tried again.

"They already know more than enough," Gideon said, shooing Cluny out of the room with his hand and telling him to bring up some tea, too. And a sweet, if there was one.

And then the gruff, mean, mountain-of-a-man gently picked up the old green armchair with the stuffing escaping, and plunked it down silently beside the bed. After a big sigh he sat down in it, his lip firmly between his teeth. He lifted the wet cloth from her neck.

"Ah, jeez," he moaned. "Are you in much pain?"

"I think less than you," she said, trying her best to manage a little smile for him.

"Me?" he asked as if she'd lost her mind. "I'm fine. But look at you. The doc says he ain't sure if you cracked the rib some or if it's just bruised. Either way you ain't to get out of this bed. The hot water poultices ought to keep down the swelling on your arms and neck and help loosen the splinters. And he left Berris some recipe for salve that'll soothe you after we get all the thorns out."

"Long as I don't have to eat it," she said and was rewarded with the shadow of a smile that faded quickly. He tilted her head slightly by touching her chin and lifted the cloth from her neck. He looked, if it was possible, even more uncomfortable than she felt.

"Yeah, well it looks like we'll all be eating Berris's fine cooking for a while," he said. " 'Course after all my preaching morals, she'll probably be serving me crow."

He'd actually made a joke. If she hadn't felt that she'd brought the roof caving in on his head, she'd have laughed. Instead she scratched at her arm and said, "I don't care what your sister thinks of me, but I can't let her think that you—" she started, but again he interrupted her. For a man who couldn't utter a full sentence just a week or so ago, he'd surely found his tongue.

"My sister thinks this baby is mine," he said, his hand hovering over the blankets that covered her stomach. "And that's how I want it, Lissie. It's best for you and it's best for the child."

God, what she'd done to this man. And all because of Slick. When he came back, she'd kill him. She'd dote on Gideon and flaunt it in Slick's pretty boy face. She'd tell him that Gideon was better in their bed than Slick had ever been. She'd tell him it was Gideon she'd been in love with all along. Gideon poked at her neck and then picked up the tweezers to go after a thorn. "What about what's best for you, Gideon?"

He worked at a splinter in silence until she couldn't stand it any longer and put her hand over his to stop him.

"What about you?" she repeated, capturing his gaze with her own.

"Remember when you said you owed me?" he asked. Was she likely to forget their wedding night? "Not that I don't wish things were different, but wishin' never put food on the table or a roof over anybody's head, and for people to think I'd been cuckolded—I couldn't live that down, ever. And I don't see as how I could stand people knowing it was Waynick's child I was raising."

All the while he probed near her collar bone with the tweezers the doctor had left, his eyes never straying from her neck, never reaching her own eyes.

"Worse would be having people think that I was tricked, or that I'm a damn fool," he added, putting the cloth back against her neck and uncovering her arm.

"But the truth is—" she said, and once again he didn't let her finish.

"That I *am* a damn fool. And that you shouldn't be talking so much. The doc says you need to rest."

"I don't deserve this kindness, Gideon, and that's the truth of it."

She stilled his hands, and if the curtains weren't blowing in the breeze she'd have thought they were both trapped in some photograph, never to move again.

"The truth isn't going to help anyone, Lissie. It ain't gonna make you happy, or me, or let us have a decent life here in Granite. It's going to mark that baby you're carrying, and you, and me along with you. You wanna let the whole town know that baby in your belly's being born on the wrong side of the blanket? And for what?" His eyes were moist when they met hers, bloodshot and full of pain.

"I never meant to cause you all this trouble, Gideon, I swear I didn't." She tried to turn away and he stopped her with the lightest touch on her chin. "You should have let me just leave town."

"Maybe I should have," he agreed when he peeled back the cloth that covered her arm and winced at the sight of her. She reached for the blanket but he stilled her hand and tucked the covers beneath her breasts. "Stay still. We'll be here all night as it is, getting these out."

"Gideon, I'm so very, very sorry," she said, closing her eyes against all the pain that assailed her inside and out.

"I know," he said, and she could hear her own pain mirrored in his voice.

•   •   •

He was nearly done feeding her the mashed bananas Berris had brought up when Lissie pushed away the spoon and tried to sit herself up.

"Lie still," he warned her, pinning her gently to the bed. She lay there under his guard, and he thought about what it would be like to hold her there beneath him, to bend his head and run trails of kisses over her cheeks, to kiss her lips, and maybe even plunge his tongue into the warmth of her mouth.

What had happened to the decent man he'd always been? Her morning sickness, her wounds, even the possibility of a cracked rib—none of it stopped his desire. Let his family be disappointed in him, let the townfolk think what they would—if he was just free to kiss her, if she just wanted him to kiss her half as much as he wished he could, he'd be a happy man.

Instead of kissing her, he worked at the splinters in her left arm, stopping only to spoon some nourishment into her before continuing on to her right arm. On the insides of her forearms the skin had already begun to turn blue from the impact of the vine. He tried to be as gentle as he could, knowing that Berris's touch would have been lighter, softer, but not sorry that he'd sent her away.

"Oh Lord, Lissie!" he said sadly, not sure which of them was in more pain as he unbuttoned her nightdress and found the thorns had dared to scratch at the top of her breasts.

"Are you very mad at me?" she asked, and her ragged breath nearly undid him.

"Mad?" he asked. Mad that he hadn't been there to stop her, to protect her, mad that he hadn't cleared the whole damn forest the night he'd decided to build the house so that she wouldn't even have been tempted to help.

"It was an awfully stupid thing to do, and you did tell me not to," she said. She bit at her lip as he poked at the remains of a thorn imbedded just at the edge of her frilly collar.

How could he be mad at her? It was what he'd fallen in love with all those years ago—that wild, crazy streak that reached out and grabbed at life with two open arms and a smile. While Gideon plodded carefully through life, Lissie skipped along merrily. While he let the possibility of dire consequences stop him from doing a hundred things, Lissie dared do all those things and more. And when something went wrong, she picked herself up and threw herself right back into life.

"I wouldn't blame you, you know, if you were mad," she said, wide green eyes glistening with tears. He poked and prodded and fought against the rising tide of his passion by rebuttoning her gown and moving on to her left arm.

"I'm not." Why was it that this little wisp of a woman would dare anything, and he wasn't brave enough to tempt fate with three little words?

"I'm sorry, Gideon," she said, then leaned her head back and closed her eyes against his ministrations. A tear slipped from beneath her lashes and he knew it wasn't the pain of the thorns that hurt her so.

He recognized the sound of his father's footsteps before the knock came at the door.

"Remember," he told Lissie, "we forgot ourselves and got carried away. I won't have people whispering behind my back that the boy isn't mine."

"The boy?" Lissie asked, her eyes still closed, but the side of her mouth twitched slightly. "And what if it's a girl?"

The thought of a tiny Lissie, one who would love him, nearly took his breath away.

"Come on in, Pa," Gideon said, his voice choking as he pulled the covers up to Lissie's chin. Nothing much had been showing before, but it felt wonderful to imagine it could have been, that he could have seen what no other man in the world had a right to see. He forced from his mind the knowledge that Slick had seen her first, had touched, had tasted, had buried his seed. She was his now, his for life, and that was all that mattered.

"You all right?" his pa asked Lissie.

"Yes sir," she said, looking like she'd been caught stealing cattle. "Just a few scrapes and bruises."

"Berris says you two put the cart before the horse," his father said.

"Berris needs to learn how to mind her own business," Gideon said.

"That may be, but it don't change the facts," his pa said. "Didn't seem to me that you two were on your way to the altar anyways, and that you just couldn't wait for the train. . . ."

"I suppose it's pretty hard for you to believe that Gideon could have been interested in the likes of me," Lissie said, "what with my wild ways and my incorrigible nature."

"Don't go putting words in my mouth, Arliss Mallard. I ain't saying that Gideon wasn't interested. I'm saying that—heck, I wish your ma was here, Gideon, to do this thing right."

"There ain't nothing to do right," Gideon said. "I'm too old for scolding, and Lissie don't deserve none."

His father shook his head. "I don't know about too old, but I can see it's too late. I sure thought I raised you better than that."

"Sir—" Lissie started, but his father wasn't about to let her take any of the blame.

"It's a man that ought to know better," he said, stepping back until he was out in the hall. "Can I see you a minute, Gideon?"

"I'll be right back," he told Lissie, tucking the covers up around her. "Try to sleep."

"Oh yeah," she said, as if he'd told her to scale Mt. Hagan. "That ought to be easy."

His father closed the door behind them and looked Gideon over, shaking his head and finding it hard to spit out what he had to say.

"It ain't right, son, you taking advantage of a girl like that. A man, a *decent* man, wouldn't have let a situation like that get outta control. He wouldn't let *wanting* a girl turn into *taking* a girl. Especially his good friend's girl."

Gideon wanted to say that it hadn't been a decent man who'd let the situation get out of control. He wanted to say that he hadn't been the one doing the wrong, not to Lissie and not to Slick. Instead he said simply, "A man makes mistakes. And a *decent* man pays for 'em. I'm doing right by Lissie, so I don't see what more you can ask."

"Well, I'm glad to see you taking responsibility for what you did, though I sure ain't easy with the fact that you did it. But what's eating my craw is that while a man's gotta pay for his own mistakes, he ought to be damn sure he isn't paying for someone else's." He rolled his eyes toward Gideon's bedroom door. "Even if you're sure you were the first one—and that sure as hell galls me, son—it still don't mean you were the *only* one."

Gideon squelched the urge to shout at his pa. Lissie was just on the other side of that door, hurting enough without knowing what her new father-in-law thought of her. "The child's mine," he said through clenched teeth.

"Sayin' a mule's a mare don't make it so," his pa cautioned. "And everyone knows that Arliss Mallard only had eyes for Slick Waynick since she was old enough to figure out the difference between boys and girls."

"Watch what you say, Pa. You're talking about my wife and my son," Gideon replied, his hand on the doorknob to his room.

"Wishin' it ain't gonna make it so," his pa insisted.

Gideon turned the handle. Before he opened the door, he turned to his pa. "I suppose you'd have said the same thing about Lissie ever becoming my wife. But she's lying there in my bed, ain't she?"

He slipped quietly into the room and tried to close the door behind him, but his father stood in the way, clearly fighting with himself. "I suppose I could work on that land some tomorrow with Cluny," Thaddeus said. "And maybe the Pielman boys would like to earn two bits or so helping out while their pa's laid up. We could probably get the whole thing cleared before Arliss here is outta mothballs."

It was, he supposed, his father's way of apologizing, or at least accepting the situation.

Lissie made no sound upon his entrance, and he thought she might already be asleep. "That'd be real good," Gideon whispered, agreeing to the tenuous truce with his father as he took his place in the chair by the bed. "I'm betting Cluny's got a little bill over at Hughes' Mercantile that needs paying and he could use some money."

"Then it's settled," his father said quietly, making it

clear as he came to the foot of the bed that this was something that would never be discussed again.

Under Gideon's watchful eye, Lissie shifted uncomfortably and blinked up at him. A small pink tongue traced her upper lip and she smiled sleepily.

His stomach jumped up past his heart and right into his throat.

"Pa, would you close the door on your way out?" he asked, pushing back Lissie's hair from her brow and fussing with her covers. "I gotta get Lissie fed and ready for bed."

"You do right by her, son," his father said, stroking the wedding ring quilt which had adorned the bed he'd shared with Gideon's mother.

"Dead set on it," he agreed, returning his attention to her cuts and bruises while his father backed out of the room and shut the door quietly behind him.

He pulled back the covers and without asking permission, or even explaining, he folded back her nightdress high up on her thighs and pulled the cold cloths from her left leg. Her ankle had been protected by her boot, but her leg and knee looked like a road map of Butte. And each thorn was a saloon. No one had ever bothered to count the number of saloons in Butte, but as he pulled at the thorns with the tweezers, he counted every little cry of pain that escaped her lips.

"We'll get through this, Lissie," he told her softly, hoping that saying the words could make it so.

Her answer was a soft breath, and he realized she was asleep.

# Chapter Eight

AFTER A WEEK OF SLATHERING BALM OF GILEAD Ointment over a good portion of Lissie's body, Gideon was clearly on the verge of going off his rails. Touching her every morning and every night, her body slippery from the lard-based salve . . . running his hands up her thighs to within inches of her womanhood . . . down her arms, letting the back of his hands brush her breasts without apology . . . it was a slow and tortuous road to the asylum. He'd even had to remove a thorn from her softly rounded bottom! How much was a man expected to take?

Still, no amount of torture could stop him from seeing to her himself, taking care of her needs before he left each morning and hurrying back to her side each night. Something had somehow shifted the day she'd been hurt—something which gave him certain rights that thrilled and excited him. Since the accident he had seen every part of her—had touched almost every one. He'd brushed her hair, washed her face, bathed her down, and dried her off, and his hands went wherever they needed to go to do whatever she needed done.

And it wasn't simply a matter of intimacy. At meals he'd taken to answering for her—making sure she was eating properly—and no one questioned his authority. He saw to her porcelain bowl in the morning and helped her into her sleeping gown at night.

And the torch he had once carried for her was now a raging fire. He burned for her with a flame that only grew hotter with each passing day.

The fact that Berris charred his meals, that his father was suddenly too busy to so much as play a hand of cards with him at the office, that Cluny badgered him with questions, all paled beside the something special he felt growing between himself and his Lissie.

That was it, he thought. She was *his* Lissie now.

So what was he supposed to do with the letter Miss Kelly at Hughes' Mercantile and Post Office handed him, along with the usual inquiries and announcements? A letter from Helena addressed to *Arliss Mallard* in an all-too-familiar handwriting? There'd been nothing for him to do but smile politely and slip it into his pocket, then get rid of it as soon as he could.

So why hadn't he?

Why was it still waiting, now in the pocket of the fancy dress shirt which Berris had bought him last Christmas? And why hadn't he mentioned it to her?

The doctor had been in just hours ago and to their great relief had declared that the rib had been bruised, not broken, and was healing well enough for her to resume her daily chores, with caution, of course. He'd taken Gideon aside and told him that *all* of Arliss's normal activities—including marital relations, he'd added in a very low voice—could be resumed. Naturally, he'd added, Gideon should avoid inflicting even a portion of his weight on Arliss, considering her accident and her condition.

*All of her normal activities, including marital relations.* So really there'd been no point in giving her the letter from Slick tonight, not when they should be celebrating her recovery.

And really, there was no point in giving it to her at all, he told himself, as he slipped under the covers beside her.

"How do you feel?" he asked her, playing with his pillows to hide his nervousness. If he touched her with the salve tonight, he vowed there would be no stopping at the top of her thigh.

"About the same as I did ten minutes ago," she answered, turning on her side to face him. "Stupid. And guilty. I've been lying here being pampered and petted and playing the princess, when it was my own fault and I never even broke my rib and . . . well, you know what I really deserve."

He knew what she thought she deserved, being what others might call a "fallen woman," and he knew that for all his spouting ideals and morals, he deserved no better. But none of that mattered with her next to him in the dim light of the waning moon.

"You really feel fine?" he asked, shifting to face her and stretching so that he could let his arm drop, oh so casually, somewhere around her hip. All right. Exactly at her hip—just as it dipped toward her waist.

She nodded solemnly.

"Think any place needs more balm?" he asked, running his hand up her arm and pulling at her nightgown to reveal the creamiest shoulder imaginable, marred only with the faint reminders of her accident and two of the many freckles he'd come to know well.

She shook her head. "I'm fine," she repeated.

"It doesn't hurt when I touch you?" he asked, this time letting his hand trail down beneath her collarbone several inches.

"No, Gideon. It doesn't hurt."

He let one fingertip trace the swell of her breast, accentuated by the fact that she was lying on her side. She was his—his wife, and this was his right. In fact, it was his duty as a husband.

He edged a bit closer to her, so that if he were to just dip his head his lips would meet hers. He wanted to tell her how pretty she was, how soft. He wanted to tell her that her glow warmed him, that her smile could slay all his dragons of doubt. "Warm night," he said instead and cursed himself for being such a bumbler. He'd managed in the few weeks they'd been married to talk to her, really talk to her, about things that mattered and some that didn't at all. But words of affection belonged to smoother men—men that brought flowers and candy and—and one in particular, whose letter was in the shirt not ten feet away from the bed in which he lay with Lissie.

*His* Lissie.

He let his hand creep further down her chest until he actually cupped her breast. Beneath his palm he felt the nipple pearl and he let his fingertip trace its hardness while Lissie closed her eyes and drew a sharp breath.

He snapped his hand away. "Does it hurt?"

She shook her head slowly and opened her eyes to meet his. "No, it doesn't hurt," she admitted shyly, waiting for him to continue.

And he knew better than to keep a lady waiting.

The tiny little buttons on her sleeping gown were lost in his huge hands, but he managed to get the top two open. Slipping his hand inside, he felt the silkiness of her skin meet the roughness of his own. It had been a strangely quiet week in town and he spent every spare moment he could find clearing the field. His hands were calloused and hardened from the labors, but it didn't seem to bother her, those rough hands of his, taking her weight and measure.

He pulled his hand from the gown, hoping to release the rest of the buttons, but her breast seemed to stick to him and when he looked, it was free of her nightdress. Nearly as white as the cotton that framed it, her breast was full, a blue vein visible beneath the surface as it zigzagged toward her nipple and the dark pink, nearly brown, area that surrounded it.

He wished he had the nerve to kiss her lips, to look into her eyes, to say how much touching her thrilled him. He wished he could survive it if she lay silent in response, but he knew that the crush would be too great, and so he settled for taking from her body what he could never get from her lips.

He bent his head and kissed her breast gently, almost reverently, and eased her onto her back. He was ready now, to make her his wife in every sense. He'd been ready day and night since he'd bent his knees to kiss her in the Granite Methodist Church. But he'd heard that women, like pumps, took priming, and he wanted her ready, too, wanted her eager and willing and wanting.

And so he toyed at her breast with his tongue, fanning his own flames as he tried to ignite hers. And he listened to her breathing and knew when the fire caught. He freed her other breast and let his fingers imitate what his tongue was doing.

And she liked it. He knew she did, and he let his other hand roam over her ribs, testing, finding her sound, then trailing his fingers down her belly.

He could hear his father insisting that a decent man didn't take advantage of a woman, but this was his wife, after all. He had a right to do this. This was *his*.

*His!* he told himself as he spanned the slight rounding of her stomach. Lissie need never know about the letter from Slick. *His!* he thought as his fingers reached her curls. The letter wouldn't change what was building between them. Slick had left her. Gideon was here, now, keeping her safe and warm and building her a home of her own.

He slipped his finger further. He was the one that was seeing that she ate and slept. He was the one that was cleaning her face after she heaved. Not Slick, who'd used her and thrown her away to fend for herself.

He slipped his knee between her thighs and she spread herself for him.

God only knew whose bed Slick was sleeping in, while Gideon had offered his own to Lissie with no strings attached. He could have left her there at the church as Slick had, but he hadn't.

He touched her softness.

While Slick was off in Helena making hell pop loose, Gideon was here, lying to his family to save Lissie's honor, enduring their disappointment and distrust.

Now she was his, to have and to hold, whenever he wanted her, however he wanted her. And he wanted her now, beneath him. even if he wasn't the man she loved, he was the one she'd married, and she was his for the taking.

He raised himself above her. He'd take her now.

She owed him this.

He didn't have to be any more decent than Slick.

*She owed him this.*

He rolled away from her, horrified at his own thoughts.

All in one motion he got out of bed and slipped into his pants as if the house were on fire.

"Gideon?"

He didn't answer her. By the light of the moon he

went straight to his shirt and felt blindly for Slick's letter. "This came for you," he said, trying to keep the anger and the horror from his voice. "From Slick."

He tossed the letter onto the bed and opened the door to the hallway where he gulped in a breath of air that didn't smell of Lissie, didn't feed his want.

He took one last look behind him at her sitting up on their bed and then silently stepped into the hall and closed the door behind him.

Her father was wrong. Juliana was wrong. Even Gideon, the problem himself, was wrong. Things were clearly not getting better, as each of them had promised they would. If Gideon didn't regret the day he'd met her, he surely regretted the day he'd married her. And time didn't appear to be what her marriage needed, despite what her father had told her when he'd brought by the sewing she'd asked for and she'd cried on his shoulder about the mess she'd made of their lives.

"Everyone," he'd said, "in the first few weeks, thinks their marriage is a terrible mistake. Imagine your mother, giving up the life she had, to be with me. And don't think I was without my doubts. Could I make her happy? Would I be all she'd ever need? But love can be a lot like flowers, honey. You remember those deep violet irises I sent for from the catalog for your mama's grave? You remember how the first year you and I didn't think they'd make it, and all we got was a bunch of leaves?

"You wanted me to pull them out, remember? But then the second year we had that one flower, and it hung on while that awful storm drowned all the plants around it. And every year those flowers come back, more of them, stronger, taller than they were the year before."

Arliss had nodded, but she knew her marriage wasn't like the irises at all. No amount of tending and caring could yield some beautiful love in the end because the seeds of love had never been planted in the beginning. But her father, as he'd stared at the bruises on her arms, seemed to need the comforting even more than she had, and she'd wound up reassuring him that her doubts were no worse than her mother's, and that she honestly believed things would all work out.

*Honestly.* The word should have burned her tongue. Somewhere amid the comforter that covered her, the letter from Slick was lost. She searched for it in the darkness, hungry for kind words and promises. She heard the crinkle of paper and clutched the letter to her chest for a moment before turning up the lamp.

"Just look what you've gone and done, Slevin Waynick. Leaving me here to ruin Gideon's life, all because of you." She turned up the lamp by her bedside and stared down at the familiar writing on the envelope. "I hope you're sorry now—so sorry you can't sleep nights for worrying about me, can't eat, can't think. I suppose you thought I'd just hang around waiting for you to see the error of your ways and come home. Well, I couldn't really do that, now could I? Not when there was more than me to think about."

Sitting back against the pillow, she slipped her finger under the lip of the envelope. "And anyways, it's done," she said as she pulled out the letter. "And poor Gideon's probably even sorrier than me."

She read the letter, a quick note scribbled on stationery from the Helena Hotel telling her he was fine and asking her not to worry about him. As if that was all she had to think about these days! He said he'd sat in a game with Nathaniel Hill's son and nearly bluffed him out, but in the end he'd learned a lesson, anyways.

Well, that was dandy. She'd learned a lesson, too. That her mistakes didn't disappear for wishing. They just grew and grew, like the baby in her belly, and she had no doubt that there'd come a time when there'd be a hurt that would be more than she could bear.

He ended with how much he loved her, how he saw her face each night on the back of his eyelids as he drifted off to sleep, and how he thought of her each morning when he rose. He said he burned for her with a fire that he feared would be his undoing and that the other women he was with paled in comparison. He said he hoped that she was taking real good care of herself considering her condition, and that he'd be back soon to make things right and to carry her away. He said he was sorry, and he'd signed his name under the words "until we can be together again."

"So then we're all sorry," she said softly, hugging the letter to her chest and turning down the lamp. She imagined Slick burning for her, wishing she were there beside him, wanting to take her in his arms and fill her with his love. He saw her when he closed his eyes, just as she saw him.

In the dark she stared toward the crack of light under the doorway and tried to picture Slick coming through the door. He was so devastatingly handsome, even if he was slight compared to Gideon. And even if the brown of Gideon's eyes was warmer than the cool blue of Slick's own. Funny how she could hardly remember what Slick looked like anymore, even though she could hear his words loud and clear. *I love you, Arliss, honey, more than any man ever could. I love you more than all the trees in Montana and all the silver in the mines. And I'll keep on loving you always. Don't you never forget that. I'm gonna love you forever.*

Well, he sure had an odd way of showing it. But oh,

could he ever say the right things. Not like Gideon.
When Juliana had come to help with the poultices she'd
said that Gideon was not much of a talker, but that he
sure did love her. Her new sister-in-law had taken the
news about the baby well. In her own sincere way, she'd
admitted that she was a bit surprised to learn that Arliss
had obviously returned Gideon's feelings. She hadn't
questioned why it was that Arliss had been at the
church to marry Slick. And she'd taken Arliss's abject
misery to be the result of her stupid accident.

So Gideon loved her, huh?

Well he sure had a queer way of showing it, too.
When a man loved a woman he wanted to show it with
his body, to plant his crop in her field. Of course, Arliss's field had already been planted. Slick's seed was
bearing fruit. Maybe when Gideon had offered to marry
her he'd figured it wouldn't bother him any to sow a
row someone else had plowed.

And maybe he'd figured wrong.

She rose stiffly and dragged the covers with her to
the big arm chair by the window where she curled up
and tried to go to sleep. After all, now that she was well,
there was no reason for Gideon to give up his bed for
her. Clearly he didn't wish to share it with her in the
way that mattered.

Not that she blamed him. She was what her ma
would have called "used goods" and she knew that
while a man liked his hat, his boots and his woman well
broken in, he liked to start with them new and do the
breaking in himself.

She was nearly asleep when she heard the bedroom
door open, heard his footsteps as he crossed the room.

"Ah, Lissie," she heard him sigh as he slipped his
hands around the cocoon she'd wrapped herself in, lifting blankets and pillows and her, too, in his arms to

carry her back to his bed. She was too tired, too sad to argue, and so she let him lay her down with exquisite care and straighten the covers around her. He brushed the hair from her face and twisted it back the way she did each night, securing it with the ribbon on her night-stand. Then he walked around to his side of their bed and sat at the edge for some time. Every now and then, from the way he took a deep breath and turned toward her, she was sure he was going to say something, but he never did.

Finally, he got up with his pillow in hand, and sat in the armchair from which he'd just carried her.

Arliss thought of all the flowers in her father's garden that never made it through the winter. She thought, too, of how Juliana had said that Gideon was just being mindful of Arliss's needs and condition. She had based her caring advice on one little assumption. That Gideon Forbes had married her because he loved her. But the fact that she was more than willing to believe it didn't seem to have the power to make it so.

Except for that moment in the church when God and the congregation demanded it, Gideon had never kissed her lips. And unlike the hundreds of times she'd heard the words from Slevin Waynick, Gideon had never said "I love you." He would never say it, either. Never feel it. He couldn't love her, and she knew it deep in her rounding belly and deep in her breaking heart.

Well, she'd just have to learn to live with that. He was good and kind and caring, and a woman could do worse than be married to Gideon Forbes. A lot worse.

And after all was said and done, it wasn't as if she loved him, either, so it hardly hurt at all. She sniffed back the tears and clutched Slick's letter to her chest, not caring whether or not Gideon heard the crackling of the paper. Even if Gideon didn't want her, someone did. She was sure Slick was wishing right now that he was lying beside her, where she could stretch out and touch him, even if Gideon was out of reach.

∘  ∘  ∘

Slick glanced once again at the cards he'd drawn and slipped the second jack in next to the first. He studied the faces of the men around the table, watching as they decided whether or not to fold. With two pair, he surely wasn't about to throw in his hand.

If he took this pot he just might move on to Anaconda. Helena hadn't turned out to be half as wild as he'd expected, nor half as lucrative, but a few more nights like this one and he'd be able to move on without looking back.

It was like he'd told Arliss in his letter—he owed her better than he was in a position to give just now. Hell, better than he'd ever be in a position to give if he'd stayed in Granite like she wanted, or even in Helena. Once he got to Anaconda he'd clean those tables so fast the miners wouldn't know what hit 'em. Then he could head on back to Granite—and Arliss—a rich man.

He wondered if anyone knew about the baby yet. Arliss had been flat as a board when he'd left. Maybe she was wrong about the baby. Or maybe she was lying. Women were known to lie about such things, and he'd poked a passel of women and none of them ever turned up on his doorstep claiming to be past their time. He'd been as careful with her as he'd been with the rest of them, or nearly, anyways. She could have been bluffing just to force his hand. And anyways, it was a woman's job to see to it that she didn't wind up wearing her bustle backward, not a man's.

"It's up to you, Waynick," the man to his left said.

Slick knew the man had a pair just from the way he

held his cards, but it would be hard to beat jacks up sixes. "Deuce to stay in, a sawbuck to raise," the man added.

It wasn't that he didn't love Arliss—he just knew better than to trust a woman.

With no chips in front of him where his stack had been and very little in his cassimere jacket, he fished around the pocket of his trousers and placed the garnet earrings into the pot. "These ought to be worth ten bucks," he said, tapping the cards that were stacked neatly in front of him.

"Three," someone at the table said, and Slick knew he was lucky to have them valued that high.

"Three," he agreed, confident that his hand would beat any at the table. The thought of winning and eventually going home to Arliss warmed him. He'd leave for Anaconda in the morning. Darcy put some jackass brandy down by his elbow, staying just long enough for Slick to take a long deep swig and squeeze a bit of her bottom.

Thinking about Arliss had left him heated with wanting, though heaven knew the girl had a lot to learn before she could be called a woman. Now Darcy, on the other hand, promised to be wild in his bed, and he was looking forward to winning this hand and heading on upstairs.

Oh, the things he'd teach Arliss when he got home from Anaconda with a pile of money in his pocket and a load of desire in his pants!

# Chapter Nine
## ⊂℘℘⊃

"I'M SURE CARSON DIDN'T MEAN IT," SAMANTHA SAID AS she and Berris iced a Savoy cake. "He just gets edgy when he's cooped up here in town. Not that he ever understands that I feel just the same way, and I'm here all the time."

"Well," Berris said, nearly slashing the cake with her frosting knife. "That's a man for you. He's got yellow jackets in his drawers and so you're the one that gets stung."

"When I was little it was different. Carson let me tag along and draw against him and shoot all the cans off the rails. But now that I'm all grown up and he's a man—well, men just—" Samantha shrugged as if that was just the way of it.

Considering how Berris was feeling about Gideon, and how he'd surely taken advantage of Arliss even if she had been willing, she was happy to finish off the thought for her friend. "Men just say what they want, do what they want, and think it's their right."

"That's not really fair," Sam said, obviously feeling it necessary to defend her clod of a brother, even if he was making her life miserable by telling her where she could go and what she could wear. What was it about men that made women so loyal despite any act on their part? "He is my brother and he did raise me, Berris."

"Oh, and *brothers* are perfect," she said sarcastically, remembering just a few days ago when she was just as naive as Sam. "Unlike *men,* who can be idiots, getting themselves into ridiculous fixes! Just be careful about putting Carson up on some white charger. He's likely to fall off and leave his horse to trample you under its hooves."

She could feel Samantha's eyes on her, sizing her up, trying to guess just what had set her off. It was killing her to keep it to herself, but Berris supposed she was no better than any other woman. She'd take her brother's secret with her to the grave before she betrayed him and the popover he'd married. There was her family's reputation to worry about, and then, too, there'd be her new niece or nephew to protect from the truth.

Animals in heat showed more sense than Gideon and Arliss had. His buddy's girl! Her fiance's friend! Really! And she couldn't even discuss it with her best friend in the world.

"You have to watch men all the time," she warned Samantha. "Like just yesterday afternoon I was down at Verinda Ruth's getting my hair evened out and she told me that Mr. Pielman had sent a message to Mr. Barone down at Granite National that he shouldn't let Mrs. Pielman take out more than ten dollars from their account, no matter what she asked for."

"I hope you're saving all that hair she's cutting off for a wig, Berris. You're gonna need one if you keep this up. I don't see how Mr. Pielman's bank account is any of your business."

"Well, of course it's not my business," Berris agreed. Samantha just didn't understand that life's lessons were out there just waiting to be learned if you kept your eyes and ears open. "I bet he thinks with him laid up and all, his wife might just get a notion to take their money and run out on him while he can't up and follow her!"

"Maybe he's just worried about running out of money while being laid up and all," Samantha guessed as she put finishing swirls on the iced cake.

"If that were the case he'd tell Mrs. Pielman, not the bank," Berris explained patiently. Heck and hydrangeas, a man didn't share more than the time of day with another man unless he had a good reason.

A woman, on the other hand, could sell a few rotten bananas and feel the need to tell the entire world what was no one else's business.

But she was forgetting herself. Educating Samantha about men was a full-time job, and Berris couldn't afford to waste a minute.

"Remember, while men may have the power, the brawn, the control," she warned Samantha, "women have the brains and the wiles. And a smart woman learns how to use them to get what she wants."

"And you think this fancy cake will change Carson's mind about the ball?" Samantha asked, taking the knife away from Berris just in time to stop her from blending all the lovely crystallized violets right into the frosting of their bribery cake.

Samantha Maddigan didn't understand the first thing about handling men. Having only her brother, she thought that Carson's behavior was unique to him, and not something he held in common with every other man in Montana. Did she think women actually liked spending half a day making a Savoy cake that was going to be consumed in five minutes by a man who would grunt his approval and then leave her with the dirty dishes and little more?

"A woman makes a fancy supper cake for two reasons," she explained to Samantha, sharing the expertise she'd culled over a lifetime of living with a father and two brothers. "To say 'thank you'—which, take it from me, is rarely necessary, but which, in the long run, helps reinforce her other use for such a magnificent offering." She stood back and pointed to the confection on the platter before them. The chocolate icing glistened, the crystalized violets sparkled atop the cake like amethysts on brown velvet.

"Which is . . . ?" Sam asked, running her finger around the plate to clean up any drips and popping her finger into her mouth to hide the evidence.

"Guilt." Carson Maddigan's voice was quiet as he appeared in the doorway, leaned against the doorframe and nodded to Berris.

"Do you walk on air?" Berris asked him, looking at his spit-shined calfskin boots and wondering how it was she hadn't heard him come in. Any other man would have announced his presence, purposely or otherwise, with the clomping of his boots.

The left side of Carson's mouth curved up, more a smirk than a smile. "Only when you're around, Berris, my love. But I wouldn't count on those feminine wiles working on me. I don't corner so easy." He reached out his finger for a bit of icing and Berris batted it away. With a flourish, careful to wave it beneath his nose, she picked up the platter and moved it to the counter near the back door.

"Oh, this isn't for you," she said as sweetly as she could manage. "It's for Gideon and Arliss. A sort of wedding present for them."

The mask of superiority Carson Maddigan always wore slipped for just a second. Berris, having practiced such skills in the mirror often, kept her smile in check.

"Of course, if you want one . . . " Berris added, her look as open and innocent as she could make it.

Carson shook his head and headed for the doorway from which he'd come. "I don't care much for anything that rich," he said, looking her up and down and sneering at the fine French Valenciennes lace collar she'd worked so hard at attaching. "But I'm sure Gideon will enjoy it immensely."

"I'm sure he will," Berris agreed, tying on her bonnet like she was heading out into a tornado. For the life of her, she didn't know why she wasted a thought on him. Carson Maddigan was simply impossible.

"I don't think it'll take the cake, Berris honey," he said, his whiskey-colored eyes meeting hers and reminding her once again why it was she couldn't get the man off her mind. "I suspect the good deputy has already got a serious case of the guilts about now."

So Gideon had been telling the truth about taking advantage of Arliss. She didn't know how Carson had found out, but it was a while after he left the room before either Berris or Samantha could find their tongues.

"Better shut your mouth, Berris," Sam said gently. "You're liable to catch a few flies."

Lissie managed two bites of Berris's cake that evening, a feat Gideon might have applauded if things had been different. As it stood, Lissie was hardly even talking to him. He didn't know what was in Slick's letter, but Lissie had barely said two words to him since he'd woken up more twisted than a pretzel from his night in the armchair and found her gone from his bed.

She'd served him breakfast, even eaten some herself, which made him happy. Lord almighty, it didn't take much to make him happy. Lissie up and about, eating, and maybe a smile aimed every now and then in his direction. But Lissie wasn't smiling at him today. Nobody was.

She'd managed to bring a light lunch for Lester and him and his pa, but she'd merely handed it to him before she left, saying something about visiting her own pa. When he'd suggested she ought to go home and rest, she'd told him she'd slept like a log and didn't need any more sleep. After that he'd been busy trying to cool down Mr. Belmont and three of his miners who'd been accused—falsely it appeared—of stealing ore.

And he hadn't seen Lissie again until he'd come home for dinner. Lord but that woman could cook! And that Savoy cake on the counter looked mighty good, too, even if Berris had helped Samantha Maddigan bake it.

His sister cut him a sliver of cake so thin two ants could carry it back to their hill without any help. Cluny sat glaring at the tablecloth when he wasn't drooling after Lissie, his eyes fastened on the straining bodice of her dress. The boy had brought her another one of those stupid bouquets—if you could call a bunch of wildflowers that—and they stood in the center of the table like they could compete with the stewed shin of beef Lissie had made for dinner.

"Got rounds," his father said, pushing back his chair and putting his napkin on his plate. His piece of cake had been twice the size given to Gideon. Even Lissie's piece had been bigger, but when she'd tried to trade with Gideon, Berris had kicked up an awful fuss, assuring Lissie that there was little point in watching her waist now. Lissie had just shrugged her shoulders, taken a bite, and struggled to swallow it.

"I'm ready," Gideon said, rising along with his father to check on the town.

"I think I can handle rounds myself," his father said sadly. "You best stick around and mend fences."

"Our fences are fine," Cluny said, taking great offense. "Saw to 'em last week and all they took was a coat of whitewash to look good as new."

Thaddeus patted his younger son's head. "Sometimes it's hard to see the cracks, but a fence can come down easy if you don't see to it."

"But I—" Cluny started, and then appeared to realize that Thaddeus was talking about something else entirely.

"Why don't you tag along with me, butch?" Thaddeus said, a hand on Cluny's shoulder. "Never too soon to break a new lawman in."

"Can't," Cluny said. "Got other things to do."

Gideon just bet he did. "You thinking of going up to Coppertown?"

"Maybe," Cluny said with a shrug of one shoulder.

"Think again," Thaddeus said, and his heavy hand held the boy in his seat.

"Pa, there's gonna be a—" he stopped in mid-sentence, his eyes real round while he sucked in his lip like it could bring back the words.

"A what?" Thaddeus asked at the same time Gideon did.

"A . . . a . . . practice for the dance, the ball," Cluny lied.

"Bull droppings!" Thaddeus said, then turned red and nodded at Arliss. "Begging your pardon."

"Don't you know how to dance?" Lissie piped up, cutting the heavy air with her soft voice. Gideon wondered if she'd fallen for Cluny's line. "Why don't you stay home tonight and I'll teach you?"

Did she want to keep Cluny out of trouble? Or did she want to avoid being alone with him? "Berris can teach Cluny," he said, but it came out sounding as if he didn't want her help or interference. Just as he started to suggest that Lissie could teach him, Berris was on her feet.

"You know how to dance, Cluny," Berris told him, taking the dishes from the table without regard to whether anyone was done. "He just wants to go up to Coppertown and help the miners plan something."

"What if I do?" Cluny shouted, nearly throwing his plate at Berris and kicking back his chair as he stood. "What if I think they're getting a raw deal and no one's looking out for their rights?"

"I'm looking out for their rights," Gideon said. He saw his father's jaw tighten, knew that Thaddeus felt Mr. Belmont's money kept the town flush and paid his salary, and he owed him his allegiance. From Gideon's way of thinking, the town had elected both him and his father, and the miners were part of that town. But then, so was old man Belmont. "I'm looking out for everybody's rights."

"And I'm doing rounds," Thaddeus said once more, grabbing his hat and shoving it on his head. "And I'm doing them alone."

"Are you going down to the office?" Lissie asked. Her voice was so small, what with him and his father and brother and sister all yelling and huffing, that it took them by surprise. "If you are, maybe Lester would like a slice of the cake? If Berris doesn't mind, of course."

"Lester!" Gideon had figured he'd come back down to the kitchen after everyone had gone to bed and help himself to a decent size piece of cake. But no, Lissie wanted Lester to have it. And Berris, who'd never had a use for Lester or any other prisoner before, was up on her feet and boxing the rest of the cake for her father to take to the poor bastard in his jail, before Gideon could even protest.

"I suppose," his father said, waiting impatiently for Berris to finish boxing the cake.

"Aren't you the thoughtful one," Berris said to Lissie so sweetly she almost choked on the words.

"Yeah," Gideon said, pushing away from the table in disgust. "And if *you* were thoughtful, Berris, you'd leave a piece of that cake for me. The portion you gave me didn't fill the space between my two front teeth."

"Well, I figured if you wanted it, you'd just take it," Berris snipped at him. She handed the box to her father.

"Don't you leave this house, son," Thaddeus said to Cluny. "Help your sister see to the dishes so Arliss can get some rest."

"Oh, I can do them," Lissie said and rose, but Cluny and Berris seemed to have it all in hand and she looked lost in the hubbub around her.

"Wanna see how we're doing on the house?" Gideon suggested.

"I should help with the dishes," she said, but he could tell she was interested. There wasn't much up yet, but it was all he had to offer. He wished she'd accept.

"It's getting dark," he said. "You can help when we come back in." Then he pulled her shawl off the peg by the door and handed it to her despite the fact that the cool air had been avoiding Montana like a prairie dog avoids a coyote. He helped her wrap the woolen cloth around her shoulders and felt her shudder at his touch.

Ah, one step forward and two steps back. What a dance he and Lissie were doing. Last night's intimacies had cost him today's casual contact. Slick might have been gone for weeks, yet still he'd been there in the bedroom with them. And even though Gideon had wedded Lissie, she still wasn't his wife.

It wasn't a dance, he thought, but a battle. And both sides were losing the war.

He showed her the outline of the house, helping her step over the strings he and Cluny had attached between the stakes that marked its four corners. It wasn't anything fancy, but it would be their own.

"You're standing in the parlor," he said and pointed off to his left. "The dining room'll be there, the kitchen behind it."

Marmalade, who'd kept Lissie company during the days when she'd been forced to stay in bed, now tagged along after her, winding around her legs. In another month or two, she might not be able to see him down there.

"Go on now," he told the cat—yet another male who had fallen under his wife's spell. "You're liable to trip her up."

The cat moved away to the far corner of the house, where he took up residence as if the fireplace had already been built and he was the king of the hearth. Lissie watched the animal like it was her best friend sent off to the salt mines. When the cat began to lick himself, she returned her attention to the house.

"It's bigger than I expected," Lissie said, but it was unclear to him whether that was a good thing or not.

"The stairs will go there," he said, pointing to his right. He looked up at the sky above them and took a deep breath. "I was planning three bedrooms upstairs." The way he figured it, Lissie and he would share the biggest room, the baby would be next door, and someday there'd be a brother or sister for it.

He looked down at her. "Does that suit you?" he asked. She had to know what he was asking. *Are we*

*gonna have children of our own Lissie? Will you really*
*be my wife?*

She bit at her lip, her eyes avoiding his gaze and
looking at the rooms that had yet to be built. Rooms
that they would spend the rest of their nights in, and it
was up to her how they spent them. She sighed joy-
lessly, the way she seemed to do everything since Slick
had run out. "Yes, Gideon," she agreed, her voice
barely above a whisper. "If that's what you want."

Three bedrooms for three people. One not even
born yet. Separate bedrooms, then. Well, what did she
expect when he couldn't even bear to touch her. Where
were the *needs* Slick had told her about? The *needs* her
mother had warned her about when she'd become a
woman, when her mother had impressed upon her—
apparently not well enough—that a man was excused by
the nature of those needs from coming to his wife pure,
but a woman had no such excuse.

She couldn't say she hadn't been warned where her
wayward behavior would lead.

"Then three bedrooms," Gideon said as if he needed
to drive home the point. "For now."

"Whatever you say, Gideon," she repeated, hanging
on the promise of his words. So even he realized that
someday he might want her, might need her. Heaven
help her, but she'd liked the feel of his hands on her,
even if his gentleness hadn't stemmed from anything
more than a concern for her fragile condition. Couples
had based marriages on less than that, she supposed.

Gideon had taken more time to work his way down
her ribs than Slick had taken to plant a baby in her belly
and change her whole life. And she'd liked it, even
though she knew she wasn't supposed to. It had almost
been as if he was doing what he was doing to please her,

and not himself—as if he had wanted her to enjoy his touch.

"Is there anything you want different?" Gideon asked. "I mean since we haven't started yet, we could change things. . . . "

She wanted everything different. She wanted to be married to a man who would say the sun didn't rise until she smiled at him. She wanted to be married to a man who would tell her that her body was like some sculpture by that famous Italian whose name she could never remember. She wanted to laugh about ridiculous names for her baby and admit how frightened she was that a life was growing inside her.

She wanted to feel free to admit that she was even less prepared to be a mother than she was to be a wife, especially Gideon's wife. She wanted to tell him that she loved the baby inside her, but was afraid to ask if he thought he ever could. It was Slick's baby, she knew, but she wondered if she loved the child because of that or in spite of it.

"We could put the steps in the middle and have the parlor on the other side of them," he said.

"It's fine the way it is," she said, reminding herself that she had more to be grateful for than most women who had done what she had done. Gideon was a good man, trying his hardest to be a good husband. He gave more and asked less than anyone she'd ever known, and she couldn't help but admire him even if she didn't love him. She probably never would love him—just as he would never love her.

"I like the house just fine," she said with determination. "I think it'll be a fine place for us."

He smiled and she was surprised to see a deep dimple in his left cheek. Now how had she never noticed that? She must have seen him smile before, when she

and Slick and Gideon were together. Of course, her
eyes would have been glued to Slick, but still . . .

"Have you always had that?" she asked, reaching out
and touching his cheek, drilling a tiny hole where his
smile had put one.

And the man could blush. Imagine that! "Poked it
with a fork once," he said, staring down at how the hem
of her dress was hiding his boots. "Cut it up pretty bad
from the inside and when it healed, it left a reminder
not to make a hog of myself."

"Really? I never knew that."

"There's lots you don't know," he said, but he didn't
elaborate.

"It's nice when you talk to me," she said softly. "I
like it a lot. Slick used to talk all the time. He used to
tell me all kinds of things, like how he'd have the biggest house in town and—"

"Ain't you learned by now that talk's cheap?" he
asked, all traces of the smile gone from his face as he
helped her over the string that went where their threshold would someday be. And then, with a warning stare
at the kitty, he stalked off as soon as he'd seen her safely
to the other side. "I don't need the biggest house in
town," he shouted over his shoulder as his long strides
pulled him away from her and back to his father's
porch.

She followed along after him, through the last spires
of brussels sprouts and spent soil, the cat following a
safe distance behind. Around her house she would plant
lilacs, and buddleia, too. She supposed that the Forbes
were too practical for something that only smelled good
or provided a home for passing butterflies. She supposed that if you couldn't eat it, they wouldn't see the
need to plant it.

But her pa had always said that the soul needed

nourishment, too, and she meant to plant a whole field of flowers in the spring. And she meant to teach her baby how to tell a weed from a flower and not be fooled by some fancy first leaves.

She expected that Gideon would take a seat on the porch glider, but he didn't. Instead he stood by the door until she caught up with him, opened it for her, and waited while she entered the kitchen. Then he nodded at her curtly as if he were saying good-bye, waited until she'd hung up her wrap and picked up a dishtowel to help Berris. After she'd taken the first dish from her sister-in-law's hands, he turned on those big heels of his and returned to the porch. The screen door slammed behind him with a finality that warned them all to leave him alone.

"What's he so mad about?" Berris asked her after the echo had left the kitchen in silence.

Arliss shrugged. "Something I said. Or, something I didn't say. Or maybe it was something I did. Or, quite possibly, something I didn't do."

Or maybe it was what Gideon hadn't done. He'd wanted her, in their bed—she knew he had. But not any more than she'd wanted him.

Dear God! How she'd liked the feel of his hands, so powerful and yet so gentle. His lips had been softer than she'd expected and the way he'd touched her had been careful, respectful. She'd told him nothing hurt, and still he'd treated her like one of those fine crystal vases her mother was always losing her heart to.

Until it had grated too hard on his nerves and he'd turned away from her in disgust at what she was, instead of what he wanted her to be.

"You look positively stricken," Berris said. "Gideon didn't—"

"No Berris, he didn't," Arliss said, almost laughing at

her private joke as she put down the cloth and picked at a dinner roll in the basket near the sink.

"You know, Arliss, this isn't easy on any of us," Berris said. "Your little romantic moment with Gideon hasn't just affected the two of you. If you had just kept your skirts around your ankles—"

"You know it's pretty easy being virtuous when no one's interested in your virtue, Berris," Arliss snipped. Lord, if she wasn't weepy these days, she was angry. And if she wasn't angry—

"Well, I guess you'd know about being easy," Berris snapped right back.

—She was sad. She could feel those stupid tears welling up as she traded insults with her sister-in-law. "Didn't your mama ever teach you it was wrong to go judging other people? My mama sure did."

"Well maybe you had to be taught not to judge because you were never in a position to," Berris said, crossing her arms over her chest and staring at Arliss's belly as if the proof was resting there. "Maybe when you do so many thoughtless things—"

"You have that last glass of milk yet?" Gideon called in from the porch, interrupting them. "Bring it out here and drink it in the fresh air."

Berris handed her a clean glass with a look that said she was sorry, and Arliss accepted the glass, and with it, the apology. Not that Berris owed her any, despite what she might have thought.

"I shouldn't have snapped at you," Arliss said as she poured the milk and replaced the pitcher in the oak icebox.

"No," Berris said, taking the shawl from the peg and wrapping it around Arliss's shoulders. "I guess I'm kind of glad you did. I mean, if Gideon's not sorry about what happened, I don't see where I've got a right to be."

Arliss shook her head and let an unhappy sigh escape her lips. "Yeah," she agreed. "If Gideon's not sorry . . . " Her voice trailed off as she headed for the porch with her glass of milk.

She felt Berris's eyes boring into her back, but didn't dare turn around as she sniffed back tears.

Sheriff Forbes was just rounding the back corner of the house as she stepped outside the door. In her home, they would use the front door—and not just for company, either.

"Town's tight as a pair of new boots," the sheriff said as Gideon sidled over on the swing to make room for her. Warmth poured from his body, enveloping her, and she cradled her tumbler of milk as she squirmed back into the cushions. "Coppertown's quiet, too."

"Pa, Coppertown is part of Granite. If the town's quiet, that ought to include Coppertown. And if there's trouble up there, believe me, there's trouble in town."

Arliss eased a little closer to her husband. Maybe it was to show she agreed with him. Maybe it was because it was getting colder out. And maybe it was because it felt good, felt right, at least to her. She sniffed and felt Gideon's eyes studying her.

"How'd Lester like the cake?" he asked his pa while he adjusted her shawl. "Is he feeding it to the cockroaches?"

"Said he wasn't hungry," Gideon's father said. "Left it on the desk for tomorrow."

"Wasn't hungry for iced cake?" Arliss asked. She'd seen him eat half of one of her mama's famous genoise in one sitting. "Is he sick?"

"Man's sick in the head, if you ask me." The sheriff

opened the back door and nodded in their general direction with what Arliss figured was "good night."

"Sure was a waste of good cake," Gideon grumbled next to her.

"A piece would go nice with this milk you're always making me drink," Arliss admitted.

"Yeah," Gideon agreed.

"A big piece," she said wistfully and saw the return of his dimple for a brief moment.

"Yeah."

They sat in silence for a while, Arliss's stomach rumbling and Gideon pretending not to notice.

"Maybe Lester will want it in the morning. Seeing that man in jail just breaks my heart," she said when she had finished her milk. He was a fixture in her mama's kitchen when hard times had reduced him to begging for a meal. Losing his father's farm had broken his spirit, and his wife going back to her people had broken his heart.

"Well, having him out wouldn't help you or anybody else, believe me. The man's where he belongs, and till that judge tells me otherwise, that's where he's gonna stay."

He was rigid just like Slick said. Absolute. He was just like Berris. The whole family had cornered the market on righteousness and woe to those who didn't live up to their standards, whether they'd lost their minds or their purity. "I didn't think you needed a judge to tell you anything," she said, coming to her feet wondering how low a woman of her soft morals must fall on his list.

She went inside, hung her shawl, rinsed her glass. Gideon remained on the porch. She thought about telling him she was going up to bed, thought about asking him to come up with her.

She almost laughed out loud at how ridiculous she could be.

He'd given her enough time to fall asleep before climbing the stairs and crawling into the bed beside her. *Slick used to talk to me all the time,* she'd said, *about how we'd have the biggest house* . . .

Was it Slick building her a house, he wanted to know. Was he coming through on any of those promises and dreams he'd filled her head with?

Beside him, beneath the covers, Lissie's tummy rumbled. There'd been a change in her today, in her condition. She'd been downright feisty out there on the swing, and even if she was wrong about Lester, it was good to see her old hackles rising. And then, too, there'd been no porcelain bowl to start the morning and she'd eaten everything that was put in front of her. Hunger, he thought, must be a good sign in a woman expecting. Maybe she'd develop an appetite for other things . . . maybe even for a big oaf of a man who might not be a smooth talker, but who meant every damn thing he said.

She smelled warm, musky. Like the floor of the forest in the summer where a ray of sun has found its way in. She smacked her lips in her sleep in much the same way that his little niece used to. She turned and scratched at her belly, still lost in her dreams. He wouldn't have guessed how much pleasure, how much contentment, could come from just watching someone sleep. She rubbed at her breast, as if that, too, itched, and made a little sound of discontent before smacking her lips again.

He wondered what he did in his sleep that she was privy to. Did he pass wind, or snore, or scratch at his privates? It was a funny thing, this marriage that gave them an intimacy without being intimate. He knew so much about her that he hadn't expected to ever know: she said her prayers before she made her last trip down the hall each night. She had the coldest feet in Montana. She sucked her thumb.

And she was hungry. If he let her keep at it, her finger would be half gone by morning. Gently he eased it from between her lips and held her hand for a moment before rising and slipping into his pants. It would be a shame to let that fancy iced cake go to waste. And he'd be damned if poor old Lester would have it, when here was Lissie, hungry as a she-wolf and eating for two.

And whatever she didn't finish, he'd be happy to take care of. Besides, if he stayed in bed beside her, he'd explode with want.

And not for chocolate cake, that was for damn sure.

Granite was quiet as he walked down the main street to the sheriff's office. A cat howled somewheres, and something—a coyote, maybe—answered back. Things scurried about beneath the wooden sidewalks as his boots thumped on them, but for as far as the eye could see, there wasn't a soul about.

It was the way he liked it. He never hungered for the excitement of Virginia City, never wanted the bustle of Butte. Everything he wanted was either back asleep in his bed or waiting to be built not a hundred yards from his father's house. Maybe he wasn't what some might call "expansive," but he thought that wanting more than you had was a sure way to wind up disappointed. Or maybe it was just that he appreciated what he had.

He'd never believed that having money could buy anything that really mattered or that money guaranteed security. In the dark of the sleeping town he admitted that maybe it hadn't been his place to go making those sorts of decisions for others. Maybe Lissie was right about him. Maybe he did judge others too easily.

The moonlight shone on the door to the office and Gideon slipped his key into the lock. Tiptoeing so that he wouldn't wake Lester, he went straight for the cake box.

"Who's out there?" Lester yelled from the back. "And whaddya want?"

"It's me," Gideon answered, coming to the door and looking through the barred window.

"Can't sleep? Bet that pretty little wife of yours is sleeping like a log, her being knocked up and all," Lester said. He was sitting on his cot pulling hairs from the top of his head.

"She ain't 'knocked up,'" Gideon corrected, though he ought to know better than to bother. "She's 'expecting.'"

"Ought to be just about beginning to show," Lester said. "I'd say 'knocked up' if it was someone else's bun in my wife's oven."

"You ain't got a wife no more, Pincus," Gideon said, a knot twisting his stomach tight.

"She come to see Hedda pretty early in August," Lester said.

Lester's sister, Hedda Clovis was the woman the ladies of Granite went to when they didn't want to see Doc Agrin for one reason or another. He figured feminine troubles were private, and a woman might feel more comfortable with another woman poking around or whatever it was they did. Hedda was from the back country somewhere and had a weed for whatever ailed a body. He'd heard that she had poisons, too, and that women who found themselves carrying when they came to her were often relieved of the burden soon after they left. The thought that Lissie could have gotten rid of her troubles crossed his mind. He wondered if she wished now that she had.

He'd forgotten all about how Hedda had taken her brother in when he'd lost his job at the livery . . . just before landing in jail because he'd gone back to shoot the horses he claimed ratted on him.

"Heard tell old Slick had gone and gotten himself in some tight spot, if you know what I mean," Lester said, dropping the hairs he pulled and chuckling to himself. "Guess it ain't so tight now," he added.

The knot in Gideon's belly rose up his throat and he choked out his words. "Lester, it might be best if we both forgot what you just said. How about it?"

"You got any hair, Gideon?" Lester asked, picking at his scabs, unfazed by Gideon's threat. "Don't know how this here dog's gonna make a nest without more hair."

"You don't have a dog," Gideon answered. "And dogs don't make nests."

"Shh! Keep your voice down. He don't know he ain't a dog," Lester said, pointing at a dark spot on the floor of his cell. Gideon stamped his foot, hoping to scare the rodent, but the dark mark remained where it was. He opened the door and came close enough to get a better look.

"What is that?" Gideon asked, looking at the dark circle next to a ball of hair that sat on the floor.

"Spot," Lester said simply.

"I can see it's a spot," Gideon said. Lester had requested a pen and paper earlier in the day and had clearly spilled the ink onto the floor in a circle which appeared to have two ears.

"Not *a* spot. Spot. My dog. Remember the Mallards' dog? Now he's mine."

He'd forgotten that Lissie's family had once owned a

dog, and surely couldn't remember whether or not its name was Spot, but he made some noises of agreement just to end the discussion.

"I had to kill him, him knowing and all. But don't you worry none, Gideon. I'm willing to take our secret to the grave. You just gotta worry about Hedda's mule talking. He's the one that told me all about it."

"Ain't nothing to tell," Gideon said calmly. He was getting better at the lie every day, and out it came, as natural as wool on a lamb. "Lissie and me are expecting a baby early next summer. Simple as that."

"That'd be after she delivers Slick's brat, I guess. Mule heard her tell Hedda she could come to the wedding, and the mule told me. But you let me out of here, Gideon Forbes, and I'll take care of that damn mule. Always did talk too much. And Hedda, too, if you think that'll help you any."

"I don't need any help," Gideon said, while Lester practiced his draw with imaginary pistols. "Short of you dropping off the planet, that is."

"I'll do my best," Lester said amenably. "But I don't think I've got enough ink." He traced the spot on the floor. "Poor little fella."

Gideon turned to leave.

"Think the little one'll look like his papa?" Lester called after him.

Gideon shut the door that divided the cell room from the main office and looked back through the bars. "Go to hell," he said, then turned and picked up the cake box, slamming the outer door behind him. "Just drop dead, Lester, and go to hell."

# Chapter Ten

ARLISS'S PA HAD ALWAYS TOLD HER THAT NO MATTER how straight you plant a tree, sometimes you still had to stake it to make it grow right. Her father was always talking about people when he told her about flowers and trees, so she guessed what he meant was that even though she and Gideon had been honest with each other when they married, the course of their marriage wouldn't necessarily always be straight and true.

Which meant that if she wanted their union to be a strong, straight one, solid like an oak, she would have to ask him where he'd gone off to in the middle of the night—where he'd been that left him all out of breath and with his heart pounding so hard she could feel the bed pulse for minutes after he'd lain down.

She stood at the stove frying Lester's fish, remarkably unperturbed by the odor. Berris had gone off to Hughes' Mercantile, and Cluny, after the same old argument about him being too old, had finally left for school. Cluny was now the oldest boy in class, since so many of the other boys his age had already quit school to work on the farms or in the mines. It wasn't until Arliss pointed out the fact that girls tended to like their boys older that he'd grabbed up his books and left with a huff. His father left with him to make sure he got where he was supposed to be going.

Now that she was alone in the kitchen with Gideon, she supposed there was no putting it off. Better to know than to guess, her mama always said. *Deal with what is and don't worry about what might be.* Her biggest fear was that he might have gone to Miss May's place on Lilac Row. Back when Slick was trying so hard not to ruin Arliss, he'd spent a lot of time, and money at Miss May's, at the edge of town. Not that he ever blamed Arliss. He understood that she wanted to save herself for her husband.

Of course, that hadn't worked out quite the way he'd promised.

"Gideon?" Her voice sounded like that of a little girl, and she cleared her throat and was about to call him again when he turned from the window to face her.

"I'm gonna try to come home early and get the frame laid out," he said, fidgeting with the cotton cloth that covered the table. All morning he'd fussed and fiddled and acted like a man with something on his mind. Guilt, no doubt. "If I get a side done each day, Cluny can help me get it up after church on Sunday."

"Is that what you been thinking about all morning?" she asked. " 'Cause it seems to me you got something on your mind."

"I got a lot on my mind," he said. "We're inches away from trouble at the Columbia. Ain't that fish ready yet? I gotta get over to the office and see what else has gone wrong since yesterday."

"Going by way of the edge of town?" she asked. "Maybe Lilac Row?"

There didn't seem to be much point in pretending Miss May's didn't exist, as did all the decent women of

Granite. And if her husband had been there, it was best that she know now, before someone went and threw it in her face.

His jaw dropped. He stood staring at her, unblinking. His face was so open, so utterly surprised, that she wondered how she could ever have supposed that was where he'd gone. "I heard you get up in the middle of the night," she explained. "And I thought that, what with the way things were between us . . . "

"That I'd be unfaithful?" His mouth still hung open but he couldn't seem to find any words. He sat in the chair without looking for it, shaking his head at her as if she'd asked him if he were out teaching the coyotes to sing.

"Well, it wouldn't be like that, since—"

He cut her off. "You're my wife Lissie. I won't forget it, and don't you, neither. For better or for worse, we promised each other and God." His arms were crossed over his chest, but his hands were fisted as he stared at her.

How ever could she have thought that Gideon Forbes—a man who stood head and shoulders above the rest of Granite—would have needed any propping up to be sure he was straight and true? "I'm sorry," she said, tears tickling her throat. "I didn't know what else to think. I heard the back door, saw your clothing gone . . . "

"Open the breadbox, Arliss," he said, her name sounding formal, chastising, on his lips. "Go on, open it."

She lifted the wooden lid that fit over the cutting board on the counter and looked from the cake box to the man at the table.

"You said you wished you had another piece of cake. I thought if you woke up hungry in the night—well, I

went over to the jail and got it for you." He shrugged
and rose from the table. "That fish must be ready by
now. Where's the basket?"

"You went to the jail? But you were nearly heaving
when you got back into bed. What was I supposed to
think, Gideon? You sneak off in the night and come
back breathing so heavy that the rafters creak."

"I had a run-in with your friend down there." He bit
at the side of his lip.

"Lester? What kind of run-in could you have had
with Lester?" she asked, putting the man's breakfast
into the basket and taking off her apron. "You didn't
hurt him, did you?"

As soon as the words were out of her mouth she
wanted them back, would have cut out her tongue to
have never uttered them.

"Anything else you figure I did while I was out last
night?" he asked, more sad than angry. "I mean when I
got done carousing with the women on Lilac Row and
beating my prisoner to a pulp? Do you want to ask me if
I broke into the Wet Whistle and drank up all their best
whiskey? And whether that was before or after I kicked
Marmalade down the stairs and set his tail on fire?"

"I'm sorry, Gideon. I don't know what makes me say
things like that. I don't think them. You're probably the
best man I know—honest, decent, hardworking." She
really should have known better. After all, this was Gideon Forbes. He didn't cut up. He didn't carouse. And
above all, he wasn't deceitful, like Slick had been. "I
really am sorry. I shouldn't go tarring you with the same
brush I'd use for a lot of other, not-so-honorable men."

He looked pleased, but his hands were still fisted.
"No, you shouldn't," he said, and his fingers began to
uncurl.

"I won't do it again," she said, a small smile teasing

the corners of her mouth. "If you won't go off in the middle of the night anymore. I got cold. Especially my feet."

She was rewarded with a quick flash of his dimple. "So it ain't an accident that they keep winding up against me in the night."

"No," she said, stroking the chocolate icing on Berris's cake and sticking her finger in her mouth. "Do you mind much?"

*Mind?* He wanted her body pasted to his with not so much as a pillow feather between them. *Mind* warming her feet? He wanted to warm her feet and work his way up the rest of her, warming every inch of her.

He watched the iced finger disappear into her mouth, come out streaked with chocolate, and disappear again. His heart clutched to a stop.

"No," he said, reaching out and taking a fingerful of the cake himself. He wished he could offer it up to her, watch and feel her mouth around him, licking, tasting. Jeez, it was all he could do to answer her. "I don't mind much."

"Can I walk with you to the office?" she asked. "I thought I'd go over to my pa's house and see if there's any cloth I could use for a dress for the Miner's Ball. I'm thinking that what I have probably won't fit me by then." Her gaze fell to the floor sheepishly.

He had no doubt the dresses she owned would hide the belly that was beginning to round on her, but the bodices would be another story. Her buttons were already straining to the point where he thought someone could lose an eye when they popped. It was a losing battle to keep his eyes from always finding their way to her chest, and he purposefully looked around the kitchen as he spoke.

"I figure sometime in April. That about right?" It would be if Lester had really seen Lissie at Mrs. Clovis's at the end of the summer. It was sooner than he'd expected, but then he should have expected that Slick had been dragging his feet for a good long time before even agreeing on a church date.

"Maybe late March," she admitted. "Along with the crocuses." March. Jeez, she was four months gone. And that damn fool Lester knew more about his wife's condition than he did. Numbly he helped her adjust her wrap and bonnet.

"You see Doc Agrin when you suspected?" he asked, wondering just how many people knew that it was Slick's baby he was building a room for in his brand new house.

"I saw Mrs. Clovis. Doc Agrin's a good friend of my pa's and I didn't . . . " She took a deep ragged breath and looked up at him, her lip disappearing between her teeth. "I guess I was ashamed, pure and simple. I couldn't even get the truth out when he came to see about my scratches. Just asked him if I was lucky enough to be carrying, if I might have hurt the baby."

He nodded, satisfied with her answer, and held the door open for her. "So then he don't know. You tell Hedda who the father was?" he asked, guiding her down the steps.

She looked at him guiltily as if she couldn't quite decide whether or not to tell him the truth. On the bottom step, she stopped and said, "Doctors don't tell on their patients, Gideon, and neither does Mrs. Clovis. There ain't a woman in this town she's ever betrayed, and she's got no reason to start with me." She spoke with determination, but he noticed that she pulled her shawl more closely around her, and he, too, felt the first chill of winter settle in around them.

* * *

She didn't know what it was about this husband of hers, but even though they walked in silence, she could hear him telling her that she wasn't alone. It was a remarkable thing for a man who said so little. Just his hand beneath her elbow, guiding her, made her feel as if he'd stay by her side and face whatever came along with her.

At the door to the sheriff's office, Gideon leaned one shoulder against the wall and looked down at her. He was so much bigger than Slick, standing there with his hands buried in his pockets, towering over her.

"If you don't find what you're looking for at your pa's, go on over to Hughes' Mercantile and get what you need." As he spoke, his eyes drifted over her bosom then snapped abruptly back to her face. A blush crept up his neck from his collar. "Just tell Miss Kelly to put it on my account."

"I can probably find something at home," she said, wishing that she didn't have to take anything more from Gideon than she had already. She had piles of cloth which she used for quilting, but she was unsure if she had something wonderful enough for the wife of Gideon Forbes to wear to the Miner's Ball. "Bertie Waynick gave me some real pretty cloth when her rheumatism started getting too bad for her to sew."

He pushed himself off from the wall and nodded curtly at her, grunting about getting to work. When he found the door still locked, he said something about his father and Cluny that only his keys could hear and stabbed them at the lock like he wanted to draw blood.

"Well, go on then," he said, frowning at her as if she'd asked for the finest satin instead of trying to save him money. Lord, he could be so temperamental! She knew the lumber for the new house had to be costing him a pretty penny, and that once the baby came there'd be more expenses she had no right to ask him to bear. So maybe she shouldn't have mentioned that the cloth had come from Slick's mother. It wasn't like Slick would be there to see her in it, after all.

"And you might as well pick up the mail while you're there," he added, clearly still irritated with her.

Well, let him be peeved. Maybe there'd be a letter from Slick waiting at the mercantile, a letter saying how much she meant to him.

Of course, if she meant so much, why was he writing her letters instead of coming home to her? She stood still and motionless in the doorway of the sheriff's office. There would be no coming home to her. She was Gideon's wife. Forever. And she'd best remember that.

Gideon flung the door to the office open with enough force for it to smack up against the wall behind it. "It's me, Lester," he yelled, loud enough to wake the dead. "Got your breakfast here."

"Is there a particular color you like?" she tried asking him, hoping to leave him on a better note. She really didn't like to make Gideon mad. Or to disappoint him. In fact, if she could just see that dimple of his again, she might make a dress that even he couldn't resist complimenting. "For my dress, I mean. Slick's mama—"

She saw him stiffen at Slick's name and cursed herself for bringing up Bertie again. Wouldn't she ever learn? "I've got some blue, I think," she quickly corrected. "Light. Kinda like the sky." It had matched Slick's eyes, but she didn't add that.

"Lester?" he yelled again, rattling the lamp that hung down so far he nearly banged his head on it every time he walked beneath it.

There was no answer from the cells.

Gideon's eyes darted around the room and a grimace touched his lips. "You go on now," he said to her, trying to shoo her out and close the door behind her. "Blue'd be real nice. Now go see your pa."

Arliss slipped past his arm. "Maybe Lester's mad at you from last night," she guessed. Gideon had been upset enough when he'd come home. Quickly overtaking her, he crossed the office with her on his heels. "Lester?" she called out over his shoulder. "You awake?"

The back of Gideon's head blocked the small barred window in the door that separated the office from the cells. "Christ almighty!" he whispered, then turned and seemed surprised to see her. "Stay here," he ordered, grabbing the ring of keys from the peg beside the doorway and rushing into the cell rooms.

The key clanked loudly in the lock, the door's hinges squealed, and the metal bars rang out as they swung back against the cell. But Lester didn't make a sound.

Arliss took two steps forward before she heard Gideon shout at her to "Stay out!" but by then it was too late.

Lester, suspended at the neck by his belt, hung from the pipe that crossed the ceiling of his cell. His face was white, and his eyes were closed.

"Get out!" Gideon shouted as he twisted around and lifted Lester's limp body to rest on his shoulder, all the while working to free the belt. "For Christ's sake, Lissie. Think of the baby!"

She whirled around, stuck her thumb quickly into the waistband of her skirt to ward off the evil spirits, and fought to catch her breath. Pressing her forehead against the damp stone wall, she felt her breakfast rising, the room swaying, and her ears exploding from the quiet which surrounded Gideon's grunts as he strained to get Lester down. "Is he dead?" she whispered.

"No," Gideon answered cautiously. "But he ain't fine. You think you can get the doc all right?"

She peeked over her shoulder to see Gideon gently lay Lester on his cot and clear his shirt away from his throat, exposing a dark line that crossed his neck.

"Don't turn around, Lissie, please! You ain't supposed to—"

"Hey, Gideon," Lester said, his voice a raspy whisper. "You dead, too?"

"You ain't dead," Gideon said, pulling a blanket up over him. "Your buckle got caught on your collar button. Near as I can guess, you probably fainted up there."

Lester looked over at her. His voice came out like an old saw on green wood. "Aw no, not you, too. This sure as heck don't look like heaven. Leastwise, not like I expected. 'Course, I didn't expect to ever see heaven, but the two of you . . . jeez, how'd you two die? Did the Columbia explode?"

"Nobody's dead, Lester," Gideon said. "And Lissie, stop lookin'! A mama ain't supposed to see nothing bad when she's carrying."

"Berris's cooking?" Lester rasped. "That what did you in? Or did old Slick come back and find Lissie here with her knees around your waist?"

"*Nobody's dead*," Gideon shouted. "Leastwise not yet."

Lester looked at him suspiciously. He poked Gideon's chest. "Really?"

"What did you think you were doing?" Gideon asked him just as Sheriff Forbes came in.

Her father-in-law took one look at the belt still hanging from the bar and at Lester, his throat a mottled red and brown, and smacked his hand against the cell bars. "Jeez," he swore under his breath.

"I tried, Gideon. You gotta give me that," Lester said. "Just like you wanted. Ain't my fault Hedda sews on buttons tighter than knots on trees."

Arliss inched closer to Lester and Gideon, her hands covering her belly. "What do you mean, 'just like he wanted'?"

"Best way to keep my mouth shut," Lester said, turning his head as if he could protect her baby by not looking at her, since she refused to keep her eyes from him. "Take what I know to my grave, just like them horses. But you know, Gideon, that woulda still left that old mule of Hedda's . . . and Hedda, too."

"Just what do you know?" Thaddeus Forbes asked Lester, leaning over Gideon and running a finger across Lester's battered neck while Arliss blinked frantically trying to make the room stop spinning.

"Don't know nothing," Lester said. "Leastwise not about Lissie here and that baby she's carryin'."

Arliss rested against the wall, afraid her own legs might fail her.

"Damn right you don't know nothing," Gideon barked at Lester before turning to look at her. "This is the last time I'm gonna ask you, Arliss Forbes, to get yourself out of this room. And if you don't go willing, I'm gonna just pick you up and carry you out."

Sheriff Forbes looked first at her and then at his son. He gestured with his head for her to go into the office.

"Pa, could you get her out of here?" he begged, blocking her view of Lester as if that would stop her from knowing what he'd done. "Now?"

"We're going, son. Rushing ain't gonna make a bad situation any better," Sheriff Forbes said as he put an arm around her, pivoting her toward his office and gently leading her to his desk chair.

With her arms on the sheriff's desk, she let her head fall down while she struggled against tears that threatened to choke her. She felt the sheriff's hand on her back, patting softly, and held her sob in check until he went back to Gideon and Lester, closing the door behind him.

"Can't say as I like the way you order her around," his pa said when he came back into the row of cells. His eyes narrowed as if he were looking back at Gideon's whole life through a new pair of spectacles that let him see things he'd never seen before. "It ain't the way I raised you, anyhow."

"I'm real sorry, Gideon," Lester said after a long and heavy silence. "If that damn mule had kept his trap shut and not gone and told me what he heard, we wouldn't be in this pickle now and you wouldn't be wishing me dead."

"We ain't in a pickle," Gideon said. He wondered how much Lissie could hear out there in the office. Heck, there were quiet days when he could hear Lester pulling hairs. What was she making of all this? After the scene in the kitchen, he supposed that she thought he'd told Lester to kill himself. "And I don't wish you dead," he added, though the words were purely for Lissie's ears and he wasn't so sure they were true.

"Not no more?" Lester asked.

*Drop dead, Lester,* he'd said. *And just go to hell.*

"You see something you shouldn't have?" his father asked Lester from over Gideon's shoulder.

"A mule told him, for Christ's sake!" Gideon shouted. Lester, of all people, could confirm what his father already suspected, that he'd gone and married a woman who was carrying another man's seed. And that the child who was to be born as his son and Thaddeus's grandson was the product of his wife's love for another man. The hurt was even greater than the shame.

"So what exactly did this mule hear?" Thaddeus asked.

Gideon shook his head and let his eyes roll toward the ceiling *"What did the mule hear?"* he repeated incredulously.

"Nothing," Lester said, looking at Gideon like some puppy who'd peed on the good rug. "He didn't hear nothing."

"Good," Thaddeus said to Lester. "That takes care of the mule. And you? You hear something you weren't meant to hear?" he demanded.

If Lester looked guilty before, he looked twice as guilty now.

"The man hears things all the time. He sees things. You've seen him have conversations with raindrops on the windowpane. Now suddenly he's got the right end of the stick?" Gideon was shouting, but he couldn't help himself. His father was looking for trouble, and Gideon wasn't sure that all hell wouldn't break loose if Thaddeus found it.

"It ain't an easy secret to keep, Gideon," Lester said softly, as if his father wasn't leaning over the two of them. "She'll be showin' soon enough. Why her whole figure's rounding out already. Cyrus, that's Hedda's mule, says—"

"That mule musta kicked you in the head one time too many," Thaddeus said, apparently content that all Lester knew was that Lissie was already carrying when Gideon had married her. "Or maybe it was one time too few." He laid a hand on Gideon's shoulder and patted him. Gideon got up from the low cot, every joint crack-

ling, every muscle aching, and followed his father out
into the office.

"I'll send the doc over and then walk Arliss over to
her pa's," he told his father as he put a hand beneath
Lissie's elbow and eased her to her feet before Thaddeus could ask her any questions. "After that I'm going
up to the Columbia to check on things. Send someone
if you need me. Otherwise I'll be back around two."

"That'll be fine," his father said, his gaze settling on
Lissie. "You rest some at your pa's, and I'll stop by later
to walk you home."

"I'll pick her up on my way back," Gideon said. He
was clutching her arm tightly, and she winced beside
him and jerked her arm away.

"You don't need to, Gideon," she said, but for all her
bravado she was white as a fresh-laid egg. "I can get
myself home."

" 'Course you can," Thaddeus agreed, his hand re-
placing Gideon's near Lissie's elbow in the same propri-
etary manner. "I just thought it might give us a chance
to get to know each other a little better. You know this
whole marriage of yours kinda took us by surprise and it
seems like I hardly know you at all."

"I—" Gideon started, but Thaddeus cut him off.

"*You* know her well enough," he said to Gideon with
a bit of a grimace before he smiled again at Arliss.
"Come on now. How about giving an old man a turn to
shoot the breeze with a pretty young thing? Been a long
time since I escorted a woman around town—at least
one who lets me get a word in edgewise."

Lissie looked as if a kitten's breath could knock her
over. Gideon felt the same way. "Think it might be best
if you stayed here, Pa. We'll send the doc over to take a
look at old Lester."

"He'd probably prefer his sister seeing to him,"

Thaddeus said, watching Lissie and putting out a hand to steady her when she began to sway a little. "You all right, Arliss? Wanna just sit for a spell while Gideon goes on up to the mine? Wanna just sit and talk a while?"

"No, she don't," Gideon barked. If Lester knew Lissie was out there in the office, the Lord only knew what he might say. And if his father knew the truth it could well be the end of it all. Lissie would never let him bear the shame of raising Slick's child, and he'd wake up in an empty bed, alone, for the rest of his life. And even if his family loved him again, it couldn't make up for what Lissie would go through when it all came out. And how much he'd miss her.

Hurt glinted in his father's eyes. "I ain't the enemy, son," he said softly.

But Gideon already knew that. The enemy was inside him, taking pieces of his heart, eating him up alive.

# Chapter Eleven

AFTER THEY STOPPED AT THE DOCTOR'S, GIDEON said she should go home instead of to her father's house, to which she'd replied that her father's house *was* her home. He hadn't liked that much and had pointedly reminded her that it wasn't anymore. She'd said, and loudly, too, that it wouldn't be long before it was again, figuring that if Lester knew, and the truth came out, there wouldn't be much point to the charade of being married to Gideon and calling the baby his.

He'd flinched at that, warning her to keep her voice down and come on home like a good girl.

And she'd hissed at him that she wasn't a *good girl* and that everyone would know it soon enough, and had headed up the street toward her pa's house, tears blurring her way. Somehow he'd managed to plant himself like a tree in her way, and every time she'd tried to get around him, the tree up and moved. Finally she'd kicked his left shin and dodged to his right.

Her pride was still smarting from how he'd caught her, scooped her up, and carried her down Main Street right in front of Berris and Samantha and Miss Kelly. She had kicked and screamed about how he'd tried to kill Lester, and he had said in that low steady voice of his that the man was just plum crazy.

Back at the house, he deposited her on a blanket near the clearing and told her to stay put and stay still while he went to the pump to get her some fresh water. And then he stood over her while she drank it, hovering like some sort of mother hen.

Like *her* mother hen.

And he didn't go to the mines like he'd told Thaddeus he would. Instead he started in on the clearing with a vengeance, shaking the ground with each swing of the ax, then stopping to fuss and fret at her.

"I shouldn't have let you come with me," he said finally, throwing the ax down on the ground and coming over to where she sat on the blanket, handing her yet another dipper of fresh cool water.

"Wouldn't have changed things," she said, accepting the cup from him and taking a sip. "It wasn't me that told Lester to—"

"It would have changed everything," Gideon said, crouching down to stare at her as if she'd gone and lost her mind. "Then we wouldn't have to worry about what might happen."

"Maybe it would be better for everyone if it did," she said, arching her back and then rolling over to kneel and push herself up. Merciful heavens, she felt heavier and bigger every day, and she was only starting to round.

"Don't say that," Gideon said, giving her a hand and then keeping hold of hers once she'd risen. "You don't really wanna lose this baby, do you Lissie?"

"What are you talking about?" she asked him, looking down into such very soft brown eyes that it was hard to believe that he'd told Lester to kill himself. "How could Lester's telling the truth about me do that?"

"Seeing him, Lissie," he almost shouted at her. "You shouldn't have been seeing him hanging there like that."

"Because now I know the truth? Because I heard him tell you that he tried to do what you asked?"

Gideon let go of her and covered his face with his hands. His shoulders sagged. Finally he looked up at her and said, "I told the man to go to hell, Lissie. To drop dead. I remember you telling me the same thing once, and I'm hoping you didn't mean it any more back then than I did last night."

"I never . . . " she began, wracking her memory for when she could ever have told Gideon Forbes to go to hell. And then the moment was there again, as shiny and painful as it was the first time, when Slick had left her at the Miner's Ball and gone off with Abby Rose Belmont to the big house on Silver Hill.

Gideon had offered to see her home, and she'd insisted on waiting for Slick to come back for her. He'd sat watching her silently for almost an hour after everyone else had left and had finally come over to her and held out his hand. "He ain't comin' back," Gideon had told her.

And what had been her answer? "Drop dead, Gideon Forbes," she'd said.

"I'll see you home," he'd repeated.

"And go to hell!" She'd stuck her nose in the air and marched out of the empty Grange Hall as if she were the queen of France.

Unlike when he'd seen her home from the church social, this time he'd merely followed her all the way, close enough to hand her over a fallen log, far enough away so that, except for that, he never touched her. It was as if they'd both been scared of what might happen between them if they'd gone by way of the creek again, if he'd taken her hand again, if there'd been a silver moon.

This time when she'd reached her door he'd stood at the bottom of the porch steps, looking up at her. "He'll do it again, Lissie," he'd said. "And again."

She'd thought him a fool, mean-spirited, and unable to understand a boy like Slick, who needed room to swing his wide loop. Where was he soaring now, her handsome lover? Virginia City? Helena?

*He'll do it again,* Gideon had warned.

"I meant it then, Gideon," she admitted, pressing her hand to her lips as if she could take the words back now. "But that was a lifetime ago. You have to know that."

He let the admission pass, the way he did so many of her trespasses. "Where are you going?" he asked, rising to accompany her.

She smiled at him and shook her head. Nature called her often, but she had the feeling he knew that already. Sometimes she had the feeling he knew everything about her. And sometimes she just felt he knew everything there was to know.

"I'll be back in a few minutes," she said. "I'm all right. I promise."

He nodded reluctantly, but she felt his eyes on her even after she was in the house and as she climbed the stairs.

*The baby was slipping from Lissie's body, the pain so strong that Gideon could feel it in his own and knew in his heart that she couldn't survive it. It was snowing outside and Gideon was alone with her in a house he didn't recognize. Some piece of his brain told him it had to be the new house he was building, but he didn't care. All he knew was that she was in pain.*

*And then the baby slid into Gideon's arms. Around
its neck squeezing the life from it, was the cord that
connected it to its mama. He studied the child, whose
face was round and soft and framed with Slick's black
hair.*

*Lissie lay quiet and still, the screaming done, her
eyes fixed on the ceiling and unmoving.*

*He let the baby slip from his hands, the cord around
its neck tightening until its blue eyes, too, stared at the
ceiling.*

*And then he screamed.*

"Gideon!" Lissie was beside him, alive, reaching for
the lamp in the darkened bedroom when he came fully
awake. "What is it?" she asked, touching his damp forehead, her eyes wide with fear. "Are you sick?"

Footsteps filled the hall outside their room, with
shouts accompanying them.

"Just a dream," he called out to his family. "Sorry!"
And then more quietly he repeated the words to Lissie.

She touched his face, running soft cool hands down
his neck and across his chest. "Are you sure you're all
right?" she asked. "You're soaking wet."

Her hands felt wonderful, and he let her minister to
him as he tried to calm his breathing down from a pant.
"Just a dream," he repeated still again, trying to convince himself that it had no meaning.

"I'll get you a fresh shirt," she said, throwing back
the covers so that the cool night air hit the sweat on his
body and chilled him to the bone.

"No!" he shouted, grabbing handfuls of her nightdress to hold her back. "Don't get up!"

"Arliss?" his father shouted through the door. "Everything okay in there?"

It was a reasonable question, he supposed, considering that they thought he'd take advantage of a little bit

of a girl like Arliss. He loosened his hold on her just a little.

"Fine, sir," she shouted back toward the closed door, as she shifted back on to the bed and wiped at his face with the cuff of her gown. "Gideon's having trouble letting a dream go, is all."

They waited, he and his wife, for the footsteps to fade, before either of them spoke again.

"Are you all right?" he asked, stilling her hands and holding her shoulders while he got a good look at her. Lord, but she was pretty when she first woke up, her hair all tumbling around her face and shoulders, her lips still swollen from sleep.

"*I* didn't cry out, Gideon. *You* did. Stop watching me so. It makes me nervous."

"I'm sorry," he said, but he couldn't pull his eyes away. "You're sure you feel okay?"

"Yes, I'm sure," she said, shaking her head at him. "Why shouldn't I?"

Gideon wiped at his brow and traced a line of sweat down the side of his face. Try as he might, he couldn't shake off the fear.

"Let me get you a dry shirt to put on," she said again, inching off the bed in an attempt to fool him.

"Please, Lissie," he begged softly, sounding more like the boy he'd once been than the man he was. "Stay in the bed. Stay still."

"For how long, Gideon?" she asked him, still edging off the bed as if to say that his simple request was too much to ask.

"Until the baby's born," he mumbled, wishing he could lash her to the bed and keep her there, keep her safe. And when the baby came he'd like to wall them both in together like one of those mud birds that built a nest around his family and cracked it open when he thought them ready to fly.

"You're not serious," she said, stopping in her tracks to stare at him. "That's months away, and I'm perfectly fine. It's not like you to be so ridiculous."

"Until we know that nothing's happened, then," he bargained with her.

"Nothing's happened?" she asked. "What do you mean?"

"Seeing Lester like that," he admitted nervously. He never should have let her come to the office with him. Never, never. "It coulda hurt the baby, Lissie, you getting a scare like that."

"Oh for heaven's sake, Gideon. That's just an old wives' tale. Why Frenna Reynold's oldest boy died when she was carrying little Tim, and he's right as rain with a little of the devil mixed in."

"I didn't say it *had* to happen," he told her, watching as she pulled a shirt from the wardrobe for him. "I said it could."

"Nonsense," she insisted as she held out the shirt.

"Where'd this come from?" he asked, noting the fine stitching on the soft white cloth. She was always sewing something, but he'd never supposed in that pile of odds and ends she worked on that there was something for him.

"I didn't suppose Berris would miss one old sheet," she said with a mischievous grin. "Nothing I had seemed big enough for you." The sleeves were full and they reached to his wrists as he slipped the wonderful smelling shirt over his head.

"Lavender," she said as he sniffed at his shoulders. "I hope that's all right. It's supposed to help you sleep." She stood there expectantly, waiting for his approval.

"It's good," he said. No woman outside of his mother

and sisters had ever made anything for him. It warmed him, just thinking of her hands on his nightclothes, even if there were sort of flowery-looking things at his cuffs.

"It's a basket stitch," she pointed out. "My mama taught me how to do it when I was very little." She stood awkwardly beside the bed and he wasn't sure what she was expecting him to say.

"Your mama taught you good," he tried. It got a smile from her.

"Then you like it?" she asked. "And you'll wear it?"

"I'll wear it," he agreed, wondering if the truth was simply that she minded him sleeping beside her in the altogether when his long johns were too warm.

"Do you feel better now?" she asked, touching his brow again and stirring unwelcome passions low in his belly. "I used to have nightmares all the time after my mama died. Got so that I was afraid to go to sleep."

"I ain't afraid to go to sleep," he said, wishing it was morning and they could just get on out of bed and start their day.

She crawled back into bed next to him. "Should I turn down the lamp?" she asked.

"Don't see how we're gonna sleep otherwise," Gideon answered, his heart beginning to pound wildly in his chest.

They lay in the dark for a few minutes, Lissie waiting for sleep, he supposed, while he just waited for morning.

After a while his eyes adjusted to the darkness once again. Now he could make out Lissie's boots in a pool of moonlight by the stuffed chair. He could see the handle of her silver hairbrush glinting from the top of his mother's highboy.

His mother. Lord almighty how he'd loved her. He remembered how his sisters would tease him when he'd race through his chores just so that he could brush her hair or fix her something to eat. And when she died, he thought he'd never get over it, never heal from the awful wounds her dying had left on his heart and soul.

"It ain't just an old wives' tale," he told Lissie in the darkness.

" 'Course it is," she said, surprising him. He'd thought her fast asleep and had only spoken out loud to chase away his demons and because he thought she couldn't hear him. The last thing he wanted to do was worry her.

She sidled over against him, one hand on his chest. As fast as she put it there, she pulled it back. "You're trembling, Gideon."

"It's cold in here," he lied.

She pressed herself closer to him. "I'll hold you. Try to go back to sleep."

"I'm fine," he said, but it was a lie and he could tell she knew as much. "You remember my mama?" he asked her when he couldn't keep his breathing calm.

"No one could forget your mama, Gideon," Lissie said, brushing the hair off his brow. "Was that what you dreamed about?"

"No. I was just remembering," he said. For years all he could remember were those last few days before she died. How his father had gone off with a posse, leaving Gideon to watch after her and the girls and Cluny. How he'd found Wayward with his leg caught in a trap and carried him home, crying all the way, to his mama. How his mama'd tried to save the dog and couldn't, and had helped him bury the dog in the yard.

And then how her pains had started that night, and how over the course of three long days, his mama's screams had turned to moans, and the moans, to whimpers.

And how at the end of it, the baby and his ma were both dead.

His pa had never held it against him, had never brought up his stupidity in the years that followed. In exchange, Gideon had never asked his father how he could have left a young boy to do a man's job. And by tacit agreement, neither of them had ever mentioned the circumstances of his mother's death, and both of their roles in it.

"Slick ever tell you the part about Wayward?" he asked, knowing that anything he'd told his friend in the strictest confidence turned into public knowledge before Slick ever made it home.

"It's an old wives' tale," she said. "Your mama's death had nothing to do with Wayward and nothing to do with you."

Despite her words, he felt her hand slide between them to cradle her belly and felt her lips move against his arm in silent prayer.

And then, as if in answer to his own prayer, she clung to him tightly, and he wrapped his arms around her and kissed the top of her hair.

"Gideon?" she asked, her warm breath rippling across his chest and turning his insides to mush. "Do you think that maybe you might consider letting Lester go?"

He'd seen Berris do it a million times with his father—bat those big eyes, give his shoulders a squeeze, and dance away with permission to buy yet another dress or whatever else she wanted. With a few well-placed kisses, Juliana got a house that was twice what Ezra, the town's only barber, could afford. It was a woman's way. Still it grated on his nerves that the head against his chest was only there for Lester's sake.

He ran his fingers through her hair sadly. How far would she let him go, for Lester's sake?

"Couldn't you let him go, Gideon? For me? I mean he's not a bad man and you know it. He's just a little crazy. Couldn't you release him, Gideon, if you wanted to?"

"I don't want to release him," he said, smelling the flower scent in her hair, feeling the warmth of her body beside him, listening to the sound of her lips moving in silent prayer. "Now go to sleep."

There was silence, cold and isolating around them. She waited in the dark, willing herself to sleep, wishing that she couldn't feel the heat rising off Gideon's body, couldn't smell the bay rum he wore lingering in the air. If she were laying with Slick, she'd know what to do, what he'd want. But here she was with her husband and she hadn't any idea at all about how to make him happy. It seemed to her from Gideon's hmphing and pillow-punching that he, too, lay awake in the darkness unsure about what was going on between them.

She decided right at that moment that it was time to put Slick into a compartment in her memory and start her life with Gideon. It was past time. "I can't fall asleep," she said finally. "I keep thinking about things."

"What things?" he asked. He thumped the pillow again with a vengeance. "Lester?"

"And other things," she said, sure that bringing up Lester now would only end in an empty bed. She wished she could tell him that she was blowing out the torch she'd been kindling for Slick, but that, too, would chase him from their bed. And so she told him about the other things, things that ran through her head and rattled her heart. "My father's flowers, and how there are none here. A stitch my mother taught me that I think you'd like better than the flowery ones. What it would feel like to hold Marmalade at night like I used to hold Pansy, and whether Berris would mind. Whether you would. Everything and nothing. And Lester, too," she added to the accompaniment of a heavy sigh from Gideon. "I just can't sleep."

"Do it anyways," he ordered, as if she was just being obstinate.

"Yes sir, Deputy Forbes," she answered, willing for him, wishing for him, praying for him to call her "Mrs. Forbes" in return—to claim her, bind her, want her.

His breath rippled the top sheet and sent chills down her spine. "You at least trying?" he asked after a while.

"I can't help *thinking*," she said in her own defense.

"Fine," he answered. "Your father's flowers are done blooming and I like the shirt just fine. The cat's happy sleeping on the porch and if we let her sleep in here we'd have to leave the door open, which we ain't doing. All right?"

He'd actually been listening to her, not just dismissing what she said. She smiled in the darkness.

"Now go to sleep. You need your rest."

"Is that what I need?" she asked him, the smile still on her lips as she twirled within his arms so that his hand, which had been resting on her waist, now rested on her midriff. She shimmied down until it was just beneath her breast. Her nipples tensed at the contact, while her chest tightened and her inners went soft. She tried to breathe in and out like a normal person, but the ins were sharp and short, and the outs were ragged. Gideon, if not her one true love, was a good man. Better than good. So much better. He deserved a good marriage.

And while he hadn't gotten a good one, she could at least give him a real one—and a real, if flawed, wife.

She backed herself up against him, hoping, praying that they could start a life together. That with all her faults, all the stupid and careless things she'd done, Gideon could still want her. She could feel his hardness behind her, his body hungry for her, even as his will resisted.

"Are you sure rest is what I need?" she asked, her heart lodged so firmly in her throat that the words were hard to force around it.

Then slowly, the way she imagined the girls on Lilac Row did it, she rocked slightly against him, hoping he'd understand that she was willing if it was what he wanted. Her thought had been to make him want her, to force him to give in to the needs she'd heard so much about, but her selfless plan was turning on her like a thankless child. Because for every inch she moved closer toward his body—the rock hardness of his chest, the heat of his belly—the more she wanted him.

She made one more press of her bottom against his manhood, held her breath, and waited.

It was an invitation, pure and simple. An invitation, or more precisely, a bribe. With just a slight turning of his hand he was able to cup the bottom of Lissie's breast. It was warm in his hand. Firm. Full.

"Got a wire this morning that the judge'll arrive tomorrow, Lissie," he said, ashamed of himself, but too needy, too hungry, to resist. "I'll try to explain to him about Lester."

"Thank you, Deputy Forbes," she said in a whisper. Then she pushed her head back and took a ragged breath while he scraped his knuckles across the sweet, sweet pebble that beaded on her breast. Millie had always been accommodating, but he'd often wondered how genuine her sighs and moans had been. How could

a man know if he was a good lover when he was paying
for the privilege, and the woman beneath him wanted
him to think he'd gotten his money's worth?

Lissie's moan came from deep in her chest. He could
feel it beneath the palm of his hand, along with her
quickening heart. He rolled her onto her back and
painstakingly fought each and every button, until her
breasts rose naked and free for him to see and touch
and taste.

Her skin was damp, sweaty, slightly salty, as he
tasted and coaxed her nipples harder still. Her breath
came in short little pants when he finally lowered his
lips to suckle. A sharp gasp escaped her as he latched
on, and he raised his eyes to make sure that she was all
right.

Her head was thrown back against the white pillow.
Her eyes were closed. One hand clutched at the sheets.
She thrust her chest up toward him, searching blindly
for the sensation to continue. Her free hand swiped at
the hair which lay against her brow and then made an
idle descent down the side of her face and across her
bodice. She rubbed at the nipple of one breast and then
cupped the whole of it and offered it up to him.

He dove for it like a fish hooks onto a lure. He circled the nipple with his tongue and suckled and released and started again.

Beneath him she began to buck, lifting her hips
toward him until he knew she was as ready and as eager
as he was. "Ssh," he said when she clutched wildly at
him as he pulled away from her slightly to position himself between her legs. She grabbed at him, making him
feel as if he was as necessary to her as the air she
breathed.

He was a big man, with big hands and feet and,
while he'd never compared, he supposed everything in

between was scaled to the same large size. Gently he took Lissie's hand and wrapped it around his manhood, the pleasure so great he almost didn't concern himself with hurting her.

"Make sure I don't go too far," he said, wishing he could see her face, grateful she couldn't see his. And then he slid into her, his key within her lock, the two of them joined from this moment on. Suddenly all the things his mama had ever said about loving became crystal clear to him in that one instant—the feeling of home, of safety, of rightness.

Slowly he moved his hips and she followed him, stroke for stroke. He didn't know when she let go of him, only that her arms were both snaked around his neck nearly cutting off his air, and that her own breaths were stilted and short. And they were coming faster and faster, until she reached up for the rods of the brass headboard and pressed herself up against him with a startled cry that did him in.

She was his wife.

Gingerly he rolled off her, careful not to let his weight fall against her. Clammy, awkward, they lay silent on the bed, Gideon wondering what she was thinking, wishing he could bring himself to tell her what she meant to him, struggling to find the courage to bare his soul.

Lissie was turned on her side away from him, balled up. He reached out to her and heard a small sob. It scared the living daylights out of him.

"Did I hurt you?" he asked, leaning over her to find her fist stuffed into her mouth. Millie was nearly six feet tall. What was he thinking, making love to this woman who barely reached his shoulder and whose body was already strained with her condition?

She shook her head.

"Are you all right?" he asked, hearing the sobs multiply and become interspersed with ragged snorts. "What is it? What's wrong?"

She shook her head at him, unable to talk. Wild thoughts went through his head. He'd hurt her or the baby. She didn't like the way he felt or smelled or sounded. She never wanted to do it again.

A shuddering sob rocked the bed. Hell, it rocked the whole damn house.

"What is it, Lissie?" he demanded. "What's wrong?"

She pulled a pillow against her stomach and curled into a ball so small there was room for a horse to crawl in between them.

"Are you hurt? Should I get help?" he asked as he rose from the bed and began to search for his pants. "I'll wake Berris," he added.

"No," she said, her first words since he'd forgotten himself and impaled her to the hilt with his bulk. "I'm fine."

"Then why are you crying?" he asked, standing by the bed and looking down at her tear-streaked face.

She sniffed and buried her head against the pillow by her chest, mumbling something.

"What?" he asked, leaning closer to hear her.

"It was never like that with Slick," she said softly, and he felt his insides crumble, felt every wish he'd harbored since he was a boy fall to pieces which lay heavy in his stomach.

And then, just when he figured there was no hope left, she reached out and gently ran her fingers down the side of his face.

"Thank you, yet again, Deputy Forbes," she said, scooting over and pulling the covers back so that he could crawl into bed beside her.

*Thank you yet again Deputy Forbes.* The words rang

like a death noll in his head and his heart sank right down to his big heavy feet.

He should have known better than to think that after all the years of knowing him, Lissie could suddenly actually want him, welcome him, love him. She'd only given herself to him for Lester's sake, a bribe for which she'd just thanked him for his compliance. Oh, he'd taken her to the heights, all right, but it was sure clear she regretted the trip.

He'd been so damn desperate for her that he'd jumped at the offer, allowed himself to enjoy the feel of her, revel in the sounds of her moans and sighs, enjoy the taste of her on his tongue and lips—when all the while he'd no intention of trying to talk the judge out of shipping Lester Pincus as far from Granite as possible.

He'd let her sell herself.

And he'd bought her, as sure as he'd ever bought Millie.

At least he'd seen to it that Lissie had enjoyed herself. He wasn't sure he'd ever even noticed with Millie once he'd gotten going.

Asleep now beside him, Lissie rolled over and threw her leg across him. Her belly was growing fast and he felt it press against his hip with the same weight her breasts placed on his chest. Her gasps and whimpers had all but undone him before. Now, even in her sleep, the little catches in her breath were causing his own to quicken.

He supposed it wouldn't do any harm to recommend that Lester go to the Insane Asylum at Warm Springs instead of Deer Springs State Prison. Anything that would get him out of Granite. For the town's sake.

And Lissie's.

And his own.

*Chapter Twelve*

SLICK WAYNICK AWOKE SUDDENLY IN THE NIGHT WITH a pain in his chest that felt as if someone at least the size of Gideon Forbes was sitting on top of him. He wheezed in a breath, and the woman beside him shifted, snored softly for a moment and then was quiet again. He supposed it was a dream, or maybe the two bottles of whiskey he'd downed before bed, that made his head swim and his stomach feel like nothing was right with the world.

Hell. He'd surely thought that life in the big city was going to be a lot more fun than this. But then, he'd been stupid enough to think that Helena was the Big City.

Anaconda hadn't proven much better, and now that he was in Virginia City he was getting close to admitting that maybe he was chasing a wild goose. Marjorie—or maybe it was Margaret—had been full of loose talk down at the gaming tables, but when he'd brought her up to his room last night, she'd spread her legs and bitten at a ragged fingernail while he'd buried himself within her. She hadn't agreed that he was the best, the way Arliss always did. Of course, he was the only one for his Arliss, and there'd been real excitement in knowing that.

He wondered if Marjorie—or Margaret—had a notch in her corset for every man who'd helped her out of it. And where it was he fell on her list.

And what it was she meant by asking him if he wanted to "try again."

At least the gaming tables had been good to him. He'd won enough to buy Arliss a genuine gold and garnet necklace to match her earbobs. And he'd made a vow not to bet the damn things again now that he'd managed to win them back. He thought if he took enough hands in the morning, he might just send her a telegram to brag a bit about his success. The gully jumpers back in Granite would be pretty surprised to see the stack of chips he was sitting behind now.

He thought maybe he should tell her, too, that her grandfather was dying a slow death not too far out of Virginia City. He'd thought about going out to see the old man, show him the picture of Arliss he always carried with him and see if he couldn't soften the old man's heart. But he'd heard the man was a lost cause and was lying about with all the brains of a boiled potato.

Not that that would have stopped him from trying. A smile curled the corner of his lip as he remembered the conversation he'd had with the brother of the old man's lawyer. While he couldn't bet for shit, he was kind enough—and drunk enough—to let Slick know that the old man's will was signed and sealed just days before a stroke. It was that news that kept Slick from immediately renting a horse and riding out to see the old man himself.

The man had all but passed out at the table before finishing his story. Now in the dark Slick wondered if it might be worth it to go on out to the old man's place and tell him that he'd seen to it that the man's line would reach into the next generation. That ought to be worth something to the old coot.

He shivered and reached for the quilt, pulling it from Margaret's back and wrapping himself in it. He always got gooseflesh when he thought about Arliss carrying his seed.

*Better be a boy,* he thought as he ran his finger down Margaret's naked skin. Wouldn't do to have a girl as pretty as himself. Pretty girls needed watching twenty-four hours a day to make sure no nasty fellows took advantage of them.

Margaret rolled over and reached for him, her hands sliding down his chest and searching out his manhood.

A pretty boy, on the other hand, had the world at his fingertips . . . and all night to enjoy it.

Arliss woke up the way she always did lately, urged by nature to acknowledge her condition. She eased herself away from Gideon's side and ran her hand down her body, gently wishing her baby good morning before she slipped out of bed and fumbled for her slippers.

"Feelin' all right?" Gideon asked as she sat on the edge of the bed.

Lord, but she'd scared the daylights out of him with all that crying she'd done when they were finished last night. She hadn't meant to cry. In fact, she'd been as surprised as he'd been. If that was making love, what was it she'd been doing with Slick all those nights down by the creek? Slick had called it "panning for gold," but it was Gideon who'd struck the mother lode.

And it had taken her by surprise. After all, it was Slick that she loved, so why was it Gideon's touch that had taken her breath away, melted her insides, and left her in tears?

And just what did that say about her? She'd given herself to Slick because she loved him and given herself to Gideon because a wife cleaved unto her husband. Wouldn't logic and common sense say that it'd be heaven on earth with the one that owned your heart and only seeing your duty through with the other?

"Lissie? You okay?" She could hear the worry in her husband's voice.

"Just going down the hall," she said, keeping her back to him. She could probably never look him in the face again. Not after she'd moaned and sighed and slithered under him like a paid-for lady. Some proper wife she was for Gideon.

Why couldn't she have just lain there and let him do what he needed to do? That's the way it had been with Slick, and he'd said she was doing it just right.

"I'll find your slippers," Gideon said with a sigh, throwing the covers off and coming around the bed to stand buck-naked in front of her, which was no more than she deserved. Once a woman had touched a man, wrapped her fingers around his manhood, her legs around his waist, she could hardly expect him to observe the proprieties that ought to exist between a man and his wife.

She kept her eyes glued to the floorboards, but felt the flutter in her chest all the same. Even his feet were strong-looking—big, solid, ready to bear any weight.

And she was a weight all right. She and the baby in her belly that was somehow swelling even her ankles and feet so that Gideon had to help with her slippers.

"Don't take all day in there," he said as he stood again and offered her a hand up. "I gotta get down to the jail and get your friend Lester over to the courthouse by nine."

"I was wondering," she said, more or less thinking aloud, "if maybe I could give Lester's hair a trim and get him washed up to face the judge."

One look at Gideon's face and she knew she'd ventured out onto thin ice. The muscles in his jaw were doing an Irish jig in double time, and daggers were shooting from his deep brown eyes.

"It's just that the judge might not understand about him, Gideon," she tried to explain. "And I thought that—"

"No."

She waited for him to go on, but he didn't.

"I could bring him your razor and some soap and maybe even a clean shirt of Cluny's and—"

"No," Gideon repeated, his anger clearly under control now. Not gone, perhaps, but simmering well below the surface. He stood staring at her, his gaze drifting down from her face to her chest, where he reached out and silently buttoned several of the buttons that he'd opened the night before.

His hands brushed at her breasts, and without her consent she felt herself responding to his touch. She took a quick breath and held very still.

"No, Lissie," he said, taking a few steps back as if he didn't want to know what he was doing to her. "I said I'd talk to the judge, and I will. Don't ask me for more than that."

"Thank you for that, then," she said softly, knowing that to argue with him would only get his back up. A man didn't like it when his wife didn't agree with him, support him, bend to his will.

Botheration! When had she started thinking like Berris? *A man doesn't like this, a man doesn't like that.*

What about what a woman liked? What about what *she* liked? And what about what was just plain right?

"Maybe your father—" she began.

"You need to go down the hall . . . or should I?" he asked through gritted teeth. "Told you already I got no time to waste this morning."

She'd have liked to tell him she wasn't fond of wasting time herself, nor of wasting words. She'd have liked to tell him that he was stubborn and bullheaded when it came to Lester and that his heart was harder than his . . .

She'd have liked to hurl a morning's worth of insults at him, starting with the fact that he'd turned her insides over beneath him and hadn't so much as said he'd enjoyed himself.

And she knew it had been good for Gideon. That was something a man couldn't hide, even if he hadn't held her afterward, even if he hadn't stroked her hair, or even said "good night."

She'd have liked to tell him a hundred things, but when he took a step toward the door she said the only thing that she could. Nature wasn't one to be denied. "I won't be a minute," she blurted out as she slipped under the arm that held open the door, her face beet red as she hightailed it down the hall.

Gideon stood outside the door to Lester's cell watching the man devour the breakfast Lissie had sent as if it was the last supper. He supposed that in a way, for Lester, it was.

Lissie was right. The man was a mess. His hair hung in thin greasy clumps from his head and his beard had a week's worth of food clinging to it. Every morning Gideon brought him a bowl of fresh water to wash in, and every night he took the same clean water away.

Unless, of course, Lester had given Spot a bath.

He was a sorry excuse for a man, but Gideon supposed that it was his pathetic qualities that made Lissie champion his cause. He supposed Lissie remembered the sweet man Lester had been and had pity for what life had made of him.

And it was hard to fault her for her caring, though her methods—hell, Gideon couldn't fault her for her methods, either. Not when he'd been party to them. Aiding and abetting. Well, "abedding," anyways.

Lord, it had been good. So very good. And unless she was a better actress than that Lily Langtree, Lissie had enjoyed herself right fine. She'd been a party to the whole thing, a partner in the act.

Good Lord, they'd made *love*. With paid women it'd been fornication—satisfying needs that demanded meeting. With Lissie, well, it had been different. A romp between the sheets with Millie and he'd be good for a few weeks, the urge gone from his body, the thought gone from his head.

But he'd wanted Lissie again just minutes after he'd exploded within her. He'd wanted her still when he'd woken up this morning, flagpole hard and straight, with the scent of their lovemaking hanging in the air, clinging to his mama's wedding ring quilt.

He wanted her now as he stared at the pathetic creature for whom Lissie had seen fit to barter her most precious gift.

"Finish up, Lester," he said, feeling as if he had no choice. "We'll stop at Ezra's and make you a little more presentable before we see the judge."

Lester looked up from Lissie's melt-in-your-mouth biscuit and cocked his head.

"Spot knew, you know," Lester said. "I was sorry to have to kill that dog."

Gideon wondered why he was bothering with a haircut and a shave for a man that was mourning an ink spot and had to admit to himself that it had nothing to do with Lester. He owed Lissie for a night he would never forget, and this was the price.

Or maybe he just wanted to show Lissie that she wasn't the only one who could bend the rules. When she walked into that courtroom to see Lester face Judge Gowdy she would see that he'd kept his part of the bargain and then some.

"You done?" he asked, unlocking the door and taking Lester's plate from him.

"I been done for since '76," Lester said, putting his hands out in front of him. "Wanna put them iron cuffs on me, Gideon?" he asked before scratching at a scab on his scalp.

"Come on," Gideon said, grabbing him by the arm and leading him out of the cell. "We don't have all day. The stagecoach was due in twenty minutes ago."

"Yer pa meetin' the judge?" Lester asked. "And trustin' you with the prisoner?" He looked hurt, this helpless little shell of a man, as if he'd been insulted to be left to only the deputy.

"Figure I can handle you, Pincus." He nearly lifted Lester off the floor as he hurried him to the door. His father wasn't going to like the fact that he was taking Lester to Ezra's, and he had no intention of it making the prisoner late to the courthouse. " 'Less you're thinking of making trouble."

Lester smiled up at him, allowing himself to be pushed through the door and out onto the wooden sidewalk. "You got enough trouble, I reckon," Lester said. "Been keeping secrets for more than twenty years now. Figure I can keep 'em a little longer. Unless . . . Jesus

H. Christ, Gideon! You don't suppose that judge'll make me swear to tell the truth?"

Gideon could see his dreams go up in the cloud of dust that signaled the arrival of the stagecoach from Helena. He steered Lester in the opposite direction, heading him toward Ezra's barber shop. "Best you keep your mouth shut and let me do the talking."

"Ain't that lawyer fella you brought to see me gonna be there?" Lester asked, looking over his shoulder toward the hotel where no doubt Gideon's father was helping the judge down from the coach. Gideon wondered if his father had seen him walking Lester down the sidewalk.

*I'll meet the stage and see to it that Judge Gowdy gets a decent breakfast and a chance to wash up. I'll have him at the courthouse around nine. Then I'll come over for Lester,* his father had said as he'd loaded a bullet in each chamber of his Winchester.

*You see to the judge and I'll see to Pincus,* Gideon had told him as offhandedly as he could.

He hadn't had the energy for an argument with his pa, too, when he'd already gone three rounds with his conscience.

He put his hand on Lester's dirty collar and opened the door to Ezra's shop.

"Sit," he directed Lester, shoving him toward a line of vacant chairs. "Morning, Ezra," he said to his brother-in-law who was clipping stray gray hairs from Marcus Mallard's balding head. "Morning, Marcus."

"Morning, Gideon," they answered in unison.

"Morning, Lester," Marcus added.

"Ain't told a soul," Lester assured Marcus, as if the man had the faintest clue what he was talking about.

"I'm sure you haven't," Marcus answered, as if he truly did.

"Even though I ain't had one of Honey's cakes in longer 'n I can remember."

"Honora's gone to her reward, Lester," Marcus said patiently. The man was a saint. It surprised Gideon to realize how much Lissie was like her father.

"I didn't do it," Lester said, eyes all wide and darting about the shop. "I swear I'da never hurt Honey, nor the little one, neither."

"Soon as you're done," Gideon said to Ezra, "see what you can do about him." He gestured with his head toward Lester. "He's going before the judge this morning and Lissie thinks he ought not look like he's been bitten by a mad dog."

Ezra nodded and indicated he'd be done in a minute. Heck, Marcus only had a few hairs on his whole head.

"How's Lissie?" Marcus asked as Gideon looked out the window nervously. He hadn't counted on anyone being in Ezra's chair this early, and he was worried about being late.

"Fine," Gideon answered absentmindedly, seeing his sister Juliana coming down the street with his niece in tow and giving her a wave.

"Good," Marcus said. "Hard not to worry about your children, you know, but it's good to know she's in safe hands."

Gideon kept his eyes glued to the window and hoped there was no indication of his thoughts as they ran to just where his hands had been on Marcus's daughter, what they'd touched and kneaded and explored.

Juliana struggled to open the door to the shop, making the bell overhead ring. Ezra had found the bell in Springfield, Illinois, on his only trip east and Gideon knew he was damn proud of it because it didn't tinkle like the one in Hughes' Mercantile.

"Well," she said, her delight written on her face and in her voice. "Half the family's here! Good. I can get everyone's opinion on the cloth I just bought. Now don't be afraid to say you don't like it," she continued, handing the package to Gideon and fussing at the strings to it. "Jeannie loves it, but Lissie said she'd switch with me if you thought it was too—"

Jeannie let out a little cry just as Juliana's eyes went wide and her mouth dropped into a small 'o.' Gideon followed the line of her stare.

"Lester, what the hell—" he started, seeing the fool's dirty hands wrapped around Jeannie's small shoulders, shaking uncontrollably now with her tears. He stopped when he saw the sun glinting off the edge of one of Ezra's razors. It was poised a hair from his niece's neck.

"Oh God!" Juliana said, her voice a whisper. In Lester's grasp, Jeannie's sobbing grew louder.

"Put it down," Gideon said, his voice hard though his insides had been reduced to sludge. "You're scaring her, Lester. Making her cry. You don't want to hurt a little girl, do you?"

Lester shook his head and gave Gideon the kind of smile the devil himself might give. "Come on, Gideon, do it. You gotta do it, son. Kill me."

"Put it down," he directed, taking a step toward them. For every step Gideon took, Lester took one in reverse, carrying Jeannie with him, until he was backed up against Ezra's counter.

"You don't have to hurt her, Lester," Marcus said, coming slowly out of the barber's chair and turning to face Pincus. "She doesn't know anything."

"The dog knew," Lester said. "Maybe he told her."

"Dogs can't talk," Jeannie said, her big brown eyes overflowing with tears. "They just lick you if they like you, but they don't say nothing."

Juliana's face crumbled before she lunged toward Lester. Ezra grabbed her just as the razor drew a bead of blood from Jeannie's neck and the child screamed out in pain.

"Don't do it!" Gideon shouted, throwing one of Ezra's pomade jars just above Lester's head so that the pieces rained down on him and he had to raise his hands to shield his head.

The minute Lester released her, Jeannie came running, screaming and crying, toward her mother. Gideon pulled his gun from his holster and aimed it where Lester had disappeared behind the counter.

"Get up now, you piece of shit, or I'll shoot you right through that counter until no one'll recognize you." Gideon saw the blood from his niece's neck seep into the lace of her collar and meant every word he said.

"Get up!" he shouted. "I ain't warning you again."

Lester's answer came in rapid succession. Four shots came from Ezra's New Central Fire Revolver—the one that Gideon had begged him to get rid of when Ezra had first shown it to him, the one that Gideon had told him shouldn't be left behind the counter, the one that Gideon had warned him would be more a danger than a help.

One bullet rang Ezra's deep bell. Gideon didn't even look to see what damage the others had done. He just stormed the counter and took aim over it, ready to empty his gun into Lester's already demented head. He was one shot too late. Lester had saved him the trouble.

He lay on the floor, one eye staring blindly at the ceiling, the other blown away along with the side of his face, the gun still in his useless hand. Behind Gideon, Jeannie was still crying, but there were no reassuring sounds from Juliana.

The mirror behind the counter reflected only him

still standing, and he had to force himself to turn around and see what taking Lester for a simple haircut had cost them all.

Juliana lay in Ezra's arms, blood covering her breast, Jeannie burrowing herself into her mother's skirts. Ezra appeared shocked, but unhurt.

Marcus Mallard lay facedown on the floor, a puddle of blood growing by his side.

Outside a crowd was gathering and Gideon could hear Doc Agrin fighting his way through the throng.

The door slammed open and hit the back wall with a thud. "What the hell . . . ?" His father's voice boomed. "Oh dear God, Gideon!"

Behind his father, Lissie gaped at the scene, then turned away to catch her breath.

Gideon heard the crowd muttering and knew the moment Lissie found out that it was her pa's body that he was hiding as he knelt beside his sister.

Doc Agrin took a quick look at Juliana. "Just a flesh wound, here. Get her over to my office and I'll see to it there. Keep your hand clamped down on it tight until I get there," he instructed Ezra who nodded silently and struggled to lift his wife while their little girl clung to her dress.

Lissie stepped into the shop as if she were walking on eggs, soundlessly, carefully. She kneeled beside Jeannie and pried her fingers from her mother while Doc Agrin and Gideon eased Marcus over onto his back.

"Shit," the doctor muttered softly. "In the gut. Think you can carry him to my office? Least I can make him comfortable before he—" He looked over at Lissie and let the end of the sentence hang.

Marcus was a big man, but his age and sorrow had

left him a shell. Even dead weight now, he was lighter than Gideon expected.

"See to Jeannie's neck," he said to Lissie who blinked furiously in his direction before nodding.

"What in the name of bloody hell was Pincus doing in here?" his father asked, getting in Gideon's way as he tried to grab hold of Marcus's legs.

"I can manage," Gideon said, shrugging him off. "See to Lester."

"Pincus is dead," the doctor said, rising with difficulty and leading the way out the door.

Gideon shook his head. "Just a haircut," he said. He looked down at Arliss, who was pressing a damp cloth to Jeannie's little neck, trying to wipe the girl's tears and her own with her other hand. "I was getting the harmless old fool a haircut."

*Chapter Thirteen*

*E*VEN UP IN ARLISS AND GIDEON'S ROOM, WHERE
Berris was hastily rummaging through the drawers for whatever Arliss might need at her pa's
house, she could still hear her father ranting in the
kitchen. Poor Cluny was taking the brunt of their father's outrage, while Gideon was seeing to things with
the undertaker.

Jeannie was curled up in a small ball on the old
green chair, nearly hidden in its lumps and bulges and
piles of cloth patches that Berris supposed would someday be a quilt. Around the child's neck, tied with a fancy
bow as if it was there for decoration, was a ribbon of
cotton to protect the thin cut she'd received from Lester. She was still sniffing back tears and had resorted to
sucking the thumb that Juliana was so proud she'd finally given up.

"Your mama's gonna be just fine, sweet potato," Berris told her little orange-haired niece, as she plucked
several of Arliss's white cotton combinations from her
mama's old highboy and threw them in the general direction of the satchel on the bed. "You know Doc Agrin
wouldn't have promised if it wasn't so." At least Berris
hoped he wouldn't. The doc had assured them that the

bullet had barely nicked the fleshy part of Juliana's shoulder, and Berris had been so upset she hadn't even thought to say that every part of her sister was fleshy now. Despite all his reassurances, Juliana looked as white as the bed sheets and Berris didn't blame Jeannie one bit for being scared.

Truth was, Berris was scared, too. Scared for Juliana, and oddly enough for Arliss and Gideon. Not that she'd changed her mind about Arliss not being good enough for Gideon, but as sad as he'd seemed since he'd married her, Berris couldn't even imagine what her brother must be feeling now that he'd let Marcus Mallard get shot.

"That idiot judge actually suggested that I ask for my own son's resignation!" her father was yelling down in the kitchen. "Now there's a goat-getter if ever I heard one! As if all the good work Gideon has done in this town, the calming down, the setting to rights, the God damn *civilizing* of Granite, could be undone by one stupid error of judgment!"

Berris hurried to get the rest of Lissie's things together so that she could get Jeannie out of the house. She wondered if Gideon would be moving into the Mallard house while Lissie was there to see after her father. Her brother hadn't asked her to pack his things. Of course, he could certainly do that for himself.

If he was welcome at the Mallard place. Oh, heck and heifer dust, with all that had happened, Berris wasn't sure he was still welcome in his own home.

As she shoved Lissie's nightgown into the satchel, she heard the crinkling of paper. Unfolding the soft cotton fabric with the delicate embroidery, she found an envelope addressed to Arliss Mallard and bearing a Helena postmark. The fight with her conscience didn't last as long as it took to bat an eyelash.

"Why don't you go down the hall and make the potty sing while I finish up," she said to Jeannie who looked up at her with big reluctant eyes. "Go ahead and leave the door open so that I can hear the tinkling, sweetheart."

As soon as Jeannie was through the door, Berris pulled the letter from its envelope. With a beginning like *My darling Arliss,* there was no need to check the signature at the bottom. So Slick had written to Arliss. From the greeting, he still hadn't heard that his *darling Arliss* was now Gideon's darling wife. She skimmed the letter, not surprised that Slick was off gambling and learning still more lessons. What did surprise her was that Slick didn't seem angered by Arliss's betrayal. There were no recriminations for her night (if that's all it was) with Gideon, and the child that was a result of it.

And apparently he knew about the child because he told Arliss to take care of herself, especially in her condition . . . and then there it was, clear even in Slick's chicken scrawl.

*I'm planning on coming back to make things right and see my duty through as soon as I've found a place for us to live. You ain't to worry none. I'll keep my promise.*

"Did you hear?" Jeannie asked, coming back into the room.

Shoving the letter back into the satchel, Berris nodded and said something like "good girl." She wasn't sure what she said. Her head was reeling as she tried to sort out all the possibilities. So the baby was Slick's after all. That didn't really surprise her. Did Gideon know? Could the baby just as likely be his? In fact, was Arliss even sure? Just what had Arliss told Gideon that had made him stand next to her in church and vow to love her until death did them part?

"I'll resign myself before I'll ask your brother to turn in his badge! You go tell that idiot judge from Helena that! Tell him he's got no law enforcement in Granite anymore!" Her father's yell was punctuated by the slamming of the screen door. "And don't you go telling Gideon about any of this, Cluny. Boy's got enough on his mind. You hear me?"

"Half of Granite hears you," Cluny shouted back.

"And I bet they agree with me!" her father shouted before slamming several doors and banging around in the kitchen like he was herding bulls.

Berris grabbed the last of Arliss's things and shoved them into the valise. She hoped she'd found everything, since there was a good chance Lissie wouldn't be welcome back in Gideon's bed once he found out the truth. "Come on, Jeannie," Berris said, extending her free hand to the quivering mass of blue calico and baby fat balled once again in the chair. "You wanna go with me to Arliss's house?"

The little girl's eyebrows came down hard over bright brown eyes. "Doesn't Aunt Lissie live here anymore?" she asked.

Berris squeezed the small plump hand within her own. It was a good question, and while she certainly had an opinion on the subject, she wasn't really sure she knew the answer.

Gideon had made arrangements for Lester's burial and taken care of Marcus Mallard's bill with Doc Agrin. He'd gone to the pharmacist and gotten the medication the doctor had ordered for his father-in-law and dropped it at Marcus's with a shout to Lissie that it was on the table in the hall. He'd seen Juliana settled at home and had told Ezra where to find him in case his sister needed anything—anything at all.

And then he'd taken up residence on the Mallards' porch.

That had been several hours ago. It had been before Cluny had come by and told him what the judge had said, and he'd given Cluny a message to bring back to his pa. It had been before Berris had dropped off Lissie's things and begged him to listen to her, and he'd put her off with promises of listening later. It had been before the sky had gone from brilliant blue to a fine soft pink and had eventually grown dark and left him hidden in the shadows.

He didn't know if Lissie even knew he was there.

He just knew it was where he had to be, within her reach if she needed him.

Besides, he had nowhere else to go.

He could hear the sounds of her moving about inside the house. He smelled the heat of the stove, though there was no scent of dinner. Not that he could have eaten anything. But Lissie needed to eat. She would need to keep up her strength. He'd never forgive himself if something happened to her or the baby.

When the hush that always fell over the better side of Granite descended, and the tinkle of the piano keys from the dance halls on the other side of town crept his way, he stood and stretched. His left foot had fallen asleep, and he shook it until the pins and needles that twitched it gave up and disappeared.

There was a cold wind blowing in from the north, carrying with it the stench of the refinery. Heck, he supposed he could become a miner. There was plenty of work up at the Columbia, he thought, as he lowered himself to the front step and let his head rest on his hands. He could get three dollars and twenty-five cents a day to hide himself in the bowels of the earth if he was willing to work ten hours instead of the eight the union was fighting to keep.

Wouldn't that just put a burr under Cluny's saddle?

Poor Cluny. Gideon could hardly remember being fifteen. He was damn sure he was never as passionate as his younger brother was about the world's injustices. He sure as heck hadn't cared about whether the miners were getting a raw deal. And he was no keg of dynamite just searching for a match the way Cluny was.

He'd written his resignation on the only paper that was handy, a one dollar bill, and wrapped his badge in it, giving it to Cluny to deliver home. That had been rash. What did he expect to live on now that he wasn't on the town's payroll anymore?

"Gideon?" Lissie's soft voice stirred him. It always had. It always would. "What are you doing out here?"

"How's your pa?" he asked her, standing once again and coming to face her through the fancy screen door with the bright white fretwork that gleamed in the moonlight.

"Resting," she said. Her face looked worn, the light in her eyes dulled by the hour and the circumstances.

"Did you eat?" He kept his hands behind his back, clasped, so that he couldn't simply yank open the door and pull her against him, no matter how much better it would make him feel.

"I had a little tea," she said wearily. "I managed to spoon a bit into him . . . " Her voice trailed off.

"You gotta eat something, Lis," he said. His fingertips touched the screen that separated them like bars on a cell.

"I'm not hungry, Gideon," she answered, sighing softly and tilting her head to stretch out her neck.

"Maybe *you* ain't," he said, pulling open the door

and stepping into the parlor. "But that baby you're carrying might be. You ever think of that?"

Her hands cradled her rounding belly.

He walked around her toward the back of the house. It hadn't changed much since he'd been inside it last, though he suspected it had to be a good five years or so. Still, he didn't suppose they'd moved the kitchen. "I'll make you something," he said. "And you can try to eat it."

"Gideon, I don't want—" she started.

He couldn't let her finish. He knew damn well what she didn't want—him here in her house, him in her life, him in her future. "I'll make you a couple of eggs and then sit with your pa while you eat 'em. I won't be in your way, Lissie, and I won't stay, if that's what you're worried about."

"I'm worried about my pa," she said, and as she did, her lip quivered. "He keeps talking about mama and how they'll be together now, and I . . . "

"Lissie?" Marcus Mallard's voice was a croak as he called to her from upstairs.

All Gideon wanted to do was take her into his arms, hold her tight against him, and tell her everything would be all right. With every ounce of strength he had, he stood stock-still, knowing that she wouldn't want it, wouldn't want his touch or his comfort after what he'd let happen.

"I'll go see to your pa," he said softly when it was clear that she wouldn't be able to keep her tears at bay. "Then I'll make you something to eat."

He looked at her, waiting for her to say something, order him to leave, demand his apology, anything—but all her efforts were geared at stemming her tears.

"Sit here," he directed her. "I'll be right back."

❖ ❖ ❖

Marcus Mallard lay on the bed he'd shared with his wife, her pillow still beside his own, *Mother* embroidered on its face. His face was ashen, and when Gideon stepped into the room Marcus licked at his lips.

"I need some water, son," Marcus said, his voice a mix of gravel and rust.

Gideon swallowed hard, his own mouth suddenly gone dry. He hurried to the bedside and fumbled with the pitcher and glass.

"What happened to Lester?" the old man asked. Gideon cradled the back of his head while he held the glass to his lips.

"Dead," Gideon said, offering Marcus more of the water. "By his own hand."

"There are some late lilies," the man said with a sigh, "out back near the old pump."

"For Lester?" Gideon asked. "After what he did to you?" He eased Marcus's head back down onto the pillow and stared at a man he'd have liked to know better but would probably never get the chance.

"They'll look nice on his casket." His eyes were closed, as if he were envisioning it. "With ferns."

"The man doesn't deserve nice," Gideon said. "He and I both don't deserve nice."

Marcus opened his eyes and gave Gideon half a smile. "How do you figure?" he asked.

*"How do I figure?"* Gideon repeated, wondering if Marcus was delirious. "The man shot you, and I didn't lift a finger to stop him."

"Lester was a crazy old fool." Marcus took a ragged breath before continuing. "I don't hold him responsible for what happened any more than I hold you. He couldn't have been trying to shoot me—the shot came right through the counter."

Gideon hadn't thought about that. "Still, the fact is that he shot you and Juliana before he—"

"Managed to kill himself. I figure that was his plan all along, don't you? To get you to kill him? He asked you as much, didn't he? And when you wouldn't do it for him, even when he tried to force your hand . . . "

"I should never have taken him to Ezra's," Gideon admitted. "It was only . . . " That he owed Lissie, but now it wasn't for the night of passion that he felt he owed her, but for all the days in which she'd offered him a smile, all the times she'd touched his heart and softened it with her own.

"You couldn't help it. You're a compassionate man, Gideon Forbes," Marcus whispered, his body limp with exhaustion. "Thank the Lord for that."

"A lawman ain't supposed to be compassionate," Gideon said, more to himself than to Marcus.

With his eyes closed, Marcus smiled. "A man of the law is as close as you can get out here to a man of God. He can't be *too compassionate*. Compassion has no limits. I was sure from what you'd done, you knew that."

"I don't know how you can forgive me," Gideon said, falling to his knees and taking Marcus's bony hand in his own meaty one. "I'll never forgive myself."

"Forgive you?" Marcus said wearily. "I've been dreaming about a man as good as you since the day Hedda Clovis put that little girl into Honora's waiting arms. I'll sleep good now," he added, and his chest rose and fell heavily as if in proof.

Gideon watched Marcus sleep for several minutes. How could Lissie ever forgive him if her father didn't get well? And the chances of that were smaller than finding mouse droppings in the woods. Oh, Doc Agrin had gotten the bullet out, stopped the bleeding and sewn him back together, but Marcus's innards had spilled into his gut. He'd seen enough miners, enough gunslingers, enough senseless death and destruction to know that it was likelier than not that within a few days an infection would set in.

Funny that Hedda had delivered Arliss, when just about everyone in town had slid into Doc Agrin's hands when they'd started life. But Honora and Marcus had always had a soft spot for Hedda, and for Lester, too. Like Lissie, they had soft spots for every poor wretched creature that came along.

"I'm so sorry, Marcus," he said, the words coming from deep in his belly. "I should have never let this happen."

When finally he came back downstairs, Lissie was asleep in the armchair by the window. She started in her sleep, her head falling forward before she righted it, swallowed, and slept on. Maybe she needed her rest even more than she needed nourishment, he thought.

Should he carry her upstairs?

Her head fell forward again and she jerked it back, shifting slightly. Still she slept.

He could put her on the sofa, stretch her out, and put a cushion beneath her head.

With her shoulders slumped, her head hanging limply down, nearly resting on her breasts, her belly looked rounder. Should someone catch a glimpse of her now, resting and unguarded, he would know in an instant that within her she carried the seeds of a new life.

Guilt cut like a dagger into his chest. Slick, for whom he'd had nothing but contempt, had given her a new life to cherish. Gideon had more than likely taken away her father. He didn't know how she could stand to have him in her house. Quietly, so as not to disturb her, he moved a chair closer to her and lifted her feet onto it. She stirred, inching down a bit, and a paper drifted to the floor while she shifted to her side and went still again. He waited a while longer to make sure she was soundly asleep then he lifted Slick's letter and placed it on the side table without reading it. He could pretty much guess what Slick had to say for himself and couldn't begrudge his wife whatever solace she could find. With a deep sigh of regret for what might have been, he laid an afghan over her, tucking it beneath her chin before placing a soft kiss on her warm brow.

"To dream on," he whispered and thought he saw the hint of a smile touch her lips before he walked out to take up his post on the porch, closing the door silently behind him.

Arliss came awake reluctantly. Her neck hurt. Her arm was sore. In her mouth, a field of cotton grew wild. And Mother Nature had thought it funny to glue her eyelids shut.

When she managed to open them, she found herself sprawled on two chairs in her father's parlor. Alone. She covered her eyes with her hands, hiding from the sunlight that pierced her lids, hiding from the truth.

"Lissie?" her father called from upstairs, his voice stronger than he had sounded the day before. He didn't fool her. She knew he wouldn't live to see his grandchild brought into the world. He would die, just as her mother had died. And she would be all alone in the world.

Her fault. Her fault, she thought, righting herself and pushing off the arms of the chair to get to her feet. *He's not a bad man, Gideon. He's just sick. He shouldn't even be in jail. Let me cut his hair Gideon. Let me give him a shave.*

What had she done? And who would pay for it? Her

father, Juliana, and Gideon. Always Gideon. Good, honest Gideon.

"Coming, Pa," she said, stepping down cautiously. Each step was agony. Her ankles had swollen within her boots and she could hardly walk. She should have remembered to take off her own shoes. Botheration! Married to Gideon for two months and she was so spoiled she'd forgotten how to see to her own needs.

She took a deep breath outside her father's door, then entered the room as cheerily as she could. "You're looking real good this morning," she said, finding him wide awake, a bit of color returned to his face.

"Where's Gideon?" he asked, straining his neck to look behind her. "Gone to the office already?"

She shrugged. "He was gone when I woke up," she answered, not mentioning that he clearly hadn't spent the night. "I'm so sorry about this, Papa. It's all my fault."

"The way Gideon tells it, it's all his fault," her father said and took a few shallow breaths as if the effort of talking was too much for him.

"I pushed him into it," she admitted. "You don't really believe that he'd have taken Lester to Ezra's if I hadn't begged him to let me fuss over the man and make him look presentable, do you?"

"I do," her father said, letting his eyelids fall. "Your husband's a decent man, Lissie. A good man. Promise me that you won't forget that no matter what happens."

"Are you hungry?" she asked, ignoring his request. Of course Gideon was a good man. And to show her deep and abiding appreciation for all he'd done for her, she'd brought ruin crashing down around his head.

She'd heard Cluny down on the porch last night through the open window in her father's room. The doctor had given her pa plenty of laudanum so that he could bear the move back to their house, but *she* wasn't deaf to the conversation. The judge had demanded that Gideon resign as deputy of Granite. And despite his father's reaction and Cluny's begging and pleading for him not to, Gideon had agreed.

"Pa? You think you could eat a little something?" she asked, trying to push the overheard conversation from her mind. She had her pa to worry about. Gideon would see to himself.

"Maybe a little of that bacon you're frying up," Marcus said, "or a bit of soft egg."

Arliss breathed in deeply. There was indeed bacon frying somewhere, and with heavy steps and a heavier heart she brushed the hair off her father's brow and then headed for the kitchen.

She pushed open the door and surveyed the mess. Pots were scattered willy-nilly around the counters, their handles pointing in every direction. There were several bowls on the table, a pitcher, her egg basket, a half dozen spoons. There was a dishtowel over the back of one chair and Gideon's jacket over another.

He stopped what he was doing when he heard her, but he didn't turn around. It was a kindness she appreciated. "Hope you're hungry," he said, waving his hand at what appeared to be enough food for most of Granite. "How's Marcus?"

"He thinks he can eat," Arliss said.

"That's a good sign," Gideon answered back. He still hadn't turned around.

Arliss stood awkwardly in the doorway, as if the kitchen space now belonged to Gideon. She ran her booted toe across the cracks of the floorboards. "Have you checked on Juliana?" she asked.

Gideon nodded his head. "Between Ezra and Berris she's getting so much attention I'm not sure she's ever gonna recover!" His shoulders perked and fell, as if to tell her it was just a joke.

"And Jeannie?" Oh how she would miss Jeannie who loved to climb up onto Arliss's lap and ask her to sing a song to her. That child could cram so much love into a hug and a snuggle. And Arliss needed every drop.

"Berris can't keep her outta Juliana's bed. Cluny's supposed to be keeping an eye on her, but—"

"Oh, please bring her here," Arliss begged. "Please, Gideon. I'll take good care of her, I promise!"

When he turned to look at her, his eyes were red and watery. His nose was rubbed raw from his handkerchief and he needed a shave.

She wished she was dead.

He wiped his hands on a dishrag and shook his head. "Now why would you wanna go watching Jeannie? Ain't you got enough to do looking after your pa and yourself?"

She noticed he didn't mention himself, not that it was any surprise that he wouldn't want her taking care of him. "I can manage," she said, grabbing a plate and spooning some egg onto it for her father. "Tell Cluny to bring Jeannie over and I'll keep an eye on her."

A knock at the back door startled them both, and they looked up expectantly, as if Cluny had somehow gotten the message already. But it wasn't Cluny's silhouette that was framed in the door's window, and Arliss put down the plate and opened the door with her heart in her throat. Somehow she just felt that it could only be more bad news.

Hedda Clovis was scrambling back from the door, as if after she'd knocked, she'd changed her mind, or that she had startled herself as well. She wore her usual layers of clothing, men's trousers beneath a skirt that was pinned up so that she could ride her mule, several shirts and a shawl over it all as if she clung hopelessly to some measure of femininity. It appeared, as it always did when she left the lean-to she called home, that everything she owned was on her back or hidden within folds of clothing. Covering her graying hair was an old felt hat, and rather than tipping it back, she tilted her head until she could see who had answered the door.

Arliss put her hands over her belly, remembering how Mrs. Clovis had offered to help her rid herself of the baby, if that was what she wanted. She'd said there were herbs, plants, ways to undo what had been done. When Arliss had told her she could never do that, Mrs. Clovis had smiled and said that there might be someone she knew willing to take a strong healthy baby, willing to make the baby—and all Arliss's troubles—disappear. It wasn't the first time, she'd said. And it was *more than fittin'*, she'd added.

Arliss had told her, and haughtily, too—if she remembered right—that Slick was going to marry her just the moment he found out. Mrs. Clovis had simply nodded, but her look had turned soft and sympathetic. She'd told Arliss to come back whenever she needed her. A month later, when she'd gone back for some tea to stop the morning sickness, the old woman had asked about the wedding.

Proudly, foolishly, Arliss had told her how it was going to be the following Sunday at the church, with half the town in attendance. Hedda had seemed happy for her and had told her the tea would stop her heaving.

They were both liars. And now they stood facing each other with Gideon looking on.

"Is he dead?" Hedda asked, as blunt as ever. "Yer pa?"

"No, he ain't dead," Gideon said coming up behind Arliss and putting a hand on her shoulder that warmed her to her toes. "Go see to him," he said gently. "I'll see to Mrs. Clovis."

"I come to ask if Lester spilled the beans before he croaked," Hedda said, rubbing her hands down her skirts.

"There are no beans," Gideon said, handing Arliss her father's plate and giving her a gentle push toward the hall.

"No beans!" Hedda tilted her head and looked at Gideon askance. "You really believe that, Mr. Deputy?"

Arliss's heart pounded in her chest.

"You wanna say otherwise?" Gideon asked, taking several steps out onto the back porch. With Hedda still on the ground and Gideon up three steps, he looked like a giant about to slay some poor villager.

"I don't wanna say nothin'," she said with a sigh. "I came to find out if that crazy brother of mine held his tongue or not. You think yours are the only beans in town? You think that there aren't pots on every family's stove?"

"I think you're talking in riddles," Gideon said, attempting to shoo Arliss from the room. Rather than argue, she took two more steps toward the front hall, but stayed where she could hear. "I don't like riddles much."

Hedda came up the steps, her footsteps shaking the pans on the stove. She was broader than she was tall, and with one hand on her hip and the other holding up her skirts, she looked more like a coal scuttle in need of shining, than a woman. "Is Marcus up to visitors?" she asked, peering around Gideon to ask Arliss.

"You want to see my father?" Arliss asked, steadying herself against the wall. Just when she'd thought nothing could get worse, Old Lady Clovis had come to tell Marcus about his daughter's fall from grace. She'd promised to keep her secret. She'd kept plenty of other women's secrets, Arliss was sure. Mrs. Clovis wouldn't turn on her now that her father was on his deathbed, would she? She couldn't. Swallowing hard, too ashamed to even look Gideon's way, Arliss clutched the plate in her hands.

"I gotta see Marcus," the woman said, tilting her head back to look at the giant Gideon guarding the house, then circling around him to the door. "Gotta see him now before it's too late."

Lissie felt the cold air come through the open doorway along with Hedda Clovis. Her voice was hardly above a whisper as she pressed the word past her lips. "Why?"

# Chapter Fourteen

"SHE SAYS IT'S PERSONAL," GIDEON TOLD MARCUS Mallard, every bone in his body wishing he could just toss Hedda Clovis back up on her mule and send her into the hills from whence she'd come. "She keeps saying that you'll wanna see her, so I figured I'd just ask you before I send her packing."

"She didn't say anything to Lissie, did she?" Marcus asked, his face ashen, his fingers kneading the white cotton blanket that covered him. "Lissie's all right, isn't she?"

"I'm fine." Lissie stood in the doorway blinking back tears. "I'm just sorry I wasn't a better daughter to you, Pa. I'm sorry I didn't listen and I was wild and I—"

"Hush," Marcus said, reaching out for her. Lissie flew toward the bed and came to her knees beside it. "You were everything your mother and I prayed for and a lot more. You've never been a disappointment to us. You—"

Hedda Clovis stood in the doorway, filling it. She took off her hat, much as a man would, and moved to the foot of his bed where Marcus could get a good look at her. "I come to be released from my promise," she said.

"No," Lissie answered, but it didn't seem that Hedda was talking to her. "Please, Mrs. Clovis. My father is very sick. I don't want him upset."

"Marcus," Hedda said, ignoring Lissie altogether, "I gave my word, and I ain't one to go back on it, but I'm thinking that circumstances being what they are, you'd have to be a damn fool not to know time's come for the truth."

Marcus nodded solemnly. "I'm no fool," he said. "I just thought there'd be a few more seasons. Thought I'd get to see the next crop, and know they understood, but it looks like that ain't to be. I'll see to it."

Hedda reached out and touched Lissie's hair gently, then took a step toward the door. "They'll understand. And it was a good bargain, Marcus, all around. She'd have been right pleased," she said.

And then, like some witch in a fairy tale, she was gone.

None of them said a word as the door downstairs opened and closed noisily. They stared at their own feet while Hedda yelled at her mule to "git." Marcus closed his eyes, Lissie held her breath, and Gideon listened to the sound of dried autumn leaves hitting the window as they fell from the trees.

Gideon shook his head at the wonder of it all. Here he was, a secret of his own burning a hole in the love he had for Lissie. And there she sat, her secret building a wall between her and her pa. And wasn't it just fitting that Marcus, too, had been hiding something—something that at this very moment kept him from reaching out and touching Lissie as a tear rolled down her cheek.

"She's a crazy old lady," Marcus said finally, waving a hand in the air as if Hedda had disappeared in a puff of smoke. "Everyone's been saying for years that all that time she spent in the mines with that husband of hers left her half crazy. And that when he died she went over the edge."

"Fix your pa some soup," Gideon told Lissie, coming to help her rise from her knees. Maybe it would be best if he could talk to Marcus alone and let him unburden himself without Lissie being privy to his secret. "And you have some, too. I'll sit with him a while."

Lissie looked at her father and then at him. As if it were just too much for her to take, she came to her feet and left the room without so much as a word.

"Love don't come from flesh and blood," Marcus said after they had listened to Lissie's soft footfalls on the stairs and were certain she was out of hearing range. "I hope you know that."

"Yes sir, I do," Gideon said. So Marcus did know. As Hedda had said, he'd have been a fool not to. But there was more to it, more that Gideon sensed rather than understood.

"You can be a man's flesh, his blood, his seed, and he can turn from you like he would a stranger. Only it hurts a lot worse when he does. It tore my poor Honey to pieces when her pa didn't want no part of her for loving a man like me." Marcus's eyes glistened with the memory of his wife. "And then when a family was denied us, I thought her poor heart would just give out and I'd lose her for sure.

"Blood's a fickle, unreliable bond. And in the end, love is stronger than any substance you can see or feel. And it'll still be there after the blood and bones are rotting in the ground." The sun glistened on Marcus's upper lip, and he swiped at his nose absentmindedly. "You think I love Honora one drop less than the day I married her just because her body isn't here beside me anymore? That love I felt when I married her was nothing compared to what followed. It grew with every year.

And when I thought I couldn't love any more than that, Lissie came into our lives. And all the love I felt for Honora just multiplied, the way a few flowers can turn into a whole field."

Marcus's eyes shone with a fire as he spoke, and when he was done he leaned back heavily against the pillows. Gideon suspected he knew Marcus's secret and wondered if he could be half the man his father-in-law was.

"Do you know what I'm trying to tell you?" Marcus asked, his breathing labored.

Gideon reached out and took Marcus's hand in his, squeezing gently, willing his own health, his own strength into the spent body on the bed. He gave him what comfort he could to a man who had loved a child not his own, even as Gideon hoped to. "I love your daughter, sir. I suppose you've known that since the days I helped you weed your garden, pretending to care about which flower was which." Marcus, his eyes shut now, smiled. "And I'm anxious to share that love with the child—my child, the way you did," he added.

"You think you're the one giving, but it turns out different in the end." Marcus said, a look of surprise and pleasure spreading across his pained features. "It turns out you're the one getting it all."

"I'm not interested in what I can get out of it, sir," Gideon said.

"I guess she turned out more like Honora than we had any right to hope for," Marcus said. "I'd have given up anything for Honey—my dreams, my hopes, my pride. And when I did, she became all those things for me."

"I'd already given up my hopes and dreams," Gideon said softly, more to himself than to Marcus.

"Pride don't count for much in light of that," Marcus answered with a wan smile.

"No," Gideon agreed. "Pride don't count for much anymore."

They sat like strangers, Gideon and she, listening for a call from her father, waiting for Cluny to bring Jeannie along with word of how Juliana was doing, watching for the gray haze of the day to lift and reveal a brilliant sun.

"You're sure your sister likes Nun's puffs?" Arliss asked for the third time. The truth was she'd never made them and hated the thought of failing in front of Gideon. "Maybe something like arrowroot biscuits would be better while she's recuperating."

"Ma used to make Nun's puffs when we were sick as kids. Said all those eggs were good for us." He looked off into the distance, maybe into the past, and then nodded. "I think Juliana would be real happy to see 'em again."

Arliss sighed, blowing the hair from her forehead, and rolled up her sleeves.

"Unless you don't wanna bother." He was on his feet again. Lord, but he was up and down more than a quilting needle. "You sure got plenty to do without fussing with some silly cakes. And there's enough food around here to feed the better part of Granite for a week." His arm swept the counters where offerings from all her neighbors and friends sat silently wishing her father well. She supposed that Juliana's kitchen looked much the same. But it was good to do something that would remind Juliana of her mother. It was a kindness Lissie wished someone would do for her.

"If it wouldn't offend them, I'd send Cluny up with some of this to Coppertown," she said, knowing that even if her father were well he couldn't consume even a small portion of what kept appearing on her doorstep. Despite that, she began to pull out the bowls and cups she'd washed and put away earlier and lay them out on the table.

"I'll take up whichever ones you tell me to later myself," Gideon said. He worried so about Cluny getting into trouble up at the mines. He worried so about everyone. And who, she wondered, was worrying about him?

She wished she could find a way to come to his rescue the way he had come to hers. She couldn't imagine what her father would be feeling now if he still had her to worry about. Without looking at Gideon, almost to herself, she asked, "You suppose my father knows what I've done?"

Gideon busied himself in the icebox, pulling out milk and eggs and looking out the window with each trip to the table. When instead of answering her, he said, "Here's Cluny and Jeannie girl," she knew that in his own way he'd told her what she didn't really want to hear.

Of course her father knew. All of Granite knew, no doubt. And along with thinking she was no better than trash, they probably thought that Gideon was a fool. It was a shame, too, because Gideon Forbes was no one's fool. He was the best of men, as good as her father.

Cluny knocked on the door and opened it without waiting for an answer. "You're looking right fine today, Arliss," he said, staring, as he always did, at her ever-expanding chest. That was another thing about Gideon. He didn't drool over her breasts or seem put off by her expanding waistline. Jeannie wrapped her legs around Arliss, silhouetting her rounding stomach. Cluny's jaw dropped slightly, but he quickly closed his mouth.

"Whoa there," Gideon cautioned, pulling gently on his niece's braids and swinging her up onto his shoulders. "Don't go knocking your aunt over."

"Shave and a haircut?" Jeannie asked, her hands already weaving into his hair.

"Absolutely," he said, grateful for a moment away from the sorrow that surrounded them all.

"Two bits," she demanded, putting her hand down on his shoulder.

He reached into his pocket searching for the quarter he always kept there for her, forgetting for the moment that he'd slept on the porch and hadn't emptied or checked his pocket in days.

"This one's on me," Lissie said, reaching into a baking tin on the counter and handing Jeannie a quarter. "You want to help me make some biscuits for your mama?"

"Papa made her breakfast," Jeannie said shyly. "And he gave her a bath just like Aunt Berris gave me."

She felt Gideon's eyes on her even as he lowered Jeannie to the floor, and she tried to keep herself from blushing. Once Gideon had bathed her. Once he'd touched her everywhere.

Since that day at the barber shop he had held nothing but her arm.

And her heart.

"And I taught him to braid mama's hair like she taught me," Jeannie said, looking over all the preparations on the table. "I mix good. Let me mix."

"Maybe later you could teach me how to braid," Gideon suggested. Then he quickly mumbled something that sounded like, "If we don't have anything else to do."

Lissie felt a bubble of excitement in her stomach, almost as if the baby had clasped its hands in prayer.

"I could show you on Aunt Lissie's hair," Jeannie said, sticking a finger into the crock of butter and licking it.

In the middle of all this, Cluny stood, watching and shifting his weight as if he were waiting for something. Finally, he said, "Pa needs some time to find a new deputy. He told me to tell you he expects you to stay on till he finds someone."

To see the shadow cross over Gideon's face was like watching the sun go behind a cloud. The soft smile he had been wearing hardened into a thin white line. His Adam's apple bobbed convulsively. "No," he said when it appeared he couldn't get out any words at all. "I couldn't do that."

"You gotta, Gideon, else who are Sessa and Beattie and all the other miners gonna turn to? You gotta be that voice of reason you keep throwin' in my face every time I wanna just blast old Belmont to Kingdom Come. Pa says . . . hell, Gid—" He looked sheepishly at her and shrugged. "Sorry. *Everyone* says you're a fine, fine deputy. The unionists like you, the Temperance Society ladies like you. Even the girls down on Lilac Row like you, and if you can get all those people—"

"Now how would you know what the ladies on Lilac Row are thinking?" Gideon demanded.

"See, that's what I mean," Cluny said, reaching around Arliss to push up Jeannie's sleeves, which were getting covered in flour and butter and anything else she could reach on the table. "You don't miss anything. But you don't make too much out of it, neither. You know how to calm down a man whose feelings are on fire and how to light a cracker under someone else who ought to care . . . "

"I asked you what you know about the ladies down on Lilac Row," Gideon repeated.

Cluny handed Arliss a tin that was well within her reach. "See? And you hold on to a horse's tail no matter how deep the water gets."

"I find out you been down to Lilac Row, you're gonna have some fancy dancing to do to get yourself out of your room before you hit sixteen. Them ladies know better than to—"

"Because you laid down the law," Cluny said, tipping an imaginary hat at Gideon. "You're a great deputy. You're gonna make a finer sheriff than Pa ever did."

"You ain't changing my mind. A man makes a mistake, he's gotta expect to pay for it." As always, Gideon was shouldering the burden of her mistakes. She watched as every one of his muscles went rigid, as his hands fisted, as his jaw twitched.

"But the mistake was mine," she said to Gideon. Then to Cluny she added, "What happened wasn't Gideon's fault. It was mine."

The boy looked at her like she was sprouting an extra set of ears.

"It's true. I pushed him into it. I—"

"Pa was right. I ain't got what it takes to be a lawman. I cost Lester his life yesterday, Cluny. I put Marcus in harm's way and there's no telling how that'll end. And Juliana—you know anybody sweeter than Juliana? And she's lying in her bed on account of me being careless. I've ruined enough lives. I ain't ever risking any more."

He stormed past Cluny and out the door before Arliss could even argue about the mistake he was making.

"Can we still make biscuits?" Jeannie asked. Her little bottom lip was quivering and her big brown eyes begged Lissie to put an end to the awful words she should never have been hearing.

"Did your father really ever say that Gideon didn't

have what it took to be a lawman?" Arliss asked, drying her hands on a dishcloth.

Cluny made a face that looked like yes and no. "He said that a lawman had to know the law, and enforce it, right or wrong. And that Gideon knew right and wrong, and had let his feelings get in the way of the law."

There was a time when Arliss believed that Gideon thought that things were either right or wrong. But that was before she knew Gideon, knew that he was quicker to forgive than to judge, knew that he was harder on himself than anyone. "Will you go after him for me?" Lissie asked Cluny as she pushed the hair off Jeannie's forehead and then reached for an apron to tie around her waist. "Will you tell him that I have to stay with my pa, but that I'm so very sorry that I ever got him into this mess?"

Cluny shook his head at her. "You're the only thing in his life that ain't a mess, Lissie. I ain't gonna tell him no such thing."

He didn't know where else to go, but back to Lissie's porch. She was his North, and no matter how lost he seemed to be, how turned around and confused, his heart, his compass, headed back toward her.

Through a window, opened just enough to let out the smell of sickness and let in a bit of fresh air, he could hear her talking softly to Jeannie. He could hear Jeannie chirp back in answer.

"Mama says I shouldn't talk with my mouth full," Jeannie said, her words muffled no doubt by several cookies.

"Well, I think we can make an exception this once," Lissie said. "We'll keep it a secret, all right?" Gideon stifled a laugh at Lissie's words. It was clear from the garbled sound that she was stuffing herself as fast as Jeannie was.

"We could let the snake talk," Jeannie suggested, and Gideon groaned and opened the door. "Uh oh," the little girl said when he pretended to be angry at her for giving away their secret. With Lissie smiling the way she was, he'd have let Jeannie give away his gun and the hip it rested on.

"What snake?" Lissie asked.

"It's something dumb," Gideon admitted sheepishly, feeling a warmth in his cheeks.

Jeannie raised her arm and made a little head out of her hand. "This is the snake," she said. "It can talk when I'm not supposed to. Right, Uncle Gideon?"

Gideon nodded. His cheeks were now burning.

"No," Jeannie chastised him. "Show her."

Gideon's shoulders sagged, but he raised his arm and nodded his fist.

"See?" Jeannie asked, delighted at bossing around her uncle. "Can I play with your bullets?"

The snake at the end of Gideon's arm opened his mouth wide in shock and shook its head. Jeannie doubled over with laughter. She grabbed two cookies and, pulling on his sleeve until she could reach his face, shoved them into Gideon's mouth, prying it open with her tiny soft fingers.

"Can I sit on your lap?" Jeannie asked, not looking at his face, but at his hand. Gideon had the snake look at his legs and then at Jeannie and then at his own face. Obviously the snake was confused. "Sit down," his niece ordered.

Gideon sat, risking a brief glance at Lissie, who appeared delighted with the show.

"Now, can I sit on your lap?" his niece asked again,

reaching for two more cookies to keep his mouth full so that the snake would have to answer for him.

The snake nodded. *Yes.*

"Can Aunt Lissie sit on your lap now?" Jeannie asked, jumping up and running across the parlor to grab Lissie's hand and drag her toward Gideon. Both girls stared at Gideon's hand.

Slowly the snake nodded. And just as slowly another snake began to raise its head, and Gideon hurried to change his position slightly before Jeannie pushed her aunt into his eager lap.

"It was our way of talking at the table," Gideon started to explain, but before he could finish Jeannie shoved another cookie between his lips, and Lissie caught a crumb from the corner of his mouth with her fingertip.

Jeez, he'd have been happy to show her his snake ages ago if he knew this was what it would lead to!

"Wanna learn to braid?" Jeannie asked, leaning over Gideon's arm to pull out two pins from Arliss's hair and let it tumble free against his chest, the sweet smell of baking wafting up as if it had been trapped within her bun.

Gideon swallowed hard and nodded hesitantly.

"You can talk now," Jeannie told him, but he doubted he could. Lissie was light in his lap, and she was soft, and warm, and her hair was like silk in his hands as Jeannie tried to tell him what to do.

"Hold this part," she said, handing him a hank of hair. Gently he smoothed the section, gathering it from its roots, running his fingers through it.

"You need three parts," she instructed, lifting the center section and exposing Lissie's bare neck. The sight was as provocative, as thrilling, as if she stood naked against him. He stiffened beneath her and prayed she was unaware of how base he was that with her father dying upstairs and his little niece nudging his elbow, he still was overwhelmed with desire for her.

She sat very still against him and let him amuse Jeannie with her soft tresses until Berris knocked on the door, making her nearly jump out of her skin as well as his lap.

"Come on in," Gideon said, keeping Lissie trapped by holding onto the half completed braid and asking Jeannie which part went to the center next. Of course, he'd braided leather strips often enough to strengthen a strap, even done some decorative plaiting once when he'd gotten his first full-size horse. He just hoped Berris knew better than to point out his abilities in front of his niece. And his wife.

It looked like he didn't need to worry. For the first time in her life, Berris was speechless as she took in the scene in the parlor.

"No, this one," Jeannie said, her hand over Gideon's, guiding it.

"Thanks for bringing over Lissie's things," Gideon said when no one seemed to have anything else to say.

Berris just nodded. She'd had a bee in her bonnet for three days now, ever since he'd brushed her aside, refusing to listen to something she wanted to say. "How's your father?" she asked Lissie.

"He's holding his own," Gideon answered for her. Lissie rose from his lap, the poor excuse for a braid hanging over her shoulder. She had enough to deal with. He could at least see to Berris.

"When was the last time you shaved?" Berris asked him, looking him over from his unkempt hair to his worn boots. "Or changed your clothes?"

Lissie studied him as if she hadn't actually seen him in the three days he'd been sleeping on her porch to be within earshot if she needed him. He didn't even know if she was aware he'd been there and couldn't say whether it had been for her or for himself that he had been.

He leaned down and whispered to Jeannie to get some cookies for her aunt from the kitchen, waiting until the little girl was out of the room to ask, "How's Juliana doing?"

"I don't know the last time I saw her this happy," Berris said. "I just don't understand it. And Ezra's making an absolute fool out of himself, jumping up at her every sigh, carrying her here and there as if she didn't weigh more than Jeannie does. She sends her good wishes for Arliss's father," she added, looking between Lissie and him like there was something she was trying to see and disappointed that it wasn't there.

Finally she asked Arliss softly, "Did you find everything you left at our house?"

"Lissie?" her father's voice quavered down the stairwell and crawled hoarsely into the parlor. "You still here?"

" 'Course I am," she shouted back up at him. There was a hesitancy as she answered her father's call that had nothing to do with the man's condition, though surely it weighed heavily on her mind. This reluctance was born of a fear of leaving Berris alone with him, and he smiled at her and gestured with his chin that she should see to her father.

Before she left the room, just so she knew that he was well aware of everything and that despite it, she was safe, he answered Berris for her. "Yeah, she got the letter, if that's what you mean."

Sure, he was sorry she hadn't thrown it out. Sure, he wished that Slick was as gone from her thoughts as he was from her life. And while he was at it, he wished for a nice thick vein of silver right where he was putting up his house, and for there to be peace on earth and good will toward men. And for his wife to love him.

And if wishes were badges, everyone would wear a star.

And in the meantime, he could live with one lousy letter.

"Did you read it?" Berris asked him, an eyebrow raised.

"Of course not," Gideon replied, coming to his feet and looking down at his sister accusingly. "I don't read mail that isn't addressed to me. Do you?"

* * *

Virginia City was as old as his mama's threats and only a little younger than its grass. Slick was as disappointed with the ramshackle town as he had been with Helena and Anaconda. The whole idea was wearing thin. He was hungry and not just for fortune and flesh.

As he made his way down the dusty road, his stomach growled, as if he needed reminding that it was empty. He fingered the velvet pouch in his pocket which contained Arliss's necklace. After losing it twice he'd vowed not to risk it again. The weather was turning raw and before long he was going to need a warm duster—which meant renting a horse was out of the question for now.

Lord! Who'd have thought he'd ever be a man who'd count his pennies and acknowledge the necessity of putting a few aside. Life was turning out hard for a man with a broken nose and a broken dream. And Gideon was to blame for that. The women weren't so quick to put an arm around his shoulder or a drink beside his hand now that his profile resembled a dimpled milk pitcher. Scrawny Rhea said it was because there wasn't a heck of a lot of him to hold onto, but he knew it was the nose. And he couldn't help that any more than he could help it if the tables had turned on him.

The women on Lilac Row always gave him one on the house when he was down and out and hard up for cash, knowing he'd take care of them when he was flush. Rhea had demanded payment and called out for the management when he'd offered her a dollar on Friday for the two-bit lay she'd given him on Wednesday. Some giant named Mac had sent him flying down the fancy twisted stairway on his ass and told him if the dollar wasn't on the bar on Friday his jaw would make his nose look good. With each step he took, Slick's ribs ached, but that was nothing compared to his pride.

It was four miles to the Bar L Ranch and Lissie's grandfather, and from what he'd heard not much hope waited out there. Old man Flynn was hanging on by a thread, and most of his marbles, along with his money, were long gone. Still, Slick was the father of the man's great-grandson. He was the one that had seen to it that the man's line went on, that he didn't perish from the earth with no issue to his name. And he was bringing him the news himself. On foot. Wasn't that worth something? Maybe Slick could offer to name the little bugger after the old coot.

There were worse names than Alaric Waynick.

Slick just couldn't think of them at the moment because he was tired. And hungry. And he still had over three miles to go.

*Chapter Fifteen*

⟡

HOPE, LISSIE THOUGHT, WAS LIKE A CANDLE IN YOUR soul that kept on burning when the ocean of tears you've cried should have drowned it out, when the winds of doubt you can't help feeling should have blown it out. And sometimes it burned so brightly that it blinded you to the truth.

And even knowing that, she couldn't help looking at her father and letting the pink in his cheeks and the steady sound of his voice convince her that he was getting well. For five days she had sat beside him and tended him and listened to the doctor say that he was doing as well as could be expected and that only time would tell. For five nights she had fallen asleep on sofas, in chairs, anywhere but in her old bed. She was a married woman now, and a wife didn't go off and sleep in a single bed, even if her husband wouldn't care if she did.

As for Gideon, he kept spending his nights on the porch, but whether it was out of guilt for what had happened or anger at her for her part in it, she wasn't sure. And it didn't matter, really. She was just grateful he didn't go home, didn't abandon her. He was there when she woke, there when she nodded off to sleep, pretending to be cheerful. But she saw the sadness out of the corners of her eyes when he thought she wasn't looking, and she knew it merely mirrored her own.

Her belly was a little round ball now, and she stroked it gently and spoke to her baby softly in the quiet when her father slept and Gideon was nowhere to be seen. She was telling the baby about Gideon's deep brown eyes when Cluny came banging on the kitchen door.

"Gideon? Gideon are you in there?" he yelled, opening the door and letting in a blast of cold air. She wondered when the weather had turned, or when last she'd gone beyond the porch, where Gideon's warmth had no doubt sheltered her from reality. She was going to have to insist that he sleep inside now that it was turning so cold. And then she realized what it was that was keeping him on her porch.

With all that had come between them, the guilt they shared and the guilt they clung to separately, where exactly was he going to sleep?

"He's up with my pa." Arliss reached for her shawl and Cluny helped wrap it around her quickly, his breaths short and rapid as if he'd been running.

"He doing okay?" Cluny asked, already in the hall and waiting with his hand on the newel post for an answer.

"He's better," Arliss said as she gestured for him to go on upstairs. "What's wrong?"

Cluny didn't answer, he just hurried into her father's room and started talking to Gideon. "You gotta come up to the Columbia," he said and then caught himself, saying hello to Marcus and asking how he was doing.

"I just might live," her father answered with a hint of a smile. "What's got your branches gnarled?"

"That thief Belmont told the miners last night that starting Monday they'll be working ten hours for the same three dollars they're getting now working for eight." Cluny waited for Gideon to respond. When he didn't, the boy continued. "He said anybody that didn't like it could find another way to earn a living."

Gideon's jaw tightened as he fought a losing battle to pretend the matter didn't concern him.

"Maybe you better go up and talk to Mr. Belmont," Arliss suggested.

"I ain't the deputy no more," Gideon said, while everyone could see plain as day the blood coursing in his veins was a lawman's blood and that it was his heart, not the star on his chest that made it pump.

"Go on," her father said to Gideon. "I'll take care of what needs taking care of."

"Gideon, Beattie says he'll hear you out. Pa's talking to Belmont and trying to keep him from closing the mine to anyone who won't resign from the union, but you know Pa ain't got the knack you do. Or the conviction. The men are talking about blowing up the mine, and I think Old Man Belmont's thinking about beating them to it."

"You should go," she said, proud of this man who was her husband, proud that he had both compassion and strength, and that he, and no one else, might stop the men from doing harm to themselves and their land.

"It ain't a good time," Gideon said, but his eyes were darting around the room.

"Your hat's in the front hall," she told him, slipping her hand within her father's grasp.

"About what we discussed, Marcus," he said as he stood in the doorway, "it might be best if you waited for me. I'll be quick as I can be."

Marcus nodded and shooed Gideon and Cluny with a wave of his hand. "You be careful," he called after them, raising himself from the pillow and sinking back against it only after they heard the door slam shut.

By the time Gideon made his way to the center of the crowd, John Holmes, a man who'd been mining underground since the new tunnel was dug, was coughing up blood. He held the stained kerchief out for the others to see.

"Ten hours a day and you won't last more than five years, I guarantee it," he said. "And what'll your wives and babies live on after yer gone?"

"What are they livin' on now?" someone from the crowd asked. "Can hardly feed 'em on the three bucks I'm getting now."

"Toplanders ain't got a right to complain here," John Holmes said. "You ain't down in some dark winze behind a widow-maker. You guys above ground can see that the sun shines the rest of the week while it's only there on the Lord's day for all I know."

"You think you're the only one starving? Dying? You think the stench from the refinery ain't in our lungs up top? And in our kids' lungs?"

Gideon didn't know who threw the first punch. He only knew that he damn well wanted it to be the last. And so he shot one round into the air and waited for the dust to settle around him, while Cluny kept telling everyone that his big brother was there to set things right. It must be nice, Gideon thought, to be young enough to believe that anything could be set right with a few words and the best of intentions.

"You're fighting the wrong enemy," he said when the crowd got quiet enough to hear him. "You men are on the same side. You wanna use up your strength fighting each other? Ain't you tired of this yet? You're like some old couple arguing about who ought to shut the window while the rain is leaking right through the roof."

While some of them took offense, he knew they were listening, knew they were ripe for someone to tell them what to do. And Lord help them all, they were looking to him to be that someone.

"I don't know nearly as much as you do about mining," he allowed and got more agreement than he really wanted on that score. "And I know a lot less about owning a mine and making it turn a profit for stockholders who are sittin' in cushy leather settees back on Park Avenue in New York City, smoking cigars and lighting 'em with dollar bills." Hoots and hollers greeted that picture. "But I do know about trouble, and I know about acting hastily and I know about paying the consequences."

What he didn't know was what he was doing up in Coppertown when he wasn't even deputy anymore and when Lissie was probably getting her heart broken down in Marcus Mallard's bedroom.

"I say the enemy is Belmont," someone shouted.

"A few days down a shaft might make him more than ready to see the light," someone else yelled to a chorus of "yeahs" and suggestions of "a few weeks" and "a few years!"

"A battle like this can't be fought with your hearts and your guts," Gideon said. "It's gotta be fought with your heads. You go after Belmont, you'll pay for the pleasure, and that security you're seeking for your kids will be down the shaft and in the gumbo."

"We can't just take this lyin' down," Beattie said. "We do, what's to stop him from upping the hours to twelve and lowering the pay to two bits? We gotta do something!"

Gideon wasn't surprised that fists punched the air around him.

"I agree with you," Gideon said. "The first thing you gotta do is think. Then you gotta plan. Then you gotta lay out that plan open and honest and give Belmont the opportunity to do the right thing."

"The time for thinking is long past," someone yelled, but Gideon was considering his own advice. Maybe waiting and watching was the coward's way, the way he had taken with Lissie. Maybe he needed to lay his cards on the table when he got back to Lissie's house and see if she wanted to stay in the game.

"I say we go up to that damn palace of his and bring a bit of blasting powder with us."

"And I say that you rotting in prison ain't gonna put food in that new baby's mouth, Getz," Gideon said, his hand clearly resting on the handle of his gun. "So let's sit down and figure out what will."

Cluny produced a chair from what appeared to be thin air, and Gideon sat on it while the miners made themselves comfortable, or not, around him. Seemed like he was in for a heck of a long night for a man who wasn't even the deputy anymore.

Arliss had fed her father, bathed him—noting that his skin held more warmth than it had for days—and helped him change into fresh nightclothes. She'd sat by his side while he reminisced about her mother and what it had been like when they were first married. He talked about the sadness in their lives, the emptiness with which they waited for a child.

His voice, strong, clear, confident, had lulled her to sleep.

When she woke, cold in the darkness, her father's breathing was labored. Struggling to find the lamp and turn it up, she wondered if Gideon had come home. No, there'd been no blanket tucked over her, no cracker left beside her. Her boots, which he'd taken to easing off her feet after that first night had left her nearly crippled, were still on her feet. No, Gideon hadn't come, and this wasn't his home.

Sweat glistened off her father's brow with the first gleam of lamplight. Her hand reached out to his forehead, but it took her minutes—hours, it felt like—to lay her hand against his skin.

He moaned at her touch, pulling his eyes open until he could look sheepishly at her as if to say he was sorry. "I didn't want to wake you," he said hoarsely. "It was good to see you sleep."

"You should have woken me," she snapped, unable to keep the anger out of her voice. How could she keep the fever at bay, keep death from the door, without someone sounding the alarm? And what good did it do to chastise him? She changed her tone and laid her hand on his shoulder gently. The heat poured through his nightclothes and seared her soul. "I'll get some cool water and a cloth and have you cooled down in no time."

He nodded, but defeat danced on his face like a candle in the wind. And why shouldn't it? The doctor had told them that should infection set in, and he suspected it would, there would be little he could do to save Marcus's life. He'd dug out the bullet, he'd cleaned and sutured and wrapped, and then he'd shaken his head and said that God would have to do the rest.

And it seemed that God was busy elsewhere. Why ever should He be concerned with the prayers of Arliss Forbes? Why should he listen to her, when she'd never listened to Him?

Her back ached as she carried the pitcher full of cool water down the hall from the washroom. Her arms were wet and the chill of the night rose on her flesh in tiny spikes. Her eyes burned with tears she refused to shed.

And she was sure her lips would tremble and her voice would quiver when she spoke.

"Pa?" she asked. "Does it hurt you anywhere? You want me to send for Doc Agrin?"

"Nothing he can do," her father said. "And the only pain is in saying good-bye."

"Then don't," she said sharply. "Anyone can have a little fever. I've seen worse with a cold, and nobody ever died from that."

"You're right," he said, but his eyes were glassy and the cool rag heated the moment it touched his body.

She poured him a glass of water from the tumbler on the bedside table and raised his head to help him drink. The water dribbled down his chin and she climbed onto the bed and pushed herself against his back until he was nearly sitting upright. "Try," she begged him. "Try to drink."

He coughed and choked and sputtered instead, and she let him back down, tenderly dropping his head to the pillow.

"It could be that I don't have much time," he said, taking her cool hand in his feverish one. "So there's something I've got to tell you. Something you ought to know."

"Ssh," she answered him back, wringing out the cloth and trying to stem the raging fire with little more than a kitten's spit. "Don't you wanna see your grandchild? Don't you wanna rock that baby on your knee like you used to do with me? Don't you wanna—"

"I wish I could, Lissie," he whispered, his voice

straining with the effort. "I'd have loved him . . . nearly as much as I loved you. And your ma and I couldn't have loved you more if you'd been our own."

Lissie stood there, just stood there, waiting for him to explain. She stood a good long time, knowing that he'd probably spoken his last word. His breath rasped in and whistled out unevenly.

"Pa?"

His eyelids fluttered. She thought she saw his fingers reach out to her, but she didn't take them. She didn't fall to her knees, or keen, or even cry. She just stood silently and watched, knowing that all his energy was being spent knocking on the gates of heaven, begging to let him in.

"Please, not yet," she whispered toward the ceiling, toward the sky, toward God Himself. "Please don't take my pa."

*Your ma and I couldn't have loved you more if you were our own.*

She wrung the damp cloth in her hands, water dripping onto her skirts like a baptism for the child within her. "Don't take my pa," she said, her voice raised now in anger. "Don't you dare take my pa now."

## Chapter Sixteen
### ⟨⟩

GIDEON WAS AS DEAD AS THE SUMMER GRASS WHEN he dragged himself back to Marcus Mallard's house on High Street. The night had been raw, the cold seeping through his jacket and into his bones. As soon as he checked on Lissie, he'd have to get over to the office and tell his father that the miners were headed for a strike, and that if Belmont lost his head, the miners would have it on a copper platter.

Only a lot of fast-talking last night had left Belmont still breathing, and the jail cells empty. Gideon pulled off the copper star that Beattie had hastily cut up and handed him when he'd told them he wasn't deputy of Granite anymore. They'd declared him deputy of Coppertown and demanded that he protect them from harm. And then they'd traipsed him from hovel to hovel and showed him such poverty that his guts ached from holding back his outrage. He had known most of their names, he'd seen their wives in town, prayed with their families in their church. But before last night he hadn't known them at all. And from the looks of the familiar embroidery on several of the tablecloths in Coppertown, it seemed he didn't know his wife all that well either. How long had she been sending her sewing up this way? One thing he did know for sure about her, she'd never have let these poor folks pay her for her work.

He came into the house as quietly as he could, tip-toeing on the hardwood floor so that he wouldn't disturb his wife and his father-in-law from their slumber. He felt guilty over the squalor he witnessed in Coppertown. Not because he had more, and better than the miners, but because not until that moment had he been truly grateful for what he had. And he'd been too shy, too scared, to share it with Lissie, to tell her that he was the luckiest man on earth.

The house was silent. Lissie wasn't on the sofa in the front room. She wasn't stretched between two chairs in the kitchen, where the stove had gone cold. He laid his hat down on the counter and reached for some wood to stoke the stove. He heard soft shuffling sounds coming from the parlor behind him and he turned to see Lissie in the dim morning light.

Her eyes were sunken in deep purple sockets. Her hair was pinned this way and that to keep it off her face, spikes of it sticking out, strands of it clinging to her cheek.

"He's dying," she said flatly, coldly.

"Oh Lissie," he said, wrenching the words from his gut. "I'm sorry, I—"

"You should be," she said, eyes dry, lips straight and hard. "You're the one that put him in harm's way. You're the one who let a man you knew was dangerous, that you told me was dangerous, that you said needed to be kept under lock and key, pick up a gun and shoot my father."

Gideon said nothing. Lissie needed to yell at him, needed to shout and rail, and maybe even pummel him with her fists if that was what she wanted to do. And then, it wasn't as if she was saying anything that wasn't true.

"I asked you to let me do it, didn't I?" she demanded, hands on hips, accentuating the slight rounding that bulged beneath her damp apron. "This never would have happened if you'd just let me see to Lester myself."

"I was trying to be kind to him, to do what you wanted," Gideon started.

"Are you blaming me for this? Are you saying this is my fault?" she shouted at him, pointing toward the ceiling. "That it was because of me that my father . . . "

She stumbled over the word and Gideon wondered if Marcus had managed to tell her the truth.

"My father," she repeated, this time with conviction, "is dying."

"I never meant for this to happen," Gideon said. "You have to know that, Lissie." He wanted to add that he would never hurt her, that if he could have, he'd have taken the bullet himself before letting her suffer.

"Yeah, well, we can put that on his headstone. *Gideon didn't mean for it to happen.*" She flailed her arms and then froze, a look of shock painting her features.

"What is it?" he asked, coming close enough to smell the sharp fear in her sweat mixed, miraculously, with the flowery smell of her hair. "What's wrong?"

She took in a deep breath and then another. "A stitch," she said and bit her upper lip. "In my back."

He grabbed a chair and somehow managed to get it behind her. "Easy now," he said, his arm supporting hers as he lowered her down into the seat. "Slow."

When he had her seated he rubbed his hands together to make sure they were warm, then slid them behind the small of her back, hoping to ease the muscles that were knotting there. Her waist had thickened since he'd held her last. He was ashamed that it still, despite her anguish, still felt so good to him.

"Don't," she said, breathing more easily.

"Does it hurt when I touch you?"

She turned her head to look over her shoulder at him and gave him a wry, sad smile. "More than you know," she said and pulled at his hands until she was free of them.

She might as well have slapped him. He was sure it would have hurt less. But then so would a needle in his eye. Coming to his full height, he reached for his hat. "I'll get the doc for your pa."

"Tell him he best bring a miracle in that bag of his," she said.

"I'm sorry I wasn't here." He didn't know what more to say.

She nodded, acknowledging his apology and shrugging as if to say it wouldn't have made any difference. Then, rising gingerly and grabbing a stack of clean towels, she left him standing in the kitchen very much alone.

◦   ◦   ◦

Verinda Ruth Tenbrink stood poised with the scissors by Berris's ear. "My, but I bet it must be hard for your poor brother," she said, running a comb through Berris's hair. "I mean what with the shooting and Arliss's own father lying at death's door. Doctor was there this morning and things don't look good at all."

Berris watched in the mirror as a good inch of hair fell onto her shoulder. "Not so much!" she told Verinda Ruth. At this rate she'd be bald before the Miner's Ball. Bald, but up to the minute on the latest gossip. "You were up at Arliss's place this morning?"

Verinda Ruth waved the scissors, and another clump of Berris's hair tumbled down her arm and hit the floor.

"Had to bring a telegram up for Mr. Tenbrink. I swear that man is lazier than an old hound in the August heat. Why, it's gotten so that every morning I've got to go down to the Western Union and deliver telegrams for him. Claims that he can't leave the office, but he's just gotten so fat that a trip down the street leaves him gasping for air like some miner after a cave-in."

"Oh, Verinda Ruth! He'd never have you deliver telegrams for him. Would he?" Berris knew for a fact that indeed he did. It was why she'd come in to Verinda Ruth's yet again, complaining that her haircut wasn't straight. And just like legs on a table, Verinda Ruth kept shortening one side or the other and then needing to take off a little more to make it come out even. It was actually working very well. Because the woman hadn't gotten it right the first time, Berris didn't have to keep paying her for the information she gleaned as Verinda Ruth cut.

Of course, Berris's hair was getting mighty short.

"So you were at the Mallard place?" Berris asked.

Verinda Ruth's tongue was firmly between her teeth as she held a lock of Berris's hair between her fingers. "Mmm hmm," she agreed.

"My poor sister-in-law," Berris said, trying to remind Verinda Ruth that they were family. Everyone knew that families shouldn't have secrets. "How did she seem?"

"Oh, I didn't even get to see her. Doc Agrin was just leaving when I got there and he said it'd be best to just slip the telegram under the door."

Berris caught Verinda Ruth's arm and held it. "You brought Arliss a telegram? From who?"

Verinda Ruth shrugged apologetically. "Now you know I can't say," she said. "I sure would love to try that Annesta May's Hair Curling Fluid on you Berris,

honey. You know it's even guaranteed to keep the curl
in the rain!"

"I sure hope it wasn't more bad news for my poor
sister," Berris said, clucking with sympathy for poor,
poor Arliss, when it was really Gideon she was worried
about. "Where did you say it was from?"

Verinda Ruth lifted Berris's hair with a grimace. "It's
so limp. It'd look just like the picture on the bottle if
you'd let me try that curling fluid. And I didn't say. But
it was from Virginia City. The one here in Montana."

"Virginia City?" she asked while Verinda Ruth carefully uncorked the bottle.

"Shall I?"

"Was it from Slick? Did Slevin Waynick send my
sister-in-law a telegram?"

Verinda Ruth tried to be noncommittal and failed.
"You want me to try this stuff?" she asked.

"What did it say, Verinda Ruth? It's important."

Verinda Ruth held up the bottle and looked at Berris.

"All right," she agreed reluctantly.

Verinda Ruth poured a small amount onto the center
of Berris's head.

"Now what did it say?"

"Told her to take good care of herself," Verinda Ruth
said, pouring the foul-smelling liquid on Berris's hair.
"Real solicitous, he was. Told her good times were coming."

*Jesus H. Christ!* How dare he! And she just bet Arliss
would keep that telegram, too. In her underthings,
where Gideon would never go looking for it.

"Don't know why she never married him," Verinda
Ruth wondered aloud.

"Because my brother is ten times the man Slevin

Waynick can ever hope to be," Berris said, jerking her head away from Verinda Ruth. "This stuff burns."

"And now I'd be willing to bet she's already carryin' his baby," Verinda Ruth said. "And that it ain't gonna wait till the summer to show its face."

"And is that any of your business?" Berris asked. Her scalp was on fire. "You better get this stuff off, Verinda Ruth, before my hair burns right off my head."

"What flea's biting your bottom, Berris? Gideon's child won't be the first nine-pound premie born in Granite. Nor the last."

"How long is this stupid stuff supposed to be on?" Berris asked, wiping at drippings that ran down her forehead and directing Verinda Ruth to catch any rivulets that were headed down her back.

"Just think about the nice curls you're gonna have," Verinda Ruth told her, shoving the bottle with the wavy hair on it in her face. "I think there's something romantic about Arliss and Gideon. The way no one knew the affection they were harboring for each other. Why even I thought she was in love with Slick all this time."

"Get it off!" Berris said, the burning now overshadowed by an incredible itch that made her want to tear the hair from her head.

"Try not to think about it, dear. Put your mind on something else," Verinda Ruth advised, dabbing at Berris's neck. "So what do you think about what's happening up at the Columbia?"

"My pa was out there half the evening," Berris said. Talking about the mine was not going to stop the itching, but beauty had its price and she was willing to pay it. "Cluny didn't even come in till this morning. He and Gideon spent the whole night up in Coppertown."

"You think there'll be a strike?" Verinda Ruth asked,

fingering Berris's hair and then suggesting, in a very quivery voice, that it might be time to wash it out.

"Is something wrong?" Could hair get too curly? Samantha's ringlets were her crowning joy.

Verinda Ruth didn't answer. She just adjusted the slant board behind Berris's back and began pumping cool water into the sink.

"Cluny seems to think that it might come to a strike," Berris continued, all the while watching Verinda Ruth's face for some indication of what her hair must look like.

"Don't think it'll do 'em much good," Verinda Ruth said, frowning. "Old Man Belmont sent a telegram this morning to the *Kirkville Register* placing an advertisement for miners and toplanders for immediate hire."

Berris hadn't lived in a family of lawmen all these years for nothing. She could smell trouble along with the best of them. Even over the throat-gagging, stomach-turning smell of Annesta May's Hair Curling Fluid for Soft Curls in All Weather.

"Finish getting this stuff out quick," she told Verinda Ruth. "I gotta find Pa and Gideon."

Verinda Ruth put a clean towel around Berris's head. "I can't guarantee the results if you don't let me do my job slow and complete."

"I really gotta tell my pa there could be trouble."

"Well, if you must. But you might wanna put this on," Verinda Ruth said, handing Berris her hat.

"I have to go," Berris said, tying the ribbon beneath her chin and putting her coat on right over the full-sleeved apron Verinda Ruth had covered her with, and which now smelled like Doc Agrin had lost a litter of pigs in her very lap.

⁂ ⁂ ⁂

Juliana, sufficiently recovered, came to see if there was anything she could do for Arliss. Neighbors, who couldn't really spare it, came all the way down from Coppertown dropping off still more food her father would never touch. Her father-in-law came, offering a shoulder to cry on and what he hoped were words of wisdom about life going on and what her father would want. Gideon was on the porch through it all, despite the cold rain that fell like God's own tears for her father's quickly failing body.

"You've got to lie down and get some rest," Juliana insisted when Arliss came down into the kitchen in search of more clean cloths. "You can't keep going like this. Not now." She gently placed her hand on Arliss's apron beneath which a tiny heart was beating while Lissie's own was breaking.

"He needs bathing," Arliss said, swiping at her brow and arching to stretch out her aching muscles. "I've got to keep one step ahead of that fever, or—"

Juliana tried pulling her toward the table, but she didn't have time to sit, to chat, and certainly not to think.

"I have to get back to him," she said, trying to shrug Juliana off.

"Have you eaten a single thing today?" Juliana demanded. "Have you fed that baby that's depending on you?"

*We couldn't have loved you more if you were our own.*

He was delirious. People with fevers said the craziest things. Once when Slick was down with the influenza, he kept telling his ma that Priscilla was one of the three kings. Her father was probably dreaming something.

"Arliss Forbes! You are to sit down right now and eat some of this wonderful food that everyone's left here."

"My father," she said, but the words choked her.

"Sit down before you fall down! Gideon will be more than happy to see to your pa. Lord knows he's just aching to do something for you." Her face was full of questions that Arliss had no intention of answering.

"He's done enough. How's your shoulder, anyways?"

"Sore," Juliana said, touching it with her hand. "But it doesn't hurt me nearly as much as Gideon's guilt is paining him. As if it was his fault! Imagine him thinking that!"

Arliss let Juliana's comment hang in the air, let her stare and raise an eyebrow and guess at how Arliss felt.

"Eat," she said, putting something warm and brown on a plate in front of her before going out into the hall, opening the front door and instructing Gideon to see to Lissie's pa.

It was Gideon's fault. Yes, Lissie had put the bug in his ear, but she'd never suggested, never meant to suggest, that he take a man as dangerous as Lester Pincus, who everyone knew was crazy as a rabid raccoon, into a crowded barber shop and let him shoot innocent people. She'd only asked Gideon to let her clean up Lester. It hadn't been her fault that Lester had shot her father. It wasn't her fault that her father now hung between life and death and that only her will was keeping him alive.

"That fork's still shiny as a new quarter," Juliana noted when she came back into the kitchen. "Don't make me feed you like a baby, Arliss, just 'cause you're having one."

Footsteps sounded above her and she could hear Gideon's low voice upstairs speaking words of comfort.

"Pa," she heard herself say, wondering if maybe he'd woken up for Gideon.

"He'd call you honey, if there was any change," Juliana assured her, taking the seat across from her and pointing at her food. "For better or for worse," she added.

Which naturally made Lissie think of her wedding vows. If only Gideon hadn't married her, none of this would have happened. Who asked Gideon to come to her rescue anyway? If he'd just loaned her the money to leave town. If he'd just done his job as a best man and gotten Slick to the church, none of this, none of it, would ever have happened.

"You want me to play horse in the stable?" Juliana asked, picking up the fork and holding a piece of stew up in the air. "Here comes the horsie. Better open the barn doors—"

"I'm not hungry."

Juliana dropped the fork against the plate with a clatter. "Who cares if you're hungry?" she said sharply. "Who cares if you're sad, or angry, or scared out of your mind? That baby needs you, Arliss Forbes. You and no one else. I can't feed him for you. Gideon can't carry him for you.

"You're the only one that child can count on, Arliss."

Arliss picked up the fork and pierced a potato.

"You'll see," Juliana said while Arliss chewed on the dust in her mouth. "A baby is a gift from God. A child of your own makes everything all right."

"How is he?" Lissie's voice was a whisper of hopelessness. Gideon put down the rag for a second to steal a look at her standing behind him. Shoulders sagging, her dress rumpled, her sleeves rolled up and wet, she looked used up and discarded. His beautiful Lissie with the ready laugh and the shining smile stood beaten and bruised by everything that had happened in her life since he'd come into it.

How Slick could make her giggle with abandon while the other girls only tittered behind their hands! How Slick could make her smile climb right from her lips to her eyes! Gideon had been wrong to let him leave Granite. You could heap the best intentions it seemed, one right on top of the other, and still wind up with nothing more than a pile of dung in the end.

"He hasn't woken up," Gideon said. "I'll get some fresh water. You eat something?"

She nodded. He was grateful she didn't waste any more words on him. The ones she'd already said had hurt deeply enough.

"Lissie? Did your pa get a chance to . . . that is, did he say anything before the fever hit?"

Again, she nodded. Once upon a time he was the one whose lips couldn't relinquish more than a word or two. Once upon a time nothing could stop Lissie's thoughts from jumping out on her tongue.

"I . . . there was something he wanted to . . . " How could he ask her if Marcus had told her that she wasn't bone of his bone and flesh of his flesh? That she'd been the child of his heart and not of his body? "I'll get fresh water."

Flatly, the way she said everything lately, she said, "He said that he and my mother couldn't have loved me more if I was their own."

It was his turn to stand mutely and nod.

"You don't seem surprised," she said, picking a cloth out from the bowl Gideon held and touching it to her father's brow. She stiffened at the contact with her father's burning body, fear as plain as the freckles on her face.

"He can rest easier having told you," Gideon said aloud, though he meant only to think it. Keeping secrets from Arliss bored holes in your soul. He knew that from experience.

"You knew?" He hadn't thought there was room for more hurt in her eyes, but there it was—the pain and the anger. "And you didn't tell me? Something so important, so essential to me, and you just kept it to yourself?"

Lord, it was just what he needed—he already had horns and a tail in her eyes. Now he stood with a burning pitchfork in his hands.

"You know," she said, shaking her head in disgust, "when I married you I was surely aware that I didn't really know you so well. But I did think I knew what you stood for. I knew what everyone in Granite believed about you. Like you'd never lie, for one thing."

It was a low blow, and he didn't deserve it. "I've never lied to you," he said. "It was your father's secret to tell, not mine. He kept the truth from you, not me."

"You knew, Gideon, and you didn't tell me, and that's the same as lying. Sins of omission count in my book as well as in God's. My father was trying to protect me. What were you trying to do?"

"I wasn't trying to do anything," he said, grabbing the cloth from her hand and throwing it into the bowl. Water splattered around them but neither of them paid it any mind. "God knows what the heck I was trying to do, 'cause I sure don't anymore. I didn't know about Marcus not being your pa until yesterday, Arliss. He told me just before I went up to Coppertown."

"Well, going up to Coppertown was certainly more important than telling me I didn't belong to my own parents!"

He released a heavy sigh, acknowledging that he simply couldn't win with Arliss. As always, he was only a distant second. "I'll get you that water now, before you find something else to blame me for."

"Is there more?" she asked his back. "Beside putting my father here, keeping his secret. Is there more you've done?"

Gideon stopped in his tracks. He turned and watched Lissie kneel beside her father's bed and clasp her hands in prayer.

This wasn't the time for confessions.

It was the time for prayers.

# Chapter Seventeen

GIDEON WAS SITTING ON THE MALLARDS' BACK porch wondering how the best intentions had landed him in hell, when Berris and his father came circling around the house. His father's strides were long, eating up the distance and spitting it out at his feet while Berris took six or so itty bitty steps for each of his, hurrying to keep up with a man on a mission.

"Trouble," his father said. "Your sister—"

"Is always looking for trouble," Gideon ended for him. If Berris had more bad news for him, he just wasn't interested in hearing it.

"Belmont's sending for help from Kirkville," his father said.

"Scabs!" Berris informed him with more pride than contempt. No doubt Cluny had told her the name for men who refused to join the union and who would work when the strikers would not. Gideon, and Cluny, too, he was sure, had a few other names for them, as well.

"Verinda Ruth Tenbrink told me," Berris said, tugging at her bonnet as she spoke. For some crazy reason, her hair looked green to Gideon—not bright shamrock green, but the green of brass that's seen too much water and too little polish. "She was in the Western Union when Belmont sent someone down with an advertisement for the *Kirkville Register*. And," she started.

"Keep it to yourself, girl," his father said. "Western Union's just like the mail, near as I see, and goin' and tellin' tales is like tamperin' with the mail."

Berris wasn't one to be thwarted easily. "Is it a crime to tell someone they got mail?" she asked. "Regardless of what was in it?"

"No one here got any mail, girl, and Gideon and I have got some fast talking to do or the Columbia just might blow for real." His father's attempt was noble, but he'd as good as told Gideon just what Berris had in mind.

So Arliss had gotten another telegram. He didn't have to wonder who sent it, what with Thaddeus trying so hard to hide the fact, and Berris nearly gloating about it. Too bad he hadn't broken Slick's fingers along with his nose. It would have made it a lot harder for him to write, at any rate.

"Pa, I ain't the deputy no more. I don't see what any of this has to do with me." He was as annoyed with his father for trying to protect him from the truth as he was with Arliss for withholding it from him. She was a great one, standing up there giving him a tongue-lashing for keeping Marcus's counsel when she had her own little dirty secret burning a hole in her pocket and warming her heart.

"That's just so much nonsense," Thaddeus said, pulling out of his pocket the star Gideon had worn for the last four years and holding it out to him. "Might as well take it, son. With it or without it, you're still my deputy."

"Some things, Gideon," Berris said as she put a soft hand on his forearm, "are in your heart and your blood.

Sometimes it's a job, like being deputy, and sometimes
. . . well, sometimes it's a man, like Slevin Waynick."
Her gaze lifted up toward the house, and for the first
time Gideon noticed how cold it was outside, how Berris's words were wrapped in little white clouds as she
spoke to him. They didn't hurt any less for the coating.

And they didn't go down any smoother just because
they were true.

He could hang around on Lissie's porch like a sick
puppy or he could do something useful. Or at least try.

"All right, Pa. I'll talk to Belmont." He thought
about going in and telling Arliss where'd he'd be, but he
was sure she wouldn't care. "And Berris," he added,
pulling her shawl tighter around her just so as he could
get a closer look. "I ain't one to criticize, but if God had
thought green hair would be becoming, somebody
would probably have had it before now."

Pa had trouble stifling his laugh and it came out
through his nose, kind of like a sneeze.

"I told you all that pumping Verinda Ruth Tenbrink
for gossip would get you into trouble, and it looks to me
like it finally did." He pushed back his sister's bonnet.
Twisted strands of wet green curls lay plastered against
her head like river kelp. His pa covered his mouth, but
his eyes were smiling like he'd seen the cat catch his
own tail and take a good bite.

Berris looked a good deal less amused. She touched
her hair gingerly with a gloved hand and tried to see her
reflection in Arliss's front window. She pulled a curl
forward and tried to see it, but as Gideon had been
warning her, it was now too short to get a good look at.

"When it dries," she said, trying to assure herself as
well as Gideon and their pa, "it'll be—"

"Like prairie grass instead of seaweed," Thaddeus

said, a guffaw exploding from him and knocking him sideways against the porch rail.

"Maybe Juliana can fix it," Gideon offered. "She was always good with vegetables and the like."

Berris bit at the side of her lip, irritation warring with her better judgment, it seemed.

"You can laugh, but without me you wouldn't know about the scabs," she said haughtily. Then she lowered her voice and said, confidentially, "And if you're interested in the other telegram, I know a bit about that, too."

"That telegram didn't come for me and it didn't come for you, so I don't see how it's either of our business," Gideon said with a finality he certainly didn't feel. He'd give half of Granite to know what Slick had told Arliss. And half of Montana to make it just go away.

"Our business is up at Belmont's," his father agreed, fingering one of Berris's curls and shaking his head. "And if I were you, child, I'd tell Mrs. Tenbrink to do a little less talking and a bit more fixing."

He and his father headed up to the house on Silver Hill. He tried to keep his mind on Belmont and the miners, but his thoughts kept returning to Lissie.

"You aware that Arliss wasn't Honora and Marcus's natural child?" he asked.

"That so?" his father said in response. "Woman was round enough to hide a litter, so I suppose it went unnoticed. Your ma always suspected as much, though. Said Honora seemed awful healthy for a woman after her first birth. And then there was the way they let that girl run wild. Your ma used to say it was almost like they didn't feel it was their place to stop her."

The words sounded like his mother's. He could sure use her good counsel now.

"Marcus is dying, Pa."

"That don't surprise me much, either," Thaddeus said. "Man's been pining for his wife a long time, making ready to join her soon as Lissie was settled."

Gideon said nothing.

"Now, thanks to you, she's settled." He said it like saying it could make it so.

Gideon ran his tongue over his teeth.

"Settled and then some. . . . Yup, Marcus can rest easy now."

Gideon felt his father's eyes sizing him up. Still it was hard to find the right words.

"She hates me." God, saying it aloud hurt, like shooting holes in his heart.

" 'Course she does," his father said. "Her father's dyin' and that's got her shakin' in her shoes. She's roundin' out and scared about the pain that's waitin' for her if all goes right—even more scared that maybe it won't. Fear feels better when it's dressed in anger—it can hide there till it's gotta be faced."

"She blames me," Gideon admitted, then quickly added, "for what happened to her pa."

"You remember when you was little how you used to bang your shin here, your knee there, and that big head of yours everywhere else? Remember how your ma used to hit the furniture back and yell at it for hurting you?

"She'd tell that table in the parlor she'd chop it up for fire wood if it ever did it again, you remember that?"

Gideon couldn't help smiling at the picture in his mind of his wonderful, warm mama smacking that table with her wooden stirring spoon and warning it to behave when her son was around.

"You felt better when she did that, didn't you?"

"Pa, it was my fault, what happened at Ezra's. When

I think about what could have happened—Juliana, Jeannie—I—"

"You told Ezra a million times to lock up that gun of his," his father said. "Why not blame him? Wouldn't that feel good?"

"It wasn't his fault," Gideon argued. "It was mine. I never should have brought Lester over there in the first place, but—"

"That man sat in our jail for four weeks without either of us paying no mind to how he looked. Suddenly you notice he needs a shave and a haircut? My guess is someone put a bug in your ear to get him cleaned up before he saw the judge—"

"I'm the one that brought him there," Gideon insisted.

"And my guess is," Thaddeus continued as if Gideon hadn't said a word, "that that particular someone is feeling mighty guilty about setting in motion something that wound up outta control. Your ma couldn't get rid of every piece of furniture in our house, so she had to take to beating it up. Made you feel better, made her feel better if something else beside you were to blame."

Gideon turned up his collar. On the other side of the heavy iron gate with the cast iron "B" on it stood two of Belmont's men. Gideon nodded to them and waited without answering his father while they opened the gates.

Just as they were entering Belmont's estate his father put an arm around his shoulder. "She'll come around, son. Ain't a person on the planet who could hate you for long."

Arliss decided that she didn't hate just Gideon, though he was at the top of her list. She also hated God, even if it was blasphemy. She hated her father, even if he couldn't help the fact that he was dying. She hated Berris for leaving Lester's meals to her so that the old feelings she had toward the poor man were rekindled, and she hated Lester himself for fooling her with his sweetness.

"Arliss? You've got to lie down a while."

And she hated Juliana, who was being so good to her only because she had no idea that it was Arliss's suggestion that had led to the whole ugly business at the barber shop.

"Why don't you and Jeannie both take a short nap while I sit with Marcus?"

Because her father was too close to death's door for her to desert him now. Because she didn't want him going off to God without someone who treasured him beside him to take note.

"I don't need a nap," Jeannie said from the hallway where she was playing nurse with Lissie's old dolls. "I'm too old."

Juliana, with the utmost care and respect, replaced the sheet over Marcus's sweating body. "Well, your Aunt Lissie ain't too old," she said. But Lissie knew she was. She was the oldest, saddest woman in all of the United States. Maybe in all the world. They could put her in *The Annual Cyclopedia*. Was there a category for the woman who made the most wrong choices in the shortest time?

If only Slick hadn't left her, none of this would have happened.

"Here comes the doc." Juliana had been peering out the window from the moment she came, as if Doc Agrin's arrival would change what they all knew could not be changed. "Why don't you go get the door, Jeannie?"

"She doesn't need to," Arliss said. "The doc lets himself in and out now. He doesn't want me climbing the stairs more than I have to."

They listened to the doc's footfalls on the porch, Jeannie's banter in the background. They heard him open the door and shut it again. They heard him mount the stairs.

"Why Jeannie Bryant! What a nice surprise to find you here. You looking after your aunt?" he asked. His words were cheerful, but his voice held the deep sadness of resignation.

"No, but I'm looking after her dolls," Jeannie said. "They're all very sick and I have to nurse them. Then they'll get well."

"I'm sure they will," Doc Agrin agreed with a deep sigh.

There was a smile pasted on his face as he entered the room. "Any change in our patient?" he asked. As if in answer, Marcus flailed his arms and kicked at the sheet with one foot.

"How long can this go on?" Juliana asked him. "Doesn't the fever have to break sometime?"

The doctor came forward and handed a yellow envelope to Lissie. "This was under your front door," he said. Lissie put the telegram down on her father's dresser and watched the doctor take her father's pulse, pry back his eyelids, press on his abdomen. "If the fever doesn't break this evening, I can't say as there's much hope."

"What can we do?" Juliana asked. "Is there anything?"

"Is he still taking the tincture of aconite?" he asked Arliss.

"Maybe a little," she said. More dribbled down his chin than ever made it down his throat.

He put his hand on her shoulder. "One way or another, it'll all be over soon. Where's Gideon?"

"Wasn't he on the porch?" she asked. Like a sentry he'd stood guard there since he'd carried her father home. She couldn't imagine that he wasn't still there. A coil of new fear wound around the old one.

"Didn't see him," the doctor said. He tucked the covers around her father's chest tightly, as if getting a chill would somehow make a difference in the end.

He could have been on the back porch, she supposed. The Forbes all seemed to be more comfortable coming in the back way. The hope, feeble as it was, didn't fool her. Gideon, like Slick, like her pa, would be gone from her life sooner or later.

"Try getting him to take more of this later on," Doc Agrin said as he pulled a dark brown jar from his satchel and magically managed to get a spoonful of it into her father's unresponsive mouth. "It'll keep him quieter. And don't look so sad. He hasn't left us yet, Arliss. There's still room for hope. Why he might just surprise us all."

Maybe men just weren't able to tell the truth, like women couldn't wield an ax.

"I could warm you up a little supper before I go," Juliana offered. "Ezra's stopping by here on his way home to get Jeannie and me, and we could just as well eat here with you, if you'd like the company. You've surely got food for an army stacking up in that kitchen. Maybe you'd like to stay, too, Doc."

"Take some of the food with you, Juliana, but go," Arliss said softly, she hoped not unkindly. "I need some time alone with my pa."

"Go on downstairs," the doctor said to Juliana. "And go home and get some rest yourself. I'll stay a bit with Lissie and her pa."

Lissie figured she could deal with them one at a time, so she hugged Juliana and Jeannie good-bye and turned to ask the doctor to go on ahead as well. He was staring hard at her apron, a grimace adding lines to his already craggy face.

"Four months?" he asked. "Five?"

Lissie shrugged in answer.

"I should have realized how far along you were when I saw you at the sheriff's place and you were so worried about what might have happened to your insides. Can't believe I was fooled by you carrying small to start."

"It wasn't foolish to assume a bride would wait for her wedding night, or near enough. Except, of course, when that bride was me."

Doc Agrin smiled a sad, knowing sort of smile. "If I told you how many babies with wide open eyes and healthy strong bones were coming into this world a month or two younger than expected, you'd never scrape your jaw up off the ground. 'Course, you look to be farther along than I'd have thought Gideon would— well, it ain't any of my business. I only brought it up because I'm worried about you."

"I'm fine," she said, rubbing at her itchy belly and catching herself.

"You're so tired the circles under your eyes are touching your knees. Nothing's going to happen to-night, child. It's the night to rest before your strength is truly tested."

Arliss thought that if her strength hadn't been tested yet, then there was no hope she would survive. "Do you remember when I was born?" she asked the doctor who had delivered nearly every child in Granite for longer than Arliss had been alive.

Doc Agrin caught his tongue between his teeth as he thought, his brow coming down hard over his eyeglasses. Finally he gave a slow shake of the head. "Can't say as I do," he admitted. "Do remember how pleased your mama and papa were, though, the first time they brought you to church."

"Why didn't you deliver me?" she asked. Even if she wasn't Honora and Marcus's baby, she had to be someone's, didn't she?

"Now that was a long time ago," the doc said. "And my memory ain't what it was, but I seem to recall that your mama went to see some special woman's doctor in Helena or Butte a couple of times. Your ma was having difficulties, best I can recall. Why?"

"Nothing," Lissie muttered more to herself than to Doc Agrin. "Just something my pa said that got me wondering, is all. It's not important."

"What is important is that you get some rest. That baby's a heavy burden, pulling on your organs and taking all your nourishment. I'm orderin' you, as your doctor, to get some rest, and I ain't leaving here till I see you safe in bed."

"But what if my pa needs something? Gideon isn't here, and I—"

"He's sleeping easier now," the doctor said, pointing out that he had stopped thrashing about on the bed. "I'd spoon some of that into you, young lady, but I think just letting your head hit the pillow will probably be all the encouragement you need for a good night's sleep."

"He won't—in the night—he won't . . . ?" She couldn't bring herself to say the word, but the doc knew what she meant.

"Not tonight," he said, urging her from the room. "I'll leave a note downstairs for Gideon telling him where to find me if he needs me."

Her father did seem to be resting more comfortably, and so she reluctantly, with grave misgivings, and only out of concern for her baby and not herself, agreed to lie down for a half hour's rest.

Back in her old bed in her old room, sleep didn't come easily. She listened for her father, but she listened for Gideon, too. Once, in the twilight, she crept down to look out onto the front porch for him, got all the way upstairs and went back down to look out the kitchen door as well.

Her father was still resting easy and she curled onto her side and spoke softly to the child beneath her heart.

"Your grandpa's dying, sweet baby, and your papa's gone off who knows where. . . . " For a moment, just a moment, she thought she might have meant Gideon, and not Slick. After all, it was Slick's seed that was growing within her. Gideon was no more her baby's father than Marcus—

Beneath her hand, deep, deep inside her belly, she felt the flutter of one small butterfly wing. And then, nothing. She waited, her breath held so that she would know for sure. A second wing fought its way out of the cocoon.

"It's all right, sweet baby," she crooned softly, rocking herself and her child. "I'll be enough for both of us." Her eyes searched for anything to light on in the darkness, but there was nothing.

She and her baby were all alone.

# Chapter Eighteen

⚜

*S*HAFTS OF EARLY MORNING LIGHT MADE WAVY STRIPES on the rug by his wife's bed. They made lacy patterns across the comforter he'd laid over her when he'd found her peacefully dozing. And now they were all but prying her reluctant eyelids open.

From the looks of it, she hadn't meant to sleep long, if it all. But sleep she did, and deeply enough not to notice his coming, to barely stir when he loosened her bootlaces, to only sigh when he brushed the hair from her face and placed a kiss on her forehead.

He'd watched her for nearly an hour now, knowing that sooner or later she'd wake up. And that whether she wanted to or not, she was going to need him. He knew the minute she came awake, before she opened her eyes, and his gut twisted so tight he could hardly draw a breath.

All in one moment she was alert, throwing back the covers, reaching for her shawl, feeling for her slippers with her bare feet.

"Morning, Lissie." His voice startled her. Her eyes found him and he stood up straighter, praying she would allow him to be her rock, grant him this one small thing to make up for what he'd done. "I've got some coffee up. Why don't you sit a minute and I'll get you some?"

"Sit a minute? I don't have time to sit a minute." The truth hit her right then. It was in her face, but she fought it. "I have to see to my pa, see if he needs anything, see if the fever's broken."

She studied him while he fought to hide the years he knew had crept up on him overnight, the anguish he felt pulling at his lips, the pity that was stinging his eyes.

"Oh no," she said, forbidding it to have happened. "Doc Agrin said he'd be all right overnight."

He used his big hulking body to block the doorway. "It's over, Lissie."

"You're lying." Her little hands balled into fists and she raised them to him. "The doc said—he promised . . ."

"He's gone."

The little fists landed on his chest like moth wings, barely fluttering, but striking again and again until they were spent. With each blow came the accusations, the recriminations, the guilt. He let her rail, let her hurl her arms and her words, because, after all, he deserved it.

"Will you get out of the damn doorway," she ordered him after taking a step back, away from him. "I've got to—"

He moved out of her way, then followed after her into her father's room. He stood at the foot of the bed allowing her to inspect the job he'd done.

"You look nice, Pa," she said softly, fingering the white cotton shirt Gideon had put on him beneath the Sunday suit. "Right handsome for your date with Mama."

He moved a chair so that she could sit beside her father's body and headed for the door.

Behind him, softly, came kind words. "Thank you, Gideon, for seeing to him."

"Least I could do," he admitted. "Don't suppose you want me to bring you anything to eat before I go take care of the arrangements with Mr. Wood?"

"No," she said. "You go ahead. I need some time alone with him."

"Figured you would," he said, fingering his hat and watching as she held her father's hand and raised it to her lips. "I'll take care of the coffin and such."

She nodded.

He swallowed hard and pushed out the words that needed saying. "I'm sorry, Lissie."

She nodded, but instead of telling him he ought to be, instead of telling him it wasn't enough, she just kissed her father's hand and laid it back down on his chest. "Aren't we all?"

Everything in the Mallards' kitchen had flowers on it. The dishes had little pink roses, the glasses were pressed glass with a daisy-like pattern. The dishtowels were embroidered with violets and the shade that hung over the lamp was painted with lilacs or something like them. Berris had never seen anything like it.

"That green hair of yours fits right in here," Juliana said, not bothering to hide her amusement. "We could just stick a few flowers in your ears and plant you in the corner."

She and Juliana had come as soon as they'd gotten word from Gideon. They were to see about the food that would be needed to serve those people who came back to the house after Marcus Mallard's funeral. Not that any of the mourners would come empty-handed. Still, things needed to be set out and there was little else for them to do.

That, and offer comfort, though it wasn't likely Arliss would want any comforting from Berris, who hadn't been exactly kind and understanding even before she had good reason to mistrust her sister-in-law.

"Why don't you go up and see if she needs anything," Berris suggested to her sister. She'd taken off her shawl, but left her bonnet in place. Damn that Verinda Ruth Tenbrink! And now with Mr. Mallard dying she couldn't exactly go get her hair seen to. "I'm probably about the last person Arliss wants to see."

"And whose fault is that?" Juliana asked over her shoulder as she headed down the hall and toward the stairwell.

Berris didn't really think the fault was entirely her own. After all, if Arliss loved Gideon the way she was supposed to, Berris would sprinkle rose petals on the ground for her sister-in-law to walk on. It was for Gideon's sake that she was wary of Arliss, but there was no explaining that to Juliana until she got to speak to Gideon and find out just what he knew.

"Now you just sit down and we'll feed that baby of yours," her sister, the saint, was saying as she led Arliss into the kitchen. "Why it's so cheery in here you can't help but feel a little better. And then there's always Berris's new hairdo to make you smile."

Berris was prepared for a nasty comment and was trying to come up with some snappy answer when Arliss shuffled in, giving her no more than a civil nod. Arliss's eyes were glassy and red, but her cheeks were dry.

"I hope it's all right to use these," Juliana said, holding up one of the embroidered towels they were using around some casseroles. "I couldn't find any plain ones."

"There are no plain ones," Arliss answered, her voice

sad and dreamy. "Mama used to say a plain towel never made anyone smile while she worked."

"She musta felt that way about everything," Berris said, waving her hand around the room before she could stop herself.

"I might have taken it a bit too far," Arliss said with a shrug.

So the flowers were Lissie's doing? Berris hadn't ever changed a thing in her mother's kitchen, though the woman had been gone for more years than Mrs. Mallard.

"You make the tablecloth?" she asked as Lissie fingered the richly embroidered cloth that was awash with a hundred wildflowers.

"Practicing for my hope chest," Lissie answered flatly. "Mama said she wanted to be served a meal in my house off a cloth I'd made in hers."

"That's sweet," Juliana said when Berris couldn't find any words. "Now are you gonna eat that biscuit or just tear it to shreds?"

Berris put a mason jar of Mrs. Gaffney's jam on the table. Kathleen Gaffney made the best jam and preserves in the county and it seemed from the array of jars lining the pantry shelves that she'd given Arliss and her father some from every canning.

"How come you didn't bring a tablecloth to our place?" she asked her sister-in-law. "I mean, since they were for when you got married?"

Lissie played with the biscuit on her plate. Not a piece had found its way beyond her lips. "Wasn't my house," she mumbled, putting a dab of peach preserves on the biscuit and playing with the knife instead of eating.

"Of course it was," Berris corrected her, just imagining what Juliana was thinking.

But the truth was that she knew Lissie was right. It wasn't Lissie's house, hadn't been Lissie's home.

And neither of them mentioned they were using the word "was."

After making arrangements with the undertaker and going up to the house on Silver Hill, Gideon stopped off at the sheriff's office. He found his father going through a stack of mail, sorting the inquiries, the posters, and the bills into neat stacks on his desk. Ordinarily Gideon took care of all that, but things were hardly ordinary anymore.

His father looked up and then gestured for Gideon to take the seat by his desk. "It's all over then?" he asked.

Gideon nodded. "Went in his sleep. Saw Mr. Woods about the casket and the Reverend Lambert about the funeral."

"Arliss doing all right?" He played with the corner of an envelope as he spoke. Gideon glanced at the return address, noticed that it came from Honey Mallard's father, and wondered at the irony of it all. He supposed the old man had been stubborn enough to hold off letting the grass wave over him until Marcus himself was dead.

"She's hurtin'," Gideon said. It was a tough admission, since he'd been the one to cause the pain. "It ain't easy to watch."

"Well, it'll be nice to have her back under our roof," his father said. "I swear Berris's cooking has gone from just plum lousy to blue ribbon worst. And then again, there's nothing like hearing a woman humming."

"Berris hums," Gideon answered. Truth was, he didn't know if Lissie would be coming back to his father's house. When he contemplated the future at all, which he tried not to do, he saw himself sleeping on Marcus Mallard's porch until a good blizzard kindly did him in.

"Berris howls," his father corrected. "Now your Arliss has the voice of an angel. Face of one, too."

"I thought you said she was wild and always asking for trouble," Gideon said. It was bad enough Gideon had gone and turned her into a dream—he didn't need his whole family feeling that way, too. It would only make matters worse when . . .

He put his hands on his knees and pushed himself up. He wouldn't think about when Lissie sent him away, banished him, left him in the same wilderness that life had been before her.

"I'd better get back," he said just as his father began to speak.

"I never meant that she was no good," Thaddeus said. "Only that maybe she was no good for you."

"Yeah, well," Gideon said, for want of anything better to say. Lissie hadn't exactly been good for him, he supposed. Still he wouldn't have traded a minute of being her husband, lying beside her in bed and hearing her soft breath, watching her every move and marveling at how it could make his heart dance inside his chest just to see her smile.

"I was wrong, son," Thaddeus said, coming to a stand and tossing the envelope he'd been toying with onto his desk. "I can see she genuinely cares for you, and that's surely a start."

"Well, I ain't exactly easy to care for," Gideon said. It wasn't as if he'd ever asked her for love. He'd have happily settled for fondness.

"Well, she seems to be making a fair go of it, son. Those eyes of hers look like dew on the meadow every time she looks at you."

"Pa!" he said, when what he wanted to say was more like "hogwash."

His pa pointed at the cuff on Gideon's sleeve, just jutting out of his coat. "Ain't seen such fancy stitching in all my days. The woman fairly dotes on you."

Gideon looked down at the spot his father was pointing to. Just last week the cuff had been badly frayed and he'd mentioned to Arliss that he needed a few new shirts. Now his shirt sleeve was banded by a fancy zig-zagging that looked kinda Indian. "She's good at sewing," he admitted. Lissie hardly doted on him. Hell, she hardly tolerated him.

"Lord but she puts me in mind of your mama. Only a woman can get a shine like that out of an old pair of boots. Don't sound right saying I miss your mama after a comment like that, does it? A woman's a lot more than what she does, ain't she?"

Gideon stood by the doorway, anxious to leave. He wasn't the kind of man who could open his mouth and let his heart fly out.

"I always thought I loved your mama because of who she was, but after she passed on, rest her soul, I came to realize that I loved her for that, but I loved her even more for who she made me think I was."

He was waiting for Gideon to say he understood. His father's marriage had been different. His ma had wanted a dependable man and his pa had been one. Lissie wanted some swasher, some bravo, some ladies' man. She was a feather in the wind and he was a rock in the muck.

He opened the door and nodded good-bye to his father without words.

What could he say? That he'd have given anything to

be the kind of man who could dance on the wind with Lissie?

He pulled his jacket closed.

Damn but it felt like snow.

# Chapter Nineteen

⌒⟨ℬ⟩⌒

EVERYTHING WAS WHITE BUT THE FRESHLY TURNED earth. Like a festering wound, the dark hole gaped an ugly brown against the freshly fallen snow. The hill of displaced soil, apparently dug the night before, rose up glistening despite the lack of any sign of sun.

Her father would have liked the sun to shine down on him, but God didn't seem to care what the Mallards wanted. He never had, Arliss supposed.

The flowers on the oak casket bearing her father's body were as white as the snow. Only their waxy green leaves stood out against the white air that surrounded them as the snow continued to fall.

Her arm, the one she'd broken in the fall from the roof when she'd rescued her cat, ached. Snow did that to her still. So did sadness, when just breathing seemed an effort.

Gideon adjusted her shawl, wrapping it securely around her neck so that the wind could find no passage between her bonnet and her coat. He'd been waiting on the porch for her when she'd emerged with Juliana and had helped both of them down the icy steps and out to the buggy. He'd gotten the buggy for them so that they wouldn't have to walk up to the cemetery.

He hadn't said a word, just taken her arm, and led her to the waiting carriage.

And now they stood in the snow, the wind buffeting them, and watched together as four men used plow harness leathers to lower her father's coffin into the cold ground. Her mama had passed on in the springtime and they'd been able to turn her over to the flowers and trees and land she loved. The smell of gardenias carried in the air as the coffin, covered with every manner of white flower, disappeared into the ugly scar in the earth where her father's body would spend eternity.

"Here," Gideon said, pulling off his jacket and wrapping it around her, leaving his arm on her shoulder to hold it in place.

There was no point in arguing with him, no point in telling him that he needed his coat himself, no point in saying that the coldness she felt would not be warmed by a hundred jackets laid upon her. The cold was inside her, freezing her heart.

And then, when she was sure that she was dead inside, the butterfly spread his wings. Oh, it was the slightest quiver, but it was there.

"What's wrong?" Gideon leaned down and whispered against her ear, his words warm as they brushed her cheek, and going cold as the moist air slapped at her face. "Are you all right?"

Her hand was pressed against her belly, an unconscious gesture, and she dropped it at once. "I'm fine," she said.

He stood upright again, but wound his arm around her so that she could lean on it.

"We return to the earth the remains of Marcus Mallard, who loved his wife, his daughter, and his fellow man. Ashes to ashes, dust to dust," the Reverend said, shoveling the first of the dark earth into the ground. The rest of his words were drowned out by the sound of rocks and grit hitting the wooden box until he finished with, "his soul to heaven."

"Do you want to go now or wait?" Gideon asked.

"I want to be alone," she said softly.

"I'll wait by the carriage," he said. "Just wave at me when you're ready to go. You shouldn't walk alone on the ice."

Footsteps crunched in the snow as the mourners began leaving, but it was Gideon's steps she heard, and she turned and called out to him.

"Wait!"

He jerked back. In two strides he was beside her, his face full of hope.

"Your jacket," she said, shrugging it off and holding it out to him. "It's too cold for you to be in your shirt sleeves."

His shoulders sagged as he took the heavy deerskin jacket from her and pushed his arms through it. "Don't be long," he said, tying her shawl over her chest and lifting the collar of her coat. And then just as he was turning, he said the strangest thing. It took her quite by surprise and seemed at once ordinary and yet somehow profound for this man she thought she'd come to know. "He'll hear you wherever you are, you know."

There was solace in his words and strength. She said her peace to her father and then called for Gideon again. She took his arm and headed for the carriage.

He helped her climb the carriage wheel, settle into her seat, and take his own. Then, he flicked the reins and the horse took off at a slow walk. *He'll hear you wherever you are.*

And where, she wondered silently, would that be?

◦ ◦ ◦

People came to the Mallard house throughout the day, all of them remarking on the storm and hoping that it would lessen up some by evening so that they could make it home. By four o'clock the house was overflowing and the snow showed no signs of letting up. Those that lived nearby ventured out. The ladies from Coppertown fretted, insisting their husbands would come for them while Gideon's father saw several of the more local women home safely in the carriage Gideon had rented from Malcolm's Livery.

Through it all Lissie sat stoically, smiling, nodding, listening to her father's praises nearly raise the roof on high. Gideon had stayed close enough to hear the most remarkable things about Mr. Mallard. How he had fixed Frenna Reynolds's pickling barrels for some pansy seeds he had said were rare. And how she hadn't been fooled, but was grateful. How he had repaired the church bell for Reverend Lambert and asked that it not be announced in church.

"It would have been enough that your father fixed that buggy seat," someone was saying to Lissie now. "But to find a new cushion for it so that my poor Natty's bottom wouldn't . . . well, I never expected such kindness from him after I went smashing through your lilacs on that blunder-headed new mare that spring!"

"My father would never hold anyone responsible for something they didn't mean," his Lissie said, one hand holding Mrs. Nathan's hand, another patting it.

"But to give me that cushion," the woman continued. "Imagine finding something so beautiful just lying beside the road the way he did! I've never seen stitching like that in my life! And it fit like it had been made for my buggy!"

It wasn't the first Gideon heard about fancy stitched

things falling from the sky through Marcus Mallard's hands to land on someone's doorstep. It was amazing Lissie didn't need little glasses to see after all that work.

"I suppose you know what a lucky man you are, Gideon Forbes," a miner's wife told him. "To have such an angel for your own. I'd have surely thought that with all of Coppertown praying for her pa, he might have made it."

"Sometimes it takes more than prayer," Gideon said, amazed that half of Coppertown would be praying so hard for Marcus Mallard.

"You be sure she knows that if there's anything any of us can do, we want to help," the woman continued. "Not that we can ever repay her kindnesses." Gideon recognized her now as Beattie's wife. She'd aged fast, but then Montana was hard, and mining was harder.

Ella Nathan pulled back the window curtain near Lissie's chair and sighed. "Well, I guess the snow ain't letting up, and what with dusk falling like a stone, I best be getting on."

Lissie told her to be careful getting home and to take some of the food that was going to spoil if she didn't. She stood up to see her to the door when Gideon's pa came through it looking like some mountain man who'd lost his way and thought his life had been saved by finding the Mallards' house.

"Blizzard," he said, "or near enough. Can't see Eula Mae's place across the road." He took off his scarf and put it on the rack by the door. Ice crystals on the scarf glistened in the lamplight.

"I've got to get back to the missus," someone said.

"I left the children with Mrs. O'Donald," someone else said, and several mothers added that they had, too.

"I'm telling you I only found this house because every light is on and there's tracks left from the last people that come. At least there's plenty of food," he added as he slipped off his jacket and looked down at the puddle it was leaving on the floor.

"I'll see to it," Berris said quietly. She'd been quiet all day, and Gideon was hardly aware that she was there. If he'd known that having green hair on her head would keep her mouth shut, he'd have paid Verinda Ruth Tenbrink ten dollars to do it back in early September.

"You ought to go upstairs and get some rest, Arliss," Frenna Reynolds said. "Don't look like you'll be able to wait for us all to go on home, and I wouldn't have your pa thinking we wasn't looking after you."

"Yes," someone agreed and pushed at Gideon. "You better take her on upstairs and see she rests."

He hesitated, watching Lissie as if he half expected her to tell all their neighbors and friends that he was the last person in the world she wanted by her side.

"Go on now, Gideon," someone behind him said and gave him a shove. "A woman needs her man at a time like this, needs holding and tending to."

She gave him the smallest nod—permission to see her up the stairs, at any rate, it seemed. He was tempted to just lift her up and carry her from the room, save her the effort of rising and walking and climbing, but it wasn't what she'd want, and so he offered her his hand and assisted her up the steps.

Touching her hurt him as surely as if her skin was covered with quills. He wished it was, as the softness was driving him crazy. He wanted to fold her against him, but he wasn't sure if that was for her sake or his own, and so he let her lead him to her bedroom and had to be content to follow.

"You look like you could sleep for a week," he said, his hands stuffed into his pockets as she took the shawl from her shoulders and placed it on the back of the rocker. He'd never seen her room before Marcus died, and he wished they were anywhere else now but surrounded by remembrances of her life before she'd become his wife.

He picked up a fancy glass-framed photograph of Slick and Lissie taken at the Granite County Fair by a traveling photographer. Without a word he tried to set it back down on her dresser, but the back that it rested on was broken. So he leaned it against the wall where Slick's cocky smile seemed in danger of sliding right off the dresser and on to the floor. He wedged the rifle he'd brought up with him against it.

"You know he thought they didn't like him," she said, before noticing what he was looking at. "Pa, that is," she added, sitting on the bed and curling over herself to reach her feet. He took a step forward. "I can manage," she said with a sigh.

"I'm sure you can," he agreed, but damn it all, she was still his wife. And what good was that if he couldn't even unlace the poor woman's shoes after all she'd been through? No damn good at all. "But I'm gonna do it anyways."

He refused to look at her face and concentrated on the tiny boot she allowed him to cradle in his hand and the soft calf that swelled above it.

"Unbutton your shirtwaist," he said, his voice gruffer than he meant it to be as he placed her shoes on the floor beside the bed. "I'll get your nightdress."

Again he didn't look at her, didn't dare risk seeing the swell of breast that strained her buttons, the small mound of belly that puffed out her apron, the sadness that wrinkled her brow.

He rifled through her dresser drawers looking for a sleeping gown while behind him he heard the rustling of black mourning cloth. The envelope with Slick's letter was in the second drawer. He should have expected as much from the looks of her room, where Slick's presence was as easily felt as the cold seeping in through the windows. In the third drawer there was a good size stack of letters tied with a tattered pink ribbon. Apparently words rolled off Slick's pen as easily as they did his tongue.

The nightdress she'd worn on their wedding night was in the bottom drawer. He turned to offer it to her. He'd expected to find her watching him or falling asleep from exhaustion. Instead she sat with silent tears streaming down that lovely face of hers.

Well, God damn Slevin Waynick for not being there for her when she needed him. For pressing Gideon into service as a very poor second. Still, he was all Lissie had, and for all Slick's words, it was clear that the man didn't love her more than Gideon did or he'd be there, wouldn't he?

Dragging his feet, he came to stand by the bed, his arms hanging helplessly by his sides. The most pitiful face he'd ever seen looked up at him, eyes swimming in tears, and he had no choice but to hold her head against his thigh and stroke her hair while he told her that things would be all right.

She shook her head against him. Hot tears seeped through his Sunday dress pants.

"I'll take care of you, Lissie," he said softly, prepared for her to tell him that she thought his promises meant nothing, that he'd already let her down.

"My . . . my . . . ," she let out a shuddering sob and clutched his leg so hard that he nearly lost his balance. "I can't even call him my father! Gideon, I loved him so much, and he wasn't even mine!"

"He raised you," he said, pulling her away from him

and squatting so that he was eye to eye with her. "He saw to it that you were fed, and dressed, and had what you needed. He worried about you when you were sick and he punished you when you did wrong. He taught you all he knew about flowers and birds.

"He was your pa, Lissie, sure as I'll be this one's," he said, laying a hand on her stomach. "If you'll still let me."

She covered his hand with her own. "I felt him moving at the burial," she said. "Like he was telling me I wasn't all alone now."

"You ain't alone," he said. "Neither of you."

She touched his cheek, a feather-soft glancing of silk against stubble. "I don't deserve you, Gideon. I said horrible things to you I know you can never forget."

"We ain't never gonna forget any of it, Lissie, but we can move on, have a life, a good life, if you want. I could make you a good husband, and I could be a good pa."

"Like my father was," she agreed.

"We could name him after your pa, if you like," he offered, unfolding the quilt at the end of the bed and wrapping it around her to keep her warm.

"You're so sure it'll be a boy?" She cocked her head at him. "Would you be terribly disappointed if it turns out to be a girl?"

Gideon closed his eyes for a moment, trying to calm the racing of his heart. "A daughter is too much to hope for," he admitted softly.

"She could be a terror, Gideon, like me," Lissie warned him.

He touched the end of her nose. "A daughter like you would be much too much to hope for."

"There's nothing wrong with hoping," she said, pulling the quilt tighter around herself.

There were footsteps and small voices in the hallway

and Gideon rose and went to the door. He opened it a crack and found Juliana surrounded by several tired-looking children.

"Is Lissie asleep yet?" she asked. "I just need some blankets and pillows to settle down these little ones."

He slipped out the door, closing it behind him and rummaged with Juliana in cupboards and drawers until they had a mound of bedding.

"Lissie holding up all right?" she asked him.

He nodded. "I think things are going to be just fine."

She was just loosening the corset cover beneath her shirtwaist when Gideon slipped back into her room. In the morning she would get rid of all the remembrances of Slevin Waynick that dotted her old room. She'd dressed for her wedding to Slick here, and now she was undressing to crawl into her bed with Gideon. Maybe, just maybe, her father had been right about love growing. She could smell the flowers already.

"You want me to wait outside?" he asked, turning his back on her dishabille and staring out into the snow.

"Until when would that be, Gideon?" she asked, wondering if this awkwardness between them would ever end.

"Until you say otherwise," he said. His shirt was tight enough to see his muscles tense beneath it. The knuckles on the hand that gripped the doorknob were white.

"There's a houseful of people that'll notice you standing guard outside my door," she said. "Your pa, your sisters. Don't you think they'll wonder about us?"

He turned around then, his gaze taking her in from head to booted toe. "Honey," he said with the closest thing to a drawl she'd ever heard in his voice, "they've been wondering about us since Reverend Lambert joined our hands and we said 'I do.'"

Gideon Forbes looked big and strong and downright handsome standing there in the lamplight. He was as honest and as trustworthy as the day was long. And today had been the longest of days.

"I do," she said, reaching out a hand to him. "I promise to honor and obey, Gideon, to have and to hold."

There was nothing tentative about him as he flipped the lock beneath the doorknob and came to her on the bed. He lifted her in his arms and when he sat down on the bed, she was curled within his lap. "I'll hold you Lissie," he said.

"To *have* and to hold," she repeated.

His arms held her own in place. After a moment he said, almost plaintively, "There's a houseful of people Lissie, remember?"

She twisted around in his arms, making a big pretense out of searching the room over her shoulder. "I only see you and me, Gideon."

"I just thought, what with your pa and all," Gideon began to fumble. "I don't want to be taking advantage of you, Lissie. A decent man—"

"You don't want to hold me?" she asked him, sure he must want to, but not caring really whether or not he did. She only knew that she needed to be held, needed to lose herself and her misery within his warmth and strength.

"I am holding you," he said. He tightened his arms around her as if to prove it.

"And to have me? Don't you want that, too?" Beneath her she felt the stirrings of his desire. "Don't you?"

He didn't bother denying it, though from his groan as he eased her back onto the bed, she knew he wished he didn't want her so badly.

Well, she wished she didn't want him, either, not now. It seemed a sacrilege what with her father's passing, to want him, to need him. But it all hurt so much, too much, and Gideon was a rock to cling to in the storm.

She reached out, lacing her arms around his neck, and pulled his face toward hers. Lifting her mouth to his, she offered her lips as she stared into his warm brown eyes. He kissed her, softly, tenderly, exploring her lips with his own, tasting them with his tongue, holding her head gently in place with his big hands. He pulled back, studying her, and then leaned forward to kiss her again, this time with passion, with eagerness, with hunger.

Quickly he eased her out of the black muslin blouse that had barely made it around her. In the flickering lamplight she could see her breasts, hard and full, straining at her corset cover. He touched her tentatively through the fabric.

"God almighty, Lissie!" he whispered when her breasts filled his palms, and she pressed herself against him, seeking his warmth, his closeness. If there was a way, she'd have slipped inside his shirt with him and let the tight cloth bind her to him. While he gently traced the contours of her breast, one finger raising a response from her nipple, she worked at unfastening his buttons.

A floor below them, the murmur of voices quieted as people no doubt settled themselves for sleep or contented themselves to wait out the weather silently.

Here in her bedroom, away from them all, Gideon's breath was soft against her neck. It teased her skin and danced down her spine. Through her skirts and petticoats, through his trousers, as well, she could feel his hardness pressed against her thigh, and that, too, set her skin to tingling.

He was slow with her, deliberate. Each touch was singular, and yet melted into the next one. His breath turned to kisses—little soft gifts laid against her temple, the base of her neck, the lobe of her ear. His hands, big rugged hands that could grip an ax or fell a man, explored the bun she'd wound her hair in, searching for pins with the gentleness of a child.

He asked for no help and she offered none. She lay there and let him confound her senses until the tinkling of ice crystals against the windows became a melody that Mother Nature had written just for them—a rhapsody of solitude.

He kissed her eyelids shut, kissed her in places where there had been clothes and now there were none, though she had no recollection of shedding them. He kissed the inside of her elbow and let her wrap her arm around his head as tightly as she could while his other hand played against her ribs, her waist, her belly.

Outside it glowed bright, the moon lighting every flake of snow and filling the air with winter candles. Inside, deep within Arliss, something glowed and burned so brightly as to put the moon to shame.

His hands rested gently on her belly, measuring. His intake of breath filled the room, and she opened her eyes to find him staring into her face.

He believed in miracles. Could he say that to her? Could he say that the child that was growing in her was no greater miracle than that he had been allowed to share it with her, that his big clumsy hands could stroke her nakedness, that she welcomed his intimate touch? Could he tell her that here, with her in his arms, all his dreams had come true?

"Hold me." She reached out and tangled her arms around him, pulling him toward her.

He'd undressed her easily, women's clothes being all ribbons and strings and such. He wasn't even sure she'd noticed. Getting himself out of his pants would be a lot less graceful, not that much of what he did fell into that category anyway.

She was beautiful and willing, wanting. And he was worried about getting off his pants with finesse. What was the matter with him anyway? It wasn't as if she didn't know the real Gideon, the man whose big feet were in his mouth as often as not, the man who made the china rattle in the cabinet when he crossed a room. He didn't need to be afraid of waking her with his awkward movements. He was the one dreaming, not her.

He forced himself to shelve his cares for tomorrow and shifted this way and that to rid himself of the Sunday pants he'd worn for her father's burial. If she still wanted and needed him after all he was and all he'd done, he wasn't going to be foolish enough to talk her out of it now.

And so he lowered his lips to hers, nipped and tasted and touched until her lips weren't enough and his mouth moved lower and his hands lower still—stroking, smoothing, stoking fires that would warm them both for years to come if he built them right.

He bent to the task with vigor—cradling, caressing, feeding the flames, wishing he could give her more than all he had, all he was, all he ever hoped to be.

He had surely planned on making love to her again—some time when soft breezes rustled the curtains, and the call of night birds floated in on the scent of roses. Some time when things were so right that she, too, would feel it, want it, need it, as he had every night since he'd known he was hopelessly in love with little Lissie Mallard.

He hadn't expected it would come like this, hard

upon her pain, her loss. He hadn't anticipated a house-ful of people who were close enough to hear them if they weren't careful—to hear them and think less of his Lissie for wanting to hide from the hurt.

He listened to her breathing quicken with each ad-vance he made and knew what it must be like to play a fine instrument and be pleased with the music being made. Her sighs encouraged him, her gasps nearly did him in.

Skin like silk brushed against his own. The scent of flowers filled the air. Warm fingers played against his back, drawing him closer, drawing him in.

"Lissie, I—" he started, wanting to tell her that a man, *this man,* could only take so much.

"Now, Gideon," she said, her words echoing his own thoughts as if they were one. She thrust her hips up toward him. "Please."

And with all the gentleness he could muster, he slipped within her waiting folds and let himself be her refuge, as she was his.

"Closer," she begged him, slipping her arms within his undershirt, burrowing against him, demanding all the warmth he was only too willing to give. She pressed her rounded belly against his own, pushed her full breasts against his chest, set a rhythm all her own as she bucked and tossed beneath him.

"Slow," he warned her, holding himself slightly away from her so that it was only their sweat and not their skins that touched. "Careful," he said, wishing that only for the moment there was no baby to watch out for, no reason to be cautious.

Her fingertips dug into his back, little rounded nails grasping onto his flesh as if she might drown if he ever let her go. Keeping his weight off her with one hand, he slipped the other beneath her bottom. With a deftness he didn't know he possessed, he flipped them over so that she was astride him. For a moment she floundered like a fish just landed, but then she found her knees, pushed up with her hands, and crouched over him with her breasts tantalizingly close to his lips. He raised his head enough to latch on with a gentle bite and felt her stiffen above him.

Fearful that he'd hurt her, he opened his mouth to let her go, only to be nearly smothered by her attempt to make him take her once again. Dear God, if he lived through this night it would be one he would never forget.

Bracing her hips with his hands, he rocked her gently against his manhood, showing her the pleasures that slow and steady had over fast and furious.

She took his hands in hers and pinned them up around his head. He supposed he could have broken her hold with the least effort. But her breasts were within reach of his tongue, and her bottom was doing things to him that would keep the smile on his face hours after he was dead, so why should he fight her? Instead he lay beneath her like the prisoner of her heart that he was and let her do what she wanted with him.

And oh, what she wanted to do, and what it did to him. And all the while there was that hair of hers like a curtain around them when she let him take her breast, like a million feathers when she arched her back and let it tickle against his thighs.

Just when all his staying power was melting on her furnace, she stilled on him, her fingers lacing into his, her breath nearly a keening by his ear.

"Let it go, Lissie," he said gently, moving within her despite how tightly her thighs were clamped together. "Let it go," he said again, when what he really meant

was *this is all I've ever wanted, Lissie, for you to want
me, need me, love me.*

The fingers that were clamped around his tightened
convulsively, and with his eyes wide open so that he
wouldn't miss the wonder in hers, he took his love
home.

He was praying that this time she wouldn't cry, that
whatever he'd done wrong before he had made up for,
and he waited for her to tell him so. He waited, listening to the ragged breaths calm and become even and
deep. He waited as the heat rose off their bodies and
the sweat left behind chilled them. He waited, her hair
tickling his nose and her breath sending gooseflesh rip-
ples across his chest.

And then he pulled the covers up over them without
waking her and sighed a contented sigh. He had seen it
in her eyes, the look of wonder he'd been afraid to hope
for in Lissie.

But it had been all he'd wanted, all he'd ever imagined, he thought as he watched the snow pile up on the
windowsill. He listened to the quiet humming of a
houseful of people who loved his wife and her father
enough to brave a snowstorm to pay their respects. He
shifted onto his side, cradling Lissie against him.
Through the lace curtains a beam of moonlight struck
the photograph of Lissie and Slick on the dresser. He'd
best put it away in the morning before it got knocked
over and broke in a million pieces she might step on.

It wouldn't do to let Slevin Waynick hurt his Lissie
again.

# *Chapter Twenty*

*T*HE COMMOTION DOWNSTAIRS WOKE *GIDEON* FROM A deep sleep. He reluctantly clawed his way to consciousness and dragged himself from the warm bed where Lissie had been pressed up close to him. The first strains of daylight were peeking through the lace curtains, the snow making so much of the light that he had to squint to see outside.

In the stillness he could just make out fresh tracks cutting an uneven path toward the porch, like some animal crazed with the cold and blinded by the snow had forced his way up to the house. The noise from downstairs grew, and he heard the front door creak open.

Just what he needed, some brave fool going out after a grizzly to protect the womenfolk. He was in his pants in a moment, and with a glance at Lissie, who was just coming around, he grabbed for his rifle.

"Sounds like trouble down there," he started to say just as the photograph of Lissie and Slick went crashing from the dresser to the floor. The clatter sent Lissie half out of bed, her eyes wide. "I'll pick it up later," he told her, shrugging his apology.

She nodded, gesturing for him to go, but he didn't

miss that lip of hers caught between her teeth as she stared down at the shards of glass he was crunching to get to the door.

"I'm sorry, Lis," he said, opening the door to an unnatural silence that quickened his step. With his rifle raised, he hurried down the stairs.

The door stood open, ice and wind swirling around a snow-covered mound.

"Oh my Lord," someone said, reaching out and trying to pull the figure into the house. "Slick Waynick! As I live and breathe!"

They hurried him in, someone taking his hat, someone else trying to find his coat buttons under the layers of ice and snow he wore like a blanket wrapped around him.

Juliana said she'd get him some tea. Samantha ran for a dry blanket.

And Gideon stood, frozen where he was, the rifle still raised in his hands, his feet still several steps from the landing.

"Slick's here?" Lissie's soft voice came from behind him, her slippers swishing against the wooden steps as she came down them.

Why hadn't he told her to stay in bed? Why hadn't he demanded she just stay put? Why hadn't he stayed with her in that bed and to hell with the rest of the world? "It's cold down here," he told her without turning around. "Go on back upstairs."

But it was too late. Slick's face was raised to the top of the stairs, his cheeks bright from the cold, his eyes moist with emotion.

"I came," he said as if there wasn't a God damn houseful of people standing around watching him. Watching them all. Watching and waiting for Lissie to say something.

"Pa would've appreciated it," she said finally. She came down a few more steps so that she was just behind Gideon.

"Pa?" Slick asked, looking Gideon up and down and raising an eyebrow at his bare chest.

"Marcus Mallard passed on," Frenna Reynolds said softly. "Laid him to rest yesterday."

"I'm sorry, Arliss," he said, beginning to shiver as the snow melted around him and the wetness seeped into his clothes.

"You better get out of those wet things," Juliana said, handing him a steaming cup and paying no mind to the fact that everyone else had lost their tongues and stood gaping at Gideon on the stairs.

What were they expecting him to do, anyways?

"Your ma'll be glad to see you," Lissie said awkwardly.

"I'm hopin' she ain't the only one," Slick replied, but it didn't come out smooth, the way it always had. The teacup in his hand was chattering in the saucer.

"Gideon, he's freezing to death," Lissie said. Still, she didn't try to get past him, didn't run to her true love's waiting arms.

"Gideon, wait!" Berris said, climbing up a step or two toward him. "You don't know—"

"Shut up, Ber," Gideon said, tensing when he felt Lissie's hand on his shoulder.

Slick coughed a couple of times and Gideon could hear his teeth chattering clear across the room. "If you ain't gonna use that thing, I'd sure appreciate your putting it down," Slick said. He pointed at the rifle that Gideon had forgotten he was holding.

Gideon put the rifle down slowly, feeling Lissie's hand lift from his shoulder as he did. Once the rifle was

lowered everyone seemed to leap into action and every
manner of advice was hurled Slick's way.

"Don't let him warm up too fast," someone said as
Juliana examined ten very white fingers.

"Can you bend 'em?" Hank Warner, a dear old
friend of Marcus's asked.

"Can you feel your toes?" Samantha asked, coming
from the kitchen with a basin and towel.

Beside Gideon, Lissie sidled down the steps, clinging
to the wall rather than touching him. She had a shawl
wrapped around her nightdress, hiding her rounding
belly, but Gideon was aware of where Slick's eyes were
looking when he looked her over.

"You better come on upstairs and get out of your wet
rags," he said. "Lissie'll find you something of her pa's
to put on."

Slick nodded, snow melting and dripping around his
face, his black hair matted down, his hands cupping his
drink. He let Lissie hold a blanket around his shoulders
and lead him up the stairs. When they got to where
Gideon was standing, Slick slipped his arm around Lissie's
shoulder.

"Sure is good to be back," he said.

It could have been worse.

Lissie could have said, "It's good to have you back."

Arliss ran her hand gently over her father's worn
blue shirt before taking it out of the dresser drawer for
Slick. Behind her, Slick's teeth were chattering as he
mumbled about how cold he was and how good it was
to be home.

Gideon, a frown creasing his features, stood in the
doorway with several towels in his arms. "Picked a hell-
uva time to come back," he said as he put the towels
down and took over the job of unbuttoning Slick's wet

shirt. Standing there shaking, Gideon having to bend his knees to see to him, Slick looked like a small boy who had fallen in the lake after being warned. And Gideon, well, Gideon looked huge. And strong. And if his gaze didn't keep darting Lissie's way, she'd think he was in perfect control of the situation.

"Couldn't wait another minute to get here," Slick said. His shoulder was twitching and his head shook as he spoke. "Couldn't let some blizzard stop me from seeing my girl."

Lissie waited for Gideon to say something, but it seemed like he was waiting for her. "I'm not your girl anymore," she said as she handed the clean shirt to Gideon so that he could help Slick into it.

His chest was bare and hairless. After Gideon's soft curls, it seemed almost unmanly. "Now Arliss, honey," he said, one arm struggling to find the end of her father's sleeve. "You ain't still mad, are you?"

"She ain't mad," Gideon said, dropping the rest of the shirt and picking up the towel Slick had dried his midriff with.

"Well, that's a relief," he said, fumbling with the buttons, his fingers too stiff to get the job done. "I sure don't like it when you're mad at me. 'Specially when I brung you a present all the way from Virginia City."

A present. Well, that was certainly going to change the fact that he'd gone and deserted her. "You're gonna have to get those wet trousers off," she said, digging in her father's drawers for some long underwear. Did he think he could just waltz back into her life with some token and pick up where they'd left off? Did he imagine that nothing had changed while he was gone?

"I'll see to him," Gideon said in the same steady voice that had seen her through her morning sickness, had helped her face her father's death. It was the voice she'd come to rely on. "You go on and get yourself dressed. People will be heading out and they'll wanna take their leave of you."

"Sure would like it better if you stayed," Slick said to her. The purr in his voice was crackly from his shivers. "No one can warm me up quite like—"

"I'm married now." She turned and caught the flash of wonder in Slick's blue eyes before it disappeared. She'd expected, when she'd pictured his return, that she'd lord it over him, flaunt the fact that she'd not let any grass grow under her feet. She'd hoped to hurt him, back in her dreams, but here, now, all she wanted was for him to understand how things stood.

"Married? You are not," he said with a shake of his head while Gideon stood back and let him try to dress himself with frigid fingers fighting him every step of the way. He gave her that lopsided grin that used to make her heart do flip-flops. "But you ain't lost your teasing way."

Her heart wasn't flipping as she held out her hand and showed Slick the band on her third finger. She could see that he recognized the ring he'd bought for her, and anger flared in his eyes.

"Son of a bitch!" he said to Gideon. "How long did you wait? A couple of weeks? Less?"

"Married her the day you left her," Gideon said, his arms crossed as he leaned his shoulder against the wall. "Same church, same minister. Even used your ring," he added.

"I shoulda known you would. The minute my back was turned—"

Gideon pushed himself away from the wall and glared down at Slick. "You never should have turned your back on Lissie," he said. He reached out and rubbed her arm gently, reassuringly. "You go on, now. People will be waiting."

She handed the long johns to Gideon and brushed back her hair, trying to pull herself together. Three months she'd waited for Slick to come back for her. She'd rehearsed what she'd say to him, what she'd do, and now she stood mute and confused. Of course, in her dreams they'd been alone: she'd open the door to find him standing there, or maybe she'd see him across a field of wildflowers. And she would rush into his arms and feel at home.

It had been a while since she'd imagined that. Long enough so that home was next to Gideon, now. Good golly! Who'd ever have thought she'd feel that way about honest, good, kindhearted Gideon Forbes? Who'd ever have thought she'd grow up?

"Turned my back on her?" Slick shouted just as she was opening the door to leave. "Is that what you told her? That I wanted to leave? That I just walked out on her?"

"What did you expect me to say?" Gideon asked. "That crap about you coming back for her? Making it up to her?"

Lissie fought to swallow. When Gideon offered to marry her, he hadn't told her that Slick ever intended to come back home.

"You made her think I wanted to go, didn't you? And then you took advantage of her and—"

"*I* took advantage of her?" Gideon bellowed. His hand reached over Lissie's shoulder and slammed the door shut, reminding them that there was still a houseful of people downstairs. "*I* did?"

"I never wanted to leave you, Arliss," Slick said, sitting down on her father's bed shaking and rubbing at his arms and legs. "Never." His clear blue eyes looked at her sadly, staring at her belly. " 'Specially not now."

"But you did leave," she said softly. "You left me to face a whole church full of people, and my pa, and—"

"Not by choice, I didn't," he said, glaring at Gideon.

"The hell it wasn't your choice," Gideon bellowed, and Slick put up his hands to shield his face.

"You gonna hit me again, Gideon?" he asked, touching his side and then rubbing at his nose, which she realized with a closer look, was crooked and bent.

"What happened to your nose?" she asked, while Gideon squeezed his eyes shut and his lips became a thin line.

"Why don't you ask your *husband?*" Slick said, lowering his trousers and reaching for the long johns before she even had the chance to turn her head. "Why don't you ask him about how he took his best shot and then ordered me, bleeding and all, to catch the next train outta town?"

"Gideon would never—" she didn't get to finish her thought before Gideon grabbed Slick and lifted him to his feet.

"I shoulda broken a lot more than your damn nose," he said. Slick raised his eyebrows at Arliss as if to say *see?* "After what you did to Lissie, I shoulda broken your balls."

The knock at the door startled all of them. Arliss's heart, already lodged in her throat, jumped up several notches and cut off her air.

Gideon cracked the door. "Not now, Berris," he said and tried to close it again.

"Ow!" Berris had wedged her foot firmly in the doorway and wasn't taking no for an answer. "I have to talk to you. Now!"

"Not now," Gideon barked at her.

"Right now!" she hissed back at him.

With a warning look first at Slick and then at her, Gideon slipped through the doorway and shut the door behind him.

"You look good," Slick said, taking in her new figure and finding that it pleased him much more than he'd expected.

"Considering," she said, looking down at her expanding middle. Then she gestured at his nose. "Does it hurt?"

With a wink, figuring one more lie wouldn't put him any deeper in hell, he said, "No more than a herd of buffalo taking a stroll across my face."

She tilted her head and stared at him. She was worrying her lip with her teeth and damned if it didn't stir him just the way it always had. After a while she said, "I don't believe that Gideon did what you said."

"You hear him deny it?" Gideon hadn't just not denied it—he'd corroborated it. Damned if Slick wasn't luckier than a fox in a deaf farmer's henhouse.

Arliss's eyes widened a little and she put her hand against her belly. Her mouth, those wonderful lips of hers, made a little "o."

"Something wrong?" he asked. It would be just his luck to have come all this way in the snow for nothing. He was counting on that baby being just fine.

She smiled shyly. After the women he'd been with in Helena and Anaconda, she was like a fresh drink of water—clean, clear, refreshing. The others had been rot gut compared to her. "No," she said, rubbing a surprisingly rounded stomach while he watched. And he'd be damned if that didn't warm his inners, too. "He just moved."

"You hoping it's a boy, too?" he asked. Not that a

little girl wouldn't be just as good. Offspring, near as he knew, was offspring. There hadn't been anything about the child being a boy.

"Everyone thinks the baby is Gideon's," she said nervously.

"Do they?" he asked, stalling for time. He'd always believed the people of Granite had gone stupid from the refinery stench, and this just proved it. Well, thinking it was Gideon that had picked her fruit before it was ripe would save him from being stoned while he was still in Granite and wouldn't make a damn bit of difference once he and Arliss were gone. He could live with it. For now, anyways.

"He's a good husband, Slick. And I've been a good wife." She played with the ends of her shawl, twisting the strings around her fingers. "He's building me a house, too."

"A house. Well, I don't blame you none," Slick said, sniffing. Man, he was still cold as ice. He just prayed his brains hadn't frozen, 'cause he was gonna need them to fix this mess the way he wanted it. "Not knowing the truth and all, I guess you didn't think you had much choice. 'Course, you coulda waited a few days, at least."

She put her hands on her hips, accentuating that round belly that was his future. "Seems like I'd have had to wait a lot longer than that," she said. "And I couldn't."

He'd gone too far, and he backpedaled as fast as he could. "You didn't have no way of knowing how much I wanted to be there, how bad off I was, coughing up blood and all from the broken ribs, and still trying to get back to you."

Arliss looked at him skeptically, and so he pointed at his left side. "Three ribs," he said. "Doc told me I could punch a hole in my heart if I moved around."

"But if you sat still at the tables you'd be all right?" Arliss asked, tapping her foot impatiently. Damn, what had ever possessed him to tell her about the gambling in those letters?

"I had to win enough to get a ticket back here," he said. "And I didn't want to come empty-handed, neither." He thought that maybe the edges of her mouth were softening just a little. "And I wanted it to be something real special for my girl."

"I told you. I'm not your girl anymore," she said, but her foot had stopped tapping and she was tracing the floorboards with her toe.

"You'll always be my girl," he said softly. "You got my baby in your belly to prove it."

"I told you, people think this baby is Gideon's." There was an edge to her voice, like saying it could make it so.

"Don't matter what people think," he said. "Unless . . . Gideon don't think—"

"Gideon knows the truth. That was why he married me," she said. He was glad that she hadn't changed any. She was still foolishly honest, and her red cheeks showed she still embarrassed easy.

"Then we ain't got nothing to worry about," he said, fumbling through his wet clothes to find the necklace and earrings he'd brought for her. "Marriages that ain't been consummated ain't really binding. We can just—"

She wasn't looking at him anymore, and her cheeks had gone from pink to scarlet.

"Arliss? You and Gideon didn't . . . I mean, with you carrying my seed and all, you two haven't . . . ?"

That chin of hers jutted out just a little, almost defiantly. Almost as if she was asking him to make something of it. Almost like she had just as much right as he had.

*Shit!* He didn't like that at all. Gideon making deposits in his bank.

He slammed his fist down on the nighttable and had to catch the lamp before it skidded to the floor.

*God damn it all!* Arliss was his. Gideon had no right to go messing with what was his. And Arliss—he supposed she was so grateful that she just spread her legs and took whatever Gideon dished out. It wasn't much consolation that it probably didn't take long, anyways. What with Gideon's experience and Arliss's abilities, he figured five minutes and it was all over.

But it grated, just the same.

Well, he'd have to put it behind him. For the fortune he expected, he supposed he could learn to forgive and forget.

Berris had to keep her hands wrapped around Gideon's arm to keep him from going back into the bedroom.

"You better give them a minute," she said, her heart breaking for her brother. "And I guess I better tell you why."

"She's carrying his child," Gideon said matter-of-factly. "That what you need to tell me, Berris? You think I'm so stupid or Lissie's so deceitful that it'd take you to tell me that?"

"Oh Gideon, I'm so sorry. If only I'd known before you married her, I could have—"

Gideon shook his head at her. She drew a breath with more effort than it ought to take and fought to swallow.

"You knew? You knew before the wedding?"

"Lissie might have been a little foolish, Berris," he said as if her giving herself to Slick Waynick was some bitty mistake, "but she's honest and good in her heart and her soul. And I can't say that about everyone."

He looked back at the door and grimaced.

"Maybe I will give them a minute," he said, trying, she supposed, to prove how much he trusted Lissie.

"Gideon," Berris started, but he waved her words away with his hand.

"I got a mess to clean up in Lissie's room," he said as she walked away.

She made her way down the stairs slowly, holding onto the railing to keep from keeling over. Heck and heliotropes! Gideon knew. He'd known when he'd married Arliss that she was carrying Slick's baby.

"Are you all right?" Samantha asked her when she reached the bottom of the stairs.

"He really loves her." Berris shook her head as she said it, unable to understand how anyone could love that much, forgive that much.

"Who?" Samantha asked. "Slick? Did he say that? Was Gideon there?"

Berris felt like she'd been riding in a stagecoach for days and that even standing still the ground moved beneath her. "Gideon. He loves Arliss. He really, really loves her. I mean not just want-to-be-with-her, want-to-bed-her love."

Samantha cocked her head and looked at Berris. "Well, of course he loves her more than that. It's Gideon."

Berris's fists curled, and she struck the wall beside her with the heel of her hand. "Well then," she said with quiet determination. "She had just better love him back!"

# Chapter Twenty-one

"DID YOU REALLY BREAK HIS NOSE?" LISSIE ASKED him after everyone was gone from her father's house and she and Gideon were alone in her room. He'd picked up the pieces of glass from the frame her mama had given her, and it hurt to let one more piece of her childhood go.

He nodded. He'd already said as much. And there was Slick's face to prove it.

"Why?" she asked.

"Because he was asking for it. Because he deserved it after what he done to you," he answered, seeing one more piece of glass glinting on the floor and reaching down to pick it up.

"You didn't know what he'd done then," she said wincing as the glass joined the rest of the frame with a clink in the bottom of the can.

"If I had, I'd a broken his legs and carried him to the church just like I threatened to," he said. Lord, if he'd known, he'd have hog-tied him and made him do right by Lissie. He admitted to himself he was glad he hadn't known, more than glad.

Of course, Lissie didn't look glad. She sniffed loudly and bit at the side of her lip. "So you beat him up and put him on the train to Helena," she said as if she were trying to get it all straight in her mind. "And then you came to the church and you married me instead."

She waited for him to answer. "I didn't put him on the train," he said with a shrug. "I let him go. Simple as that, Lissie. I just let him go."

"Why?" she asked again.

"Because he wanted to go. Because he was packed and ready when I got there. Because he—"

"And so you came to the church and married me. Why?"

"Why what?"

"Why did you marry me, Gideon?"

He threw his hands up. How many ways could he prove he loved her? Wasn't he proving it every day? "Why do you think?" he asked, coming to his feet and pacing.

"Because of the baby," she said. "Because after you got rid of Slick you felt guilty and so you—admit it, Gideon. You'd have never asked me if it hadn't been for the baby."

"Well, you *are* having a baby, and I *did* marry you and what's done is done. And Slick's coming back here don't change what's between us."

"I don't need reminding of any of that," Lissie snapped at him, banging platters around the kitchen. "I know what I did, and I'm not sorry!"

"Well, I'm not sorry neither!" he shouted back, picking up platters, too, and having no idea what he was supposed to do with them.

"No?" she asked, stopping her scurrying around to raise a doubting eyebrow at him.

"No!" he said, reaching for his hat and coat. "I gotta go meet the train and see if them miners from Kirkville are on it."

The frigid air rushed into the kitchen as he opened the door and he grabbed his rifle. He was about to shut the door behind him when he heard Lissie's small voice.

"Wait!" she said. He turned and her hands were on her hips, her eyes narrow. "You're not sorry you broke Slick's nose, or you're not sorry that you married me?"

"I done a lot of stupid things I regret, Lissie, like what happened to your pa. But I ain't sorry for a second about either of those."

She was wearing a smile when he shut the door, and he took it with him down to the train station. The kiss kept him warm despite the cold, and despite the dozen men that came off the train, half of them clutching newspaper advertisements and all of them chattering in some language Gideon didn't understand.

Gideon spoke a spattering of German, a few words in Italian, and he found nearly understandable the old Gaelic that some of the miners used. And while the men had every right to go up to the Columbia, they also had a right to know what they were getting themselves into. Gideon supposed he didn't have a salmon's chance in bear country of telling them just what they had been hired to do.

He followed them up toward the mine, the stench and the smoke a road map for the foreigners. He took only a moment to stop and talk to Berris and Samantha as they passed. Green hair sure did make a change in his sister, as she kindly offered to help look after Lissie while he looked after the whole damn town.

"You know, you were right about Gideon being the sweetest man on earth," Samantha said as they stamped the snow off their boots on the Mallards' porch. "You could see that he had more important things on his mind, what with those—what did you call them? Scabs? And still he was worried about Arliss."

"Well, it's a little more complicated than that," Berris said vaguely. "You know, what with Slick back in Granite."

Samantha shook her head. "He said he was worried about her being alone what with just losing her pa. He didn't make any mention of Slevin Waynick, Berris, and you'd be wise to keep those kind of thoughts to yourself or Arliss is liable to—"

Arliss opened the front door and Samantha held her tongue.

"Yes?" Arliss finally said when Berris and Sam just stood there like they were soliciting funds for the new library.

"Berris and I were just passing by and we thought we'd check in on you and see how you were today," Sam said pleasantly, nudging her friend toward the door.

"I'm still fine," Arliss answered her. "It's only been a few hours since you all left."

"Well, you've been alone a while," Berris said, leaving her bonnet in place to cover Verinda Ruth Tenbrink's disaster. "Haven't you?"

From the elbowing she got from Samantha she knew she'd said the wrong thing. Heck and huckleberries, but she always seemed to say the wrong thing to Arliss.

"I mean, Gideon, that is we, were afraid you might be lonely." She looked around the hallway, peeked into the parlor, and finally started unbuttoning her coat when she saw no sign of Slevin Waynick on the premises. "What with losing your father, and then everyone leaving you all alone and all," she added, handing her coat into Arliss's waiting arms. "You are alone, aren't you?"

"I was wondering," Samantha said, pulling some thought straight out of the air, "if you could possibly help me with the dress I'm planning on wearing to the Miner's Ball. I realize it's a bad time for you, but I'm really hopeless with a needle and I was thinking, what with you being so good at it, if you could just show me a stitch or two for decorating the bodice of my old green silk, it might look new."

Arliss stared at her like she had two heads, but Samantha just plunged ahead, bright as the sunshine on a June day.

"I thought it might help take your mind off things," she added, studying Arliss's face and seeing the same fed-up look that was clear to Berris. Sam shrugged apologetically. "Perhaps it was a bad idea. I hope I haven't offended you."

Arliss shook her head, waving away the apology. "There are a few stitches I could show you that might be nice. If you used a light-colored silk thread and did some lazy daisies, it could look very sweet."

"Oh, Samantha isn't hoping to look sweet," Berris said, glad that they'd gotten past the fact that they'd come to watch her. "She wants to be positively fetching! Maybe even a little, you know, *available.*"

Samantha grabbed her elbow and squeezed hard. "I most certainly do not want to look 'available.' And I'm sure Arliss wouldn't have the vaguest notion how to make me look that way anyway."

"Of course she would," Berris said and felt Sam's grip tighten on her arm like the plumbing wrench Gideon used to fix the pump.

"No, she wouldn't," Samantha insisted until Berris realized that she was once again being insulting.

"Oh, heck and hogwash! I didn't mean to imply that you dressed like one of the Lilac ladies," Berris said with a sigh of resignation. "Doesn't it seem like I can never say the right thing to you?"

"You know," Arliss said, crossing her arms over her chest, "you come over here, expecting—no, *hoping*—to catch me doing who knows what with Slick so that you can go reporting back to your brother. Then, when you don't find him here, you suggest that I doxy up Samantha's gown. So, no, Berris, you can't say the right thing to me, and maybe it would be best if you just didn't say anything at all."

"Gideon didn't think anyone was here. He was just worried about you, the way he always is. He's too good and kind to think anyone would be doing anything wrong, least of all you, Arliss."

"Anyway, while flowers might be nice," Samantha prattled on quickly, "I was thinking about beads, maybe. What do you think?"

"Actually, I think you came here to spy on me."

Berris thought it was amazing that Arliss could keep the smile on her face while the smoke poured out her ears.

"Now why would we do that?" Berris asked innocently as she inched her way down the hall.

"I thought maybe the same color beads as the dress," Samantha said, taking Arliss's arm and trying to steer her into the parlor. "Or maybe some kind of lace overlay. They showed us how to do that at Miss Emily's, but I wasn't there long enough to really get the hang of it."

"Slick's not in the kitchen, Berris," Arliss said. "Wanna go up and check the bedrooms so you can report back to Gideon?"

"You know I really wish we had a finishing school here in Granite," Samantha said as if there wasn't a fight going on around her. "If I hadn't missed home so much, and felt so out of place back in Chicago, I'd have loved to stay on there. I mean there's so much a girl needs to learn, and without a mama there just isn't any way to learn it all out here."

"Don't go accusing Gideon of not trusting you," Berris said in her brother's defense. "Despite everything."

"I give up!" Samantha said. "Berris, you promised Gideon you'd make sure Arliss wasn't too upset and you're making her more upset with everything you say."

"Have you eaten?" Berris asked Arliss, taking a page from Sam's book and ignoring her now. "Juliana said it's very important that you remember to eat. She said those Nun's puffs you made her were wonderful and that she would make some for you now that she's feeling better."

"A lace overlay won't make the dress look very different unless you use ecru or white," Arliss said. "If you're looking for sophistication, I think that beads are probably the best choice."

Samantha flashed Berris a satisfied smile.

"What?" Berris asked defensively. "I was nice. I told her Juliana thought those buns were good."

In response, Sam rolled her eyes and turned back to Arliss like Berris was simply too uncivilized to deal with at the moment. "What are you going to wear to the ball?" she asked.

"Oh, I don't think I'll go," Arliss answered. "With my pa and all . . . well, I don't think I'll feel much like dancing."

"Gideon will want to show you off," Berris said without thinking. She'd have swallowed the words back, too, if Arliss didn't seem just a little pleased at the thought.

Samantha jumped on the bandwagon. "Oh, it'll be your first big event since you got married. For sure Gideon will want you by his side looking lovely."

"I'm afraid I'd look a little more than lovely," Arliss said, looking down at her belly.

"All the more reason for you to be there on Gideon's arm," Berris said. She couldn't say any more than that in front of Samantha, but she figured that Arliss would know what she meant. "You could probably borrow something from Juliana that would fit you better."

"Not that you're showing much," Samantha hurried to add in. "Why, if I hadn't heard, I'd never even have guessed that you were expecting."

Berris fought with all her might to stop her eyes from rolling. A person would have to be blind, deaf, and dumb not to know that Arliss was months along toward motherhood. And a person would have to be just plain stupid not to know who the father was.

Arliss had served them all tea and some lovely little sandwiches that she found amongst the dozens of platters that people had brought for the funeral. Samantha had insisted on doing the dishes, and Berris had stoked the fire in the parlor and added a log. And then they'd both donned their coats and said they'd visit again, and Samantha had asked if she might bring over her dress sometime in the next few days.

And then, thankfully, they'd gone.

She dragged herself up the stairs to her father's room and stood for a while staring at the empty bed. *He loved his wife, his daughter and his fellow man,* Reverend Lambert had said at the burial. She'd bet the copper band on her left hand that Gideon had supplied those words. And that Reverend Lambert had no idea how very much they meant to her.

"Hello? Anyone home? You here, Arliss?" She'd been lost in thought, her fingers fondling her father's shaving mug and brush on the highboy. Anyone would have startled her, caused her heart to jump, her hands to fly away from the dresser, her words to stumble on her tongue. "Arliss?"

She heard the footsteps on the stairs, two at a time like he always took them, and stepped out of her father's room to meet him in the hall.

"Lord, you are a picture," Slick said with a sigh. "Prettier even than I remembered."

"Well, you'd have needed a good memory," Arliss said, staring into eyes that could melt a block of ice in January.

"Feels like I've been away an entire lifetime," he said, unbuttoning his jacket and slipping it on to the newel post at the top of the stairs.

"A few more months, and it would have been," she replied.

"Sure was terrible about your pa," he said, patting her gently on the back and then leaving his hand on her shoulder. She dipped down a bit to free herself without asking him to keep his distance.

"He's with my . . . with Honora, now, and I think he's happy," she said, backing up until she hit the wall.

"I heard it was some kind of accident in Ezra Bryant's shop," he said, more a question than a fact.

"Lester Pincus shot him and Juliana Bryant," Arliss said. "Thank God, Juliana is all right. My father wasn't as lucky."

"Lester Pincus? Wasn't he in jail?" Slick asked, one eyebrow raised, just waiting for her to say that it was Gideon's fault that her father was dead.

"Slick, I don't think Gideon would be very happy if he found out you were here," she said, making her way toward the stairs.

"I bet he wouldn't be," Slick agreed, not following her the way he was supposed to down the stairs. "Not knowing how we feel about each other."

"I'm a married woman now. I don't have any feelings for you."

Slick sniffed and bit at his lip. "None? Well, I got enough for us both, Arliss, honey. I got so much love for you I'm bursting with it." He fell to his knees and clutched at her skirts. "All that time I was away, missing you, wanting to get back to you, thinking you were with another man. . . . It nearly drove me crazy."

"You didn't know before you came back that I'd married Gideon," she said feeling his breath penetrate the layers of her skirts and brush hot and heavy against her thigh.

"But every moment since I found out's been agony," he said, clutching her tighter against him. "What he did to me was bad enough, but what he did to you, taking advantage of you like that, making you think I wasn't coming back. . . . He don't deserve you, Arliss Mallard, and that's a fact."

If he didn't have that sad, crooked nose, if Gideon hadn't said he'd been the one to break it and send him away, she'd have known what to say, what to do, what to feel. Gideon had been her savior, had rescued her from ridicule, and had shown her nothing but patience and kindness through the worst days of her life.

And it wasn't just gratitude that she'd been feeling toward him lately. It had been stronger, deeper, richer. Heaven help her, but she'd fallen in love with him.

Of course, just because she loved him didn't mean that those flowers her father had compared her marriage to didn't have some awful disease that just might kill them all.

"Why did Gideon make you leave Granite?"

"Because he wanted what I had, plain and simple. Because he was jealous and knew that if he got rid of me, he'd be the one to go crawling into bed beside you, he'd be the one to touch you in your private places. And he thought he'd be the one to plant his seed and bind you to him, but he didn't figure that I'd already shown you how much I loved you, and at least there's some justice in that, some consolation for me."

"But he knew about the baby before he married me, before he even asked," she argued.

Slick was quiet for a while, his hands idly rubbing her legs while he stayed pressed against her. "I guess he was willing to live with that if it meant stealing you from me. But we can get you out of this, Arliss. In a little while we can leave Granite and go wherever you want and start over. We'll just find some lawyer to get you out of this mess and by the time this baby comes along, his real daddy will be holdin' him."

Arliss stilled Slick's hands and pulled them away from her. "I'm not leaving Gideon," she said. "I don't know what happened between the two of you, but I know that what he did, he did out of the goodness of his heart, to help me. Gideon Forbes is a man I can trust, a man I can count on—"

"Didn't hear you say nothing about love, Arliss honey. You think that man could love you half as much as I do? And what about my son? You think the good deputy, who beat me within inches of my life, is gonna love a child that isn't even his? Did he promise you he'd love my son?"

Gideon had never even said he loved her, let alone the baby she was carrying. "He said he'd be a good pa," she said in answer to all Slick's questions.

"To a kid that ain't his own? Oh, Arliss, you're just

dreaming again like you always used to if you think that a man could love a child that wasn't even his blood and bones."

"Some men could," she said, going into her father's room and seeing her own face smiling from the frame by his bedside. "And Gideon's one of them."

"It's a tin star, he's wearing Arliss, not a halo."

"It might just as well be," Arliss answered. "Gideon doesn't lie, doesn't cheat, and doesn't do wrong."

"Don't be so sure of that, honey," Slick said. "Besides, maybe that there's reason enough to leave him. After all, it seems like, considering your condition, you and I just might suit better, don't you think?"

They heard the door at the same time and came out of the bedroom together to look down at Berris Forbes' dropped jaw. In her arms was a package which she let fall to the floor.

"I was cleaning out my father's room and Slick dropped by for a minute," she was quick to tell her sister-in-law. "He was just leaving."

"Yeah, well I'll just wait until he does," Berris said, pulling off her bonnet and letting her green hair shine in the afternoon sun which came streaming through the window of the front door. "And I'd be happy to keep you company until Gideon gets back," she added, fighting with her muffler and tripping over the package she'd dropped as she flung her outer garments toward the hall tree by the door.

"Your hair looks a little—" Slick began.

"Don't forget your jacket," Berris interrupted him. "I don't see it down here in the hall."

"You ain't the kind of woman a man gets over," Slick whispered to Lissie as he reached for his jacket, his back to the stairs and Berris, below. "Just like I ain't that kind of man." He winked and shrugged into his jacket while Arliss stood silent and watched him go.

"You take care of yourself now," Slick called back to her and then, ruffling Berris's hair as he passed her, added, "and you see to it that she's eating and resting plenty. It'd kill me if anything happened to that cargo she's carrying."

"Let me get the door for you," Berris said, swinging it open wide and nearly pushing him out of it. "I wouldn't want to keep you."

"Ah, Berris honey," Slick said as he pulled his jacket closed. "Nice to know that nothing's changed around here since I left."

"And nothing's gonna change now that you're home," Berris said, slamming the door shut and then looking up at Arliss. "Is it?"

"Three times in one day, Berris. I'm seeing you more now that I'm staying back at home than when I lived at your place."

"Are you and Gideon going to be living here?" she asked.

The question took Arliss by surprise. She'd been staying at her father's house, but didn't think of it as living there. Gideon, well, poor Gideon hadn't really been living anywhere, but she supposed that Berris didn't know that part of it.

"Because frankly I think it would be better for everyone if you moved back to our house. That way you wouldn't be alone so much. I mean just in case Slevin Waynick decided to see how you were doing again."

She said it all casually, as if it wasn't an accusation. And while she spoke, she picked the package up from the floor and untied the strings.

"I brought you one of Juliana's dresses from when she was carrying Jeannie." Berris shook out a brown satin dress and held it out toward her. "I figured as far along as you really are, you're gonna need every inch of room."

"Gideon and I already admitted—" she began, but Berris was coming up the stairs with murder in her eyes.

"I know what Gideon admitted, Arliss. And I know the truth. And if you dare embarrass my brother, you'd better be prepared for a little embarrassment yourself. I'll let the whole of Granite know that you were some Lilac Row accident that Hedda Clovis gave to Honora and Marcus to pass off as their own."

Arliss backed away from the steps slowly, tentatively. She could feel the floorboards shifting beneath her and she didn't trust her legs to carry her as far as the bedroom, so she just leaned against the wall and tried to breathe deeply.

"Honey Mallard was my mother." Her voice came out tiny and she tripped on the words.

"That's not what I heard Gideon tell my father," Berris said. "He said Hedda Clovis gave you to Honey and Marcus. I don't figure Hedda's growing babies out there under the cabbage leaves, do you?"

Oh, dear God! Why hadn't the truth occurred to her? Why hadn't the question even occurred? It was no wonder her ma was always warning her about what men wanted and needed. She was worried about the apple not falling far enough from the tree.

And it hadn't, had it?

Berris watched the shock turn Arliss's face white, and it was only because she was quick in mind and body that she managed to catch Arliss at all before she actually hit the floor in a dead faint.

"Arliss, wake up," she said, tapping at her cheeks.

"I'm not going to tell anyone. I swear it on my life. On Jeannie's life! I just don't want you to hurt my brother.

"Arliss? Can you hear me? Gideon loves you more than life, and I love him. Please, please don't hurt him when all he's done is love you."

# Chapter Twenty-two
ᘓᕫᕬᐁ

I T WAS NEARLY MID-MORNING WHEN GIDEON TRUDGED back to Lissie's house. He was cold, tired, and the burr that had been under his saddle since he'd lain eyes on Slick Waynick yesterday morning had rubbed him raw. Had it only been a day since Lissie's old flame had turned up like a bad penny at the door? He stomped with frozen feet on the porch to shake off the snow caked on his cuffs and clinging to his boots. Who'd have thought that so much could happen in one day.

Danish miners. Fifteen of them, and not a one of them speaking more English than "want work." He'd drawn pictures, made gestures, all of it to no avail. He'd searched the whole of Coppertown looking for a Swede, a Norseman, a herring choker who might know a word or two of Danish. And all the while he'd had to keep the miners quiet, making them promise to hold their tempers while he tried to get the tumbleweed out of the brambles.

He slipped quietly into the house, hung his jacket by the door, and sat down on the stairs to remove his boots. He was still mad as hell at Berris for upsetting

Lissie. She'd come all the way up to the mine to tell him what had happened, expecting him to fix it all.

"It must be Gideon," he heard Lissie say from the back of the house, her voice warming his insides as always. "We're in the kitchen."

So Berris had come back to watch after Lissie as she'd promised him. He'd figured he might not make it home before morning and he sure as heck didn't want Lissie here all alone.

"Just getting the snow off me," he called out. "You wouldn't have something hot on the stove, would you? Something Berris didn't have a hand in making?"

If his sister took offense, she didn't do it loudly enough for Gideon to hear.

"There's coffee," Lissie said. There was a tremor in her voice that didn't sit well, and he left one boot on and stomped into the kitchen to see what Berris had done now. As if she and Cluny hadn't done quite enough yesterday to make Gideon wish he'd been given up for adoption along with Lissie all those years ago, or that his ma had stopped having babies after him.

He stood in the doorway, one shoe on, one shoe off, his jaw no doubt scraping the kitchen floor. Slick, sleeves rolled up to his elbows as if he'd been there long enough to warm up, was seated at the kitchen table, a steaming mug clasped between his hands. On the table in front of him was a copy of *Appleton's Standard Higher Geography*. From where Gideon stood he could see the pink square that was Wyoming, the yellow rectangle of Montana and the green boot of Idaho.

"You all right?" he asked Lissie, trying to pretend that Slick wasn't there, wasn't sitting at the breakfast table across from his own wife. "Berris told me you fainted."

"Oh did she?" Lissie asked, her chin jutting out. "I suppose she acted as if she cared."

"You fainted?" Slick asked, reaching his hand out and laying it over Lissie's right there in front of Gideon like he had every right to touch Gideon's wife. "Nothing's wrong, is it?"

Lissie shook her head.

"If I'da known, I'da been here," he started.

Gideon had been there, had crept upstairs to make sure she was sleeping soundly before he'd left again to try to set things to rights for her.

"I'da been here in a flash," Slick said, looking at him accusingly as if to ask where he'd been.

"Like you were here for the heaves and the rest of it?" Gideon demanded, coming over and lifting Slick's hand by the wrist until Lissie was free of it. "Like you were here when she was too tired to put one foot in front of the other? Like you were here to marry her and save her from shame?"

"Arliss knows why I left," he said, the words tight when Gideon continued to squeeze his wrist.

"Yeah? Does she know why you came back?" Gideon asked him.

"I came back because she and the baby mean everything to me," Slick said, giving Lissie his sick puppy look.

"I'll just bet they do," Gideon agreed. He knew just what that baby Arliss was carrying was worth to Slick. It just didn't compare to what it and its mama were worth to him. "But you're a little late coming to realize that. A little *too* late, so the best thing you can do for Lissie and the baby, since you love 'em so much, is get on the next train west and just keep on going."

"Don't go pushing me too far," Slick said, trying to wrench away his hand. "There ain't a person in this town who'd believe that baby was yours if I said it was mine. Everyone knows that Arliss has been head over heels for me since all she had on that chest of hers were two mosquito bites."

"You threatening to claim this baby?" Gideon asked, pressing so hard on Slick's wrist that sweat popped out on the man's forehead. "If it wouldn't hurt Lissie and the child, it just might be worth it, if only to see what this town would do to you for running out on her."

"Gideon, let go of his hand before you break it," Lissie said. She was pale as a pitcher of milk and Gideon let go of Slick's hand to kneel beside her, trying to force her head down into her lap.

"You eat anything today?" he asked her and felt her nod against his hand.

"I made her eggs," Slick said, like he'd stayed around, married her, built her a house, and gave her baby a name.

"I want you to move back to Pa's," Gideon said. "I don't like you being here alone if I gotta be out, and there's gonna be some real trouble at the mine before much—"

Before he could finish, someone started pounding at the kitchen door. Damn, but they'd promised him they'd hold off, and now, no doubt, someone was threatening to blow Granite to pieces.

Slick got up and opened the door while Gideon came to his feet and helped Lissie straighten up, as well.

Cluny nearly fell through the door. "Pa says to tell you to come over to the office soon as you can," he said, as if nothing had passed between them the night before.

"You gave me your message, now go on home," Gideon said. The last thing he wanted to do was go on over to the office and leave Slick Waynick sitting in the kitchen with his wife.

"You ain't got no call to be so mad," Cluny said. "I'm nearly sixteen, you know." Cluny sloshed across the room in his wet boots and took himself a cup of coffee.

"This ain't the time or the place," Gideon said, gesturing with his eyes at Lissie. "I ain't gonna discuss your bad judgment in front of a lady."

"All the ladies down at Lilac Row didn't stop you from reading me the scriptures last night," Cluny barked back. "You're so quick to throw stones and spout chapter and verse."

"There ain't no *ladies* on Lilac Row," Slick said.

Gideon saw the hurt in Lissie's eyes and kept his mouth shut. Given enough rope, Slick Waynick was bound to hang himself without any help from a lynching party, no matter how Gideon itched to tighten the noose.

"Cluny, wait on the porch." He looked down at Lissie, chewing at her lip, and added, "Go pack your things and Cluny'll carry 'em home for you."

"So," Slick said with a big grin on that stupid face of his. "You're a man now, huh, Cluny?"

"That's enough outta you both," Gideon fairly shouted, using his bulk to tower over Cluny and stop the boy from answering Slick. "Go on up and get your things together, Arliss."

"So old Gideon caught you down there, huh kid?" Slick asked Cluny loudly enough for Lissie to hear as he shoved her out through the kitchen doorway. "What was he doing down there?"

Lissie stood stock-still in the hallway, staring up at him, one eyebrow raised in question.

"We've been down this road before, Arliss," he said. "I'll be damned if I'm gonna go down it again."

"It's a simple enough question," she said. "What *were* you doing down at Lilac Row last night when I was here waiting for you?"

Did it matter that he'd seen her sleeping fitfully and he'd headed out again, in the cold, to check with some of the older, more discreet women on Lilac Row who might have, all those years ago, known Lissie's mother? Hell, any of them might have *been* Lissie's mother. When women fell in Granite there was only one place they'd land. And women who weren't in that kind of trouble—married ladies who were giving birth to legitimate babies—didn't find themselves on Hedda Clovis's doorstep.

He was sorry now he hadn't just waited until morning and gone to see Hedda himself, but Lissie'd looked so distraught, tossing, turning.

He'd have been smarter, and warmer, to have just crawled into the bed beside her, than try to fix things yet again.

*Damn it all!* His whole body ached with fatigue and sadness and frustration. He clomped past her toward the door, reaching for his boot, reminding himself that just the night before, Lissie had been his, free and clear of the past.

"I have a right to know," she said, her jaw set, her arms crossed over her chest.

"I come home here and find Slevin Waynick's head bowed with yours over the breakfast table and *you* have a right to know? What about my rights, Lissie? What about the right to be trusted?"

"Are you telling me you didn't go to Lilac Row?"

"I'm telling you that I am sick and tired of defending myself—to you, to my family, to a judge from Helena and the whole damn town." He shoved his foot down into his boot and reached for his coat. "I'm telling you that I'm done. Now go get your things."

"Hey, Arliss," Slick called from the kitchen. "Can I cut you a slice of Mrs. Bailey's pumpkin pie?"

Lissie looked at Gideon.

"You're tired, too, Liss. And you've been through too damn much on too little rest. And on top of that you ain't thinking straight. Best if we put the past few days behind us and forget them. Now get your things together and—"

She pulled her arm from his grasp as surely as if it were her heart that he had been holding, and his hold as tenuous. It would have been easy to tell her what he'd been doing down on Lilac Row, but after all he'd done, after all he'd seen her through, it seemed kinda pointless to go explaining himself again. And it seemed like a task with no end, like he was one of the men in those Greek stories trying to do something that simply could never be done.

Her chin, stuck out determinedly, told him everything. Her yelling to Slick to "make it a big piece," was only another nail in the coffin.

"You going?" she asked Gideon.

He nodded, fighting the urge to just pick her up and drag her back to his pa's where she belonged until he could build her a place of her own. He couldn't make her love him, couldn't make her trust him, it seemed. "You staying?"

"Seems like," she said, turning on her heel to join Slick Waynick in the warm kitchen while Gideon girded himself to go out into the bitter cold.

"Well," he said to her back. "Things ain't always what they seem."

*     *     *

Arliss huffed back into the kitchen and rested her back against the door, pretending that she couldn't care less that the man she'd finally given her heart to had spent the night spilling his seed on someone else's sheets. That instead of coming home to her loving arms he'd crawled into another woman's bed. Maybe he'd gone and made a baby for Hedda Clovis to get rid of, one way or the other. The thought brought an itch to the back of her throat and blurred her vision so that Slick was just a blur at her table.

Way back when she'd been holding out, Slick had told her that a man liked lovemaking best with a woman he cared about, but that the truth was that for a man it didn't take caring to make it good. And in that way, a soiled dove was just like a man, only she got a few bucks along with the ride.

She'd thought it was different for Gideon. Oh, botheration! She *knew* it was different for Gideon, just as it had been different for her.

"Well, we're just gonna have to go out and celebrate," Slick was saying to Cluny, one arm wrapped around his shoulder as if paying a woman two bits to spread her legs was something to be proud of.

"You should've seen Gideon," Cluny said, shaking his head as if he still couldn't believe his brother's reaction. "At first, I thought he was gonna kill Teddie Bare. Then I thought he was gonna kill me. He kept yelling about what could happen."

"What *could* happen?" Slick asked, helping himself to the piece of pie he'd set out for Arliss.

"Babies, he told me. Didn't I know where babies came from? Like I thought the stork dropped them down the chimney or something."

"Well they don't," Arliss said, coming to the table and removing the pie to set on the counter where neither man would bother themselves to get at it. "And your brother wanted to be sure you understood that there could be consequences to your actions, consequences that everyone might have to live with."

"You better sit down, Arliss," Cluny said. "You're looking real pale again."

She took her seat and put her head down on her hands. She sure knew how to pick 'em. First Slick with his promises and then Gideon with those honest eyes. "The truth, Cluny," she said softly. "What was Gideon doing on Lilac Row?"

Cluny shrugged at Slick. "I guess he was there on deputy business."

"Yeah," Slick agreed. "Musta been deputy business. Whose crib was he climbing out of?"

"Doris Landerer's," Cluny said. "But I'm sure he wasn't—"

"Aw jeez," Slick answered making a face. "She's nearly old enough to be his mother."

Slick smiled all the way over to Hughes' Mercantile. Good old Gideon Forbes. Big enough and strong enough to dig his own grave.

He blew on his hands to warm them.

Poor Arliss was going to need a lot of consoling now that her husband was straying. Poor thing was wounded to the core. Anyone could see that.

Maybe tonight he'd drop by and check on her.

In the store, three men, miners from the looks of their clothes, stood arguing with each other at the counter.

"If *they're* going to the Miner's Ball, I'll be damned if I'll show up there," one of them said.

"Me neither," a second agreed.

"My wife looks forward to that damn ball all year,"

the third said, plunking down two bits for some tobacco. "And I promised Deputy Forbes that—"

"Who's going to the ball?" Slick asked them, a plan beginning to weave its way through his head.

"Belmont's inviting the damn scabs," one of the men answered. "And I'll see them all in hell before I rub shoulders with any of them at some silly dance."

"So all the Danes'll be at the ball next Friday night, huh?" Slick asked. "And Belmont, too."

"Well, I won't be," one of them said, a fist pounding the counter.

Slick adjusted his coat, brushing a speck off his lapel and mumbling just loud enough to be heard. "With the Danes and Belmont at the ball, who'll be up watching the mine?"

The angriest of the men found it hard not to smile. Slick was relieved that miners weren't as stupid as he'd always thought. No, something had definitely occurred to the man who grabbed the tobacco off the counter and was shoving the other two men toward the door in a hurry. He had a thought in his head—and Slick was proud to have planted it there.

Damned if there wouldn't be some trouble the night of the ball. Trouble that the sheriff and his deputy would have to go on up to the mine and check out.

And poor Arliss! Left alone at the ball. He supposed it would only be right to offer to dance with her while her husband was occupied elsewhere.

And he supposed that once he got Arliss back in his arms, it wouldn't take much to keep her there. And once he had her—and the child, of course—he'd have it all.

*Chapter Twenty-three*

"*I AM NOT SIMPLY BEING STUBBORN,*" *ARLISS TOLD JULI-*
ana four days later, handing the shoes for a fancy
doll to Jeannie. "He is." And if she did want to be
stubborn, she could be just as stubborn as Gideon.
Stubborner, even. After all, it wasn't she who'd forgotten they were married. No, it was Mr. High and
Mighty—who'd said that he'd never forget their vows
and she shouldn't either.

Of course, that was before he knew she was no better than those *ladies* down on Lilac Row.

Well, he'd known that when he married her. He just
hadn't known that her mama was—

"Stubborn? Is that what he is?" Juliana asked, handing Arliss another bead for the bodice of Samantha
Maddigan's green satin gown before tying the laces on
the doll for Jeannie. " 'Cause I'd surely have mistaken
that long face and those slow steps of his to be misery,
not stubbornness."

"He's got watery eyes," Jeannie added, nodding her
head solemnly. "I think he's coming down with something, but he won't let me take his tempitcher."

Lissie fought the urge to smile. So he was miserable,
was he? She suspected he wasn't half so miserable as

she. He didn't have one sister-in-law or another traipsing in every hour to check on him, to chide him, to tell him that he ought to—

The needle caught her finger, drawing a tiny bead of blood. She put it into her mouth and fought against tears. She hadn't cried when Gideon left, and she wasn't going to let some pin prick undo all the hard work she'd done to hold herself together. And she sure as heck wasn't going to break down in front of Gideon's sister and have her running home to tell him that she was falling apart without him. Because she wasn't.

She wasn't. And if she told herself twice a minute, every minute, maybe, just maybe, she could convince herself.

Not that it had worked yet.

"He hardly eats anything," Juliana said. "He misses your cooking."

Arliss bet he did. With what she'd done to the spice jars and the baking powders, Berris's meals ought to be inedible even by the Forbes' standards.

"We baked him cookies, too," Jeannie said. "Only we gave him the broken ones and saved the good ones for you. But you're not supposed to tell."

"No, *you're* not supposed to tell," Juliana said, taking Jeannie on her lap. "He doesn't sleep. At least it doesn't look like he does. He's got rings around his eyes that reach to his mouth. Which, by the way, is set in a perpetual frown."

Arliss shrugged, her eyes on her bead work. She was anxious for Juliana and Jeannie to leave so that she could pull out her own dress and add a bit of flare to it. If Gideon wanted some fancy woman, well, he didn't have to go down to Lilac Row to find her. "He knows where I live."

"You live, Arliss Forbes, halfway across town, where

your husband lives. You're just staying here temporarily."

"Till you come to your sentences," Jeannie said. "Only temporneverly."

Half the Forbes family seemed to be staying on High Street, *temporarily*. Apparently hers was the only place Cluny was allowed out to visit. Even the sheriff had stopped by. Twice.

"He says he asked you to come home with him and you were too busy sharing breakfast with Slick Waynick to come," Juliana said, moving the plate of cookies within Arliss's reach despite the fact that Arliss had said she didn't want any. They smelled like heaven, all buttery and sweet, and saliva pooled in her mouth. Juliana whispered something in Jeannie's ear and Jeannie reached forward and held a cookie out to Arliss.

"I wasn't sharing anything with anyone," she said, taking the cookie from Jeannie and putting it on the table beside her. "*He,* on the other hand—"

"Arliss, don't be an idiot," Juliana said, pushing Jeannie off her lap and coming to her feet. "You've dug in your heels so far that you're likely to get sucked under by the mire."

Arliss took the cookie and bit into it with a vengeance. "Well, if I'm drowning in the mire, what is Gideon's waist deep in?" she asked.

Juliana threw up her hands, wincing from a pain in her shoulder. "I give up! With the two of you, one is worse than the other. Two people so blind with love they can't see straight, and the way you're both going on, like as not you'll end up alone and miserable.

"And what about the baby, Arliss? You think you can just go on living here, have your baby and—" she stalked toward the hall.

"Does Uncle Gideon know about Aunt Lissie's

baby?" Jeannie whispered to her mother, stealing a glance back at Arliss.

"No one knows about a baby until the stork comes along with it," Juliana said to her daughter. "Most especially not little girls who promised that they would keep their ears and mouths shut if they were allowed to come visiting."

"But I don't know how to shut my ears," Jeannie whimpered, sniffing to hold back the tears.

"Thank you both for coming by and for the cookies. And Jeannie honey, I don't know how to shut my ears, either, but it might be something worth learning." She was relieved that Juliana and Jeannie appeared to be leaving and was hoping to give them a polite push.

When she heard yet another set of footsteps on the porch she really did wish she could shut her ears. "Oh, that must be Berris," Juliana said, opening the door.

Arliss thought about stabbing herself with her needle and supposed that it was only in fairy tales that it could put her out of her misery.

"Slick!" Juliana's dismay rang in the hallway like a death knoll. "What are you doing here?"

Beads flew in every direction as Lissie leaped from the chair. *God,* she prayed, *don't let him say anything that will embarrass Gideon!*

"To tell you the truth," Slick said, and Lissie thought he'd picked one heck of a time to start that and prayed it wasn't anything of the kind. "I was up to the cemetery today, visiting my pa's grave, and thought I'd pay my respects to Marcus, me not being here for the funeral and all. And then I thought it might give Arliss some comfort to know that the snow's all but melted and the place looks right nice."

"Oh," Juliana said, sounding vaguely disappointed. "I suppose she would like to know that."

"All right if I come in?"

"Of course it is," Arliss called out. "Why wouldn't it be?" She wasn't doing anything wrong, after all. No matter what Gideon seemed to think.

"Well," Juliana said, hesitating to tie her bonnet beneath her chin. "I suppose that Jeannie and I could stay a while longer."

Lissie tied the bow for her. "You've stayed longer than you should have already. Jeannie's hungry as a bear and Ezra will be growling like one if you don't get on home."

"But Gideon—" Juliana started.

"Gideon knows where I am," Arliss said, trying to get them out of the house before Slick said something he shouldn't.

"Good to see you," Slick said to Juliana, opening the door for her and patting Jeannie on the head. "And you, too, pipsqueak."

And then he shut the door behind them.

She didn't look real happy to see him, but Slick figured he'd be able to change that in just a minute or two.

"So how are you doing today?" he asked.

"Better than yesterday but not as good as tomorrow," she said with a sigh, giving no indication that she was in any mood to entertain him.

"We just gonna stand here in the hall?" he asked. "I mean, shouldn't you be sittin' down?"

"I'll sit down after you've gone," she said, watching through the window of the door behind him as if maybe someone more important might come waltzing up her walk.

He walked into the parlor and heard something crunch beneath his feet.

"Watch where you're walking," Arliss said, sitting

down on the stairs and loosening her bootlaces. "I dropped a few beads and—" She stopped when she noticed he was looking at her legs and blushed red as a beet. He tried to keep a straight face as he came over and raised her foot.

"Let me help you with these," he said as she tried to pull her foot away without falling off the stair. "Arliss honey, it ain't as if I ain't seen all that you got. Now sit still and let me help you."

"Do you think I walk around barefoot when you're not here? Or sleep in my boots at the end of the day? I'm perfectly capable of—"

He let go of her foot. "Have it your way," he said. "Whatever you want is all right with me, long as you don't go hurting yourself or this baby."

"What I want is to be left alone for just a few minutes, which seems to be too much to ask in this town." She pulled off her left boot. Her cotton stocking clung to her foot and he had the urge to reach out and trace each toe. "Why are you here, anyway?"

"I came to level with you," he said, turning his back to stop himself from grabbing at her too soon. He closed his eyes tight enough to sting. "I made a big mistake not marrying you when you first come to me and told me about the baby. I can see that now. See that I missed out on watchin' you fill out so pretty. And it twists my heart not to reach out and touch you."

"Slick, I—"

"I came to tell you how sorry I am." He turned around when his eyes were sufficiently watered. "And to tell you I could make it up to you, Arliss. Starting now."

He pulled the velvet pouch from his pocket and held it out to her.

"It's an apology, pure and simple."

He was disappointed when she looked at the pouch suspiciously and didn't reach for it.

"I owe you this, Lissie," he said, Gideon's pet name for her feeling awkward on his tongue. "Please take it."

"I don't think Gideon would like it if I did," she said.

"You lettin' him tell you what to do? That ain't the Arliss I know." She raised her chin a little, and he forged ahead. "Doesn't seem like he cares too much what you'd like. Near as I can see, it doesn't seem he cares much about you, at all."

"And you do, huh?" she asked like she didn't believe him for a minute. Still she *was* staring at the bag in his hand.

"I've learned my lesson, Arliss. I swear I have."

"It's too late," she said with a little shake of her head.

"Well, then take it as a kind of memento of what we had," he suggested, figuring that when Gideon saw the necklace and earbobs on Arliss it would be the last straw. And then Arliss would have no choice but to throw herself on his mercy. And Slick would take her back, on his terms, of course, and all of this before she even knew her own worth.

"I don't want to remember what we had," she said softly, without any anger. "I learned a real hard lesson from you, when I gave you my innocence. And I've been learning ever since, and every lesson hurts more than the one before."

She sure wasn't making his job easy. He sauntered into the parlor and fell to his knees, picking up the beads that littered the floor, thinking of what he could say that would soften her resolve.

"You making this for the Miner's Ball?" he asked, studying the satin gown that was draped over the arm of the sofa as he worked. "I was kinda hoping you'd be wearing that dark red you look so beautiful in."

"It's Samantha Maddigan's dress," she said, tiptoeing into the parlor and taking the beads from his out-stretched hand. "I'm just adding some interest to it."

"Then you'll be wearing red?" He looked up at her like the color dress she was gonna wear to the dance was the most important thing in the world to him.

"I'm not sure I'm going," she said, clearly wishing she was.

"I wish you would," he said, touching her hand as he handed her some more beads. "I wish you'd come in a deep red dress with that chin of yours stuck out like you don't owe nobody any explanation and I wish you'd wear these," he added, putting the velvet pouch into her waiting hand.

"What is it?" she asked, the bag sitting in her hand like some sick kitten, all limp and unloved.

"Open it," he said, kneeling by her.

It looked like she had to force herself to do it, but finally she opened the pouch and shook out its contents. "Your grandma's earrings!"

"Well, to tell you the truth, they're not," he said and smiled inwardly at his extreme cleverness. "I found ones near as I could to replace the ones you lost. And I kept picturing you wearing them at the ball and when I saw the necklace—well, my Arliss just had to have that, too."

"I'm not *your* Arliss," she said. She sounded determined, but if he listened just right, it could be that he detected a note of sadness when she said it.

"I suppose that now you ain't," he agreed, watching Berris through the window behind Arliss. "But maybe someday you will be again. Maybe someday real soon."

He kissed her hand and rose.

"Let me help you put that on," he said, taking the necklace from her and putting it around her neck.

"I'm just borrowing these for the ball, Slick," she told him while he struggled with the clasp. "And only because I am wearing red."

"You got the God damn longest neck I ever saw," he said, meaning it. "Like a swan. I'd give my right arm if you'd let me kiss your neck just one more time."

"It might cost you that," Arliss said with a smile, backing away from him. "If my husband were to hear you say that."

"You gotta take the bull by the horns," Gideon's father said. "All your life you been slow and steady, and Slick ain't gonna nap just so as you can mosey across Arliss's finish line first."

"What?" Gideon was standing at the counter in Hughes' Mercantile waiting for Miss Kelly to finish flirting with his pa and locate the packages that had come in for him.

"I'm saying that he who hesitates is lost, and you're he."

Miss Kelly came out from the back room with a large parcel. "Your boots, I think," she said, shoving the box up on the counter with a groan. "Feels like lead."

"That'd be the boots, then," Gideon agreed. "The other stuff come in yet?"

"Sure did," she said over her shoulder as she headed to the back storeroom again.

"You're a plodder, Gideon, and a plodder just doesn't get anywheres in life. You gotta seize the opportunity, you gotta make a few waves, you gotta—"

"Little drops of water made every damn canyon we got in Montana, Pa," Gideon said. "One slow drop at a time."

"Well," Thaddeus said, pushing back the hat on his head. "Excuse me. I didn't realize we had eons here to set things on the right course. A bolt of lightning can cut down a tree in an instant. Take all day for a man with a dull blade."

"Bolt of lightning can start a forest fire," Gideon said, reaching out to help Miss Kelly with the rest of the parcels.

"Sometimes you just gotta take a risk, Gid, or there ain't no chance of succeeding," his father said, looking over the packages and checking the labels.

"You planning on lighting a spark yourself, Gideon Forbes?" Miss Kelly asked, pointing out a shipping label to his father. "This here package came all the way from New York City!"

"You got any mail for me while I'm here?" Gideon asked, not willing to share the contents of the packages with Miss Kelly—or his father, for that matter. If Lissie wanted some fancy ladies' man, she could have one. A damn big one.

"Letter for Arliss," Miss Kelly said. "From Virgil Keker, Esquire, in Virginia City."

Gideon took the letter and put it into the inside pocket of his coat. So then the old man was finally dead. Gideon wondered if Slick knew, and supposed he did, supposed that was what drove him right through a blizzard back to Arliss's arms.

"You going over to Arliss's?" his father asked. When Miss Kelly raised an eyebrow, he added, "I mean you still staying with her at her pa's place or are you bringing her on home already?"

"Don't seem she's quite ready to come on home yet, Pa," he admitted sadly.

"The past can have a strong pull," Miss Kelly said as Berris came into the shop. "Hard to let go, hard to break free of all the memories."

"Gideon! Thank goodness! I've been looking for you everywhere!" Berris said.

He shoved the parcels he was holding into his father's arms. "Something wrong at Lissie's?" he asked, halfway to the door before even giving her a chance to answer.

Berris raised her shoulders and pulled him aside. "He was there again," she whispered. "I saw him through the window."

"Ain't you got anything better to do than spy on Arliss Mallard?" he asked.

"Not so long as she's Arliss *Forbes*," Berris said. "You got a present for her in any of those boxes?" Berris demanded. "Because Slick just gave her—"

"Berris, I ain't interested," Gideon said. He'd given her baby a name, the promise of a home of her own, he'd given her love and tenderness and caring. If that wasn't what she was after, nothing else he offered would make any difference.

"Son, you gotta put your foot down," his father said. "Draw that line and tell her what it'll cost her if she steps over it."

"I've got some new toilet water straight from Paris, France," Miss Kelly said. "They say it smells like heaven and all the women are asking for it. Maybe a bottle of that . . . "

Gideon shrugged off Berris's arm, returned to the counter to scoop up his packages, and headed out the door to a chorus of suggestions and unasked-for advice.

He made two stops on his way over to Lissie. One to drop off his bundles, which he had no intention of letting her see, and one to pick up the "thing." He refused to consider it a gift, or a bribe, though he knew in his heart that it was, plain and simple. He settled for thinking of it as a peace offering. That put guilt aside and spoke to the future instead of the past.

He stood waiting on the doorstep, unsure whether he needed to knock or could simply walk in. Lissie was, after all, his wife. He could hear his father whispering in one ear that the plan was to just charge in there, grab her by the hair, and drag her home. In the other ear, he could hear Berris telling him a very different plan—he ought to let her have it right there on the porch, tell her it was all over between them and that Slick could have her if he wanted her.

Truth was, Gideon didn't have a plan. And if he'd had one, it would have gone right out of his head when Lissie opened the door. Good Lord, but she was four days prettier than the last time he saw her. Her cheeks were rosy, her eyes sparkled.

He tried to untie his tongue while she stood in the doorway waiting. Finally she opened the door. "It's freezing out there. You coming in or not?"

Well, he hadn't really expected her to roll out a welcome mat.

*Take a risk,* his father said. He stepped into the foyer and swallowed hard. "I missed you," he mumbled at her back.

"What?" she said, turning around, a garnet earbob catching the lamplight.

"I see Slick's been here," he said instead of repeating himself. What did his father know about affairs of the heart? Gideon's mother had loved his father from the day she'd met him until the day she died—no matter what he did or didn't do.

"He dropped by once or twice to see how I was feeling," she said, trying to hide the fact that she was pulling the earbobs from her ears as if he hadn't seen them.

"And how are you feeling?" he asked, thinking that it was true what they said about women glowing when they were carrying. Thinking that she'd never been more beautiful and that he'd never wanted to hold her as much, touch her as much, taste her as much.

"Good," she said, showing him into the parlor as if he were a guest, instead of taking his hand and leading him up the stairs like a husband. "You don't need to be worried about me."

"I can't seem to help it," he said, as much to himself as to her.

"Don't you want to take your coat off?" she asked when he stood in her nice warm parlor fully dressed for the brutal weather. "Or aren't you staying that long?"

The peace offering was nestled inside his coat, and he wasn't so sure, after seeing those damned earbobs, that he wanted to hold out the olive branch after all. "Don't really know," he said. "See how things go."

Lissie bit at her lip. "That apply to sitting, too?" she asked, easing herself down into the soft armchair where Gideon couldn't sit next to her. He sat down on the sofa carefully juggling his gift.

"You wanna come home, Lissie?" he asked, unbuttoning the top few buttons.

"I am home," she said, cutting him right to the quick before she added, "You wanna live here?"

What he wanted was to pull her close to him, smell her hair, taste the sweetness on her lips, and feel the warmth of her in his arms. He was all ready to say yes when he felt a series of pinpricks in the vicinity of his heart and shifted on the sofa before opening up his mouth.

And by then it was too late. Lissie was at it again. " 'Course you'd have to give up your fancy women," she said. "No more trips in the night to Doris Landerer's crib," she added.

Well, Cluny was grounded for life now.

"I wouldn't want to give my heart to a man I couldn't trust."

"You didn't seem to have that problem with Slick," he said before the words registered in his head. *Give her heart?* Had she really said *give her heart to a man she couldn't trust?*

Her face tightened, her shoulders hunched. "I never expected better of Slick," she admitted.

"You still think you can't trust me?" he asked her, unbuttoning his jacket the rest of the way and welcoming the cool air against his chest.

"I don't know," she said mimicking his own words. "I'll have to see how things go."

"After everything, you don't think I deserve the benefit of the doubt?" he asked.

"I don't want to have a doubt, Gideon. But I can't help it."

"I don't see how I can help you with that, Lissie. I've been open and honest with you right from the start—"

"Until the other day," she corrected him.

"I could explain it, Lis, tell you how I was there just to ask some questions. I am the deputy of Granite, you know. But I don't see how that would help the next time."

"The next time?" Her eyebrows slipped under the little fringe of curls that covered her forehead. "So then you'd go there again?"

"See what I mean? And there'd always be something, Lissie." He rose sadly and held out the kitten he'd had tucked under his coat. "I thought you might want something to hold onto in the night," he said.

Her eyes welled up as she took the ball of fur into

her hands and held it against her cheek. "Looks like I'll need it," she said, and he could hear the tears in her throat.

"It's your choice, Lissie. Always has been." He stood looking down at her, watching her cuddle the kitten to the same breasts he had caressed, and knew that he didn't want to go home without her, without her and the stupid kitten and the child growing in her belly.

"Are you going to the ball on Saturday?" she asked him. Well, it really looked like she was asking the cat, but he figured she was just afraid to look at him.

"I was planning to," he said. More than planning, he'd been counting on it to show her Slick wasn't the only ladies' man in Granite. But he'd be damned if he'd tell her that. "Just in case there's any trouble there."

She nodded, huge green eyes looking up over dark fur, pleading with him for something.

"Could I take you?" he asked. "I mean, would you like to go with me?"

She nodded. "I'd be honored to accompany you," she said, walking him to the door.

"Lissie, I—" He stopped at the door and pulled the letter from Virginia City from his pocket. "This came for you," he said, handing it to her.

"What is it?" she asked, looking over the envelope.

He shrugged. One step at a time, he figured. Slow and steady.

In the meantime, he had a date with his wife.

# Chapter Twenty-four

⟨*⟩

ARLISS STARED AT HERSELF IN THE MIRROR TRYING TO see just how enormous she looked from every angle, surprised to see that she looked better than she had in months. Well, getting a letter from a lawyer in Virginia City could do that, she supposed.

She'd thought about telling Gideon just as soon as she read it, but something convinced her it would be better to wait. "You are a very silly kitten," she told the ball of fluff rolling in the hem of her dark red moire gown with the low beaded bodice. "And I am a very silly woman, hoping that my very own husband will court me and woo me and win me, and holding out that letter as his reward."

Slick's necklace sparkled around her neck. If it hadn't matched her dress so perfectly, if it hadn't made her look so extra special, she wouldn't have worn it. And since Slick had said he wasn't going to the ball if she wouldn't go with him, she figured it couldn't do any harm. Oh, maybe Gideon might get a little jealous, but the man seemed to need a good kick in the pants—or the head—to see that he belonged with her. Belonged *to* her, just as she belonged to him.

Slick had shown up shortly after her letter had arrived, but she hadn't mentioned it to him, either. She could just imagine what Slick would do if he knew. Why he'd already suggested that since things weren't going right between her and Gideon, and things had always been so fine between them, that she ought to think about maybe leaving Granite, starting fresh somewhere else, with him. Of course, Slick didn't know that now she had something to offer Gideon that just might make him stay with her even if he couldn't quite bring himself to love her the way she loved him.

She'd been peering out the window into the darkness since four o'clock, pacing, leaning against the wall, doing whatever it took not to wrinkle her gown. She wanted to be beautiful for Gideon—she wanted to walk in on his arm and have the whole town, miners and farmers and townsfolk, all think that Gideon Forbes was the luckiest man in the world. She wanted to tell him about her good fortune and tell him that the luckiest man was just what he was. And she wanted him to look at her and think it himself.

After all, she was the luckiest woman, wasn't she?

He looked like an idiot. Gideon stared at his reflection in the mirror and tried unbuttoning the fancy black on black brocade vest he'd sent for from New York City. It didn't help. He changed the collar on his shirt and tried tying the bowtie again.

He looked like a jerk.

The clothes fit all right, and they were surely true to the drawings in the catalogs. But somehow the dashing men with mustaches looked a lot better in the fancy suits than he did. He adjusted his cuffs, as if that would make the difference between looking like he belonged on the stage in Butte spouting Shakespeare and looking like a man Lissie could trust and love.

He wouldn't trust the man in the mirror as far as he could spit.

"Chew-ey, Gideon!" Cluny said, stopping by the doorway. "Aren't you the dandy?"

"Look that stupid, do I?" Gideon asked, undoing the tie and trying again.

"Stupid?" Cluny asked, his eyebrows down over his eyes, his head cocked. "Heck, Gideon, it's the first time I wished I was gonna ever get as big as you. All your hand-me-downs look like they came right off some overgrown scarecrow, but this . . . this . . . is truly magnificent."

Gideon searched his brother's face. "That stupid, huh?" he asked again.

Cluny nodded. "Worse," he said, falling against the doorjamb with laughter. "You look like someone attached one of them air pumps to Slick Waynick's toe and blew him up! You look like—"

"I think that's enough, son," Thaddeus said, looking in on Gideon and trying to keep a straight face. "I know I said you ought to grab the bull by the horns, Gideon. I didn't mean to say you had to become a damn matador!"

"Out!" he shouted at both of them, slamming the door behind them. He was gonna be late for Lissie if he didn't just go the way he was. He took the jacket off. The vest alone didn't look half bad, and with the little pocket just right for safely holding the new gold band he'd bought for Lissie, he was loathe to give it up. Besides, it was bound to be hot in the Grange Hall. Maybe he could just slip out of his jacket right away.

He looked down at his first pair of opera cowboy boots—the ones that the catalog called "The Dress Parade." Oh, but they were a sight to see! It was a good thing he'd practiced dancing with Juliana. If he stepped on Lissie's toes in these, he'd have to carry her home.

He considered that option and smiled.

Berris and Samantha were almost ready to head out the door. In a fit of bravery, and with Samantha's help, Berris had her hair in an up-sweep that had tight green ringlets framing her face. If Carson Maddigan didn't take notice of her tonight, he never would!

"Are you certain you don't want to wear a bonnet?" Samantha asked her for the thirty-fourth time.

"Jealous that my hair matches my gown and yours doesn't?" Berris teased back. "Maybe you should visit old Verinda Ruth Tenbrink and let her just—"

Samantha was busy studying herself in the mirror. "Do you think there's too much beading on this dress?" she asked. "I don't even know what's appropriate anymore. When I was at Miss Emily's we were taught that a young woman of worth didn't need to wear it on her chest."

"Well, don't worry. No one at the ball but you has ever had even one day of finishing school. They won't know any better than you about the latest styles. All the Lady Goody's Magazines around here are at least a year old." Berris gave herself one more once-over before deciding she was satisfied. She just dared Carson not to show all of Granite, Montana that he was brave enough to dance with a woman who in turn was brave enough to show up to the Miner's Ball with green hair!

"Ready?" Sam asked her.

"I think tonight is going to be the most special night of my life so far," she admitted, squeezing Sam's arm in anticipation. "Don't you?"

"I always think something special and wonderful is going to happen, but in Granite, nothing ever does."

"Sam," Berris chided. "Something will happen to-night, you'll see."

"Well, if it does," Samantha agreed, "it won't happen to me."


"What time is the game?" Slick asked, patting his nearly empty pockets.

"I figure we'll get started around ten-thirty," Bart Sommers told him. "Gotta give the ladies a few turns before we go on upstairs to 'smoke cigars,' " he said with a wink.

Ten-thirty. He could win Arliss over, see her home, engage in a little hanky-panky, stop himself out of respect and politeness, and still get to the table by then, give or take a few minutes for her resistance. "I should be there before eleven," he said. After all, Arliss needed her sleep if she was going to have a nice healthy baby.

"It's a cash-only table, Waynick," Bart said. "No markers."

"Understood," Slick agreed, biting down on his tongue. The truth was that at the moment he was a little short on cash—after the shave and haircut and visit with Teddie Bare. But soon he'd have enough money to buy and sell these chumps ten times over. In the meantime he was sure he could come up with some collateral for long enough to start winning everyone else's cash.

"And remember, not a word of this to anyone. I don't want no trouble with the law for gambling over the Grange Hall."

Slick smiled. "I have a feeling that the law will be occupied elsewhere."

What was that word the Persian beauty in Butte had taught him? Something about three princes who found agreeable things they weren't even looking for? Oh yes. *Serendipity.*

Serendipity, indeed.

Gideon stood nervously on Lissie's porch, his leg shaking as he waited for her to open the door. Through the fancy glass panes in the door he could see her approaching and a shudder ran right through him. If she looked as lovely when she got the door open, he was a goner.

She opened the door.

He was a goner, all right.

She smiled at him shyly.

He struggled to smile back.

"New hat?" she asked, opening the door for him to come in.

He wiped his feet on the mat and ducked his head slightly to enter the house. He felt ten feet tall looking down at what had to be the most beautiful woman in the world.

"Oh Gideon! New boots, too!" she exclaimed.

He nodded, struggling to get his tongue to work. "You look like a fairy princess," he said with a sigh.

And the smile she gave him made her all the prettier. "And you look like my knight in shining armor," she teased back. "Is that a string tie I see around your neck?"

He felt the pink creeping into his cheeks. "Well, it is the Miner's Ball," he said, as if she needed reminding.

"I'll just get my coat." She twirled around in front of him, making him dizzy just to watch the light sparkle off her dress.

"Let me help you." Lord, he felt as awkward as the average thirteen-year-old as he tripped over his words, his feet, the kitten, and a host of imaginary strings on his way to get her cloak.

She pretended not to notice.

"It's real cold out there," he warned her, buttoning the buttons of her coat for her, letting his hands brush against her chin, her neck, working the buttons over her breasts and wishing they were coming home instead of going out, wishing that the courting was over and the marriage had begun again.

It only took a moment or two, and all the bravery he possessed, to lean forward and brush her lips with his. It only took a heartbeat to deepen the kiss, to take her into his arms, press her against his body, taste the sweetness of her mouth, run his tongue gently along the seams of her lips, and wish that she would welcome him in.

And it felt like forever until she parted those lips, inviting him in, promising him with a small sigh more than he dared to hope for.

He'd have stood there forever, his arms around her, his mouth playing with hers, if she hadn't pushed him away gently and dabbed at her swollen lips with one gloved finger.

"Guess you wanna be going," he said, trying to rouse himself from a wonderful dream and quickly straightening his coat collar like they'd been caught doing something they shouldn't have been doing.

"I think you look real handsome, Deputy Forbes," she said, taking the arm he offered her.

"And you, Mrs. Forbes," he said, loving the sound of it on his tongue, wondering why he'd never said it before, wanting to say it again. "You, Mrs. Forbes, look like a million dollars."

* * *

Arliss didn't bother trying to hide her smile. Maybe she wasn't worth quite a million dollars, but near enough. She took back every rotten thing she'd ever thought about Honora's father, except maybe that he was a miserable old thing to ignore his own daughter's death—and all because she'd married the sweetest man west of the Mississippi.

That was, if you didn't count Gideon, who no doubt had a perfectly logical explanation for the fact that he'd been coming out of Doris Landerer's crib at daybreak. And frankly, she didn't need to hear it. Gideon was as trustworthy as her father had always been, and she was ready to tell him as much when the evening was over.

They strolled to the Grange Hall arm in arm, Gideon watching her every step on the icy streets. He seemed as lost in his thoughts as she was in her own, and Lissie was surprised that the silence was quite comfortable. A man like Gideon didn't need to say much. A woman could tell he was there beside her without him uttering a word, without his touch, without his soft breath making clouds in the dark air around them.

They could hear the strains of the fiddle from a block away, mixing with the sounds of laughter and the swish of Arliss's skirts. It was a happy sound, and she turned up her face to Gideon and smiled.

"Isn't it just the most glorious night?" she asked him. "Look at all the stars!"

"That's Orion over there," Gideon said, turning her shoulders and pointing over one of them.

"My pa used to tell me that one of the tiny stars by Orion was my mama, and that she was watching down on me," Arliss said. She watched the stars twinkling and imagined her mother smiling broadly at her on Gideon's arm.

"Why, I think I see an extra star up there," Gideon said, pointing vaguely. "Suppose that's your pa?"

But he wasn't looking up into the night sky, he was looking right at her eyes and leaning forward until his lips touched hers. Soft, velvety like the sky, her lips caressed his, making promises he intended to see she kept.

"Oooh!" someone whispered loudly as a group passed them by on their way to the hall. "Married since September and still in love!" they teased.

Gideon pulled back and tightened the woolen shawl around her neck. "Guess we best get in there," he said, but the magic of the moment was gone when he failed to tell her that he loved her.

She refused to dwell on it. After all, Gideon wasn't a man of words, he was a man of action. And if he didn't love her, why had he married her? And now that Slick was back and Gideon could easily rid himself of her, why was he still asking her to come on home?

She took Gideon's arm again and lifted her skirts to climb the steps of the Grange Hall. Cold air swirled around her legs, sending shivers up her spine as they entered the hall.

Oh, but there were chandeliers everywhere, their candles burning brightly, and women in fancy dresses twirled on the arms of handsome men beneath each of them.

Gideon helped her off with her coat while several women eyed her dress with admiration. Then he disappeared and came back looking as dashing as she'd ever seen a man look. His broad shoulders filled out a narrow cut jacket so that there was no missing his muscles. His white shirt was crisp and bright against a black vest which sparkled with gold buttons.

"My, my, my," she said, shaking her head in disbelief

that the man before her was the same sensible Gideon Forbes who had done little more than grunt at her until the day he'd come to her rescue and married her.

Scarlet crept up his cheeks. His dimple deepened. "Don't know what I was thinking," he admitted with a shrug, but Lissie knew precisely what it was.

"He don't hold a candle to you, Deputy Forbes," she said, not mentioning Slick's name as she straightened his tie. "Not in any way."

There just wasn't anything like a Gideon Forbes smile. They could blow out all the candles and the room would still be glowing bright as noon.

"Wanna dance?" he asked, and she had a vivid memory of what must have been a million years earlier when he'd asked her once before.

This time she put out her hand and curtsied. "I'd like that very much."

It seemed like forever since she'd been in Gideon's arms. He felt larger, stronger, and yet she fit against him well, completing something that was bigger than the two of them alone.

"Everybody's staring at us," she whispered to him.

He laughed, a deep rumble that she felt against her chest. "They ain't staring at *us*, Lissie. 'Less, of course, they think I look as ridiculous as I feel. They're staring at you."

"I went too far with this dress, didn't I?" she said, rounding her shoulders so that her breasts didn't stick out quite so much.

"You are the most beautiful woman in this room," Gideon said, his movements in perfect time to the music. "Ain't a woman here that even comes close."

"Why Gideon!" she said, truly stunned. "You are a new man tonight. Did that suit come full of compliments?"

"For what it cost, it sure oughta," Gideon said with a chuckle in his voice that she hadn't heard in too long.

"I wouldn't worry about what it costs," she said, wondering if now was the time to tell him her secret.

"I didn't," he said, holding her far enough away for her to get a good look at his suit and for him to take her in from head to belly if not toe. "That's a pretty necklace you're wearing. Your mama's?"

"No," she said. Good glory! She'd forgotten all about the stupid thing. Who wanted Gideon jealous when he was being just perfect on his own? "I borrowed it."

"From?" he asked just a little too calmly as he pulled her closer against him and twirled her around the floor.

"You're not going to like the answer," she said.

"You're right about that," he said. "I don't like it one bit."

"And why is that?" she asked, tensing in his arms.

"Because you oughta know better than to go getting yourself involved with the likes of . . . the giver."

"I'm not *involved* with anyone," she said, pulling back to put some distance between them.

He whistled. "Well, there's our problem, ain't it?"

"You know what I meant," she said, purposely stepping on his toe. From the look on his face, he didn't even feel it.

"Then why'd you take it?" he asked.

"Borrow it," she corrected. "Because I was mad at you, and feeling spiteful, and maybe even a little sorry for myself. Now I'm just plain sorry."

He said nothing, and so she continued.

"I'll return it. Or you can do it for me, if you like."

There was no response, but she could feel his breathing change ever so slightly against her.

"Gideon?"

"Hmm?" he answered absentmindedly while he appeared to be checking out the room. His hold on her loosened, his tongue played with his cheek.

"Is something wrong?" He'd all but stopped dancing, his head turned first in one direction and then in another.

"You see any of the miners from the Columbia? Getz? Beattie? Any of 'em?" he asked.

She looked around her. "There are some," she said, gesturing toward a bunch of men in heavy boots by the punch bowl. "But I don't recognize them."

"The Danes," Gideon said with disgust. "I told Belmont not to go and invite them or the—"

His face froze and he spun around twice, dodging the arms of other dancers on the floor, searching for someone.

"You see Belmont?" he demanded, just as his father came by with Miss Kelly on his arm.

"You look lovely tonight," he told Arliss and then leaned into them. "You two seen Berris yet? Green hair, green dress, you can't miss her!"

"Pa," Gideon said, barely keeping the lid on his voice. "You seen Belmont?"

His father shrugged. "Not yet, I don't think."

"You seen any of the men from the mine?"

The smile slid from Thaddeus's face. "Maybe they're just late," he said, but it didn't look to Arliss as if he believed it.

Gideon pulled the watch from his pocket and showed it to his father. Almost half past nine.

"Shit."

"I gotta go on up to Coppertown, Lissie. Want me to find Cluny so he can see you home?" Gideon asked.

"She looks too pretty to go sitting home, Gideon," Thaddeus said, taking his leave of Miss Kelly at the same time. "She'll be fine here for a while and Cluny

can see her home later if we don't get back in an hour
or so."

Gideon looked anything but pleased.

"I'll be fine," she assured him. "Do you think you'll
be very long?"

He fingered the necklace around her throat. "I'll be
as fast as I can. Don't you go *borrowing* anything else
while I'm gone."

Arliss put her hands on her hips. And Gideon had
the nerve to complain to her about the importance of
trust?

"And don't go dancing yourself tired," he added before nodding to his father that he was ready to go. "I'll
see if Ezra can save a slow one for you."

Arliss tapped her foot impatiently. "If you're going,
Deputy Forbes, you'd better go."


Berris stood off to a corner of Grange Hall, with a
cup of punch in her hand. She threw her head back in
laughter, pretending she was having the time of her life
with Samantha while the girls whispered behind their
hands and the boys pushed and shoved at each other,
no doubt daring one another to dance with the girl with
green hair.

"Oh, wonderful," she told Samantha sarcastically.
"There go Gideon and my pa. I haven't seen Cluny all
night and there isn't a man here brave enough to ask
me to—"

Samantha clutched at her arm and looked beyond
her. "Isn't it a lovely party?" she asked, her grip getting
tighter.

" 'Evening Samantha," Carson's voice purred from
behind Berris. " 'Evening, Miss Forbes."

"Mr. Maddigan," she said with a nod of her head as
she turned to face him. "Lovely party, don't you think?"

Carson held out his hand to her. "It would be even lovelier if you'd consent to dance with me, Miss Forbes."

Berris's heart did a handspring down Main Street. "Oh, but I'd hate to leave Samantha all alone," she said, trying not to seem too eager.

"Well, if you'd rather not," Carson said, and Samantha nearly pushed Berris right into his arms.

"I'll be fine," she assured them both. "Let's not all stand here on my account."

"If you're sure," Berris began, but Carson had already put his arms around her and was leading her in the direction of the dance floor.

"Keep it up, Berris, and I'll think you don't really want to dance with me," Carson said, stepping heavily on Berris's left foot.

"Keep that up and I won't," Berris shot back just as Carson was saying he was sorry. "Oh, no, I am. I thought you'd done it on purpose," she said just as he did it again.

"Maybe we should just quit while you've still got one good foot," Carson suggested. "I never was much for dancing."

After feeling the weight of Carson Maddigan pressing down on her foot a third time, she didn't have to wonder why not.

"Sure you don't want to just call it quits?" he asked her. "Cut your losses and let that Phelps kid give you a turn?"

"I've danced with Gideon," Berris said as she adroitly avoided yet another assault on her toes. "I think I'll survive."

"Then you wanna keep on dancing?" he asked, sounding more surprised than disappointed.

Heck and healing bunions she wanted to continue

being whirled around the floor in Carson's arms, the envy of every woman in the hall. "I think you're getting it right, now," she lied, trying to match his erratic steps and save her aching feet. She'd pay for this tomorrow, but oh, for tonight, it was heaven.

That was until she saw her sister-in-law in the arms of Slevin Waynick.

"He sure doesn't wait for the milk to spoil," she said in disgust. "Gideon hasn't been gone five minutes and he's got his arms all over Arliss."

Carson swung her around, and rather gracefully, too, to have himself a look. "She doesn't seem to be enjoying herself much," he said. "We could go rescue her and switch partners if you like." There was just a hint of teasing in his voice. As if he knew just how much she wanted to dance with him.

"If you'd prefer," she said, noticing that Carson had stopped stepping on her toes. "You seem to have gotten the hang of it now. You probably won't maim Arliss for life."

He tripped on her left foot. "I'd hate to run the risk of hurting her in her delicate condition. Especially what with that baby as important as it is to your brother, who I might add, is a lot bigger than I am."

"Suit yourself," she said, raising one shoulder as if she truly, honestly didn't give a huckleberry whether or not his breath kept ruffling the top of her hair and making her dizzy with excitement.

He pulled her a little closer to him and whirled them about several times, sending Berris's skirts in circles around them. "You are one game woman," he said, keeping time so perfectly to the music it was like he'd been born on a dance floor.

She lifted her skirt slightly and kicked his left shin with all her might. "And you? How game are you?" she asked ready to stomp away when he stopped dancing and grabbed at his leg.

"A match made in hell," he said with a laugh, grabbing her arm and twirling her body back against his.

"I'm sure you've got more experience there than I do," she said, her blood coursing through her veins and setting every part of her to tingling.

Another man might have told her she was pretty, or light on her feet, or patient beyond measure. Carson had called her "game." And it was better than any namby-pamby thing Johnny Phelps had ever said. It was better than any man had ever told any woman.

"Most women would have worn a bonnet," Carson said.

"I'm not most women," she replied.

"It only takes one," he said softly, his movements perfect, his words warm on her temples, his hand firm against her back as he turned her again and again.

"Some people need more than one," she said with a sigh. "At least my sister-in-law seems to."

Carson turned his head. "She was always one to flirt with danger, and in a town like Granite, Slick's about as dangerous as they come."

"I don't know what he ever came back to this town for anyway," Berris said. "It was always too small for his plans."

"That was before," Carson said. "What I can't figure is how he expects to get her away from Gideon. Why would your brother give up Arliss and her money now?"

This time it was Berris who tripped over Carson's feet. If he hadn't had a strong grip on her, she'd have fallen clear over. "What money?"

"Arliss's inheritance from that grandfather of hers. From what I heard it could be as much as a hundred thousand dollars."

"A hundred thous—" Berris shrieked and Carson put his hand over her mouth.

"Keep it down will you? I was told in the strictest confidence," Carson said, eyeing Slick and grimacing.

"Who told you?" Berris demanded. "And what makes you think Slick knows?"

"He's back, isn't he?" Carson asked. "It was all over Virginia City that Alaric Flynn was leaving his fortune to some long lost heir."

"Alaric Flynn?" Berris asked.

"Honora Flynn Mallard's father," Carson said as if it clarified everything. And Berris supposed it did.

"Arliss is going to be rich?" Berris asked. "Won't Gideon be surprised!"

Carson was slow to answer. "Will he?" he finally said.

"Of course he will," Berris said. "Gideon is nothing like Slick. He's loved Arliss since he was old enough to know the difference between boys and girls. He's looked out for her, taken care of her . . . he's the best thing that ever happened to Arliss Mallard, and that includes her inheritance!"

"Well, maybe you just better tell her that, Berris honey, 'cause right now she's holding onto Slick like he's the papa bear."

She sure was a fool, believing Slick when he said he wouldn't be at the ball. If she hadn't been terrified of the scene he could make, she'd never have agreed to even this one dance.

But it was clear it had been a mistake. It was the only thing that was clear as Slick whispered in her ear and the room spun around her.

"Do you know what it's like for me, Arliss, knowing you're lying in another man's bed? How it cuts me in the gut to think that there's someone else for you when there'll never be anyone else for me?"

"Could you stop?" she asked, trying to focus on one point to keep her balance and losing the point every time Slick turned.

"You don't want to hear it," he said, "but truth is that I don't think I can go on without you, Arliss honey. Loving you the way I do, worrying about you and the baby, I can't just step aside and let Gideon Forbes have everything that belongs to me."

"Stop," she said, her voice ringing like a bell inside her head. "I can't . . ."

"Holding you tight like this, I just wanna take you home and—"

"Excuse me," someone said, and Arliss fought to focus on his face. Carson Maddigan? Was it Carson Maddigan tapping Slick on the shoulder? "I think it might be time to—Lord have mercy! She's white as a sheet!"

Arliss was glad to stop dancing, but disappointed that the room continued to spin without any help from her.

"She's going to faint again!" Berris gasped.

Ah! Now she recognized the feeling. She tried to nod, but her head was so heavy she couldn't get it back up.

And then she was being carried through the hot smelly room that reeked from cigars and sweat. And someone was telling her to just hang on, and she was trying to.

"Put her down here," Berris said at the same time that Arliss felt a welcome rush of cool air.

Very gently she was lowered into a chair. Then, much more brusquely, her head was forced down to her knees.

"Take a deep breath," someone said, but with her

skirts pressed against her face she was lucky to get any air at all.

"Why didn't you say something?" It was Slick's voice that cut through the haze. "Am I supposed to know everything?"

"We'd settle for you knowing where the train station is," Berris said before leaning her head down near Arliss's own. "You all right?"

She nodded, pushing against a strong hand. "Don't get him mad, Berris," she pleaded. She hadn't been nice to him this long to have him open up his mouth now and ruin everything for her and Gideon. "Please let me up."

"You're sure?" Carson Maddigan asked.

"I just needed some cool air."

"As opposed to the hot air you were no doubt hearing," Berris added.

"Maybe I ought to just take you on home," Slick said. "It's getting late anyway and you ought to be getting your rest now. Taking care of that baby."

"Oh, now you're going to pretend you care about her baby?" Berris demanded. "Don't you mean her money?"

"Berris!" Carson said, a note of warning in his voice, but it was too late.

"You know about the money?" Arliss asked Berris. "You're better at this busybody business than I thought. How in the world could you already know?"

"The same way that Slick knows," Berris said. "Or at least that was how Carson found out."

"I don't know what you're talking about," Slick piped up suddenly, when the truth was written clear across his face in dollar signs.

"You come straight from Virginia City?" Carson

asked and received only a shrug in return. "Figured you did."

Well, she surely should have known, not that it made a lick of difference. "So you come back here, telling me you love me and can't live without me and getting Gideon's hackles all raised, and all this time you were just counting my money?"

"It ain't *your* money," Slick said. "It's the baby's."

"Berris, could you get me some water?" she asked quickly. "I'm feeling woozy again."

Berris started to say something about Slick getting it, but Carson seemed to realize that she needed a minute with Slick alone and took Berris's arm. "You get her a drink and I'll get our coats. I think we better see Mrs. Forbes home."

"Thank you," Arliss said softly. Her eyes met Carson's, and he winked.

"Won't be a moment," he warned Slick.

"I don't want to ever see you again," Arliss said when she was alone with Slick again on the Grange Hall porch. She pulled the necklace off, not caring if she broke the clasp, and slipped the earrings from her ears. She placed them in a pile on the arm of the chair. As though she'd already gotten her inheritance, as though Gideon had already come back to her, as if nothing could hurt her anymore, she rose and looked at the shell of the man she had once believed she loved, before she knew what that word really, truly meant. "I don't want to see you or hear from you or know you're alive."

"The money belongs to the baby, Arliss," he hissed at her. "And the baby belongs to me. And I'm not going to let Gideon Forbes have what's mine just because he found out sooner than I did that your grandfather was getting ready to push up daisies."

"Gideon doesn't know about the money." She arched her back and came slowly to her feet, testing them.

"No?" Slick said, watching her carefully but keeping his hands to himself. "Why do you suppose he married you in the first place?"

# Chapter Twenty-five

GIDEON SAT IN THE KITCHEN OF HIS FATHER'S house with a hot cup of coffee, watching the sun rise. Nothing could have salvaged the night he'd had except coming back to Arliss's house and finding Carson Maddigan's note tacked to her door. *Deputy Forbes—Arliss is at your place with your sister. Signed, Carson Maddigan*

In his opera boots he'd tiptoed into the room they had shared and watched her sleep to make sure that she was all right. He imagined that after the baby was born he'd tiptoe in to check on him, too, just to make sure that the child was breathing. He'd tucked the blanket up around her chin and then, too fidgety to sleep after the events of the evening, he'd gone back downstairs to sit with Cluny and his father.

"I take back every damn thing I said, Gideon," his father was saying just as Lissie came through the door. "Your way is the right way. Slow and steady. That's for sure."

"Come and sit," Gideon said, rising and pulling out a chair for Lis. "I'll get you a cup of warm milk."

"I'll get it," Cluny said, rising up like a jack-in-the-box. "But first I gotta tell you about Gideon, Arliss. You should have seen him. First he took on the guards, tellin' 'em they'd be in jail before the first shot was fired if they just dared to raise their rifles! Then, when they put 'em down and the miners picked up their axes, he told them they'd have to go through him! And he—"

"Just get her some milk," Gideon said. "And Lissie, you tell us what we missed at the ball."

"Oh, you didn't miss much," she said. "Berris got to dance with Carson Maddigan, though, and she looked brighter than a firecracker in his arms!"

"Chew-ey! I bet she liked that," Cluny said. "What about Sassafras Harper? She dance with anyone?"

Lissie raised an eyebrow. It matched his own. "Sassafras Harper? I'm afraid I didn't notice," she admitted. "But then I did leave kind of early."

"You all right?" Thaddeus asked. In his eyes were all the events of the night. In his hands, which fiddled nervously with the spoon to his coffee, was one incident in particular.

"Got a little light-headed, was all," she said. "Are you all right, Sheriff Forbes?"

"Nearly killed my own son," he said, choking on his words. "Lifted my gun and aimed right into that crowd. . . ."

"He had no business being in the midst of that crowd," Gideon said, wishing his father would do some yelling at Cluny so that things could go back to normal. "And I hope it's a lesson he doesn't have to learn twice."

"You should have seen him, Arliss," Cluny started in again, holding his hand up as if there was a picture she could see. "Standing there alone and taller than all the rest of them, tellin' 'em that the mine made widows aplenty and that what they were doing would only add to the misery of it all. Tellin' 'em that money was only one of their grievances and they ought to get 'em all out on the table and addressed.

"And all in that dandy suit of his," Cluny added, shaking his head like Gideon had parted the Red Sea with Moses' own staff.

"That suit must have cost you a lot," she said, studying her coffee so that it was clear to Gideon she had something else entirely on her mind. "And the boots and hat."

"Some," he agreed. What was she fishing for? What it was worth to him to impress her? There wasn't a number he could put on that.

"Everything go all right up at the mine?" Berris asked, coming into the kitchen in her robe and slippers.

"Gideon was like the whole cavalry, stomping up the hill to save the troops from certain slaughter," Cluny said. In the next rendition, he'd likely turn Gideon into a saint.

"Well, Pa and I just explained the consequences of any action that anybody up there might happen to be thinking of taking," Gideon explained.

"Not me," his pa said. "I wasn't even listening, or I'd a thought about the consequences of my own actions."

"Did anyone get hurt?" Lissie asked and he was quick to tell her no.

"Then let's just put last night behind us," she suggested.

"Did something happen last night I ought to know about?" Gideon asked when a look passed between his sister and his wife.

"Oh," Berris said, kicking her leg about idly. "I found out a few interesting things . . . like why Slevin Waynick decided to come back to Granite."

Gideon felt the hairs on the back of his neck start crawling. He took a sip of his coffee and tasted turp.

Lissie was staring at him, reading his thoughts, passing judgment. He stood and stretched. "Guess we better get ourselves ready for church. Plenty of time to go over last night another day."

She followed him out of the kitchen and let him lead the way up the stairs. When they got to the bedroom door, he opened it and she went in and busied herself with her ball gown.

"I'll have to go back to Pa's house on the way to church," she said. "I came straight here last night without bringing a Sunday dress."

"I'll just change my shirt," he said, not looking her in the eye.

"I gave Slick back the necklace," she said. "And the earrings."

He nodded. "You dance with him?" he asked, looking in his drawers for the shirt he wanted.

"Yes."

"Close?"

"I got a belly that makes standing across a room close now," she said.

He didn't smile.

All night she'd told herself that Slick had to be wrong. That Gideon didn't know, that he wasn't cut from the same cloth. Botheration, the man wasn't simply Slick Waynick in the more-for-less economy size. She crossed her fingers and said a silent prayer, then fussed with her gown as if what she had to say meant nothing at all. "He came back for my money."

"Well, he ain't getting it."

Not *what money?* Not *that's a good laugh.* Not *you mean your father's house?*

"The letter from the lawyer says according to the

sheriff in Granite I'm the only surviving child of Honora Flynn Mallard. Are you that sheriff?"

"I'm the one that answers the inquiries," he said, slamming drawers and fighting with his buttons. "You gonna accuse me of marrying you for your money now?"

"Depends," she said, gathering up her gown to get dressed down the hall. "How long ago did you find out?"

"Long enough," he said softly, turning around to look at her and stroke her face.

She backed up from his touch while her whole body begged to be held, stroked, cosseted from the truth. "How long would that be?" she asked, knowing the answer in her heart but needing to hear him say it.

"Two days before we were married, I got a letter from Virgil Keker asking about any surviving issue from the marriage of Honora Flynn to Marcus Mallard. Said he was inquiring on behalf of his client, Alaric Flynn," he said.

"And?"

"And nothing. I wrote him back and said that would be you. It didn't take a giant leap to figure out why a man's lawyer was looking for heirs."

"And then?" she asked. "I don't believe that you beat up Slick and ran him out of town."

"You don't?" he asked. "You aren't softening now, are you Arliss? Thinking that I might have a decent bone in this big body of mine?"

"You tried to make him come to the church, didn't you?" she asked.

He nodded softly.

"But you didn't tell him about the money, did you?" she asked, fingering the silk gown in her hands and tracing the beads with her pointer.

Gideon's smile was slow and sad. He shook his head, the gesture admitting that he could have and had chosen not to. "Would he have left if I did?"

She let him walk her home, but he knew before she said it that she wouldn't be accompanying him to church.

"I need to do more thinking than praying," she said at the door to her father's house. "You go on without me."

"Do what you gotta do, Arliss," he said. "But the truth is that I wouldn't want you to be married to a man you couldn't trust."

He left her with tears in her eyes, turning before his resolve weakened, before he fell at her feet and explained away everything and begged her to love him.

He kicked at the mounds of snow on his way down the path he'd cleared to her house, wondering why he even wanted her to love him anymore. Why he couldn't just cut her loose and let the wind take her where it would.

He kicked snow from her house to his, ruining his opera boots and forgoing church. He needed time alone, time to say good-bye to all the dreams in his heart.

But he'd come to the wrong place. Instead of being in church, where they belonged, Berris and Cluny and Pa were all around the kitchen table. They went silent when he walked in, so it wasn't hard to guess that he'd been the topic of conversation.

"I guess Reverend Lambert didn't have much to say?" Berris asked.

"Or did he give you time off for good behavior?" Cluny added.

"Lissie decided to rest a bit and I . . ." He didn't

know what lie to tack on, so instead of finishing his thought he just grabbed a mug and filled it with the hot cocoa that was waiting by the stove.

"Why didn't you bring her back here to rest?" his father asked.

He hadn't any answer so he just stood there looking at his family and wondering if this was his future, here in this kitchen, with his sad, widowed pa and his green-haired sister.

"Is it over?" Berris asked. "Between the two of you? Has she finished torturing you now?"

"It can't be over," Pa said. "There's a baby coming, a house being built. This is just a pebble in the road, this trouble between the two of them. She'll see the light— you watch."

"I hope it is done," Berris said. "I hope she's out of your life for good, Gideon. You deserve a woman who'll make you happy, not tear up your insides the way she's been doing."

"Why not just shoot the sun from the sky, Ber?" he asked. "Why not just take all my breath away, 'cause I sure don't need it anymore."

"Gideon, there are other women," Berris began, pushing out his chair with her foot so he could sit. "Women who would love you. Women worth your love."

"Arliss loves Gideon," Cluny said, banging his fist on the table for emphasis. "She gets a look in her eyes, all soft and misty, every time he walks in the room. If a woman got a look like that for me, I'd move mountains."

"Sometimes there's another mountain just behind the first one," Gideon said, lowering himself into his chair. "And another one behind that one, too."

"So that's it then?" Cluny asked, the boy's eyes all wide and hard.

"Let him be, Cluny. How much does he have to put up with? How much do you expect him to stand? He shouldn't have to pay for a moment's weakness with the rest of his life," Berris added.

"Seems to me Arliss is paying for it. And the child," Pa said.

"Well," Cluny said. "It's his baby, his wife, and it's not like he could let her just waltz out of his life even if he wanted to."

"Do you want to?" Berris asked him. "Because if you do—"

"No, I don't want to. I don't want her waltzing anywhere but in my arms, so Berris you can stop cheering about the best part of my life being over, all right?"

"Arliss is hardly the best part of your life," Berris began, but he cut her off.

"Berris, you don't know squat about it, or about her. You ain't watched her paste a smile on her face and make the best of things that would have you under your comforter for a week. You ain't felt the warmth of her smile spread through you. You ain't slipped your arms through a shirt she'd made to surprise you and watched the hope in her face that you'd like it. You ain't heard her sweep away your fears in the middle of the night or include you in the prayers she mumbles before she falls asleep."

"Yes, but Gideon she's—"

"Do you know anything about a couple of new quilts that go up to Coppertown every fall? Or that the curtains I saw in Getz's little shack look just like the ones that used to hang in Lissie's front parlor? You know that nearly every home I went through that night up there had a fancy stitched tablecloth all covered with flowers?"

"Well, I—" Berris began, but Gideon was rolling on greased tracks now and there was no stopping him. This was his Arliss they were talking about, and they didn't even know her.

"You even know these things were going on? 'Cause I sure didn't. I didn't even know there was a need, and all this time she was fillin' it. The miners ain't nothing more to her than they are to us, but what have we done, cushy and comfy here in this nice house?"

"You make her sound perfect," Berris said softly. "But—"

"Hell, Berris, if you had to be perfect to be loved, there'd be little hope for most of us," he said. He looked her up and down, sighed, and added, "and no hope at all for some of us."

Cluny didn't bother stiffling his laugh. "And anyways, Arliss is perfect—"

"No, she ain't," Gideon admitted. "I never thought she was. I love her because of some of her faults, and in spite of the others. She ain't perfect, and neither am I, but somehow it felt like together we could be."

They were all silent.

"So then what are you doing here, son?" his father asked. "A woman makes you feel like that, you don't leave her alone in her father's old house."

"It's what she wants, Pa."

"So that's it?" Cluny asked. "You're just gonna throw up your hands and let her call the shots? What'd you tell all the men in Coppertown, Gideon? That they got wants and Belmont got wants and that they was gonna have to bargain to somewhere in the middle, right?"

"You suggesting Lissie and I live somewhere between our two houses? In the Grange Hall, maybe? I

don't think that's gonna solve the problems we got between us." Gideon stood up and looked down at his
ruined boots, the wet snow leaving white lines on the
black leather.

"I'm saying what she wants isn't more important
than—"

A long, low whistle rattled the dishes in the cabinets.
Two more bursts followed, and before they were done
Gideon was headed out the door, Cluny and Pa bun-
dling into their jackets and following hard on his heels.

Smoke gushed from the hill like a smoldering fire
and spired up to mix with dark clouds.

"Cave-in," Pa whispered.

Cluny's face was ashen and Gideon hoped he was
wrong. There'd been a lot of careless talk about blowing
up the Columbia when neither side wanted to give an
inch. Gideon had to wonder as he ran toward the hill if
this was where the night of bargaining had gotten them
all.

# Chapter Twenty-six

M EN WERE IDIOTS, BERRIS THOUGHT AS SHE SHUF-
fled through the snow toward Arliss's house.
Of course, women were idiots, too. And any-
one who had the incredible stupidity to fall in love, well,
there was a special level of idiot reserved for them.

But the stupidest, most asinine, most moronic, idi-
otic, imbecilic of them all, she was quite sure, were the
dummies who couldn't even see that they were in love,
and consequently risked throwing such a precious gift
away.

And that was exactly what she planned to tell Arliss
Mallard-Forbes, her sister-in-law for life, whether she
liked it or not. Nobody, nobody was going to throw
Gideon's love away as long as Berris was around to look
after him.

She rapped on the door twice, her gloves muffling
the sound of her frustration before she just threw open
the door and barged on in. She was not going to stand
on ceremony now. Not when she had an apology to get
out of the way and a marriage to save.

"I'm here!" she shouted as she closed the door behind her and pulled at the buttons on her coat. "Don't
bother hiding, I'll find you!"

"I'm not hiding," Arliss said, coming down the front hallway with a pile of cloth in her arms. Oh dandy. St. Arliss was striking again. "Unless of course, you were expecting to find Slick here, and you were calling him."

"Don't put words in my mouth Arliss. There's no room," she said. "I'm not accusing you of anything anymore."

Arliss raised an eyebrow. "Now that I'm rich?" she asked.

"Heck and honeycombs, Arliss, I swear I don't know how Gideon puts up with you," Berris said, offended to the core. "But my brother seems to think that you walk on water, and anybody who'd turn away that kind of love, for anyone, let alone for Slevin Waynick—" She wanted to say "deserves him," but she was there to plead her brother's case, not hang his wife.

"Look Berris," Arliss said reaching for her cloak by the door. "I really have to get going. There are people that are going to need help and comfort and—"

"You're going up to the Columbia?" Berris asked. The women in town never went up to the mine. It was their job to wait for the men to come back, feed them, patch them up, and send them back to help some more. "Are you going to dig them all out yourself, in your condition?"

"Berris, why are you here?" she asked, heading back to the kitchen and making Berris trail after her like a puppy while she assembled a basket of groceries.

"I came to tell you that Gideon loves you and you have to love him back," she said as Arliss dashed around her. "And that I'm sorry."

"For what?" Arliss stopped what she was doing and looked straight at her, an open expression that Berris imagined would appeal to a man like Gideon. Yes, looking at Arliss through Gideon's eyes, if she squinted and imagined, she could even see the spark that Gideon saw.

"For selling you short, for making trouble, for—"

"Hating me?" Arliss asked, the hurt shining in her eyes.

Berris could even see now why Gideon called her Lissie, her body looking soft, her cheeks rounding out a bit, her hair fighting the bun she'd tried to confine it to.

"I never hated you," she tried saying, but even she didn't believe it. "Well, maybe I did, but I don't anymore. Not that it matters. Lissie, Gideon loves you . . ."

"Really?" Arliss said, looking more annoyed than anything else. "You'd never know it, going back home to live, keeping secrets from me, never, not ever, saying he even liked me, never mind loved me."

"Maybe you aren't listening," Berris said, handing Arliss the tin she was reaching for across the table. "What were those stupid bananas, if not love? What's the house, the caring? What about the new gold ring?"

"What gold ring?" Lissie asked.

Berris blushed to her green roots. "I think that was supposed to be a surprise . . ."

"If he loves me, Berris, why has he never said so?"

"Love isn't something you say, Arliss. It's something you do. You want words, you've got the wrong man. Empty promises and easy words aren't his department. You want love, then let Gideon love you. And if you want to know why he was up at Lilac Row, ask him."

Lissie looked at the copper band on her finger, the one that Berris knew was really from Slick. "Will you come up to Coppertown with me so I don't have to make two trips?" she asked, pretending that they weren't even talking about Gideon cheating on her like she thought he was.

"Is there another basket?" Berris asked, gathering up the platters of food that seemed to cover every surface in the kitchen as if Arliss had always been preparing for just such an emergency.

"I've got one upstairs." She hurried from the room while Berris wrapped all manner of baked goods in the little flowered cloths that waited in a pile. *Did you know that every house in Coppertown has a flowered cloth?* she thought, fingering the delicate stitching before she heard the thumping in the hall.

"Arliss?" she called out. "You drop something?"

There was no answer from upstairs and she moved closer to the door to the hall.

"Arliss?" she shouted again, needles crawling over her skin as she inched her way out into the hall.

Arliss lay halfway up the steps, the pile of cloth she'd had earlier surrounding her. She didn't move.

Silently, like she didn't want to wake her, Berris tiptoed closer until she could lean over and brush the hair from Lissie's tortured face.

"It hurts," Lissie whispered, her hand so tight around the stair spindle that her knuckles were white. "Oh, God, it hurts!"

Somehow Berris managed to get her to the couch, but Lissie knew it was all over. She felt a wetness between her thighs and a pain that cut through her back like a hundred buggy whips.

"I thought I'd just take the cloth up with me," she told Berris, struggling to speak around the pain. "Save myself an extra trip."

"I should have gone for the basket," Berris answered.

"My boot got caught in my hem," she said, tears

coming even though she forbid them. "I shouldn't lose this baby because my boot got caught in my hem."

"You're not going to lose this baby," Berris said, squeezing her hand. "It would break Gideon's heart if you did."

She couldn't talk with the hot poker that seared her lower back and she prayed through it before she said, "You know it isn't Gideon's baby."

"I didn't say it was," Berris said, still holding her hand, still stroking her head. "But it will break his heart all the same."

"I'm bleeding, Berris. Bleeding bad. You better go for Doc Agrin."

Berris looked around the room as if someone would magically appear. "The doc must be up at the mine," she said. "And I don't want to leave you alone."

"I need help," she said, sure that another pain would rip her apart and leave her dead.

Berris piled pillows beneath her feet and knees. Then she covered her with a blanket and kissed her forehead the way Gideon would. Oh, but she would give the world for Gideon's strong arms now. "I'm just going to run next door and find someone who can get you help, then I'll be right back. Will you be all right for just a minute or two?"

She nodded, unable to speak as the pain increased. "Oh, baby," she said once she was alone. "I'm so sorry. Mommy didn't lift her skirts and now—I'm so sorry."

Two pains later Berris was back. "She's in there," Lissie heard her say. "Just help me get her upstairs and then you better go."

"Why is she in the parlor?"

Lissie threw her arm over her eyes and groaned. How fitting that Slick should be there when it was all too late.

"I don't suppose that you can carry her yourself," Berris said.

"You get her under one arm," Slick said. "And I'll get the other. We can't let her lose this baby."

"Baby didn't mean much to you five months ago," Lissie managed to say, but it cost her. She yelled out in pain and dug her nails into her palms.

"I made a mistake," he said. "I panicked. You gonna punish me for that forever?"

"Maybe you two could argue about this later?" Berris suggested, helping Lissie sit up and putting an arm beneath her shoulder.

"I can't make it upstairs," Lissie said, but they didn't listen to her as they both lifted her up, ready to drag her to the steps.

"Oh, shit!" Slick said. "She's bleeding. Arliss don't you go and lose this baby now. I can't be losing this—"

"I wish Gideon broke more than your nose," Lissie got out through gritted teeth. "I wish he broke your whole damn head."

"And a couple of other parts," Berris added.

"Yeah, that," Lissie said before the sharp pain froze her where she was. "Wait! Don't move me."

"We gotta get a doctor," Slick said.

Had she really ever believed she loved this man? Had she really willingly given herself to him because the moon was full and his eyes were blue and he knew how to promise her the world?

"Didn't you hear the whistle?" Berris asked.

"Think you can get her upstairs yourself?" Slick asked, putting her hand firmly on the bannister and easing out from beneath her shoulder. "I'll get that Clovis woman."

"Go," Berris said as if hurrying him out would make

any difference. As if Hedda Clovis would make any difference either.

Berris had never seen so much blood. There was a pool of it on the sofa, a trail of it led up the stairs. It was on Berris's clothes from helping Lissie out of her dress, and it was seeping through the rags faster than they could get them beneath Lissie's body.

All through the long and awful night, after Slick had deserted them for the Lord only knew what, Hedda had stayed and held both their hands. She'd been a godsend, and Berris swore she would never make fun of the old woman again. She boiled rags, she wiped Lissie clean over and over again, and most importantly she calmed Lissie down.

"Women lose babies all the time," she said, running a cool rag over Lissie's brow. "The trick is to live to have more. And that's what we're gonna make sure of. We're gonna make you a mama ten times over."

Lissie swung her head back and forth. "Never again," she said, grabbing at the bedsheets and clutching them in her fists.

"Again and again," Hedda assured her. "You're young and you're strong and you've got a good man, not like your mama."

"Mrs. Clovis," Berris said softly, hoping to spare her sister-in-law one indignity at least. "I don't think Arliss wants to hear about her mother right now."

"Your pa told you about her?" Hedda asked Lissie. "Tell you how it come to be him and Honey that got you?"

Arliss shook her head.

"What a lovely woman she was, your mama," Hedda said. While she spoke she checked under the sheets and shook her head at Berris. It was all but over, it seemed.

"So much bad luck in one family. Losing her husband and then coming down with Miner's Lung."

"Her husband?" Lissie's writhing stopped. "My mama was married when I was born?"

"Widowed by then," Hedda said, reaching for more clean cloths. By now they were using the piles of fabric Lissie seemed to have stored all over the house. "Your pa was killed by an explosion at the Columbia. Same one that took my Mac. Left her with nothing. Couldn't even afford the doctor when her time was coming close."

Lissie moaned and arched her back off the bed. Hedda pressed down against Lissie's stomach and told her to push, motioning for Berris to take over pressing against Lissie's stomach while she moved to the foot of the bed.

Lissie's cry was like the siren from the mine—loud and sad and too late.

"It's over now, honey," Hedda told her, wrapping up in a little pink towel a tiny mass that Berris supposed was her niece or nephew.

"It hurts," Lissie moaned, arching again.

"That's it. It's over." Hedda slipped some fresh cloths under Lissie, whisking away the evidence that there had ever been a baby in Lissie's womb. She tucked the covers down around Lissie tightly. "You rest now," she told her, and Berris watched the teardrops track from beneath Lissie's closed eyes down the sides of her face.

# Chapter Twenty-seven

⚜

GIDEON PULLED HIMSELF UP MARCUS MALLARD'S front steps, leaning heavily on the railing. Four men, all Danes who didn't know the first thing about explosives but needed the work bad enough to risk everything, had lost their lives, pulled from the wreckage along with eight survivors. He stamped the dirt from the mine, the snow, the death, from his legs and boots and knocked.

Berris, her eyes red and puffy, opened the door. In her hand was a rag that appeared to be smeared with blood. "Oh Gideon!" She covered her mouth with her free hand and stared at him with wide, hollow eyes.

"No," was all he could say, falling to his knees and shouting toward the sky. "No, no, no!" All those last vivid memories of his mother lying in a pool of blood came tumbling in on him like a second cave-in. "Not Lissie. Not my Lissie."

"Ssh," Berris said, falling to her knees beside him. "She's resting now. Hedda says she'll be all right."

Gideon stared at the rag in Berris's hands, then at the floor where she'd obviously been cleaning.

"She lost the baby. It was all my fault. She was going upstairs for a basket and carrying things and I should have stopped her." Tears flowed freely down Berris's cheeks and she swatted at them with the back of her hand.

"I'm sure she doesn't blame you," Gideon said, squeezing her arm and then lumbering slowly to his feet. "Will she see me?"

"She's real weak, Gideon. You might want to wait a while."

"That you Deputy Forbes?" Hedda called down, standing in the doorway of Marcus Mallard's bedroom. "You best come on up."

Gideon took the steps two at a time.

"She's lost a lot of blood, but she's young and strong. All she needs is a good reason to hold on," Hedda told him, and Gideon could only nod and try his best to swallow his pain.

He came into the room slowly, staring at her small form lying in her father's big bed. She was pale as the bedsheets, and her eyes were closed. There was no relief for him that Slick had no ties to her now. There was only the overwhelming sadness at losing something that was a part of her, and he swiped at his own cheek before coming to stand beside the bed.

Hedda scrambled in, looked over Lissie's spent body, and patted her arm gently. There was no response. "I'll just get these things out of here," she said, reaching for a basket full of rags so bloody it was hard for Gideon to breathe.

"There's just one thing," she said, motioning for Gideon to come away from Lissie. He went by the door and bent to hear her whisper, "You gonna bury the child? Or should I just . . ."

"The child will have a proper burial," he said. "I'll see to it."

"I'll clean her up then," Hedda said, carefully taking

a small package wrapped in a soft pink towel from the top of the dresser.

"Was it . . . what was it?" he asked when he could get the words out of his clogged throat.

"Little girl," Hedda said. "Ten fingers and toes, tiny as you please, but all there."

Gideon leaned his forehead against the wall and let the tears flow. A little Lissie, who he had already begun to love.

"There'll be others," Hedda said softly. "All the babies the two of you could want."

Ten babies wouldn't make losing this one any easier.

"Gideon?" Lissie's voice was barely a whisper. "Is that you?"

"It's me," he said, coming to lean over her, taking her little hand in his big one.

"Guess you're free now, huh?" she asked, each word an effort.

"Before you go tossing me on my ear, Mrs. Forbes," he said, "there's something you ought to know. Something Slick wasn't counting on even if all this hadn't happened. Your grandpa's will reads the natural child of Honora Flynn's natural child. You ain't gettin' one red cent from the old man."

Her eyes drifted open and then fell shut again. "Well then all your reasons for marrying me are gone. No baby and no money."

"I didn't marry you for your baby, and I didn't marry you for your money, Arliss," he said, shaking his head.

"No?"

"No."

"Why then?" she pried her eyes open and stared at him, a pathetic creature who looked more beautiful than he imagined any woman ever looked, even after all she'd been through.

"Because . . . because I love you. I've loved you forever and I'll keep on loving you forever."

Tears filled her eyes, but he didn't think they were from sadness with the wonderful smile that played at her tired lips.

"I've been awful to you," she said quietly. "I've accused you of everything under the sun and I—"

"I still love you," he said, sitting down on the bed beside her.

"I let Slick give me that necklace to make you jealous and I—"

"I still love you," he repeated.

"I don't see how you could," she said with the deepest, saddest sigh.

"It isn't all that easy," he admitted.

"You think it's easy loving you?" she asked.

"Loving me?" he asked. "I imagine it's damn near impossible, but I ain't askin'—"

"Damn near," she agreed, a smile curling one side of her pretty little mouth. "You think a woman doesn't need to hear that she's loved and she's doing all right by someone that really means it?"

"I mean it, Lissie."

"Well, that makes it easier."

He stretched out on the bed beside her. "Would it be all right if I held you—just real gentle-like?"

"That'd make it even easier," she said, raising her head up for him to snake his arm beneath her head. "I do love you, Gideon, a real and abiding love."

He'd never been good with words, and even now, at the most important moment of his life, they failed him. But Lissie didn't seem to need them. She just burrowed softly against him, her sad sigh breaking the silence.

"I'm so sorry we lost our little girl," he said, his hand

running up and down her arm. "I'm just so grateful that we didn't lose you."

"Truth is, Gideon Forbes, if I could leave something half as wonderful as you behind, it'd be worth dying for."

"Ssh!" he scolded her, not able to get out more than that for a while. Finally, when he'd swallowed enough tears for a lesser man to drown in, he said, "We'll have more babies, Lissie, I promise."

She nodded against his arm.

"I'll give you all the babies you want."

"I'm glad," she said sleepily, a weak arm falling across his chest. "But not tonight, all right?"

He held the laugh inside him, not wanting to disturb her sleep. The last few months they'd been to hell and back, but now, with Lissie by his side, it felt as if they'd finally found heaven.

He kissed his fingers and put the kiss on her forehead. "To dream on," he whispered closing his own eyes and welcoming sleep.

# Epilogue

LISSIE WAS STANDING IN THEIR NEW KITCHEN CUT-
ting slices of cake and handing Berris the plates
to pass out when Gideon snuck up behind her.

"Baby's sleeping like a cub in winter," he said, having been upstairs to check on their new daughter more
times than Lissie had licked her icing-coated fingers.
He waited for Berris to leave the room and then grumbled against her ear, "Do you suppose they'll ever
leave?" his words warming her insides as well as her
ear.

"No one's going to leave until the bride and groom
do," she grumbled right back, feeling the heady rush of
promise run up her spine and make her dizzy.
"Couldn't you just tell your father it's time to take Miss
Kelly on home?"

Gideon pressed his body up against her back, reaching over her shoulder to pretend that it was cake he was
after. "Not unless you want him to know why," he said
and she felt his hardness pressing against her. "I ain't in
any condition to leave this room. You go tell Miss Kelly
to take Pa home—you know, woman-to-woman."

"Tell her that the party she's been waiting for all her
years is over and she should leave because my husband

wants to take me on upstairs?" She turned and found herself safely in Gideon's embrace. Her breasts were full and aching, despite having nursed their new daughter just minutes ago, and she braced herself against Gideon, protecting them.

Gideon took a step back, reluctantly giving her more space. "We don't gotta—" he began.

She put a finger, speckled with the chocolate icing, up against his lips. "We gotta," she said, her voice husky, the want undisguised. "Or I might just burst."

"You, too? Lissie, I swear this has been the longest seven weeks of my life." He took her finger into his mouth and closed his eyes in a mixture of pleasure and pain.

"Plus the two before Addie was born," Lissie added, reminding him of how they'd had to restrain themselves because of her condition. This morning, when she was sure that her bleeding had ended, she told him she was ready to be his wife again, to lie beneath him the way she'd been able to before the baby had made her too vulnerable and she'd had to take her place atop him.

Not that they both hadn't enjoyed that, too. Not that at the moment she wouldn't let him take her right on the kitchen table if the house weren't full of her husband's family and several friends.

And as eager as she was, he was even more so. What with losing her figure, with dripping milk from her breasts and with diapers drowning them, it felt better than good to have him hungry for her. It felt like heaven.

"I'm gonna tell everyone you're getting tired," he said, gently pressing her bottom against him until he was nearly lost in her skirts. He smiled wickedly. "I'll tell 'em it's time I got you into bed."

"Well, I'll just go into the kitchen and get some more cake," Berris announced loudly from the doorway.

With a groan, Gideon backed up and busied himself at the sink, his back to Berris.

"Sorry, you two," she giggled. "It seems like lately I'm always interrupting you! Everyone's loving the cake, Lissie. Naturally, I'm taking credit."

Lissie smiled. Berris had helped with the cake, and her cooking had certainly improved since Lissie had returned all the labels to their proper jars and given her a few pointers, as well.

"And Carson asked for a second helping," she said, unable to hide the pride and excitement in her voice.

"Doesn't he have to go kill someone today?" Gideon asked his sister. "It's been a good few days since he's gone hunting scalps."

"Don't mind your brother," Lissie said, pushing two plates at Berris and aiming her for the door. "He's mad at everyone today."

"Carson Maddigan in my house," Gideon huffed, shifting his stance and shaking out a leg. "Why'd you ever agree to make this party anyways? Juliana coulda done it and we coulda left early and—"

"We'll be lucky if Juliana doesn't wind up delivering in our bed this afternoon, she's so ready to pop," Lissie argued.

"Bite your tongue, woman!" Gideon said, drying his hands on a fancy flowered towel and folding it beside the sink with care. "I'm checking on Addie one more time and then I'm sending everyone on home." He looked out the kitchen window and let out a big humph.

"Let him be," Lissie said gently. "He's just showing her what's left of my garden."

Gideon humphed again. "Since when does Cluny care about your roses?"

"Since Sassafras Harper said they were the prettiest flowers in all of Granite, and couldn't he cut just one for her," Lissie said, batting her eyelashes and mimicking the girl's breathy voice.

"I suppose he's telling her he did all the planting," Gideon drawled.

"I'm guessing he's told her he raised them from little bitty seeds," Lissie said, coming up to look out the window with Gideon.

"Roses don't come from seeds," Gideon said, having planted the bushes himself under her direction.

"You think he knows, or that she cares?" Lissie asked, watching young love bloom along with the last of the roses. Cluny reached out and brushed the hair off Sassy Harper's cheek, leaving his arm hanging over her shoulder. The two bent their heads together, pretending they were studying the flowers.

"Party's over," Gideon declared. "I can't wait any more."

Lissie reached up on her toes and kissed her husband softly on the cheek. "I'll tell Miss Kelly I'm tired," she whispered. "You go bring the ladies' wraps down from upstairs."

He smiled at her, that wonderful dimple of his just begging to be explored. "I'll just peek in on Addie and be right on down."

"You do that," Lissie said, finding it hard to breathe at the thought of being alone with Gideon once everyone was gone.

"Let me help you," Gideon said, reaching out and unbuttoning Lissie's shirtwaist. She closed her eyes and a satisfied little smile played on her lips.

"Oh, God, Lissie!" he whispered, trying to drag in a breath as he stared at her breasts, heavy with milk, blue veins crisscrossing white skin. He jammed his fists up into his armpits to keep from touching her, knowing that she was tender and not wanting to hurt her. "Oh, God!"

She took one of his hands and gently guided it until it cupped her. Her head tipped back, her eyes closed, her mouth opened and the tip of her tongue played with her upper lip.

He was undone. It took all the effort he could muster not to fling himself on her and bury himself deep where he belonged.

"I wanna go easy, Lis," he struggled to get out, but she was working at his buttons, pushing the shirt from his shoulders, fumbling with his waistband and breathing hard.

"Yeah, easy," she agreed, backing up to the bed and fighting with his trousers while he searched for the strings to her skirts. "Easy," she nodded, pushing away his hands and undoing her ties herself in one quick motion.

Her skirt fell to the floor. Her petticoat followed it.

He stepped out of his pants, letting them tangle with her clothes in a heap as he shed his drawers and stood naked in front of her.

She eased her fancy embroidered intimates down over her hips.

"I haven't gotten my figure back yet," she said, suddenly shy in front of him after the months he'd watched her grow and change with his child inside her. "But I will, Gideon. I'll—"

He lifted her up and laid her gently on their bed, lying beside her and cupping with one hand the small belly she had as a reminder of what their love had made. "This is not a figure a man minds," he said, inching up to her breasts with just a finger touching her. "Not this man."

He lowered his head and gently placed a kiss on the tip of her nose, her chin, her neck. And then, heaven help him, he traced with his tongue a path to one breast and took it lightly between his lips. One small tear of milk escaped her and he tasted the sweetness that nourished their daughter. He looked up at her, amazed, and licked the corner of his lip.

"Oh, Gideon, I'm sorry! Sometimes it just—" she began before he dipped his head back down and nuzzled against her with his mouth, running his tongue over her nipple.

She arched and grabbed for him. There would be no teasing tonight, no slow building to one special moment. The special moment they both wanted was already at hand and he slid into the place that was his alone.

Coming home.

Love was more than he'd hoped for with Lissie, more than he'd dreamed.

In the quiet afterglow, her body tucked up against his, while they lay still and expectant, waiting for a cry from their daughter, he argued with himself, just as he had in that early time in their marriage before Lissie had come to love him.

"Got a sheriff's report from Coeur d'Alene," he said in the darkness. "Slick's been arrested up there."

Next to him, Lissie fussed and he reached over her, found her chemise, and helped her wiggle into it.

"Cold?" he asked, tucking his ma's wedding ring quilt up around her shoulders.

"What did he get arrested for?" she asked. Her cold feet climbed his legs until he parted them and took her feet between his thighs, unsure whether it was her interest in Slick or her cold feet which sent a chill up his back.

"Fraud. From the looks of it he sold someone an interest in a mine he didn't own."

She nodded against him. "That'd be our Slick," she said sleepily, cold fingers burrowing into his armpits.

"You ever think about him, Lis?" he asked, steeling himself for her answer.

"Every now and then," she admitted in a small voice. "But it's the strangest thing. When I remember things, it's as if it was always you and me, and that Slick was just around, too. I remember you pulling me out of Flint Creek, and I know Slick was there. He was the one who took me out on the river in the first place, but somehow I can't see him with us in my memory. I remember the night Slick left me at the Miner's Ball and you walked me home and caught me when I tripped over the log. I know in my head that you and I weren't in love then, but in my heart . . . oh, Gideon, in my heart there's only room for you."

For a moment he thought his heart had stopped beating, the clutch in his chest was so great. Only his daughter's plaintive cry could tear him from their bed.

"Room for only you and Addie," she said with a laugh, throwing back the covers and starting the search for her slippers.

"You keep those feet under the blankets," he warned her. "I'll get her."

He had the baby wrapped up in a blanket and smelling fresh and sweet when he laid her down in the crook of Lissie's arm. He climbed under the covers himself, sandwiching the baby between them. In the soft light of a million stars he watched his wife bare her breast and offer it to their baby, and could tell from the stiffening of Lissie's body the moment the baby latched on. A tiny fist pushed against Lissie's chest before Adoration Forbes got down to the serious business of draining her mama dry.

He watched the whole process, fascinated that love could produce this miracle, that his love alone had brought a miniature Lissie into the world. When she was done, her mama's nipple slipped silently from her lips and she lay there contented and ready to be returned to her cradle.

Gideon eased off the bed and reached down for his daughter. With the little blanket wrapped tightly around the baby, Lissie touched her lips to Addie's forehead.

"A kiss to dream on," she whispered softly, handing the baby up to Gideon.

"And one for her mama," Gideon added, kissing Lissie's brow as he bent over his girls.

"What about you?" Lissie asked him as he straightened up. "Don't you want a kiss to dream on, too?"

He looked down at his wife, stretching and settling down to sleep, her eyes already beginning to close, a slight smile touching the corners of her mouth. "Don't need it," he whispered, clutching Adoration to his chest. "I've got everything I ever dreamed of already."

# If you are
# *Wishing For More*
## Stephanie Mittman's
## two FULL-LENGTH NOVELS
## are just what you need!

"Stephanie Mittman might very well be
the standard against which all future
Americana romance is judged.
**Five Stars!"**
—*Affaire de Coeur*

**The best of American romance."**
—*Romantic Times*

\_\_\_\_\_ 22181-1 THE COURTSHIP $5.99

\_\_\_\_\_ 22180-3 SWEETER THAN WINE $5.50

\_\_\_\_\_ 22182-X THE MARRIAGE BED $5.50

Available wherever books are sold or use this handy page for ordering:

**DELL READERS SERVICE, DEPT. DSM**
2451 South Wolf Road, Des Plaines, IL 60018

**Dell** Please send me the above title(s). I am enclosing $_____.
(Please add $2.50 per order to cover shipping and handling.)
Send check or money order - no cash or C.O.Ds please.

Ms./Mrs./Mr._____

Address_____

City/State_____ Zip_____

Prices and availability subject to change without notice.
Please allow four to six weeks for delivery.                    DSM-9/97

# HARLEQUIN

## *Presents.*

Next month, look out for Kelly Hunter's Harlequin Presents
debut! Her sinful Claimed by a King quartet stars four
powerful rulers, dedicated to duty—until they meet the
only women to threaten their iron resolve! In *Shock Heir for
the Crown Prince*, Anastasia kept their child a secret. Now
Casimir will make her his royal queen...

Prince Casimir of Byzenmaach can't shake the memory of Anastasia
Douglas. With her, he forgot his royal duties in a moment of wild
abandon. Seven years later, he must wed—but in seeking out the
unforgettable Anastasia, he discovers a secret: she gave birth to his
daughter! And he'll stop at nothing to claim them both...

*Shock Heir for the Crown Prince*

Available February 2018!

**King Theodosius must find a queen—so he offers Princess
Moriana an initiation in the pleasures of the marriage bed...**

*Convenient Bride for the King*

Available March 2018!

And look for Augustus of Arun's and Valentine of Thallasia's stories

Coming soon!

he'd fallen for a sexy French girl the summer after boarding school. It wasn't until summer ended that his father had gleefully revealed that Melice had actually been a prostitute, bought and paid for all the time. *I did it for your own good, boy. All that weak-minded yearning over love was getting on my nerves. Now you know what all women are after— money. You're welcome.*

Ares's bodyguard closed the car door behind him with a bang, causing him to jump.

"Sir? Are you there?"

Turning his attention back to his assistant on the phone, Ares said grimly, "Give me her phone number."

Two minutes later, as his driver pulled the sedan smoothly down the street, merging into Paris's evening traffic, Ares listened to the phone ring and ring. Why didn't Ruby answer?

When he'd left Star Valley, he'd thought he could forget her.

Instead, he'd endured four and a half months of painful celibacy, since his traitorous body didn't want any other woman. He couldn't forget the soft curves of Ruby's body, her sweet mouth like sin. She hadn't wanted his money. She'd been insulted by his offer. She'd told him never to call her again.

And now…

She was pregnant. With his baby.

He sat up straight as the phone was finally answered.

"Hello?"

*Don't miss*
*CLAIMING HIS NINE-MONTH CONSEQUENCE,*
*available February 2018 wherever*
*Harlequin Presents® books and ebooks are sold.*

www.Harlequin.com

*She succumbed to his sinful seduction…*
*Now she's carrying the Greek's baby!*

It's the last thing he wanted, but Greek billionaire
*Ares Kourakis is going to be a father. He'll do his duty*
*and keep pregnant Ruby by his side—he'll even marry*
*her. But will his offer of intense passion and a vast*
*fortune be enough to get idealistic Ruby down the aisle?*

Read on for a sneak preview of
**Jennie Lucas**'s next story,
*CLAIMING HIS NINE-MONTH CONSEQUENCE*

*One Night With Consequences*

Ruby.

Pregnant.

Impossible. She couldn't be. They'd used protection.

He could still remember how he'd felt when he'd kissed
her. When he'd heard her soft sigh of surrender. How she'd
shuddered, crying out with pleasure in his arms. How he'd
done the same.

And she'd been a virgin. He'd never been anyone's first
lover. Ares had lost his virginity at eighteen, a relatively
late age compared to his friends, but growing up as he had,
he'd idealistically wanted to wait for love. And he had, until

# Get 2 Free Books,
## Plus 2 Free Gifts—

### just for trying the *Reader Service!*

HP17R3

### #3597 THE GREEK'S ULTIMATE CONQUEST
by Kim Lawrence

Grief-struck Nik Latsis found oblivion with a stunning stranger.
Since then, Chloe's haunted his dreams. Only another taste will rid
him of his desire, but first Nik must entice feisty Chloe back into
his bed...

### #3598 A PROPOSAL TO SECURE HIS VENGEANCE
by Kate Walker

Imogen O'Sullivan is horrified when Raoul breaks up her
engagement and makes her his own convenient bride—he's
planning a passionate punishment for their stormy past! Can
Imogen resist Raoul's delicious revenge?

### #3599 REDEMPTION OF A RUTHLESS BILLIONAIRE
by Lucy Ellis

Nik Voronov is ferociously protective of his grandfather. When he
believes Sybella Parminter is taking advantage, he strips her of
her job! But unexpected desire soon threatens to consume them
both...

### #3600 SHOCK HEIR FOR THE CROWN PRINCE
*Claimed by a King*
by Kelly Hunter

Prince Casimir never forgot his wild nights of abandon with
Anastasia Douglas. Years later, he discovers she had his daughter!
And he'll stop at nothing to claim them both...

---

# Dani Collins

---

## PRINCE'S SON OF SCANDAL

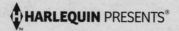
**HARLEQUIN** PRESENTS®

Recycling programs
for this product may
not exist in your area.

ISBN-13: 978-1-335-41901-9

Prince's Son of Scandal

First North American publication 2017

Copyright © 2017 by Dani Collins

**Printed in U.S.A.**

www.Harlequin.com

Canadian **Dani Collins** knew in high school that she wanted to write romance for a living. Twenty-five years later, after marrying her high school sweetheart, having two kids with him, working at several generic office jobs and submitting countless manuscripts, she got The Call. Her first Harlequin novel won the Reviewers' Choice Award for Best First in Series from *RT Book Reviews*. She now works in her own office, writing romance.

### Books by Dani Collins

#### Harlequin Presents

*The Secret Beneath the Veil*
*Bought by Her Italian Boss*
*Vows of Revenge*
*Seduced into the Greek's World*
*The Russian's Acquisition*

#### *The Sauveterre Siblings*

*Pursued by the Desert Prince*
*His Mistress with Two Secrets*
*Bound by the Millionaire's Ring*

#### *The Secret Billionaires*

*Xenakis's Convenient Bride*

#### *The Wrong Heirs*

*The Marriage He Must Keep*
*The Consequence He Must Claim*

#### *Seven Sexy Sins*

*The Sheikh's Sinful Seduction*

Visit the Author Profile page
at Harlequin.com for more titles.

Back in 2012, I received a call—*the call*—from editor Megan Haslam, telling me she wanted to buy my book. It was my first sale and terribly exciting. I have since worked with some of the other fabulous editors in the London office, but with *Prince's Son of Scandal*, I came back to working with Megan. I'd gone so far down a rabbit hole with Trella in the first three books of this quartet, I really wasn't sure I could pull off her story. Megan offered just the right feedback to help me make it work. We're reunited and it feels so good!

I'd also like to dedicate this book to you, dear reader, for your wonderful letters and support for The Sauveterre Siblings. I'm so glad you love these characters as much as I do. xo

# CHAPTER ONE

*Six months ago...*

WHEN THE GREETER at the ballroom entrance asked Trella Sauveterre for her name, she nearly gave an arrogant "you know who I am."

She bit it back. Her sister was never acerbic. Not with strangers, and definitely not with underlings. Her twin was perfectly capable of terse words and might even hurl some blue ones at Trella when she learned what she was doing right now, but Angelique's personality was one of sensitivity and empathy. Gentleness and kindness.

Trella? Not so much.

"Angelique Sauveterre," Trella lied, wearing her sister's polite yet reserved smile. She ought to feel more guilty. She ought to feel like an overused cliché from a children's movie, but she didn't.

She felt *alive*.

And apprehensive. Terror could overcome her if she let herself dig deep enough. This was like swimming toward the middle of a lake, where the bottom was too

deep to imagine. Who knew what dangers lurked in those dark watery depths? Monsters. They existed. She had met them. Had nearly been consumed by them.

But she wouldn't think about that.

Nothing in her outward appearance revealed the way her heart bounced and jostled in her chest, fighting internal battles. She moved gracefully, even though her muscles felt stiff and petrified, twitching to run.

Because, along with the trickles of fear, a tumbling waterfall of joy rang through her. It was all she could do to keep tears from her eyes or laughter from escaping her throat.

*I'm doing it!* she wanted to call her family and cry. *Look. I'm in public. By myself. I'm not shriveling like a vampire in the sun.*

But they didn't know where she was and it was best to keep it that way. This was the sort of sneaking out a window she should have done years ago, when she'd been an adolescent. Instead, she'd been a grieving survivor with an eating disorder and more baggage than a passenger jet.

Still was, if these people only knew.

She quashed the negative self-talk and moved like a normal person through the crowd. Gazes lingered, noting Angelique Sauveterre had arrived. Her bodyguard kept anyone from approaching, though. Maybe that wasn't normal for everyone, but it was for the Sauveterre twins, even the eldest set of brothers.

With her sister's aloof nod, she returned a few greetings to people she imagined she was supposed to know.

In a few weeks, she would come out as Trella and

have nothing left to hide behind. No more walls, literal or technical. No broad-shouldered brothers. No playing her sister to avoid being herself. She had determined, had sworn on the blood she had shed when she nicked her ear cutting her own hair before Christmas, that this was the year she would free herself from the prison she had created.

For now, she was still hiding behind Angelique. She had impersonated her sister a few times recently, with her sister's permission, escorted by their brother Henri to watch his twin, Ramon, race. They'd also taken in a fellow designer's latest collection during fashion week. It had been spectator stuff where they didn't interact with anyone and kept to places her sister had been seen with their brothers before.

Trella had never walked out in public alone. In her entire life, she had rarely done anything alone. As a child, Angelique—Gili to her family—had been the needy one and Trella, the protector. She had held Gili's hand so her sister wouldn't tremble and cry at the attention they had received. Their brothers had barely given them breathing space even before Trella's kidnapping at age nine, always ready to catch a tumble from a swing or to keep them from wandering too far from the group.

Then she'd been stolen and had *wished* that her captors had left her alone.

She swallowed and veered her mind away from those memories. They were guaranteed to bring on an attack and she was doing far too well. It was coming up to two years without one.

The attacks had manifested years after her rescue,

when she should have been finding her feet and moving on with her life. Instead, she had become a horrible burden. Her siblings would never say so, but they had to be sick of being on call for her. She was certainly tired of being the weakest link. She *had* to change.

Tonight was another step toward that. The press would go mad when she finally came out of seclusion at a friend's wedding in a few weeks. She had to be ready, but she had to *know* she was ready.

So she was testing herself, if somewhat impulsively, because this charity dinner hadn't been on her agenda at all when she had arrived in Paris.

She had been beside herself with pride when she'd landed, high on travelling from the family home in Spain—by private jet with trusted guards, always—but without her mother or siblings. It had taken her newfound independence to the next level.

So, when Gili tentatively had asked if she could run to London for a hot secret weekend with her new paramour, *of course* Trella had told her to go. Her sister had looked incandescent when she'd spoken about Prince Kasim. He was clearly something special.

Trella wanted her sister to be happy, wanted to quit holding her back. Spending a night alone at their tightly secured living space above their design house, Maison des Jumeaux, had seemed a perfect cherry on top of Trella's already sweet split from old fears.

As the evening stretched on, however, she had restlessly poked around the flat, picking up after her sister and teetering on feeling sorry for herself. Wistfulness had closed around her.

Would *she* ever have a romantic liaison? Her feelings about men were so ambivalent. At fourteen, she'd had the usual rush of hormonal interest, even shared an embrace with the gardener's son behind a rosebush. Then their father had died and the most terrifying predators had emerged online, threatening her in vile ways. Her fear of men, of *everything*, had compounded a hundredfold. As her panic attacks escalated, the deepest fear of all had crept into her very soul—that she was so damaged and broken, no one would ever want her.

For years, she had barely allowed men near her, interesting or otherwise. She slipped from one secured location to another through shielded walkways, accompanied by a mostly female guard detail. Occasionally, her brothers introduced her to a friend, but even if she had wanted any of those bankers or race-car drivers to make a pass, Ramon and Henri wouldn't have allowed it.

Their dearest family friend, Sadiq, was the only man she'd spent real time with and theirs had never been a romantic relationship. He was the shy, heart-of-gold computer nerd who had helped the police locate her, returning her to her family. She loved him, but as her savior, not as a man.

Which was why his engagement had shaken her out of her ivory tower. She would do anything for Sadiq. If he wanted her at his wedding, of course she would attend, even though it meant overcoming her demons and returning to the public eye.

It had been a struggle to come this far, but now, as

she stood on the cusp of achieving something like a normal life, she found herself resetting the goalposts.

She wanted her sister's anticipation for a weekend with a man. She wanted to be the person she would have been if she hadn't been stolen and assaulted, stalked and bullied, but it would never happen if she kept living behind these damned walls!

A disgusted toss of the latest fashion magazines onto the coffee table had sent a pile of paperwork sliding to the floor, revealing an invitation to this ball.

The fundraiser benefited orphaned children, something that would go straight to Gili's tender heart. Even if Gili had sent regrets, the Sauveterre checkbook was always welcome.

Not letting herself overthink it, Trella had briefed a security team and slipped on one of her sister's creations.

Where Trella loved powerful touches like strong shoulders and A-lines, along with eye-catching beadwork and bold colors, her sister's style was gentler. The champagne gown had a waifish quality in the way the sleeves fell off her shoulders. The bodice and torso were fitted to her figure, but the ruched skirt across her hips created a sensual impression of gathered satin sheets around a nude form.

She added her sister's earrings and a locket with a panic button, but kept the look simple, arranging her hair into a fall of dark locks and painting her lips a soft pink.

Now she was here, breathless and petrified, yet filled with more optimism than she'd experienced in years.

She moved to speak to the aloof Russian host and his much warmer British wife, Aleksy and Clair Dmitriev.

"I'm so glad you came," Clair said, drawing her aside in a confiding way that revealed Clair had no idea she was talking to Gili's twin. "You're not my only supporter who comes without a date, but you're the only one who won't be silly about my guest of honor. Don't even ask how I got him here. I was hideously shameless, interrupting their trade talks and putting him on the spot in front of everyone. I talked him into auctioning himself for the first dance."

Trella scanned for a glimpse of this exalted personality. Clair continued her confession as she wound them through the crowd.

"Aleksy said at least I use my power for good instead of evil, but I feel a little evil because the ravens surrounded him the minute he arrived. They'll back off if you're there, though. I know you'll put him at ease. Everyone loves you. Do you mind?"

Trella could see how Clair got what she wanted, sounding sincere in her flattery as she took agreement for granted. Still, she was curious enough to murmur, *"Bien sûr,"* in her sister's preferred French.

Clair beamed and gently pushed into the thicket of gowns.

The mystery man turned, revealing a red sash beneath his black tuxedo jacket. He was tall. Intimidatingly tall, with broad shoulders and an economy of movement, suggesting a huntsman's physique lurked beneath his sophisticated attire. The blond glints in

his light brown hair looked natural, given the hint of gold in his eyebrows.

*Those eyes.* They were such a piercing blue they struck like slabs off a glacier, peeling away to fall and rock the world. The rest of his features were precisely carved in sweeps of long cheeks under sharp cheekbones, a jaw hammered square and a mouth of two perfectly symmetrical peaks over a full but uncompromising bottom lip.

He was so compelling a force, so beyond her experience, the room faded from her consciousness. They became trapped in a noiseless, airless bubble as they took each other in.

Had she really longed to be seen as a woman? Because it was happening. He skimmed his gaze down in unabashed assessment. She saw the flash of interest in his gaze as it came back and locked with hers. He liked what he saw.

He saw Gili, though. Sweet Gili who was used to being in public, where men routinely sized her up as a potential conquest.

The strangest reaction slithered through Trella. She ought to have prickled with threat, or acted like Gili and let his male interest drift past her as if she didn't notice or care.

Instead, she took issue with her sister being seen as a trophy. Protective instincts honed since birth pushed her confrontational personality to the forefront of the image she presented.

*You'll have to go through me*, she projected, tucking Gili safely behind her.

His stare intensified. *Burned.* He saw *her.* Whatever shields she had walked in here holding—including her sister's persona—were gone. She felt completely unprotected against his thorough exploration of her face, his gaze touching each curve and dip of her features.

It felt like a spill of magic, making her cheeks tingle. She had to disguise a rush of unprecedented sensual awareness. Men didn't affect her, but the spell he cast sent invisible sensations from her throat to her nipples and her pelvis, into her thighs and terminated in a paralysis that nailed her feet to the floor. All the while, delicious stirrings swirled upward through her, making her feel drawn toward him.

"Your Highness," she heard Clair say from what seemed like another universe. "Have you met Angelique Sauveterre?"

"Ms. Sauveterre, the Crown Prince of Elazar, Xavier Deunoro."

Xavier had known exactly what he was doing when Clair Dmitriev had cornered him into making an appearance at her charity event. He was buying a future favor from her powerful husband, a man who was notoriously difficult to influence.

He had also known it would be an evening rife with what he had before him: Women in daring gowns, swishing their hips in enticement, sweeping lashes in false shyness while they twisted their hair in invitation.

As Europe's most eligible bachelor, he was used to having his pick from such an array. He only needed to

drop a claw and let it pick up one of the brightly colored toys before him. It didn't matter which one fell into his hands. They were all the same, providing brief entertainment and something soft to embrace for a night, before forgetting them in the hotel room when he left the next morning.

Given the news he had received this morning, tonight's plaything would be his last before his royal duty took precedence. It was another reason he had agreed to this ridiculousness. At least he had a decent selection for his final visit to the amusement park.

He was taking his time singling out his companion. They all had their charms. Was he in the mood for voluptuous or fair? Should he be practical and choose the one wearing enough gold not to covet his own? Or go with the one who promised some spark as she set her chin and glared at the rest?

Then his hostess presented a newcomer like a gift, one who made the rest of the women take sharp little breaths and step back.

She was taller than most, with divine features that matched her name. Her skin was soft and flushed, too warm to be called cream yet not dark enough to be olive. Golden as a sunrise glancing off a snowy peak.

A muse, clearly, since he felt poetic stirrings just by gazing at her. How could he not admire her? Her figure was goddess-perfect, her mouth sinful, her eyes fey and mysterious, colored somewhere between gray and green. If he pulled her from the cloud of perfume surrounding them, he bet she would smell like mossy forest and clean cold streams.

That was what she presented on the surface, at least. In a blink, she had shifted ever so slightly and it was as if she'd hit exactly the right angle to catch and reflect the sun. Something less tangible than external beauty seemed to concentrate and strike out in a sharp white light that pierced his eyes, like a star being born.

She was the diamond in a bowl of imitations, a woman of facets and contrasts, infinitely fascinating and priceless. If recognizing that caused him a stab of regret because he didn't have time to fully explore her depths and contradictions, he ignored it. Such was his life. He took what he could, when he could.

Tonight, he would take her, *grazie mille*.

"Good evening." He bowed over her hand, letting his breath warm her knuckles and feeling the tiny flex of her reaction. "It's an honor to meet you."

"A rare treat indeed." The tilt of her lips suggested an inside joke. "The honor is mine."

"I've seated you at the VIP table," Clair said. "Please find your way when you're ready. Has everyone seen the silent auction items?" Clair broke up the knot of disgruntled women, most of whom drifted off.

A few opportunists remained, one being the redhead with the determined chin. He sighed inwardly as the redhead flashed a too sweet smile before asking, "Angelique, how is your sister? Still keeping to herself?"

Ah yes. That's why the name had struck him as familiar. The family had a tragic history. One of the twin girls had been kidnapped as a child. She was

rumored to be batty, so they kept her out of sight. As someone who had been reported as everything from born of an alien to outright dead, he put little store in such gossip, but did wonder how she would respond to such a blatant intrusion. It was clearly meant to disconcert.

She swung a scythe-sharp glance at the redhead, revealing the compressed carbon beneath her sparkle.

"She's excellent." Her tone struck him as ironic. "What's your name? I'll tell her you were asking about her."

"Oh." The redhead was startled, but flicked him a glance and decided to take a final stab at snaring his interest. "*Lady* Wanda Graves."

"I'll be sure you're added to our list." She smiled distantly and turned to him. "Shall we find our seats?"

She didn't see the redhead brighten briefly before a darker thought struck, one that tightened her mouth. The other women who'd been standing by widened their eyes then averted their gazes before they scurried off.

He offered his arm and dipped his mouth to her ear. "You have a blacklist?"

"Nosy people do not wear our label."

Catty, ruthless, or both? Either way, he was entertained.

And now he was reminded that the sisters had some kind of design house. Women's fashion was last on his list of interests, but he took a fresh assessment of her gown, appreciating the peek of thigh exposed by the

slit and the gather of strapless satin that left an expanse of upper chest and breast swell to admire.

"This is one of your creations? It's pure artistry."

"I can tell when I'm being patronized," she warned.

"Then you'll know I'm sincere when I say the dress is lovely, but I see the woman inside it. Which is the point, is it not?"

"Do you?" She tilted a considering look up at him, something dancing in the elfin green of her eyes. He could have sworn they were gray a minute ago. Her gaze dropped to his chest, where the band of silk slashed across his heart. "I see the crown, not the man. Which is what this is meant to convey, isn't it?"

Astute, but a woman who made her living with clothing would understand such nuances.

The sash in question felt unaccountably restrictive this evening. Duty hovered in his periphery, set there by a brief news item passed along from his PA about Bonnafete, a small principality in the Mediterranean. The reigning prince's daughter, Patrizia, had called off her marriage to an American real estate mogul.

Patrizia was a longtime acquaintance. Xavier was not as sorry as he had implied when he had sent his condolences. He was in need of a titled wife. His grandmother wanted him married so she could step down. Patrizia was infinitely suitable.

He had asked that his grandmother be made aware of the broken engagement. It was an acknowledgement of his responsibility toward her, their bloodline and the crown. Loath as he was to marry, he preferred to spearhead such actions himself, rather than wait for her to

issue orders. She might be the one person on this earth
with the power to govern his actions, but he didn't have
to encourage it. He was confident she would approve
and God knew she would let him know if she didn't.

"Is it heavy?" his final sown oat asked of his sash.
The levelness in her tone told him she didn't mean
physically, proving she was even more perceptive than
he'd imagined.

Compassion was not something he looked for in
anyone, though, least of all his temporary compan-
ions. There was no room for any weakness in his life.
No one saw him flinch. No one was privy to his bitterness at the hand life had dealt him.

It was a wasted emotion to feel.

So he ignored the chance she might understand him
in a way no one else ever had and held her chair. "Nothing could weigh me down while I'm in your beguiling
company, *bella*."

She froze and looked over her shoulder. "Why did
you call me that?"

"It's an endearment. Elazar's official language is an
Italian dialect, though French and German are com-
monly spoken along with English." He adjusted her
chair as she sank into it then leaned down to speak
against her hair where it fell in loose waves against
her nape. "Why? Don't you like it?"

Tiny bumps lifted on her skin in a shiver of reaction. Her nipples tightened into peaks against the silk
that draped over them, making him smile. She liked it.

Awash in more sexual anticipation than he'd felt in

a while, perhaps ever, he seated himself, pleased he would end his bachelorhood with such a terrific bang.

Trella was a natural extrovert. The chatter and color around her, the voices and music and attention, was like standing in the sunshine after years in an *oubliette*.

But to have this man glance at her with that admiring look on his face as he seated himself next to her was a deliciously sweet accompaniment. He was clearly an accomplished seducer, wearing charm and entitlement as comfortably as his sash, but she was excited to be singled out by him all the same. It was the flirtation she had yearned for.

"What brings you to Paris?" he asked.

Although, if she was going to do this, she wasn't settling for plain vanilla.

"Surely you can do better than asking what a nice girl like me is doing in a place like this?"

"Let me consult my app." He glanced at an imaginary phone. "How about… What sign are you?" He affected sincere interest.

Her mouth twitched. "Gemini. Twins. Obviously. You?"

"No idea. August sixth."

"Leo. The lion. King of the jungle."

"Obviously," he said, with a self-deprecating tilt of the corner of his mouth.

She bit back a smile, intrigued by his position, but only because she knew what it was to be in the spotlight. He'd glossed over her query about the weight of

his crown, but surely he wearied of attention and responsibility.

"You take horoscopes seriously?" he asked, nodding at a server who offered them champagne.

"Not as a belief system, but I used it as inspiration for a collection a few years ago. *We* used it," she amended quickly, clearing her throat over the white lie and sliding her gaze to ensure the people searching for their seats hadn't overheard her. It was well known in fashion circles that *Trella* had designed that particular line.

"How?" He seemed genuinely curious. "The patterns in the fabric?"

"Not that literal. More how the nature of each sign is perceived. They fall into different qualities, like fixed or mutable, and elements, like air and fire. There's a lot to play with. I work better with deadlines so I approached one sign a month. It was an interesting exercise." She leaned closer, wrinkling her nose. "Also a terrific marketing hook."

The corners of his mouth deepened. "Beauty *and* brains. Always an irresistible combination."

This prince, causing her heart to thud-thud under a simple compliment, should have sent her running. She had learned healthy caution from her childhood, but even though most men put her on edge, this one filled her with a giddy *lack* of fear. It was like breaking out of a shell. Like discovering she had the ability to fly.

She definitely wanted more time with him before this evening ended.

On impulse, she motioned for her guard, who was

actually one of Gili's, and quietly gave him an instruction about the silent auction. He melted away.

Was she being too forward? Reckless?

Their table filled up, forcing her to wait to find out. Dinner passed in a blur of neutral conversation. Someone asked the Prince about his country's foray into green energy. She vaguely recalled his mountain kingdom between Italy and Austria had been accused of providing a tax haven during the world wars. Elazar sounded very modern and self-sufficient now. He spoke about exporting hydropower, since rivers and streams were one of their few natural resources. There was also a decade of investing in education, attracting engineering and technology start-ups, solar and wind power.

Her inner businesswoman should have been taking mental notes, but she was mesmerized by his casual command over his audience and subtly seduced with how close his sleeve came to touching her arm. Beneath the table, she imagined she could feel the heat from his thigh mere inches from her own. All she could think about was dancing with him.

*Dancing.* Tears pressed the backs of her eyes. She ached for that simple pleasure.

This adolescent reaction was ridiculous, but she let it happen. Embraced it. This is what she should have been doing at twenty, not hand-sewing sequins on mini-dresses for other young women to wear to exclusive clubs, killing hours with concentrated work so she could get through one day, one more hour, without a breakdown or the drugs that were supposed to prevent them.

Then Prince Xavier turned his terrifically handsome face toward her, bathing her in the light of his regard. "You must travel a great deal for your work? What drew you to fashion?"

He had given each of the others a moment in his attentive sunlight. Now it was her turn. He must engage in small talk with a thousand people a day, at ribbon cuttings and children's hospitals, but she would have sworn on her life the tension around his eyes eased as he met her gaze. He'd been doing his duty, impatiently waiting to get back to her. She felt delirious even as she prevaricated her way through her reply.

"Both of us are quite creative." Gili more so. She was the artist who designed out of love and ran the business out of necessity. Trella was the ambitious one, determined to turn a healthy profit. Practicality, not passion, had driven her into making her own clothes, because she couldn't bear being judged by trolls for merely *buying* something, let alone how it looked on her.

"We had some start-up help from our brothers but surprised them and ourselves with our success." Another fib. She wouldn't have rested until they were making buckets of money. She was competitive and driven by an I'll-show-you desire for revenge against those who had thrown shade.

"It can't be an easy field. I'm sure your success is due to hard work as much as anything else."

He was trying to get her into bed. She knew that with the brains he'd said he admired, but his flattery *worked*. She was ridiculously affected by his compli-

ment. She wanted to say "It was a ton of work. Thank you for noticing." Gili was the face of Maison des Jumeaux, which meant she received the bulk of the credit—not that she didn't deserve a lot, but Trella worked just as hard and was not a naturally humble person. Hearing his praise went into her like a transfusion, tipping her further under his spell.

Their hostess moved to the podium to make a short speech, thanked the guests for their donations then announced the winners for the auction items. Trella grew increasingly self-conscious as the moments ticked down, certain she had truly lost her mind this time. Maybe she should leave before—

"Finally, our most coveted prize, a dance with the Prince of Elazar, has been won by... Angelique Sauveterre!"

The applause was polite, the knives in her back proverbial, but she felt them. She privately smirked, then blushed as Xavier showed no surprise. Was he so sure of her?

"I'm flattered."

"You should be. I promised to double the next highest bid. You had better dance well enough to be worth it."

"I do," he assured her, rising to help with her chair, doing that erotic thing of speaking against her hair so tingles raced all over her skin. "For that sort of generosity, *bella*, I'll give you the whole night."

Oh, he was good. Lightheadedness accosted her every time he called her *bella*, the same nickname her family called her. Her pulse pounded so hard she

thought it would bruise her throat, but it fed the thrilling excitement washing over her. He made her feel so alluring. *Sexy.*

He made her feel as though he wanted *her.*

That was beyond captivating. She had spent a lot of dark nights telling herself how flawed she was, how she didn't want men anyway, so she didn't care if they didn't want her. She did want, though. She wanted to feel normal and alive. Happy and desirable.

The touch of his hand on the small of her back had a terrific effect on her. The awareness that had been teasing her all evening became a suffusion of deeply sensual lethargy. Dear Lord, was she becoming *aroused*?

It was what she'd envied her sister for—which was when it struck her what was happening. She and Gili had a twin connection. They didn't read each other's thoughts or anything so intrusive, but they picked up hints of the other's emotions despite whatever physical distance might separate them. The preternatural sense was stronger on Gili's side. Trella had been so messed up for years, taking anti-depressants to quash anxiety attacks, she hadn't been as receptive to her sister's moods.

Lately, however, she'd become more aware, particularly if Gili was restless or having an off day. Tonight, her sister was with a man who truly excited her. She was usually so careful, so rarely selfish, yet she was basking in something that made her incredibly happy.

Her sister's buoyant heart lightened Trella's. She was happy for Gili, happy her sister wasn't weighed

down by all the things Trella had put her through. It added another lift of carefree joy to her own evening.

"You dance well yourself," Xavier said as he spun her in a waltz.

She was too exhilarated to respond. The sparkling ballroom circled around her in a kaleidoscope of colors. His embrace was confident and reassuring, making her feel light as a fairy.

"I feel like Cinderella." It was too true. She was the smudged sister who had escaped from the attic, wearing borrowed clothing to dance with a prince.

"You look like something out of a fairy tale." The line of his brow twitched and the corner of his mouth deepened, like he both surprised and disparaged himself for saying. "You're very beautiful," he added gruffly.

Gili was the beautiful one. Trella had fought hard to get back to the same weight as her sister, wanting to feel as good as Gili looked. She had let her hair grow out to her sister's length so she could impersonate her for her dry runs going out in public, but she never thought of herself as beautiful. She too often thought of herself as broken.

Not tonight. She diverted herself away from any thoughts other than how *glorious* this was. Around and around they went. His thighs brushed hers, his fingers splayed as though trying to touch more of her. She let her fingers trail closer to his collar so she could rest the side of one finger on the hot skin of his neck. It was electrifying. The magnetic sensations grew as he kept her dancing into the second song, tugging her

toward an unknown crescendo. When someone tried to cut in, Xavier shrugged him off.

"The privilege of position?" she teased.

"I've never seen anyone glow like you. I'm enthralled." Again, misgiving seemed to flicker like a shadow across his face. He didn't like admitting to whatever he was feeling, but it added to her own exuberance.

"I feel like... I can't even describe it. Like it's Christmas. Like anything is possible." She brought her gaze down from the chandelier into the turquoise blue of his eyes.

She reminded herself that becoming over-excited could have a rebound effect. She didn't want to backslide. It would be a long fall from this height.

Then she forgot any sense of caution when he said, "I need to kiss you." The desire in his words was a sensual squeeze that stole her breath.

A very long time ago, she had been quick to agree to anything that sounded adventurous. A dungeon full of shackles and bars had kept her grounded since then, but somehow, with a few words, this man reached past all the darkness and invited her into the light. To be the impulsive, audacious person she was in her heart.

"Me, too," she said through sensitized lips. *It's only a kiss.*

His sharp gaze moved beyond her. The next thing she knew, he had her off the dance floor, through a small break in the crowd and into an alcove hidden by the giant fronds of a potted plant.

She wasn't given time to decide whether she'd been

too quick to agree. His arm tightened across the small of her back, pulling her in, arching her against the layers of his tuxedo. He was steely beneath his civilized covering. He knew what he wanted. His hot mouth covered hers without hesitation.

For a second, she was terrified. Not of him, but of how she would react. Would she panic?

Then her senses took in the way his mouth fit against hers, moving to part her lips, questing for her response. Something primitive moved in her, shaking her foundations, waking the woman she might have been if her life had been different, drawing her beyond old traumas into a place she barely understood.

Pleasure flooded her, making her stiffen, wary of such a strong reaction, but primal need quickly took over. Her brain might not be able to process what was going on, but her body knew how to respond.

Rather than put the brakes on, her hands went behind his neck. She found herself running her fingers into his short hair, shaping the back of his head as she drew herself up, parting her lips so he could plunder at will.

His arms tightened around her and she thought he made a growling noise. It should have scared her. Male aggression, especially the sexual kind, was something she'd taken pains to avoid.

Strangely, with excitement pulsing through her, she found herself thrilled by his response. She kissed him back with abandon, just as if she knew what she was doing.

Something flashed behind her closed eyes and he abruptly lifted his head.

"That was a camera," he muttered, fingers digging in near her tailbone as he pressed her close enough to feel the thick shape straining the front of his trousers. "Let's find some privacy."

Her analytical mind urged caution, but her old self, her true self, trusted her instincts. She released a breathy, "Let's."

# CHAPTER TWO

HE DIPPED HIS head to lightly scrape his teeth against her neck, urging against her ear, "You leave first. I'll follow you upstairs."

She gasped, mind going blank before a million thoughts rushed in.

"You have a room here? In the hotel?" What had she thought when he had said *privacy*? Was the idea of being alone with him intriguing or alarming?

"The penthouse, yes."

"Is it safe?"

"Of course." Good gracious he was handsome, even when he frowned. His features weren't too refined. There was just enough toughness in the intensity of his gaze, just enough stubbornness in the square of his jaw to make him look stern and rugged.

As he read her hesitation, his hand cupped the side of her head while his gaze flicked with irritation at the noise around them. "I want you to myself."

Empathy panged within her. She knew the wear and tear that being in the spotlight took on a person. She instantly wanted to give him the break he needed.

He was a sophisticated man. She had nothing to fear from him physically, but was compelled to say, "I have guards. For a reason."

She was using her sister's tonight, both to give her own a much-deserved night off as well as to maintain the illusion she was her twin. *She should tell him who she was.*

"The room is completely secure. More secure than here," he added, mouth twisting in dismay at their having been photographed. He led her back to their table. "I won't keep you waiting long."

Voices of caution crowded into her head, but when would she have a free pass like this again? When would she meet a man who made her feel anything like this? It wasn't just physical, although that part was so heady she felt drunk, but there was a rarity, too. There were other men in the world who were a safe bet, men vetted by her brothers, but when would she feel this pull? This compulsion to know more about *this* man?

Before she talked herself out of it, she let her finger press *up* for the penthouse. It wasn't that she didn't have misgivings, or that she ignored them, she *overcame* them. It was different. It was another small triumph that had her stepping lightly off the elevator onto thickly carpeted floor.

It was easy to spot the Prince's room. Two guards were stationed outside the door. Her own accompanied her as she approached them.

"Mademoiselle Sauveterre," one greeted with a respectful nod. "We were notified to expect you."

He stepped inside and invited her guard to sweep the rooms.

Both men behaved with the utmost professionalism, not betraying a hint of judgment about what they must know was a preliminary for seduction.

A smile touched her mouth as she thought about how her brothers would blow their tops if they knew where she was right now, even though they had both been on the Prince's side of this equation hundreds of times, the hypocrites.

Then she was left alone and she took in the elegant shades of ivory and sage green on the walls and the furnishings. A glass of watered-down Scotch had been abandoned on an end table, ice long melted. She sniffed, then dared a sip, thought about looking at the view, then decided to leave the drapes closed.

The double doors to the bedroom stood open. She stared at the bed, taking another quick sip of liquid courage just as the main door opened. His star power impacted her anew, making her heart skip.

"You made yourself comfortable. Good."

"This is yours." She tilted the glass, then set it aside, instantly wishing she'd kept it to keep her hands busy.

"I'll make you a fresh one. Or, how about champagne?" He moved to the bar. As he peeled the foil from a bottle, the crinkle seemed overly loud.

This was the moment she should have admitted she was Trella.

A very real fear sat within that admission—that he would develop his own misgivings. He would either want explanations she didn't care to give, or he might

jump to conclusions that made him averse to being with her. In no scenario did she imagine this exciting, lighthearted atmosphere would continue.

"You're nervous," he noted as he popped the cork.

"You're observant," she said, compelled to at least confess, "I don't do this."

It was true no matter which twin she represented. Gili running away for a weekend with a prince was as out of character as her being here with this one.

"I already guessed that." He set two glasses as he poured, canting his head to eye her. "You're not a virgin, are you?"

She choked. "No."

True again for both twins, but she had to look away, mind skipping off the dark memory like a stone off the water's surface.

No, that was another reason she was here. Being alone with a man was another snapped link in the chain that bound her to the past. She was really, really proud of herself right now. Even though her proffered excuse of "I'm just out of my comfort zone" was the understatement of the year.

He brought the glasses across the room to her and offered her one. *"Saluti."*

*"Salud."*

They sipped, gazes locked, unspoken expectations hovering between them. Her throat grew abraded by the bubbles.

"What if I change my mind about being here?" she asked in a soft rasp.

"Then I will be disappointed." His intent expression didn't change.

"Angry?"

"Disappointed. Very disappointed, *bella*." His gaze acted like wildfire, igniting her blood as he swept it across her cheek and down her throat.

He turned away to set music playing. The notes were low and sultry, matching the thick feeling in her veins, the sensual throb of her pulse.

"Either way, I'm pleased to have you to myself." He came back to her, steps laconic, touch smooth and confident as he looped his arm around her. "Whether you want to talk or dance or…pass the time in other ways."

He swayed them into a dance that was really just the press of two bodies. Foreplay. They both still held their champagne flutes. Held gazes.

"I wasn't in the mood to fight other men for your attention."

"Was anyone else even trying? I hadn't noticed." She batted her lashes.

His mouth tilted. "I like that wit, *bella*. I find myself regretting we only have tonight."

She tucked her chin and gave him an admonishing look. "You're patronizing me again. I don't need the rules spelled out. I'm not *that* green."

"See? Such sharp intelligence is the sort of thing that holds my interest longer than a few hours."

"Is that how long your liaisons usually last?"

He stopped dancing, arm remaining across her back, but loosely. "That's probably not a good topic of conversation."

"I know." Bubbles tickled her nose as she sipped, trying to wash away a strange bitterness on her tongue. It shouldn't matter what his past looked like. Whatever man eventually attached himself to her wouldn't come to her pristine. She couldn't expect it when she had such a complicated history herself. "I think I'm looking for reasons not to like you so I won't feel so…"

She frowned. The hand she'd rested on his shoulder slid down to splay on his chest as if she had the right to touch him with such familiarity, but touching him felt very natural. Her fingertips dipped beneath the ribbon of red, sliding the tips of her polished nails beneath it as she ever so slightly lifted it off the crispness of his shirt.

"I'm not a pushover. I'm normally the most contrary person you could imagine. A fighter." Her family told her that all the time, so why was she letting this happen? Her usual streak of rebellion was absent.

Actually, she realized with a spark of insight, it was directed against the life she'd been leading, pushing her to break free of old restraints. No one was stopping her from spending a night with a man except her. All she had to do was *choose* to.

"I'm not trying to pressure you. I'm sincere that I wish we had more time to get to know one another, but my life has never allowed for long term relationships." His hand shifted to splay in a warm brand against her lower back, offering a soothing caress. "For what it's worth—" He bit the inside of his cheek, seeming to weigh what he was about to say. The shadow moved behind his eyes again, telling her that he was uncom-

fortable with how revealing his words were. "If you walked out of here right now, I wouldn't go looking for someone else. You're the only woman I want to be with tonight."

"Why?" It came out of her with a pang of disbelief. "Please don't say it's because you like the way I look." She didn't want him to want Gili. It would break her heart—it really would.

His breath came out in a soft snort of disbelief. "Because of the way we make each other feel."

He lowered his head to graze his damp lips along her jaw and down to her neck, making her shiver. Her nipples pulled tight so quickly they stung. He chuckled softly at the way she audibly caught her breath.

"We're positively volatile." His hot breath bathed her ear before his teeth lightly closed on her lobe, nearly causing her knees to buckle.

She pressed her hand more firmly to his chest.

"No?" He drew back, but held her close. Held her up, if she was honest.

"I'm trying to think," she gasped, nearly overwhelmed by sensations that were the furthest thing from fear.

"And you can't? Then we feel the same." His tight smile only made the edgy fist of need inside her clench harder. "Feel, *bella*. Feel how much you're exciting me." He moved her hand all the way under the sash, so the pound of his heart slammed into her palm. "This isn't anything I've ever experienced, either."

Her scalp tingled. She dropped her champagne glass, ignoring the delicate break of crystal, wanting

too badly to touch him with both hands. She slid her fingers to the back of his neck and raised her mouth, inviting him to kiss her. It was pure instinct and he didn't hesitate, covering her parted lips as though he'd been let off his leash after having been tempted for too long.

The world stopped then spun the other way, dizzying her. She made one whimpering noise, astonished by how thoroughly such a thing could devastate her, wilting all her muscles.

She distantly heard another delicate shatter, then he picked her up, lifting his head to reveal a fierce expression. Victory? Not quite, but there was something conquering there. Something exalted.

Yet his bright gaze asked a question.

She nodded, unable to speak, just gave herself up to it, to him. She knew when to fight her body and when to surrender. Perhaps it was the silver lining to all those years of having to accept that physiology trumped logic. This was bigger than anything she could make sense of.

He set her on the bed and she watched him throw off his jacket, shaken by the feelings that were carving a valley through her. He joined her and dragged her half under him, kissing her again. Thorough, drugging kisses that set her alight, yet she felt stiff and frozen.

"What's wrong?" He lifted his head, proving himself to be attuned to her in a way that was reassuring and disturbing all at once.

"I'm shy," she admitted, ducking her head as she said it because that wasn't her at *all*. Her eyes stung with emotive tears at how monumental this was. She

was alone with a man, on a *bed*, and he had set the sun inside her. He made it radiate outward, filling her with such heat and joy she was going to burst. "I want to touch you, but I don't want to make a fool of myself. I don't know if I can contain myself."

"Don't even try." His voice brimmed with graveled warning, which might have made her chuckle, but she released her breath and let her hands move to greedily stake a claim.

He was firm everywhere, taut and strong. Hot. Her fingers discovered the textures of his clothes, then slid beneath his shirt as he yanked it free of his belted pants. He made an approving noise as she found satin skin and the tension of his abdomen, then the shape of his rib cage and the sleek muscles across his chest. The sharp beads of his nipples fascinated her.

She made her own appreciative noises, utterly rapt with the contrast of his body to her own, all flat planes and crisp hair and indomitable strength.

He released her zip and dragged down the loosened front of her dress. As he bared her breasts, something elemental gripped her. The spirit of womanhood. She melted onto her back and arched, emphasizing their differences, liking that he made a noise that sounded almost suffering, yet growly and ferocious. He opened his mouth and engulfed her in such a place of earthy pleasure, she released her own cry of agonized joy.

*Volatile.* Was that what this was? She hadn't known she could feel like this, frantic yet intoxicated. Impatient yet timeless. She wanted to stay like this forever, running their hands over each other, kissing, mouths

needing to fuse and breathing be damned. But as his hands moved on her, shifting silk with a touch so hot it burned her through the fabric, she wanted more. So much more.

His fingertips grazed the slit in her gown and she found herself offering more of her leg then trembling in anticipation, waiting for the feel of his touch on her skin. The pet of his hand on the outside of her thigh made her shiver. She gloried in the way he kissed her harder, deeper, hand shaping her hip, exploring her belly, then tracking to her other thigh. He squeezed the taut muscle then moved with delicious confidence to cup the center of her.

Breath stalling, eyes opening, she waited for panic, but before she could entertain a grim memory, he firmed his touch and rocked his hand, sending a jolt of incredible pleasure through her pelvis. Her eyelids grew heavy again and she found herself lifting, spellbound by the lightning bolts of sensation that grew in strength as they kissed and he caressed her.

How could anything feel this good?

She wanted to touch him as intimately, but she could hardly think of anything but how he was making her feel. Just as she tried to shape him through his pants, his touch changed, exploring beneath silk with knowledge and intention.

She bucked in reaction. "I can't—My heart is going to explode."

She moved a reflexive hand to cover his, not quite stopping him, because the slide of his fingers against her was so mesmerizing, but so sensitizing she almost

couldn't bear it. Her entire focus narrowed to that delicate circle and stroke.

"I want to be inside you, but I don't want to stop touching you. Like that?" He pushed a long finger into her.

She couldn't speak, could only hear a keening noise that came from her as he penetrated and circled where she was so sensitive and molten that she ached. She tightened, trying to savor, trying to hold back the build, but wanton mindlessness took over. Her hips danced against his hand, the pleasure growing too acute to bear, tension growing and growing until she couldn't stand it—

"*Oh!*" Her world exploded in a sudden release that had her shaking and shuddering, flesh pulsing and eyes tearing at the absolute beauty of it.

She pressed his hand still, trying to ease the sensation, trying to catch her breath.

He kissed her, tongue questing for hers, and continued to gently caress her, soothing and teasing so her level of arousal didn't fade, only edged into deeper desire.

With a groan, she rolled into him, strangely ravenous. She wanted the barriers between them gone. Wanted *all of him*. What was he *doing* to her?

He made a feral noise and they tugged at each other's clothing, stripping in seconds, then rolled back together, naked, gloriously naked. Now he was hers, all hers. She swept her hands over him, enamored with his broad shoulders but equally fascinated by his rock-hard biceps and the way his Adam's apple bobbed in a swallow.

When she cradled the fiercest part of him in her palm, she wasn't frightened at all. She felt powerful, especially when he looked agonized and closed his eyes and breathed, *"Bella."*

With a smile, she pressed her mouth to his throat and tried to roll him onto his back. He rolled her beneath him instead, pressing over her as he kissed her, letting her caress him as he used his tongue to mimic what he wanted to do until she couldn't take it and tore her mouth from his. "I need—"

She didn't know what she needed. She was restless and urgent, loins feeling achy and neglected. Empty.

He reached over to the night table then rose over her, knees sliding between hers and parting her legs with effortless strength.

She felt so many things in that moment. Vulnerable, yes, but strangely trusting. It didn't matter if she didn't particularly enjoy this part. She wanted to know she could take a man—

"Oh."

He paused, tip pressing for entry, the invasion startling enough that she tensed.

His head came up. His whole body was taut, his cheeks flushed, his eyes glittering, but there was a shred of man still governing the animal. "I might literally die if you've changed your mind."

Maybe that's what made her smile. Maybe it was the fact her body was so eager for his. Maybe it was simply the joy of this crazy, magical night.

With a little arch, she invited him to complete his thrust and he did with a shudder, sinking deep, gaze

never leaving hers, but glowing hot as the center of a flame as their flesh melded.

To say she became a woman under his possession was silly, but she *felt* like a woman in that moment. Mature and whole and *sacred*. She was responding exactly as nature intended under the advances of a mate. *Her* mate. With this act, he gave her back her sexuality, her desire. Her *self*.

She closed her eyes against something too big to contemplate, but it only made the sensations intensify as he took a testing withdraw and return. She shivered as though velvet passed over her skin.

"Yes?"

"Yes," she moaned, savoring the deliciousness that lingered with anticipation for another stroke. "More."

Lucidity faded as he did it again. And again.

He began to thrust with more purpose. She found her hips rising to meet his, longing for the return of his. Needing it. The dance delivered such acute pleasure, she released a strangled groan of enjoyment.

He picked up the tempo and magnificent sensations ran through her. She wanted to tell him but couldn't speak, as she was too enraptured. Tension gripped her. A kind of tortured ecstasy—her body searching for an answering call in his.

She needed him to be as driven beyond himself as she was. To come with her to this place where nothing existed but this new being they had become with their joining. Scraping her nails down his back, she grasped at his buttocks and pulled him into her. Into the eye of the storm.

They struck the pinnacle together, the climax so intense, she opened her mouth in a soundless scream. Pleasure like she had never known flooded in, drowning her as he held himself magnificently deep inside her, throbbing in her jubilant grip as he released a ragged cry of exhilaration and shuddered with completion.

Xavier swore.

"What's wrong?" Trella murmured, hands moving with endless appetite over his damp shoulders.

He withdrew and rolled away. "The condom broke."

She was glad it was dark now. After the first time, they had turned out the lights and slid under the covers to fondle and caress for ages, barely speaking, just kissing and enjoying. Bonding, she might have been tempted to think, yet something in his silence, and the condoms in the night table, told her he had done this a lot.

She had suffered a hollow ache as she'd forced herself to accept that, despite his sweet words, she was merely the woman *du jour* for him. A lady of the night, really.

Whether he had sensed her withdrawal, or she was just that easy, he had grown more passionate. The second time had been even better than the first. Her inhibitions were gone and he held out, giving her two shattering orgasms before taking her on a third ride that nearly killed her, their shared climax being so powerful.

She was too sweaty and lethargic to be triumphant, but she was pretty darned smug at having taken a lover.

She had distantly been hoping she had rocked his world as thoroughly as he had rocked hers, but reality struck like a brick through a window at his words.

"It's okay. I won't get pregnant." She swallowed, trying to clear the thickness that gathered in her throat.

"You're on the pill or something?"

Or something. "Yes."

"I have physicals all the time."

"I'm fine, too." Did people really have these conversations? It scraped the romance off a wonderful evening, leaving her thinking about the rest of reality. Guilt crawled in. She had kept secrets from him and— far worse—from her family. They'd be worried sick if they knew where she was.

As if on cue, her phone plinked with the harp notes of her sister's ringtone. Like some kind of empath, Angelique was picking up on her sudden discord.

"I have to get that," Trella murmured, then she groaned. Her muscles ached as though she'd run a marathon. She forced herself to rise and move naked across the shadowed room, finding her clutch where she'd dropped it in the lounge, then came back to the bedroom door.

She stayed there, slyly hoping he was looking at her, silhouetted by the lamplight. In a quick exchange of texts, she reassured her sister she was fine. Gili knew something was up, though. Tendrils of misgivings began working through Trella's system. It was time to call it a night. She needed to hole up at the flat where she knew she was completely safe and process all of this.

"I have to go." She clicked off her phone and sent him a smile of cheerful resignation.

"Is everything all right?" He rose to pull on his pants, not bothering with underwear, which pleased her for some reason, but he didn't invite her to stay, which depressed her as well.

"Just my sister. She needs me to get home." She texted her guard that she would be ready in fifteen minutes and stepped into her thong.

Xavier shook out her gown and brought it to her, then moved behind her as she stepped into it. Hurrying her? She pulled up the gown then lifted her hair while he zipped.

His hands lingered on her skin, not moving, not holding her in place, but his grave words pinned her motionless. "I remember her kidnapping."

She dropped her arms, letting her hair fall over his hands, as helpless and as terrified as she had ever been. Her breastbone turned to ice and her ears strained to hear what he would say next.

"I was fourteen. My father was renouncing the crown. My mother was already gone, exiled by my grandmother for their divorce. I was feeling very sorry for myself. Then I saw photos of this little girl, so pretty and happy, stolen. I stopped worrying what would happen to me. I was so relieved when she was recovered."

His fingertips stayed across her shoulders, not caressing, just resting in small hot prints. She thought she would bruise from the contact. Not in a painful way. It was the opposite of injury. Healing?

He drew in a sharp breath and pulled his touch from

her skin. "I don't know why I said that. It was far too personal for both of us. You're clearly still worried about her if you're rushing off." He bent to retrieve her shoes. "I hope she's all right."

*It was me.* She should have said it, but her throat was too tight.

She knew there were people who had rooted for her family all the way along, but it was so wrapped up in their notoriety, she didn't differentiate the kindly meant from the intrusive or downright cruel. Her family hadn't asked to be famous for the odd trick of nature that had created two sets of identical twins. They were just people, perhaps better looking by certain standards, definitely richer than average, but regular humans.

Yet the world was insatiably curious about what brand of soap they used and held strong opinions on how they should conduct themselves.

To have this man, who was completely removed from it, reveal such a personal memory connected to her affected her, changing the careful constructs inside her. Defenses that held darkness at bay while keeping her open to the people who loved her shifted and angled to provide space for him to enter.

*No.* She couldn't let him in! Tie herself to a man? Lose herself behind someone else's goals and wishes and expectations when she had so many unreached aspirations of her own? She couldn't attach herself to someone whose life was bigger than hers. She was trying to escape all the restraints that had bound her for so long.

Shaken at how vulnerable she was to him, she jiggled her bodice against her breasts, then perched on a chair to strap on her shoes, hands trembling.

"Is she really as beautiful as you?" He watched her with his fists pushed into his pockets. His naked shoulders were relaxed and outlined in pale gold while the shadows in his face suggested a brooding expression. The dark patch of his chest hair narrowed to a suggestive line, arrowing to his navel, then lower.

He was the beautiful one. She memorized this last intimate glimpse of him.

"Exactly as beautiful." She smiled, amused with her own joke, then poignant gratitude accosted her. "Thank you for tonight. I—" She stopped herself from saying something truly gauche.

She wanted to ask if he'd meant it when he'd said it wasn't always like this for him. She wanted to tell him what he had given her. She wanted to get out of here before she revealed too much.

She glanced at the clock. If she didn't show her face promptly, her guard would knock and enter. They were paid very well to be diligent and investigate when she wasn't where she said she would be.

Xavier moved to offer a hand, helping her to her feet. "Thank *you*. This was lovely." The words came off lighthearted, punching into her as she imagined the legions of other women who had heard such offhand praise. Not even, *I won't forget you*. Just, *this was lovely*. A pleasant meal. Nothing life-changing.

He brought her hand to his mouth, exactly as he had

when they'd met, except this time he turned her hand over and kissed her palm.

Trying to hide how deeply that affected her, she said, "Goodnight, sweet Prince."

He snorted. "I could have you beheaded for that."

With a lightning move, he pulled her close and wove his fingers into her hair, planting a real kiss, a final one, on her mouth. It was painfully sweet. Thorough, yet tender. Oddly heartbreaking.

For her.

And even though she was the one to draw back, her lips clung to his. Temptation to stay, to say more, gripped her, but he distracted her.

"You've lost an earring." His fingertip flicked at her lobe.

"No!" Both hands went to her ears, finding one empty. "Here? In the room? Did you notice if I had both while we were downstairs?"

"I'll buy you new ones," he offered with an off-hand shrug.

"They're sentimental. A gift from my father." *To Gili*. She clicked on the lamp and flung back the bed covers, searching.

A polite knock tapped on the main door, her guard telling her the car was in position. They avoided waiting whenever possible. It drew a crowd.

"I'll find it and send it to you at the design house."

"Promise?" She looked from his muscled chest to the sheets to his eyes. Oh, he was spectacular in the golden light, emptying her brain all over again.

"I only make promises I can keep."

"Thank you." She didn't bother worrying about him addressing it to Angelique. She would intercept it or come clean if she had to. "I really did, um, enjoy this."

His eyes warmed with laughter. "My pleasure, *bella*."

She was starting to sound like the neophyte she was. Definitely time to make her escape. She ducked her head and made for the coach before she turned into a pumpkin.

# CHAPTER THREE

*Present day...*

COMMUNICATIONS FROM PRINCE XAVIER'S grandmother fell into three categories. All were delivered by the palace's Private Secretary, Mario de Gaul.

"Your grandmother requests a meeting to discuss…" Fill in the blank. Those were routine and benign. She listened to her grandson's opinions and they worked together on a strategy for whatever event, negotiation or dignified visitor stood on the horizon. They were equals, more or less.

The second, more ominous type of appointment began with "Her Majesty invites you to join her at…" Fill in the meal. Those were more dictatorial instructions on how she wanted something handled. A parliamentarian or ambassador needed massaging. A high-level staff member needed firing. He was doing her dirty work.

Then there was—

"The Queen is in her receiving room. She expects you."

Mario entered with that missive on the heels of Xavier's Personal Assistant, who still stood before him, his speech bubble of grim news dissolving in the air above his pleading don't-shoot-the-messenger expression.

"Of course." Xavier rose from his desk. It was the appropriate response. One didn't refuse the Queen. One certainly didn't leave her waiting.

Still, his agile brain leapt to all the triage he needed to accomplish in the next few minutes, not least of which was to reassure his new fiancée, Patrizia, before she saw the headlines herself.

*Switched Before Birth!*
*Future King an Expectant Father?*
*Trella Tricked Everyone—Including the Prince!*

He should have said something a few weeks ago, of course, when the first bomb went off. Trella Sauveterre, lately returned to the public eye, had turned up pregnant. The reaction had been loud enough to shake the world off its axis, forcing him to reach out to her, again, much to his dismay. He didn't want anything to do with her after realizing how thoroughly she'd duped him.

*Why had she done it?*

The sting of chasing her to Berlin a week after Paris, like a fool with his first crush, came back hot and fresh under his skin. He'd had a very real duty to meet with Patrizia, but he had put it off, stealing an extra few days of bachelorhood, inventing excuses so he could…what? Have sex with a stranger once more?

Sex was sex. He'd had many lovers over the years and experienced varied degrees of pleasure. He put down the better experiences to chemistry, the less satisfying ones to inhibitions and incompatibility.

That night in Paris had seemed extraordinary while it was happening. She hadn't been a virgin, but she'd made sex feel new again. She'd been so responsive. So sensual. So *abandoned.* His stomach tightened just remembering it.

*So what*? He knew from his father's history that letting the brain below his belt do his thinking was disastrous.

Nevertheless, a day later, when he had read that *Angelique* would be in Berlin, he had reconfigured his entire schedule. Rather than courier her earring as promised, he had sought her out—only to find her with another man.

It had been the most lowering of moments, not because his ego was dented, but because he had revealed something of himself to her. Somehow, she had tricked him into believing they had a connection that went beyond the physical. What had possessed him to talk of those dark hours when his parents had been banished?

He didn't form intimate friendships. He was an only child raised by a grandmother whose life was too demanding to offer affection. Yet, for some reason, he had entrusted a one-night lover with his private thoughts.

He had trusted *her*. When she had said she didn't sleep around, he had believed her.

Judging by what he found in Berlin, however, she'd moved on very quickly. The innocent act was part of

her routine, he had concluded, castigating himself for acting so callow as to follow her.

Nevertheless, when he had the chance to catch her alone, he approached, waiting for the catch of excitement she had kindled in him the week before.

Nothing. She was desirable the way all beautiful women were, but whatever he'd felt in Paris was gone. It had perplexed and annoyed him, made him doubly irritated with himself for thinking they'd had something special.

He's stood there searching for whatever it was that he'd found so enthralling and she had pretended she didn't even know him, staring blankly as though he had broken into her bedroom and stolen the diamond hoop earring he was returning.

In those seconds, he had felt as though she was even more of a stranger than she had been before they'd made love—which she was, he promptly learned. He hadn't slept with Angelique. He had slept with her twin, Trella.

The revelation had been welcome and infuriating. He didn't care for dishonest people, but his desire to see Trella had renewed itself. He had asked Angelique to pass along his contact details, wanting an explanation. Wanting something he refused to acknowledge, but…

Nothing.

Not one returned call, message or text.

What did it matter? He made himself get over her, focusing on more important things, primarily his duty to marry.

He had made a concerted effort to avoid all head-

lines containing the name Sauveterre, which wasn't easy. First, the mysterious, reclusive Trella had come out at a friend's wedding. That had kept the gossip industry booming through spring and summer, along with other news within the family, making it a challenge for him to change channels or flick screens fast enough to avoid catching sight of her.

Then, just as things seemed to have died down, she'd been caught climbing from her brother's car looking less svelte than in previous photos. *Pregnant*, the avid Sauveterre watchers speculated.

So what if she was? It didn't make a hill of beans difference to anyone's life, least of all his.

Still, Xavier had looked closely at the photos that emerged, one showing her in a stunning maternity gown at her brother's engagement party. She didn't look *very* pregnant. She had said she was on the pill. If she was carrying his child, she would have returned his calls. He didn't have anything to worry about, he assured himself.

This latest inflammatory sound bite was more of the same. Had to be. He had a walk-on part in the episodic drama that was the Sauveterre serial. He had slept with her *one night*. He resented being drawn into scandal for it. He was now engaged. That made besmirching his name unforgiveable. Immediately after allaying his grandmother's concern, he would insist Trella clear him of involvement so he could reassure Patrizia their marriage plans could continue.

Damn it, he had completely forgotten about Patrizia. He paused to text.

I'll have this cleared up shortly.

Their match was perfect in every way. Not only would it strengthen both of their countries, but they liked each other. Neither had unrealistic notions like love and passion to muddy the waters. She was nursing a bruised heart and was keen for a stable, reliable situation. A civilized relationship, she kept calling it.

He was pleased to perform his duty in a way he could stand. Patrizia was intelligent, attractive, well-bred. She would have children for the same reason he would: They were expected to. They respected one another. They were on the same page.

*He wanted this marriage.*

Mario paused with him and knocked, then announced him.

His grandmother didn't rise as Xavier entered. She didn't even look up from whatever she was writing with her antique silver pen. The crackle in the fireplace became the only sound along with the scratch of her pen.

He took the bull by the horns. "I'll refute it and press charges against the source."

The pen went down and she peered at him over her glasses. She was a well-preserved seventy, her eyes were the same Deunoro blue as his own, her hair more iron than silver. She was overdue to start her morning audiences, which always made her salty.

"The Queen Mother of Zhamair is the source."

Xavier's PA had also pointed out that the story had stemmed from Angelique's soon-to-be mother-in-law. "I haven't had a chance to confirm that. If she made

a statement, I'm sure it's in reaction to some online nonsense."

"She is reacting, I am informed, to remarks made about her son and his fiancée. She wanted to set the record straight that Angelique was not the woman kissing you in the photos that emerged some months ago from Paris. Angelique has always been faithful to King Kasim. Is that true?"

"I couldn't say whether she's been faithful, but I'm told I was with Trella."

"You were *told*?"

"They're twins." He shrugged, not bothering to feel awkward discussing his sex life with his grandmother. She had had "The Talk" with him herself when he was an adolescent, explaining in no uncertain terms that royalty did *not* produce bastards and had offered explicit tips on how to prevent such a thing.

"That particular twin is pregnant." She used her most imperious tone. "A source intimately connected to her family has stated you were with her at an appropriate time for conception. Did you take precautions?"

"Of course."

*The condom broke. Are you on the pill?*
*Yes.*

"She would have told me if there were consequences." Tension gathered in the pit of his gut. He didn't know which one of them he was trying to convince. "Any woman who sets out to trap a man does not hide it for six months. Even if it was an accident, there's no reason to keep it from me. She might be pregnant, but *it's not mine*."

Her brows went up in regal disdain. "Perhaps you should confirm that."

As if that hadn't occurred to him? "Of course," he said. Dutifully.

"Because it would be a shame if this were to cause any delay in our schedule." She intended to step down the minute he was married. To Patrizia.

"Understood."

It was hot in Innsbruck, despite the elevation and the calendar showing the last days of summer. But maybe the heat was caused by this extra human she was carrying.

Trella lifted her face into the gentle breeze, enjoying the sweet scent of it. She was six months along and felt it, even though she wasn't showing much. Her mother had possessed the same tall, model-slender figure and had barely shown with twins until the very end. This was only one and with the right clothes, she barely looked pregnant.

She needed that ambiguity. Prince Xavier's texts had devolved to the two-word kind.

Call me.

She had ignored the latest, received this morning, exactly as she'd ignored every other text and call she'd received from him, the first immediately after he'd met Angelique in Berlin, and most recently after she'd been exposed by her sister's soon-to-be mother-in-law as the twin in his arms at the ball in Paris.

She had her reasons. That's what she kept telling herself, even though it was pure emotion that drove her and that emotion was cowardice.

"They're blocked by a service vehicle," her guard, Benita, said of their car, lifting her gaze from her phone to continue her scan of the street. "Let's wait inside."

Benita was as tall as Trella and had a mannish demeanor when she was on the job. No nonsense, no makeup, hair scraped into a bun, communications terse.

Trella didn't mind. She wasn't the most cooperative principal. To her occasional chagrin, she was a high maintenance person in every way. Acknowledging that about herself didn't stop her from saying, "I'd rather stay out here."

The day was gorgeous and she would be on bed rest soon. She wanted to enjoy the outside world while she could.

"Killian said—"

"I know. Take extra precautions." She scoffed at a lot of things, but not security reports. "I spoke to Sadiq. He's the one who discovered the hack and restored all the firewalls. No one even knows I'm here."

Except the handful of people inside the building who had just taken selfies with her. They were no doubt posting those as she spoke. She was a celebrity, whether she liked it or not. It was only a matter of minutes before lookie-loos began pulling over, wanting their own photo with a Sauveterre, especially the elusive pregnant one.

"My gut doesn't like it."

"Because Killian trains you to be overprotective."

Benita had tried to cancel this trip as soon as the security bulletin had come through. Trella wasn't sure why she had insisted on making what amounted to a house call for a joint venture she wasn't sure she would pursue, but she had.

Ah, she knew why she had come. For starters, her sister had been doing this kind of thing on her behalf for years. It was yet another burden she had placed on her twin and it was her turn to pay it back, now that Angelique was starting her life with Kasim.

Oh, her sister was in love. It was as majestic a sight to behold as the timeless sparkling peaks around them. Trella was deeply happy for her, but so very envious.

Her gaze tracked to the sharpest, highest peaks to the south. To Elazar.

Was he texting from inside that border, sitting in his palace office, cursing her for ignoring him?

A flutter in her midsection had her resisting the urge to press her hand across her belly. She didn't like to draw attention to her pregnancy when she was in public. Besides, it wasn't the baby that caused that stir in her middle. It was a complex mix of emotions.

She wanted to tell him she was grateful. She wanted to see him again, to discover if the magical connection she'd felt in Paris had been real or just a product of an exciting foray into independence. She wanted him to know they were expecting a baby.

She also wanted to hold their night in her memory as the ideal that it was. She didn't want the harsh fallout she would have to face once she acknowledged this baby as his. Most of all, she didn't want to be a burden

on a man who had seemed too perfect to want anything
to do with someone as flawed as she was.

Her expected black sedan with its darkened windows slid up to the curb.

"There. See?" Trella said, even as she noted a man
approaching in her periphery.

"That's not—" Benita's voice cut off.

Perhaps Trella went deaf at that moment because
nothing penetrated beyond the fact that the back door
opened and the Prince of Elazar rose from the interior.

He was as remarkable as she remembered. Like a
knight of legend, his hair shot with glints of gold, his
visage sharp and stern, his air one of heroic power.
He was so godlike, she couldn't move. She was too
mesmerized.

Then reality rushed in as a scuffling noise and a
grunt penetrated. She swung her gaze to see Benita in
a fight. A *fight*. With a *man*. He tried to twist Benita's
arm behind her back as she bent forward, trying to use
leverage to flip him.

Training, the kind Trella had attended to daily until
pregnancy had sent her into yoga and water aerobics,
jolted her into action. As Benita's attacker pulled back
his weight, dragging Benita off her feet, Trella stepped
in and nailed him with a solid, knuckle-bruising punch,
right in the nose.

The man grunted and Benita twisted, nearly escaping.

"What the *hell* are you doing?" That *accent*. Strong
hands grasped her upper arms and pulled her away
from the struggling pair.

Trella turned into him, stomach flip-flopping in response as she felt his solid abdomen against her bump. Adrenaline coursed through her, but she only felt reassurance as he drew her protectively close. Her gaze stayed over her shoulder, fixed on the fight, which seemed to be more of a wrestle for dominance. A bloody nose wasn't slowing down the man and Benita wasn't giving up, biting out in Spanish, "Run."

"Help her—Wait. What are *you* doing?" Trella cried as she realized she was being shoved into the back of the car.

Xavier easily overpowered her, pushing her in and following without ceremony.

She was so shocked that it took her a moment to resist. By then his big body had created a wall of shoulders and chest that were impossible to get past.

Before she could touch the door on her side, he pulled his own closed and the locks clicked. The car pulled away, leaving her guard scrapping on the sidewalk with a brute whose shirt was the same color as both men in the front of this car.

Far too late, she realized what was happening.

She was being kidnapped. *Again.*

# CHAPTER FOUR

"STOP THIS CAR. *Now.*"

Xavier respected her ability to sound so authoritative, but he ignored her and opened the privacy window long enough to accept an ice pack from his physician, Gunter, then tapped the button to close it.

"Hello, Trella. Have I got that right?" He knew he had the right one. It was impossible to explain, but the minute he had seen her, he had known.

He pushed aside the ridiculous high that rocketed through him as he finally had her alone and held out his palm. He wiggled his fingers, urging her to release the pendant she was pinching and let him examine her hand.

"What were you thinking, getting involved in that?" The mix of rage and fear he'd experienced at seeing her step into the fight was reflected in his tone. Even if she wasn't pregnant, it would have been a foolhardy, dangerous thing to do.

But she was pregnant. There was no denying it. The narrow waist he'd held in the crook of his arm had thickened with an undeniable bump. Her breasts…

He dragged his gaze up, refusing to let fantasies sidetrack him, but her features were a distraction all on their own. Her face was rounder, her mouth lush and pouted. The urge to kiss her struck him with a fierce pull.

Damn it, what *was* it about her?

He met her glare with his own, thinking that he would have sworn her eyes were green, but they were steely. Bright as a cornered cat refusing to stay that way.

"I thought I was preventing myself from being kidnapped. Once again, I have trusted the wrong person." Her unpainted lips seemed bloodless, which gave him a moment of pause, but too much of his life had been set off balance by her. He wanted answers. Today.

"It's not a kidnapping." He set the ice pack near her thigh. "It's an improvised meeting to discuss mutual business, so drop your pendant. I know it's a tracking device. Your guard won't be harmed, only delayed. Your car can't chase us. It's still blocked."

"Which sounds a lot like a kidnapping." A harsh ringtone emanated from her purse. "That's for you." She pulled out her phone and used her thumbprint to accept the call then handed it to Xavier. Her hand might have trembled.

Desperate times called for desperate measures, he'd told himself when he'd concocted this intervention. As he picked up on Trella's shaken nerves, he wondered if he was using a sledgehammer to kill a fly. It hadn't occurred to him she might be anything but angry at having her timetable interrupted. He couldn't be happier if he inconvenienced the hell out of her. He was

beyond incensed at the way she was impacting his life without any attempt to mitigate it.

Explaining that would have to wait. He'd been warned to expect this video call. He took the phone and met the formidable expression of a man who resembled Trella. Henri, Xavier suspected, since the other brother was in Brazil.

"Your demands?" Henri asked without greeting.

"A blood sample for a DNA test."

Trella made a strangled noise. "Like hell."

He glanced at her. "I would accept her word as to whether she's carrying my heir, but she's lied to me more than once already."

Xavier willed her to lash out with denials of his paternity. With an explanation. An *apology*.

She hitched her chin and turned her face to the window.

"Return her to where you took her. I'll see what I can do about the blood test."

"You can't even get her to return a call. I can't wait any longer."

Trella's silence was gut-knottingly damning. Whatever lingering favor he had felt toward her went ashen and bitter. A jagged lump hardened in his throat. He swallowed it, but the acrimony only moved to burn as a hot knot behind his collarbone. Each minute that she failed to deny his paternity was a tiny, incremental progression toward accepting what he had been refusing to believe. What he still didn't want to believe.

"I have your coordinates," Henri said, dragging Xavier back from staring at the woman who was ru-

ining his life. "A team has been dispatched. We don't need an incident. Return her to Innsbruck."

"If you're tracking us, you know we'll be in Elazar soon." Xavier leaned toward the window to see a helicopter chasing from the distance. "I'll close the borders if I have to, but she's perfectly safe, especially if that's our future monarch inside her. Stand down from trying to stop us."

"Unless my sister gives me her safe word, this escalates."

Xavier handed her the phone. "Your move, *bella*."

She flashed him a sharp glance then looked at her brother.

"We're coming," Henri said.

"I know." She nodded, pale and grave, then said, "Begonia."

*"Vous êtes certain?"*

*"Sí."*

"That's tomorrow's word," Xavier said.

She shot him a startled frown.

He shrugged. "I do my homework."

"Then you'll know I'm buying you twenty-four hours." She turned back to her phone, expression haughty. "I'm sure Killian knows by now who hacked him. Ask him to drop a virus into the Elazar palace networks, won't you?"

"Killian has Elazar's Minister of Foreign Affairs on the phone, along with a more aggressive team assembled."

Xavier suspected that remark was more for his benefit.

*"Gracias.* Tell him I'll handle it."

"Will you?"

A leaden silence followed where she only gave her brother a tight-lipped look.

Xavier wondered if others were also frustrated by the avoidance game she had been playing.

*"Bien,"* Henri said. "If I don't hear from you every hour, your prince may expect a gun against his temple. *Je t'aime."*

*"Te amo."* She ended the call and slipped her phone back into her purse, then folded her hands into her lap. "Why did you say I lied to you more than once?"

Xavier admired the way she attempted to take control of the conversation, but he was not prepared to give her any concessions until he had what he wanted.

"Why did you speak Spanish and he, French? Was it code?"

"Habit."

She tried to leave it there, but he lifted a skeptical brow.

"It's true. Our father was French, Mama is Spanish. We grew up speaking both. I only told one lie."

"That you were on birth control."

"That I was Angelique. You asked if I was on the pill *or something*. I said yes because that was true. At least, I thought it was." She bit the corner of her lip.

"Your *or something* failed?"

She flinched, making him realize his voice carried a thickness close to contempt or even hatred.

He grappled to hang onto his temper. "You assured me pregnancy wasn't possible. How have we arrived at having this conversation?"

Dumb question. They both knew how babies were made. They'd made love. She had come apart in his arms again and again. He'd been greedy as a starved beast certain he would die from the pleasure of being inside her when she shattered around him like that. Then, when he couldn't hold back any longer, he had joyously thrown himself into the small death of simultaneous orgasm.

In that post-climactic moment, when her breaths had still been jagged and his heart had pounded against her sweating breasts, he had felt…restored. Not just a release of tension but as though deeper needs had been met. Withdrawing had provoked a painful, abandoned sensation he had impatiently tried to forget.

"*Is that my child?*"

She jolted at the grate in his tone. "You said you wouldn't believe me no matter what I said."

"You'll submit to a blood test, then?"

Her eyes narrowed in mutiny.

"You can submit nicely or I can pin you down while my doctor takes it." He was clearly a sadist because something in him longed for her to push him into restraining her.

"Touch me and I'll break *your* nose." She started to lift a threatening fist and flinched, quickly cradling her right hand—which is what she'd been doing since her hands had gone into her lap, he realized.

He caught her wrist and held on when she tried to pull away. The backs of her fingers were an angry red, her knuckles puffy.

His heart lurched.

"Did you break any bones? Can you move your fingers? That's what this is for." He picked up the ice pack, incensed all over again that she had waded into the fight.

"I know how to throw a punch." She took the ice and flexed her fingers against it, showing only a wince of discomfort so he presumed she hadn't fractured anything.

"What were you thinking? It's a damned good thing his reflexes didn't take over. You would have been on the ground."

"My bodyguard was being assaulted."

"No, *my* bodyguard was moving into position to cover *me*. *She* attacked *him*. Then you did. Do you understand what bodyguards are paid to do? There is no reason you should have involved yourself."

Her brows flicked in dismissal of his concern.

Was this really the mother of his heir? If he'd gone to a brothel and bought a *man*, he couldn't have picked someone less suitable.

"A simple blood test could prove I'm not the father. We could have it done before we cross the border." He pointed at the sign they passed that stated they were less than a mile away.

"I'm afraid of needles."

"Be afraid of *me*, *bella*."

Her flat smile died. Something vulnerable flashed in her expression.

His conscience pinched.

"Is that the problem?" His voice still sounded gruff and aggressive. His animosity hadn't evaporated just

because he was finally getting answers. He didn't want to soften toward her at all. She was far too dangerous. But fear was an explanation he could understand.

"Have you been afraid of my reaction? I'm not happy." That was a gross understatement. A well-practiced aloof demeanor had always served him well, but it was impossible to find in the face of this life-altering situation. Still, he tried to reassure her. "Nothing bad will happen if the baby is mine. I'll recognize him or her as our future monarch. We will marry so it's legitimate. That's all. No stake burnings or feeding to dragons. Were you afraid I'd pressure you to terminate? Is that why you've kept it from me?"

Silence. She turned her attention out the side window again, so he couldn't read her expression.

"Do you not *know* who the father is? How many contenders are there?"

Her glare swung like a blade to slice through him.

"I don't *care* how many men you've slept with." Much. He was disturbed to realize he did, actually. It wasn't because of the paternity question, either. The passion between them had been unprecedented. He didn't like to think she reacted that way to every man she slept with. It would have made all of this even more intolerable.

"How pregnant are you? Let's see if that eliminates me, shall we?"

"Pregnant enough to need a pit stop. Can we stop here?"

"No." The border guard waved them through with

only a very minor slowing of their speed, recognizing the plates. "We'll be at my chalet shortly."

The car sped along the pass that formed part of the border between Austria and Elazar. As they rounded a bend, the valley opened, allowing a glimpse of Lirona, the capital, once a modest fiefdom, now a thriving city of culture, intellect and wealth. It sat like a heart against the shore of Lac Lirona, the arms of the mountains stretching out to embrace the blue water he loved with everything in him.

Over the centuries, his ancestors had fought to maintain their governance over this small kingdom many times. His great-grandmother had taken up with one of Hitler's top advisors to keep the Nazi invasion at occupation rather than annihilation.

*That is where the bar is set when it comes to duty*, his grandmother had extolled as a history lesson, explaining why Xavier's father was unfit to rule. *We are custodians. We do what we must. To put yourself before Elazar is treason.*

This, because his father had followed his libido into a high-profile affair with a topless waitress from Amsterdam then married the woman's aunt, owner of a drug café. His divorce from Xavier's mother had already been ugly and, even worse in his grandmother's eyes, *common*.

His grandmother was a hard woman—her father, King Ugo, hadn't forgiven his wife and Queen Julia had grown up in a harsh climate of blame and sacrifice. If her spare had survived, things might have been different. Instead, she had forced her only son to renounce

the throne, disowning him and keeping her grandson as Elazar's future.

It was all on Xavier to perpetuate the monarchy into the next generation. He had planned to do so through an elegant association with Patrizia, a respected princess with a degree in social justice and a pedigree that couldn't be faulted.

Instead, he had behaved as impulsively as his father, tangling with a fashion designer whose life was stained with one scandal after another.

He was running out of hope that her child was not his. Whether his grandmother could find it in her to forgive him for this transgression didn't matter.

He would never forgive himself.

# CHAPTER FIVE

As someone who had grown up in obscene wealth, Trella didn't bat an eye at the chalet that turned out to be a three-story modern fortress with a nod to its rustic ancestors in its gables and tiered verandas.

She was more interested in counting pairs of eyes—one at the gate, two at the door, the physician who followed them into the house, the chauffeur who took the car around to what she presumed was the garage, a butler who greeted them and a woman named Inga who was asked to prepare tea.

"Powder room?" Trella clung by her fingernails to control.

Ghosts—terrible, terrible ghosts—were creeping in at the edges of her consciousness, but something pressured to diamond brightness inside her kept her from becoming hysterical. *This time she would get away.*

As each of the Prince's attempts to draw her out had pulled at her laser-like focus, she had resentfully allowed that she was taking the rough road, not the high one. She could still call in a team to break her out if she wanted, but a furious, too often helpless, part of her demanded she prove she could rescue herself.

Over the last months, she had come close many times to calling him. The problem was, she wasn't as stupid as many would conclude from her behavior. She knew what would happen and he had confirmed it. He would marry her.

Which meant a profile in the public eye that was even higher than the one she already occupied. One from which she couldn't retreat at will.

Worse, it meant being honest with him. She would have to reveal exactly how crazy she was. She would have to explain these ghouls tickling across her skin, making her want to scratch herself all over. The nightmare could spring to life with a beat of her heart, the cold sweats and shaking, the profound helplessness...

She hadn't suffered an attack since well before their night in Paris, but one ticked like a bomb inside her. She could feel it. But *no*. She wouldn't succumb, even though fighting it made it worse. She knew that.

With a dry mouth, she locked herself into a bathroom that smelled of potpourri. The small space was pristine, with a porcelain sink in a cherry wood vanity. She glanced from the full bath and shower to the frosted window that, once carefully opened, looked out onto the woods at the back of the house.

No balcony below this window, but it was big enough to allow a woman with a modest six month swelling in her middle to crawl through, and close enough to the nearby balcony she could swing a leg that direction and clamber across.

Not a kidnapping? Damned right it wasn't.

* * *

"I'm sure she'll come around," Xavier told Gunter. He hadn't lied when he had threatened to hold her down, but he didn't want to. It wasn't his habit to manhandle any woman, pregnant or otherwise. "Did she look six months to you?"

Gunter shook his head. "It's difficult to say. Every woman carries differently. The fact she was able to hide it so long leads me to wonder, but…"

They needed a blood test.

"And this?" Xavier waved to where she had disappeared to use the toilet.

"Extremely common. Although…" He glanced at his watch.

That's what Xavier had thought. He hadn't taken his eyes from the closed door and she was still in there. He didn't want to be indelicate, but he moved to knock.

Silence.

Fainted? His heart swerved.

"Trella." He tried the handle, found it locked and rattled it. "She wouldn't have—" The window dropped about thirty-two feet to the ground. That's why he hadn't bothered assigning someone to watch that side of the chalet.

"I'll send someone to check." Gunter hurried away, moving through the kitchen as Inga appeared with keys and a concerned expression.

Xavier gave the key a hard twist and walked into an empty powder room. A fresh breeze came through the open window. He glanced out to see Gunter below,

holding Trella's clutch, a grim expression on his face as he tracked the distance to the nearest balcony.

At least *she* wasn't lying in the dirt below. Tramping through the alps in trendy heels wasn't much better. Damn it, this woman was turning into a nightmare.

"Alert security," he told Inga, and he strode outside to join the search.

Crammed beneath the sink was a little too much like the horrid cellar she'd been locked in during her first kidnapping. The shelf had easily moved to the bottom of the vanity, making room for her to curl herself on top of it, but she'd had to cover herself with the towels and was overheating.

Panicking.

No. One minute at a time. *Uno naranjo, dos naranjos...* She counted the seconds, counted the oranges, a scent she always associated with family since they had a grove of them at Sus Brazos. She would get through this. It was another test of her ability to move on from her past.

She did her breathing exercises while she listened for footsteps. When she was confident everyone had moved outside, she carefully opened the cupboard door and groped her way out of the small space, thankful for her yoga practice.

Carrying her shoes, she paused at the door. There were security cameras. She had noted one in the foyer as they'd entered. Someone would be watching the screens. She had to move fast, but—*thank you, Killian*—she had what amounted to an SOS flare in

her phone. It was supposed to be for signaling help, but she hoped it could have another use.

She took the device from her bra, turned on the blinding white light, and walked into the hall, aiming the beam directly at the first camera she came to. It sat like a brilliant spotlight on the dark orb. She prayed it blinded the lens as she hurried through the house to the garage.

There was no one in the kitchen and keys hung neatly on the hook beside the door. She tucked her phone back into her bra and took all the keys, deducing from a keychain which one belonged to the top-down cobalt blue Audi.

Outside the garage doors, she heard footsteps jogging across gravel.

Her entire body trembled, but she fought to keep a focused mind. She *wasn't* helpless. She *would* get away.

She set all the keys on the passenger seat and climbed behind the wheel of the Audi, then hit the button on the visor to open the garage door, ready to start the car as soon as the door climbed high enough.

There was a click, the hum of a motor and a rattle of effort, but the door didn't budge. She jabbed her finger onto the button again, glancing at the jumble of keys. Should she take a different car?

The door to the interior of the chalet opened and Xavier came into the shadowed garage.

*Nooooo!* She jabbed again and again at the stupid button, then started the car with a roar of its high-performance engine.

"The house is locked down. Don't try to drive

through the door. It's reinforced. You'll hurt yourself. And my car." He moved past the other three vehicles with smooth steps, pausing beside her to lean in and turn off the engine, pocketing the key. "But that was a very good try. I'm impressed."

She gripped the steering wheel, staring straight ahead, concentrating on not revealing the tears gathering hotly behind her eyes.

"Come back into the house."

"No."

"We'll talk here then." He moved to flick a switch on the wall. A fan came to life with a low drone, quickly sucking away the lingering exhaust.

He came back to set an elbow on the top of the windscreen. She felt his eyes studying her, but kept her nose pointed forward.

"I'm trying to be patient, *bella*, I really am, but I don't understand why you're being so combative. This doesn't have to be a fight."

"I could drive this, you know. Probably better than you."

"Not without keys."

"You'd be surprised." She worked her hands on the steering wheel's soft leather, more than a little enamored with cars, thanks to Ramon. "I can hotwire and drive anything. I've been up to two hundred and twenty on a closed circuit in my brother's Pur Sang. The Gs nearly crack my ribs when I brake from that speed, but it's quite a rush. Have you ever driven this the way it was designed to drive?"

"No." His tone was one of forced patience.

"Ramon got into racing after taking evasive driving lessons. We all had to take them." Like Ramon, she had tried to outrun herself on the track more than once, but it was never a permanent solution. At some point, she had to park the car, take off the helmet and face reality. "Because of my kidnapping."

She sensed him grow very still, indicating she had his full attention.

Had he thought that wouldn't come up? She hated that it defined her, but it did. She worked around it as often as she could, but when she did have to face it, she did it head-on with her foot to the floor, even though it also had the power to crack her ribs and shatter everything inside her.

As the silence lengthened, she suspected he was reviewing what he had said in Paris—when he had thought he was talking about her but had been speaking *to* her.

"You think *you* were worried when I was stolen." Her voice trembled against her will. She soothed herself by running light fingers across the bumps in the bottom of the steering wheel, playing over them like keys on a piano, but her hands shook.

His voice was grave. "If I was triggering you today, you should have said."

"Really?" A smile touched lips that felt so dry they might split. Her body vibrated with fight-or-flight. She was going to crash hard after this, but she couldn't think about that yet. "Because I did tell you to take me back and you ignored me. Which is exactly what happened the first time."

Her knuckles whitened where she grasped the wheel again, trying to keep a grip on herself. It was time for the head-on collision.

"I said *stop*, and *no*, and *please* so many times I lost count. I said it when they threw me in their van and I could see Ramon running after us. I said it when one of them pulled me onto his lap and shoved his hand under my skirt and *hurt* me. I said it when he slapped me because I was fighting him. I said it when he locked me in a cold, dark cellar and I said it a lot when he let me out three days later, only to put me on a filthy stinking mattress and call me lucky. *Lucky*. Because he was going to show me what men liked."

She knew it was an assault to throw that at him. It was one of the reasons she rarely spoke about it, but she wanted to hurt him. She wanted to *scar* him.

"I should check with my therapist, see if my experience of being assaulted might create a profound desire to control my own destiny. Gosh, what an enlightening moment of self-discovery you've provided, Xavier. Yes, I'm quite sure that's why I'm *combative*."

He couldn't move, wasn't even sure he was breathing, as he tried to un-hear what she'd said. Who would do such a thing? To a *child*?

He didn't have a particular affinity for children, not having had a childhood to speak of himself. Royal duties took him into contact with them, but children were just one more foreign culture with whom certain rituals were observed. He didn't live among them or desire to.

What he did understand was that they were vulnerable. Those who exploited the weak were beneath contempt. Only a true monster would hurt someone as helpless as a nine-year-old girl, especially sexually.

"I didn't think I could get pregnant." Trella's thin voice echoed off the concrete and steel of his garage, underpinned by the drone of the fan. Her profile was pale and still, grayed by the half-light beyond the row of windows in the doors. "The damage he did was that bad. Do you understand what I'm saying? Because I don't want to get any more specific."

A twisted, anguished feeling struck his middle, clenching talons around his chest and squeezing his throat, pushing fear and helplessness to such heights inside him, it became a pressure he could barely withstand. He knew his heart was beating because it throbbed with painful pounds that rang in his ears, but he couldn't move or speak.

There were no words, no reactions, that fit this situation. Only a primal scream that would have no effect whatsoever. It wouldn't reverse the past, wouldn't erase her dark memories. He was at a complete loss.

"When I realized I was pregnant, I had to give the baby a chance. Even though the odds were against it. I've been expecting a miscarriage every single day. What was the point in telling you if I was only going to lose it? Even now, I'm terrified of becoming too attached in case something happens."

It was his. The knowledge crashed over him like a wave, bringing a sharp sting of heightened awareness to his whole body. It changed everything. His en-

tire life, every decision and action, filtered in a blur through this lens of a new life they had created.

The cogs in his brain finally began turning, but with a rustiness that scraped at his detachment.

"So this is…delicate?" What if she lost it? For some reason, neat as that solution might sound, the idea appalled him. "Are you all right?" He should have asked these questions the minute he'd had her alone. "Has this put you into labor? Are you in pain?"

"No." She skimmed her hair out of her eyes and let herself relax into the seat of the car, hands settling over her bump. Her complexion was pale, but she sounded calm. "We're both quite healthy, all things considered. But I see a specialist in London and she wants me on bed rest for the third trimester. She was an intern in Spain when I was a child and knows everything I've been through. I'll let your doctor take my blood, but I'm not giving some stranger my medical history. He touches my arm. That's *it*."

He nodded, still trying to put the pieces together.

"I know I should have told you sooner, but I also knew that if I carried this baby to a stage where it could survive birth, then I would have to marry you. I don't want to."

Her gaze finally came up, striking into him like a harsh winter wind. Bleak.

"I thought if I ever married, it would be for love." Despondency pulled her brows together and her thick lashes swept down to hide her eyes again. "That makes me sound like a romantic and I'm not. I just don't want

to be something taken on in sufferance. My sister fell in love. I know it's possible."

Her elbow came up to rest on the door and she set her teeth on her thumbnail.

"Plus, my life is already high profile. Yours is worse." Her hand dropped away and she flashed him a look of blame. "Why can't you be a mechanic or something? Your life comes with even more restrictions than I imposed on myself. Why would I sign up for that? Of course I avoided telling you."

He certainly wouldn't live this life if he had a choice, but it struck him as odd that she disparaged his station. Every other woman aspired to be his queen.

"So, yes, I've handled this badly. God knows I've been informed of *that* more than once." She rolled her eyes. "I probably owe you an apology."

"Probably?" Did she have any idea the damage she had caused by avoiding him?

"I'm not sorry. I will never be sorry that I'm trying to have our baby." Her chin came up, defiant and fierce, but with deep vulnerability edging her unblinking eyes.

Something stirred in him. Gratitude? How? This baby was a disaster.

As if she read his mind, the corners of her mouth went down. "And I think we'll do enough damage to each other in the next while that if we start apologizing now, we'll be peaking way too early."

*Never trust anyone who can't make or take a joke*, his father had told him once. *Your grandmother, for instance*, had been the rest of the crack.

His grandmother. Yes, indeed, there would be hell to pay and many, many apologies to make.

Before he could fully grasp the scope of impact, a dull buzz emanated from the front of her shirt. "Goodness, an hour gone already?" She reached inside her collar to bring her phone from her bra, voice shaken but trying for lighthearted. "*Hola*, Henri. I'm fine. Just congratulating the father of my child. Does he look green to you?"

Trella could ignore the signs for only so long. The nausea churning in her belly, the heart palpitations, the hot and cold sweats. An attack was upon her. Of course it was. This was one of the most stressful days of her life and she was doing everything wrong, making it worse. Maybe she *did* self-sabotage, the way her brother Ramon sometimes accused, but she would rather eat live worms than admit he was right about anything.

She hated to admit any sort of weakness, because she knew, deep down, that she *was* weak. There was no hiding it from her family, but few others knew exactly what a basket case she was. That's why she'd spent so many years sequestered in the family compound. It had provided the security and stability she'd needed to overcome the worst of her issues, but it had kept her pride intact, too.

Ridiculous pride that kept her from admitting she was falling apart to Xavier and his doctor.

Gunter took her blood then her blood pressure, which he noted was elevated. He frowned and began asking pointed questions about her pregnancy.

She clammed up. The truth was, she wasn't combative as a result of being kidnapped. She'd been born that way, much to her family's eternal frustration. Her experience only gave her an excuse for it.

At her silence, Xavier turned from the window where he'd been standing in quiet contemplation. "Pass the readings to her specialist. She can determine if further action is necessary and advise a treatment plan. Request her doctor come to Lirona as soon as possible and stay for the duration of the pregnancy."

"She has other patients," Trella pointed out.

"None so important as you," he stated with a humorless smile.

"Flatterer," she tried, but her own sense of humor was buried beneath an onslaught of sensory overload ticking toward detonation.

"Sir, I've performed many deliveries," the doctor argued. "There's no need—"

"Sweeten the deal however you must. Our women's health initiative is due for an upgrade, I'm sure. Expenses won't be spared."

"Very generous, sir," the royal physician said more firmly. "I'm sure many Elazarians would benefit, but…" He cleared his throat. "Perhaps such an undertaking should wait until DNA results are received."

"The results are for the Queen. I'm confident this is my heir. But I do have to inform her. *Bella*, please advise your brother we'll be on the move again, but not for long. The palace isn't far."

That was when she should have said, *I can't.*

She knew what kind of self-care was needed. A

quiet, dark room. A sibling holding her hand, talking her down from her mental ledge.

She didn't say anything. Her stupid, tender pride, knocked to the ground so many times, locked her teeth while the rest of her began a slow collapse.

Now she sat in the back of his sedan, gripping her elbows as the ghouls came for her. It was going to be a bad one. She could taste it. The sheer frustration of not being able to stave it off made her eyes sting. Her mind spun down ever more scary avenues. Dark, harmful thoughts crowded in, feeding the anxiety.

*This is my life now.*

There would be no escape from the attention. It would be worse. Harsher. More judgmental. All the things she had tried to avoid by keeping her pregnancy secret and withholding the father's name were going to come true now.

The pressure in her chest grew worse, suffocating her, and even though her specialist had assured her from the beginning that suffering an attack wouldn't hurt the baby, she was convinced it would, *knew it.* She was going to lose her baby because she couldn't control these awful spells.

While Xavier watched her lose *everything.* He would reject her for being the disaster she was. Even if she managed to keep his baby and deliver it some weeks from now, he would take it from her. He might have her locked away.

*She needed Gili.* She took out her phone and gripped it so hard her hand ached. Where were Henri and

Ramon? They wouldn't let anyone take her baby. They would always keep her safe.

*No.* She couldn't keep expecting them to turn up and save her from herself.

"Why are you breathing like that? Are you asthmatic?"

She shook her head and turned her face to the window, wanting to die because now he'd noticed she was off and was staring at her.

"I'll ask Gunter if he reached your doctor." He started to lean forward.

She grabbed his sleeve. "Don't."

"You're flushed." He touched the backs of his fingers to her cheek then her forehead, making her flinch. "Sweating."

"It's nothing," she lied in a strangled voice, and was both relieved and horrified that her phone began to ripple with the heavenly notes of a harp.

It took two tries to open the call. When her sister appeared, she wasn't in focus. Tears of homesickness and failure filled her eyes. "Gili."

"I know, *bella*," she sounded equally anxious. "I can feel it. Where are you? Still at the Prince's chalet?"

"I don't know." The realization that she was in a strange land had been stalking her. Admitting it made it real and added to her terror. Her heart was so tight, she feared it was going into arrest. She clutched at the front of her shirt. "We're driving. How will you find me if we're moving? I'm so scared, Gili."

"I know, *fillette*. Breathe. Count your oranges. I'm coming. See, I'm going through the door. Henri has

been tracking you all day. We'll always find you, you know that. Are you still with the Prince?"

Trella looked up and saw Xavier staring at her like her hair was made of snakes.

It was the most humiliating moment of her life. She couldn't make it worse by having her sister come to her like she was a child. *Couldn't.*

"No." She turned back to her phone. "You're married now. You have to stay with Kasim."

"He understands. I've already sent someone to tell him and prepare the helicopter."

It sounded so outlandish. What other person had family flying in from all corners to save her from imaginary threats?

"No, Gili." She managed to sound firm, even though turning away her sister felt like plunging a knife into her own chest. "I don't want you to come. I mean it."

"*Bella,*" her sister breathed as though she'd felt the knife, too, in the back.

"I have to learn, Gili. I *have* to. I'm going to hang up and I'll call you later—"

"Wait! Let me speak to the Prince. He needs to understand."

Since there was no way Trella could explain it herself, she pushed the phone toward him.

"It's a panic attack," Gili said. "She doesn't need drugs or a hospital or strangers making her relive why this is happening. She needs to feel safe. Is there a hotel where you can secure a room? I don't mean book one. I mean *secure* it."

"We'll be at the palace in ten minutes."

"Good. Get her into a quiet bedroom, keep the lights low, blinds down, guards at the door. She needs to let it run its course without fearing people are going to see her. Keep her warm and whatever she says, remind her she's safe. If you can't stay with her, I'll come."

"I'll stay with her." His voice was grim. He handed back the phone.

She ended the call, mortified by how needy her sister had made her sound. Appalled because it was true. She hadn't tried to weather a spell on her own since they had first started. It had been a disaster.

Nevertheless, she screwed up her courage, pressed the phone between her breasts, and spoke some of the hardest words that had ever passed her lips. "You don't have to babysit me."

She held her breath, dreading the prospect of going it alone.

"I'm not letting you out of my sight until that baby is born."

The harsh words jarred, taking her brief flash of gratitude and coating it in foreboding.

# CHAPTER SIX

XAVIER HAD THE car drive to the postern gate, where delivery trucks and other utility vehicles came in. They took a lane through the back garden to the private apartments. It was a longer, slower, but much more discreet entrance into the palace built by a king three hundred years ago.

Did coming in this way also allow him to avoid Mario and any mention of his grandmother's expectation that he present himself? A man did what he had to for the mother of his unborn child.

Xavier didn't *do* emotion. Fits and tempers were signs of poor breeding. He'd been taught that from an early age. When women became histrionic, he offered space.

Not possible today. And as much as he wanted to hold himself apart from the way Trella was behaving, he couldn't. She was shaking, hair damp at her temples, eyes darting. When he helped her from the car, she clung to his sleeve and looked to every shadow.

It was unnerving. Even stranger, her sense of threat put him on guard.

He kept reminding himself this was a panic attack,

something he knew very little about except that it was a false response. Nevertheless, her fear provoked a very real primal need in him to offer protection. His heart pounded with readiness and he scanned about as they moved, fingers twitching for a weapon. He'd never experienced such an atavistic, bloodthirsty reaction. He was not so far removed from his medieval ancestors as he had imagined. He was completely prepared to shed his cloak of civility and slay if necessary.

Staff leapt to their feet as they walked through the kitchen. He said nothing, only pulled her into the service elevator.

Gunter came with them, frowning as he saw how distraught she looked. "Are you in pain?" He tried to take her pulse.

Trella shrank into Xavier.

"Leave her alone." He closed his arms around her. Her firm bump nudged low on his abdomen, reminding him that her panic attack was only the tip of the iceberg where this confounding day was concerned.

His valet, Vincente, met them as they entered his apartment. Xavier had moved into his father's half of the rooms when he'd finished university and never even glanced toward the adjoined feminine side, but it was kept dusted for the ghosts of past queens.

He pressed Trella toward the canopied bed of gold and red then started to close the doors, telling Vincente, "I'm locking us in. Leave sandwiches in my lounge. If I need anything else, I'll text. No one comes in here. *No one.*"

"Of course, sir." He read Vincente's apprehension. "But I believe the Queen—"

"Inform her I'll be along when I can, but it will be some time."

Xavier did as he'd promised, moving to lock each door and close all the drapes, turning on one bedside lamp as he went. Then he shook out a soft blanket from a chest and brought it to where Trella sat on the edge of the bed.

She clutched the blanket around her, back hunched, still trembling.

All he could see was a nine-year-old girl. Was this what that experience had left her with? He had a thousand questions, but heeded her sister's advice and only said, "You're safe, *bella*. This is my world. Nothing can harm you here."

Tears tracked her cheeks and she swiped the back of her hand along her jaw, skimming away the drips.

"I didn't want you to see me like this." Her voice was thin as a silk thread. "I wanted you to think I was Gili. She cries at proper things, like weddings and stubbed toes. She's afraid of real things, not stuff she makes up in her head."

Was it made-up? He used the satin on the corner of the blanket to dry her cheeks, not sure where the urge to comfort came from. It wasn't taught or ingrained. Manners and platitudes got him through displays like this, not affection.

But he felt responsible for her and her attack. "I only wanted to talk to you. I didn't expect things to go off the rails like this."

"Don't blame yourself. I take everything further than it needs to go." She drew in a shaken sigh. Her eyes filled again.

"Is this what you were hiding, staying out of the spotlight all those years?"

She nodded jerkily. "It started after Papa died. We were fifteen. I was starting to feel like I might be able to go back to school and have a normal life. But we were seen as sex objects, I guess, because the most disgusting men found us online. I'd already been through an eating disorder and trolls mocking me for it. Then all these men started sending photos and telling me what they wanted to do to me. It hit a switch."

A streak of impotent fury lodged in his chest. His entire life, he had struggled against this particular irony. He was a future monarch, charged with great power and responsibility, godlike in some eyes, but he couldn't control how people treated each other. He couldn't prevent the kind of harm that had Trella drawing up her knees so she was a ball of misery. His inability to help her struck at the deepest part of him.

"I'm a woman of extremes. You might as well know that about me. Give me that pillow."

He dragged it closer and she fell onto her side and buried her face in it. She sobbed so deeply, was in the throes of an anguish so terrible, he was stricken witnessing it. How did she withstand it?

*Let it run its course,* her sister had said. That seemed cruel.

He settled on the bed behind her, rubbed her arm and soothed her shaking back. It took several min-

utes for her crying to subside. She lifted her head and breathed as though she'd been running for miles.

"I keep worrying I'll have an attack while I'm in labor. My doctor says this won't hurt the baby, but I'm so scared all this adrenaline is causing damage. What if we go through all of this and our child isn't fit to reign? What if that's my fault because I can't control this?"

"Is there nothing you can take? Something safe during pregnancy?"

"No. I mean, maybe, but I can't. *Won't*." She threw her arm over her eyes. "I tried drugs years ago. They made me depressed and dependent. I was close to taking a whole bottle just to end this."

She dropped her arm and twisted to stare at him from between matted lashes.

"I shouldn't have told you that. You'll declare me unfit and take our baby away. Oh, God…"

She rolled around the pillow again, dragging the blanket with her and pulling it over her head.

"Trella." He was no mental health expert, but he knew a tailspin when he heard one. He settled on the mattress behind her, propped on an elbow, letting his body heat penetrate the blanket as he gave rubs of reassurance against her shoulder and arm. He wanted to fold right around her, absorb whatever had such a terrible grip on her.

"Let's take this one thing at a time. Hmm? The baby is well. Your doctor said so, yes? Do you know the sex?"

It took a minute, but her breathing settled to something more natural.

"I've been afraid to ask, thinking it would make me more attached. I'm so scared I'm going to lose it." She shifted, pushing away the blanket to reveal her face, then peeled the blanket all the way back, piling it on him as she exposed her bump. She smoothed her shirt over the roundness. "It's moving. Do you want to feel?"

He stalled, reality hitting him like a train. He let her draw his hand across the tense swell of her midsection. He had thought it would feel like an inflated beach ball, but she was warm and there was give within the firmness. A shape. Something that felt no bigger than his knuckle pressed outward, moving across the palm of his hand.

He almost jerked back, yet he was too fascinated and kept his hand in place, waiting to feel it again. "Does that hurt?"

"It reassures me. *Hola, bebé. Cómo estás?*"

Another tiny kick struck his hand, prompting a soft noise of amusement deep in her throat. She turned her head to look at him. Her eyelids were red and swollen, but her smile was so filled with joy and wonder, she took his breath away.

The moment snaked out like a rope to encircle and draw them together, binding them, inexorable and eternal.

He sucked in a breath, drawing back as he tried to pull himself free of what threatened to carry him into deep waters like a deadly riptide.

"How are we even here? How—Why me, *bella?*"

"Why did I sleep with you? I didn't plan to sleep with anyone." She curled around her pillow, rubbing

her face against it, drying tears. "I only wanted to practice being in public. I was so proud for having the courage to talk to a man, then to be alone with one. You made me feel normal. Safe. I needed that. I was using you. I admit that. But sleeping with you?" She craned her neck to look at him, her expression helpless. Anxious. "I couldn't help myself. You said we were volatile. That…"

He knew what he had said. It had been true. He'd never experienced anything like what he'd felt with her that night. Despite his best efforts, the memory haunted him. He wasn't a dependent person, but he was disturbingly gratified to be this close to her again. The animal inside him had finally stopped pacing with restless frustration.

He was loath to admit any of that, though. Her power to still affect him unnerved him. "It was my last night before I got engaged. We were both attributing significance for our own reasons."

The light in her eyes dimmed with hurt. She withdrew, turning away again.

He closed his fist in the tangle of blanket across their hips, lungs turning to lead.

"Either way, it gave me hope that I could *be* normal. Maybe fall in love and get married, someday. That's all I've ever wanted. To be normal. Now I never will be, because I'm carrying a royal baby and I was so happy to be pregnant, but I knew this was a disaster. You have your life and I've never had any life at all. I deserve a chance to be single and free. Free of *this*!"

Her tension returned in a contraction of her muscles

that drew her in like a shrinking bloom, fists coming up to her clenched eyes.

"I told Gili I would run Maison des Jumeaux. When we were little, she was able to count on me. I want to be that person people can rely on, but I'm always going to be this pathetic—"

"Trella. You *have* to stop escalating."

"Do you think I can control it?" Her hands went into her hair, clenching handfuls. "I try. I really try, but the fear *grips* me. Now we have to get married and you don't want some crazy burden of a wife. You'll hate me. I'm *so scared* of what will happen."

"Stop." He couldn't stand it. He pressed his body heat around her, held her in sheltering arms and willed her back to calm. "Hatred is a wasted emotion. It closes all pathways to resolving a conflict. Our situation is difficult, but hating each other won't make it easier."

Her trembling continued, but he felt the moment his words penetrated. Her hands loosened in her hair.

"That sounds very wise," she said on a sniff. "Do they teach you that in monarchy school?"

"Divorce class. My mother was a great believer in practical demonstrations."

She unfolded a few increments more. "When we were in Paris, you said your mother was sent away by your grandmother because she wanted a divorce?"

He eased his embrace, regretting his loose lips. He had learned out of necessity to be comfortable with his own thoughts, never needing confidantes, but keeping her mind engaged seemed to forestall her emotional downtrends, so he answered.

"She made a commitment then didn't accept her lot. Unhappy wives move into the dowager wing. They don't reject royal life altogether. My mother tried separation, but my father and grandmother pressured her to have another baby. Since their marriage was over, she refused. She was granted a divorce on the grounds that she left Elazar. She had family in Germany so she moved there."

"Exiled, you said. But you still saw her? How old were you?" She tried to twist enough to see him.

He used the weight of his arm to keep them spooned. Her hair tickled his lips while the scent of her went straight to the back of his brain, finding where she had imprinted herself in Paris and settling like a puzzle piece matched to its empty space.

He shook off the notion. "I was eight. At boarding school. My life wasn't affected much. We exchanged a few letters, but what was there to say?"

"You didn't see her *at all*?" She tried harder to twist, rolling onto her back and forcing him to meet her gaze. "Do you see her now?"

"We send Christmas cards." He shrugged off the jabs of rejection that still came alive when he revisited the memory. "Chosen by our personal assistants. We're not sentimental people."

Her expression grew appalled. "What about your father? You said you were young when he abdicated?"

"Renounced," he corrected, regretting this. It was becoming too intimate. Too uncomfortable.

"Do you see him?"

"It was best we didn't communicate." *This* communication ended here, he conveyed by drawing back.

"But—" She groaned and rolled to face him fully. He could see a fresh wave of emotion taking its grip on her. Her hand closed on the front of his shirt, catching at a few chest hairs, making him wince. "Now I'm worried you'll drop out of our child's life like that. Swear to me you won't."

He covered her hand, loosening her fist and holding her slender fingers. He had to consciously overcome an urge to draw her hand to his mouth and kiss her bruised knuckles, even as he acknowledged she was far more likely to disappear than he was. Royal life was not easy, especially when shoved to the fringes as his mother had been. He didn't blame his mother for extricating herself, and wouldn't censure Trella when she did it, especially if the stress of life in the public eye put her in paroxysms like this.

"Duty may have skipped a generation, but it is firmly drilled into me. I will never forsake my obligation to our child."

"Obligation." Her brow furrowed. "What about love?"

He dried her cheek with his thumb. "Love is a problem not a solution."

"Who told you *that*?"

"It's an observation. My mother loved my father, which is why she couldn't bear his cheating. My father loved the woman who cost him his kingdom. Duty is more reliable."

She shook her head.

"I don't have to argue with you, *bella*. Time reveals all. Now, let's stop talking about things that upset you. What did your sister say about counting oranges? Tell me why she said that."

Xavier hadn't had his backside handed to him on one of the palace's sixteenth-century gold platters since his teen years. He refused to allow it today.

He had had plenty of time in the night, lying awake making decisions between comforting Trella through crying spells and nightmares, until she fell deeply asleep in the early hours.

He rose to put his plans into action and by the time the Queen summoned him, he was able to preempt a shredding of his character by proving what he had told Trella—he adhered to duty above all else.

"She has agreed to that?"

"She will."

"And you?"

"Of course. Why wouldn't I?"

The Queen cocked a skeptical brow. "You spent last night with her. That implies…preoccupation."

"You think we were having sex? No." Despite having few secrets from his grandmother, her intrusive remark grated. "She was upset."

"Gunter said she's fragile." Her mouth pursed with disdain. Ruling required strength of every kind, especially emotional.

He frowned, annoyed that Gunter's report had preceded his own, especially because it was off the mark. Trella was besieged. It was different.

"She held off telling me because her pregnancy is high-risk."

"So, it would seem, is she."

An urge to defend her stayed lodged in his throat. She *was* a threat—one he was mitigating to the best of his ability.

"When would you like to meet her?" he asked instead.

"Perhaps after the baby is born?"

He hadn't slept. That's why the snub struck him as unconscionably rude.

Before he could react, Mario entered. "Deepest apologies, your Majesty, but Ms. Sauveterre's brother insists on seeing her. We've stalled him as long as possible."

"He's *here*?" Xavier's heart lurched with protectiveness and a jolt of alarm. Trella was catching up on much-needed sleep. More importantly, "We both spoke to him yesterday. She told him she was staying for the foreseeable future."

*She couldn't leave.*

"I believe it's the race-car driver. She has agreed to receive him. I thought you would wish to—"

"I would." Xavier strode from the room. When he heard raised voices as he approached the apartment they now shared, his aggression increased. With a snap of his fingers, security personnel fell into step behind him. He pushed into what had once been his mother's parlor.

Trella was red-faced as she confronted a man who looked like Henri but emanated a hot-tempered de-

meanor that was in complete contrast to his brother's air of aloof control. "No, *you* shut up—" Ramon was saying to his sister.

"Leave quietly or I'll have you removed." Xavier would do it himself. He was in that kind of mood.

Ramon snorted as he gave Xavier a measuring once-over, hands on his hips, looking willing for the fight Xavier promised.

"Don't." Trella threw herself against her brother's side, looping her arms tight around his waist. "I was saying things he didn't want to hear."

Despite the animosity that had been flaring between them seconds before, Ramon curled a shielding arm around his sister, even as he frowned at her, concern evident beneath his glare of impatience.

Trella looked as rough as the night she'd had. When Xavier had left her, she'd been subdued and exhausted, falling back asleep within seconds after he'd woken her to tell her he was leaving. She still had dark circles under red eyes and hadn't changed out of the silk pajamas he'd given her to wear to bed. In fact, she'd raided his closet for a thick cardigan to belt over them.

Xavier snapped out of searching her expression to realize she was bickering with her brother, refusing to go with him.

"All those times you showed up when I called makes it possible for me to work through this. I know you *will* come if I ask. That means everything. But until I ask, you *have* to *butt out*."

With a resigned scowl, Ramon dropped his arm from around her. "*Bueno.*"

"And be nicer to Iz—"

"No. Butting out goes both ways. And you *will* introduce me to your host."

"Did you call me a *virgin*?" Xavier asked Trella in an ominous tone as they entered his suite hours later. "You switched between French and Spanish so often, I might have heard wrong."

She tried not to snicker. "I told you it was a bad habit. Ramon and I are the worst because we get heated and grab the first word that comes in any language."

Ramon had joined them for a meal that might have been pleasant if so many questions hadn't been hanging over her like a guillotine blade. If he'd caught her alone again, he would have skewered her with all of them, she was sure, but he'd behaved. They had played verbal tennis as they always did, sticking to neutral topics like films and current events.

Sparring with her brother always helped restore her confidence. Where Gili was her security blanket and Henri was her rock, Ramon was her worthy adversary, keeping her sharp and forcing her to hold her own. She was tired and stifling yawns, but her lingering melancholy had lightened. As she looked into the cloudy crystal ball that was her future, she was thinking, *I can do this*.

Especially because, like her, Xavier seemed to be experiencing the same threads of attraction they'd felt when they had made this baby. A selection from her closet in Paris had arrived earlier and she now wore a dark blue skirt and a white maternity top. It draped her

breasts in such a flattering way, she'd caught Xavier eyeing her chest more than once while they ate, making her tingle and giving her hope.

She turned her back on him and lifted her hair, silently requesting he release the tiny clasp at the top of her spine, realizing she hadn't properly answered his question. "And yes, I did. Ramon asked me how you did with looking after me through my attack. I said pretty well, for a virgin."

"Lovely. I hope the dining staff enjoyed that." His breath warmed the back of her neck along with the light brush of his fingertips, making her shiver.

"I said worse. I called Ramon a—"

"I heard that one. Very clearly," he cut in dryly, motioning her to lead the way to her side of the apartment. "Because of his engagement to 'Izzy.'"

"Isidora, yes. She's a dear friend. Her father handled our media for years. Aside from Gili, she was my *only* friend for a long time."

Her heart dipped and rolled when he turned, locking them into her bedroom. Despite her rough night, sleeping with him had been more than comforting. She had liked the brushes of contact and the inherent intimacy, the way his strong arms had made her feel so safe. It had given her that bonding feeling she had felt in Paris, one that was incredibly bolstering.

His efforts to comfort also gave her hope for their marriage. All her flaws had been laid bare, yet he had stayed with her. She was deeply gratified. Touched.

Now all she had to explain was that, as much as she might like to, she couldn't make love. Practically blush-

ing at the mere thought, because she was so deeply tempted, she moved to take up her brush and began working it through her hair, trying to act casual as nerves accosted her.

He moved to lean on the footboard of the bed, appearing in the mirror behind her. The way he watched as she stroked her hair made her feel as though she was enticing him. The crackle of tension on the air was exciting, giving her that sense of power in her sexuality he'd instilled the first time. Oh, she wished their timing wasn't so far off.

His expression tightened before he jerked his gaze away, clearing his throat. "If she's such a good friend, why don't you approve of her?"

"Who? Oh. Um." She blushed at having her mind fixated on intimate acts while he was clearly not. "I approve of Isidora completely, but Ramon is sleeping with her."

"Stickler for waiting until after the wedding, are you?" He dropped a pointed gaze to her middle.

"Ha-ha." She tapped the brush against her thigh then set it aside. "No, their engagement is a publicity stunt. Earlier this year, Isidora took over her father's position at Sauveterre International." Trella took off her earrings and bracelet. "You'll notice Ramon's very public proposal coincides with the first photos of my pregnancy showing up online. He does that all the time, takes the spotlight off the rest of us. Izzy is so loyal she went along with it, but she had a terrific crush on Ramon when we were young. He never returned it and shouldn't sleep with her if he has no in-

tention of marrying her. She's going to get hurt. That makes me mad."

"I see. Well, kindly convey that we would prefer fewer stunts in future. My team will handle—" he indicated her middle again "—this."

She blinked, not expecting him to be worried for Izzy, not really, but his cool attention to his own interests sent a premonition down her spine like a drip of icy water.

It occurred to her that he had closed the door not because he wanted to nurture the growing trust between them. He wanted to have a conversation that was best held within the gilded cage he'd assigned her.

Logically she knew she had imprinted on her first lover like a baby duckling emerging from its protective shell. She'd spent weeks reliving Paris and imagining this reunion, dreaming up scenarios where he was as happy about her pregnancy as she was.

It was delusional. She had known that, but apparently she was still building castles in the sky because a minute ago, she had been okay with his knowing all her worst secrets. Now a grossly naked sensation accosted her, like he had leverage on her.

She tried to disguise her apprehension with a tough smile. "It's time to discuss *this*. Isn't it?"

The barest flicker of emotion reflected in his blink. He folded his arms and tilted his head in assent. "Gunter informs me your doctor has accepted my offer of a residency at Hospital del Re, with a mandate to ensure our obstetrics wing is the best in the world.

She'll be here tomorrow and has requested a private room be prepared for you."

"Bed rest." Trella had known it was coming, but still made a face of dismay.

"You'll fight it?"

"No." She wasn't able to keep the dread from her voice, though. "It's for the best."

"It is."

Something in his tone, in the subtle shift of his expression, pricked up her ears. Relief? His approval of her going into the hospital had nothing to do with the health of their unborn child. He was protecting his own interests again!

An ache of hurt spread through her until all her sweet imaginings had been pushed out and she was left with the ugly reality. She really had been deceiving herself all these months.

"Keeps me out of sight, does it? Is that the Queen's preference? Or yours?" Behind the stir of their child, her abdomen tightened.

His expression grew even more shuttered. "It's expedient for all. You said you don't want the attention our association brings."

"Don't pretend you're doing me a favor. Are we not marrying, then?" Clearly not, if he was hiding her away.

Her arms pulled into a defensive fold across her front. Her shoulders grew rock hard while she ignored the creep of anguish that began working in tendrils through her core. What did she care? She didn't want a husband anyway!

Right?

"Of course we'll marry." He mirrored her posture, arms folded, seeming relaxed in the way he leaned on the footboard, but there was a stillness to him, an implacability in his tone. "Elazar had a bastard monarch in the 1700s. It was a bloody fight to keep the reign. We've been sticklers for legitimacy ever since."

She understood she was speaking to a future king now, not the charming prince who had lulled her with something that had resembled caring. Twice.

"Our marriage will be a private ceremony. Announced, but without fanfare. No formal photos. We'll keep it brief."

"The ceremony? Or the marriage?"

"Both."

The tendons in her neck flexed as she fought a choke, doing her best to hide how deeply he was striking against her hard-won self-worth. "How brief?"

"We'll divorce by the end of the year."

Her teeth closed on the inside of her lip, biting down harder and harder until she had to consciously remind herself not to break the skin.

What had she expected after showing him her true colors? A declaration of love? A desire to live out his life with *that*? Well, she knew exactly how much *duty* he felt toward her, didn't she? Not even four months' worth.

"That's quite the virgin birth you're orchestrating."

His eyes narrowed at her shaken tone. "Is this conversation going to bring on another attack?"

Oh, she hated above all things to be managed like she was too delicate for honesty.

"I do better when I know what's coming." Her voice only trembled a little, mostly from the effort to hide the burn of disgrace sizzling under her skin. "Is this room a time machine, by the way? I feel we've gone back to your 1700s and I'm something shameful you're sweeping under the rug."

"It isn't about hiding you." He showed the barest hint of discomfort by dropping his hands to the footboard and pushing to stand. "I'm acknowledging you and the heir you're providing me, but it would be helpful if your role was downplayed, so as not to overshadow Patrizia's."

"You're still *engaged*?"

"It's been called off, since I'm marrying you, but—"

"She's still willing to marry you?" The news pushed her into falling back a step. Maybe it was the realization that he still wanted that marriage himself. Why did that hurt? So much?

"Unless a better offer comes along, she is not averse to reviving our plan after you and I divorce." He must have read the incredulity in her expression, because he said, "We're friends. Both ruled by duty. The fact we *don't* have strong feelings for each other and she's *not* hurt by this—" again with the generic wave at her middle "—is the reason we're a good fit."

"But her child won't be first in line! Or is she hoping mine's a girl?"

"Gender isn't an issue in Elazar. First born is first in line, but…" He seemed to debate whether she could handle his next words before he said, without emotion,

"Until you deliver a healthy baby, many aspects of this situation remain fluid."

Trella sucked in a gasp so sharp it went down the back of her throat like a spear, sticking in her heart and pinning her motionless. She tried telling herself the shivery clamp around her was anger, but it was anguish. Dark, blood-red betrayal.

"How *dare* you give someone *hope* that I'll lose our baby."

"It's not hope." He strode away from the foot of the bed in a sudden rush, making her jerk back another step and keep him in her line of sight. "It's caution. You said this will be your only pregnancy. There is a reason for an heir and a spare. If my uncle had lived, this conversation wouldn't even be happening. If my mother had done her duty, I would have other choices. I don't. I will accept what comes of this pregnancy, but I have to ensure there are alternatives."

She was so appalled that she wasn't even sure what the cold feeling against her lips was. Her fingers? All of her felt cold and empty and deeply furious.

She barely tracked that his hand flicked the air. Through her own haze of emotion, she had a brief impression of bitterness before he turned his back on her.

Anything close to suffering on his part was imagined, though. Had to be. Everything she had shared with this man was imagination and faulty memory. A wish. Girlish daydreaming. A rescue fantasy.

He was a spoiled prince who had sullied a maiden and was tidying up that mess the most pragmatic way possible.

"This really is medieval times, isn't it? Women have come all this way, yet I'm still just a vessel. A faulty one." She knew she was broken. It shouldn't surprise her that she was being rejected. She had thought she had prepared herself, but she hadn't. She was gutted and had to fight with everything in her not to reveal how devastated she was.

So many times, she'd wished she could go back to that moment as an impetuous girl, when Gili's math tutor had called out to her. She had run to tell him he had the wrong twin, *that's all*. It had been one second of impulse and she was still being punished for it.

Xavier's head tipped back as he aimed his gaze at the portrait of an ancestor surveying them from high on the wall.

"If I don't produce our next ruler, the crown passes to a family living in America for the last two hundred years. Rather than let that happen, our neighbors would squabble to take control of Elazar. Instability would ripple across Europe. The globe. We're a small country, but a pivotal one. I need more than one child to ensure Elazar's future. I need a wife with connections that cement our alliances."

His voice held not one iota of regret or even concern for how his plan would affect *this* child. Or her.

"Spell it out for me." She grappled for her most pragmatic tone. "Exactly how is this to work? Because I am not allowing some strange woman to raise my baby."

"Our child will be raised by nannies, tutors and servants, same as you and I."

"*I* wasn't!"

"You left for boarding school at *seven*. If you hadn't been kidnapped, you would have grown up there. Your brothers did."

"My parents traveled, but they were very involved. We knew they loved us!"

As she stared into his half-lidded eyes and read indifference, it struck her why he was being so dispassionate rather than weighing his decisions through his heart.

"You don't know what that's like, do you?" She felt cruel saying it, but everything he had told her about his parents came back to her, bringing his brutally logical plan into focus.

His brow went up in arrogant query. "What?"

"Love."

He might have flinched, but it was gone so fast that she wasn't sure. His sigh was pure condescension as he pushed his hands into his pockets. "I told you last night—"

"I'm not talking about romantic love. *Family* love."

"Love of any kind isn't real." His voice slapped her down for being so gullible. "Look around. Is it here? Keeping anyone in my life but my grandmother? Loyalty. Obligation. Duty. Those are real."

She would have argued that her family loved her, but something else struck with brutal force. "Are you saying—"

She had a flash of her mother crying with joy because Trella was pregnant. Elisa Sauveterre was worried sick and had strong opinions on how Trella had avoided telling Xavier, but beneath all of that was pure, over-the-moon love for her unborn grandchild.

# FREE Merchandise is 'in the Cards' for you!

Dear Reader,

### *We're giving away FREE MERCHANDISE!*

Seriously, we'd like to reward you for reading this novel by giving you **FREE MERCHANDISE** worth over **$20** retail. And no purchase is necessary!

You see the Jack of Hearts sticker above? Paste that sticker in the box on the Free Merchandise Voucher inside. Return the Voucher today... and we'll send you Free Merchandise!

Thanks again for reading one of our novels—and enjoy your Free Merchandise with our compliments!

*Pam Powers*

Pam Powers

P.S. Look inside to see what Free Merchandise is **"in the cards"** for you!

# W

e'd like to send you two free books like the one you are enjoying now. Your two books have a combined cover price of over $10 retail, but they are yours to keep absolutely FREE! We'll even send you 2 wonderful surprise gifts. You can't lose!

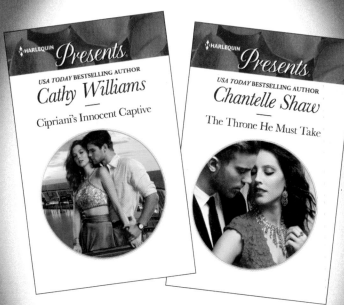

**REMEMBER:** Your Free Merchandise, consisting of **2 Free Books** and **2 Free Gifts**, is worth over $20 retail! No purchase is necessary, so please send for your Free Merchandise today.

## Get TWO FREE GIFTS!

We'll also send you 2 wonderful FREE GIFTS (worth about $10 retail), in addition to your 2 Free books!

Visit us at:
**www.ReaderService.com**

Books received may not be as shown.

## YOUR FREE MERCHANDISE INCLUDES...

2 FREE Books **AND** 2 FREE Mystery Gifts

## FREE MERCHANDISE VOUCHER

2 FREE
BOOKS
and
2 FREE
GIFTS

Please send my Free Merchandise, consisting of
**2 Free Books** and **2 Free Mystery Gifts**.
I understand that I am under no obligation to buy
anything, as explained on the back of this card.

❑ I prefer the regular-print edition          ❑ I prefer the larger-print edition
106/306 HDL GMV7                                      176/376 HDL GMV7

*Please Print*

FIRST NAME

LAST NAME

ADDRESS

APT.#          CITY

STATE/PROV.          ZIP/POSTAL CODE

## NO PURCHASE NECESSARY!

P-N17-FFM17

BUSINESS REPLY MAIL
FIRST-CLASS MAIL    PERMIT NO. 717    BUFFALO, NY

POSTAGE WILL BE PAID BY ADDRESSEE

REASER SERVICE
PO BOX 1341
BUFFALO NY 14240-8571

NO POSTAGE
NECESSARY
IF MAILED
IN THE
UNITED STATES

▲ If offer card is missing write to: Reader Service, P.O. Box 1341, Buffalo, NY 14240-8531 or visit www.ReaderService.com ▲

"Is your grandmother happy we're having a baby?" Her voice quavered with strain.

His jaw set. "That is not the word I would use, no."

"Wow." A jagged laugh clawed inside her chest. "Just wow." How did one survive such an emotional desert?

The answer was before her. They turned into this—an image of a man with a heart, but one who was actually incapable of deeper feelings. One who scoffed at love.

A fierce gleam—torment?—flashed in his gaze before he steeled himself behind a visage of hammered armor. "But she recognizes we have a responsibility toward it."

"Precious obligation," she said shakily. "Here's some news for you. I will *not* be shut out of my child's life and replaced by nannies and tutors. I'll call in the rescue team right now and barricade us in Sus Brazos for the rest of our lives if that's what you're thinking."

"Dramatics will not be necessary," he said with pithy disdain. "We'll share custody, fifty-fifty. Aside from security and education, how you meet the needs of our child is your business. Visitations to Spain or elsewhere can be worked out as they arise. But our child lives in Elazar." He pointed at the floor. "I will provide you with a home here in Lirona as part of our divorce settlement."

She shouldn't care how quickly he got rid of her. He was being so cold, acting so far removed from the man she had wanted to believe he was, she could hardly endure facing the next minute in his company let alone four months of marriage.

It still took effort to say, "Well, that's a relief." She held his gaze, saying goodbye to those moments when he had held her and touched her as if there had been more between them than obligation. "I can move on then, too."

His eyes narrowed with warning, gaze so hard and devoid of feeling she struggled to hold the contact. "You can."

How foolish of her to try getting under his skin. She looked away, thinking that she couldn't stay this close to him with her defenses annihilated the way they were.

"Where is this dowager wing of which you spoke?"

"You'll sleep where I can keep an eye on you. You were difficult enough to track down as it was."

"Confinement. How apropos. And *familiar*."

"I won't apologize. We've agreed it's wasted."

"I still won't forgive you."

"Because I'm not upending my life?"

"Because you don't want our baby!"

"I don't want our *situation*."

*You don't want me!* She didn't say it. She was appalled she had thought it and turned her face away, boiling in humiliation. Pressure filled her throat and sat livid behind her eyes.

Into the thick silence, he sighed. "What I want has never mattered, *bella*. Duty to the crown takes precedence. I learned that a long time ago."

His voice was surprisingly gentle, which made the lash of the words all the more cutting and intolerable.

"Don't call me that. It's a family nickname and implies we're closer than we are, but it's just something

you say when you can't remember the name of the woman you're sleeping with."

Another loaded silence filled the room like an acrid cloud.

"Explain to me how sniping at each other will make this easier."

"It's the *truth*." She swallowed past the ache in her throat, but it only lodged deeper in her chest. "You called me that in Paris and it made me think you saw *me*, not my sister, but all you saw was a willing partner. I need to stop thinking we're friends. Stop acting like we are."

They were still strangers and would remain so. He kept his heart behind thicker walls than she had ever hidden behind.

"If you insist. Trella."

"Thank you." She wasn't grateful. She was shattered. "Can you—" She waved at the door. "I'm tired."

"Will you be all right alone?"

She had thought he couldn't hurt her any further, but that did it. After rejecting her so roundly, did he really think she would want to cling to *him* through another emotional storm? How did he manage to sound like he *cared* if she suffered alone?

"I have to learn to be, don't I? I've known that for a long time. Goodnight."

# CHAPTER SEVEN

*I NEED TO stop thinking we're friends.*

There was no reason he should have lost sleep over that. Perhaps the *bella* endearment *had* always rolled off his tongue very easily around women, but for some reason knowing it held a more intimate connotation for her made it something he wanted the right to use. He doubted he would ever use it again with anyone else. It was hers now, which made it doubly frustrating she refused to hear it from him.

He went into his first meeting of the day, unrested and gritty eyed, only to face the woman still torturing him. They were about to negotiate their prenuptial agreement.

He introduced her to the palace attorney who fell under her spell at the first flash of her smile. She wore a pin-striped sky blue jacket over a white shirt that draped untucked over her matching skirt. It made her look smart and capable, yet sensual. Achingly vulnerable.

"I should have invited your brother to stay for this," he said as he directed her into a comfortable armchair.

"Why?" She cooled when he touched her arm and

delicately removed her elbow from his loose touch, adjusting a cushion behind her back as she sat.

"To protect your interests."

"You can email the draft to him," the attorney said with a magnanimous smile. "If he has concerns, we can address them before you sign."

She sat back and folded her hands on her lap, smiling in a way that could only be called patronizing.

"Gentlemen. Along with our mother, my siblings and I jointly own Sauveterre International. Ramon votes Gili's share and Henri votes Mama's because they don't take an interest. I vote my own, thank you very much. Maison Des Jumeaux is not the only enterprise I've asked SI to underwrite. One hundred percent of my initiatives have turned a profit because I have a brain and use it. So…" She cut a glance toward Xavier. "The Prince may show the draft to his grandmother before *he* signs, to ensure *his* interests are protected, but I'm confident I can look after my own."

The attorney cleared his throat and shuffled papers.

Xavier held her lofty stare.

He should have been affronted. It was a well-executed burn in front of the attorney and his PA, but he was darkly thankful for that scorn in her.

He had watched her all through their meal with her brother yesterday, captivated by her rallying spirit. The glimpse of her family dynamic and the new facets in her personality had only made him want to know her far better than he would be allowed to. It had taken genuine effort on his part to stick to the plan and outline how they would proceed. If he had had a choice—

He didn't. So he had said what needed to be said.

She'd been angry. Injured. She *was* sentimental. And despite his claims to be anything but, he didn't take pleasure in hurting others. If things were different…

Wistfulness was a useless emotion. He steeled himself against futile *if only*s. "Let's get started."

As promised, Trella protected her abundant interests with pointed questions and clear language. The details were hammered out with very little fuss until the attorney asked, "And the dissolution of the marriage? Midnight, December thirty-first?"

"That's fine. But if I lose the baby, the marriage ends immediately."

Her statement was jarring. Xavier swung his head to regard her, disturbed.

"There would be no reason to draw it out," she said stiffly. White tension ringed her mouth.

A strange void opened in him. Why? She was right. What else was there between them besides the baby?

*You don't know what that's like, do you?*

Her disturbing accusation last night kept ambushing him, but his parents had been disruptive forces in his life, dividing his loyalty, creating nothing but turmoil and disappointment. If that was love, he didn't need it.

His grandmother's levelheaded reason and clear outline of what was expected from a future monarch had been a welcomed relief. Taking responsibility meant taking control.

Like love, Trella was an unpredictable influence. Too much was at stake to indulge any latent desires

for either. She was right. Without the baby, they had nothing holding them in their union.

He lifted a finger, indicating the attorney should record that their marriage would end if the pregnancy did. He ignored the grate in the pit of his stomach.

They signed the contract a few days later, once the DNA results had been confirmed. Afterward, Trella hurried to greet her mother, who had arrived for the ceremony that would be held in the palace chapel.

"We agreed on a private ceremony," Xavier said when she informed him her mother would attend.

"She's giving me away." Trella hadn't mentioned her sister had cried over missing the ceremony. "All of my family wanted to be here, but neither of us is getting the wedding we wanted, are we? Well, I guess you are. Later."

His expression had hardened as he looked away.

She wasn't trying to be "combative," just stating fact. She had hoped she and Xavier would have something to build a family upon, but they didn't.

That made her sad, but all her soul-searching had been done in the months of keeping her pregnancy under wraps. Xavier had given her a chance at motherhood that she had believed was out of reach. For that, she would always be grateful.

But he saw her as, at best, one of the many staff who would tend to his offspring so he wouldn't have to. They might marry, but she wouldn't be his wife.

He didn't want *her*.

She had to ignore how spurned that made her feel. She already had people who loved her, after all.

"*Mi niña hermosa*," her mother exclaimed as she finished buttoning the gown and Trella turned to face her. "Truly, this is your *pièce de résistance*."

Trella had been working on the gown in secret, not even showing it to her mother or Gili. It was understated, like her makeup, with a high waist to cover her bump and a simple bodice with cap sleeves. The seed pearls and crystals had been the time-consuming work and she was proud of how it had turned out.

Her hair was in a loose chignon. Her mother placed a bridal comb over her ear in lieu of a veil. The brushed silver flowers with pearls and diamonds was a family heirloom, not ostentatious, just right for a small afternoon wedding.

They followed the ever-efficient Mario to the palace chapel.

Xavier was already there, speaking to the bishop. He wore a bone colored tunic-style jacket with dark gold epaulettes and gold leaf embroidery at the cuffs and hem. His royal red sash sat across it, decorated with a number of pins, including a key and a family shield. A sword hung off his hip.

*My prince*, she thought, and ached inside.

He wasn't, and he never would be.

Xavier turned and splendor kicked him in the stomach.

Her dress was white, which somehow wasn't ironic despite being a maternity gown. Perhaps it was the fact her bump was still modest, or the way the gown drew

his eye to the beading at her neckline and across her shoulders. The detailing resembled angel wings but also projected strength. Delicate armor.

The rest of her was incandescent. Her skin held the warm glow he had noticed the night they'd met, as if firelight reflected off a creamy nude. She was both waif and warrior. Goddess and maid. Infinitely fascinating.

She came forward, expression guarded as she introduced her mother.

Elisa Sauveterre was a tall, elegant woman of Spanish ancestry with sensual features and a single streak of white in her black hair.

As she held his hand in both her warm ones, shadows in the misty depths of her eyes told him she had feared this day would never come for her daughter. It made him feel churlish for bristling when Trella had informed him her mother was coming.

"It's an honor to have you here." He was embarrassed now that his grandmother wasn't attending, and that they hadn't extended an invitation for Elisa to stay at the palace. His impatience with himself sharpened his tone as he told Trella, "You look beautiful."

Her mouth tightened. "Thank you." But she might have been speaking to Mario who handed her a bouquet.

Mario was Xavier's witness, which suddenly felt like a disregard for the significance of the occasion. Xavier understood ceremony. His entire country was up in arms, wanting to witness this moment. The least he could have done was invite a friend to be his best man. He might not have many friends, but he had some.

Friends would come next year, though, when he married Patrizia in a spectacle he already dreaded.

Today's occasion was far more to his liking, even though the exchange of words seemed to hold extra power when spoken in such an intimate setting, heard only by the three witnesses. Even those few extra pairs of eyes and ears fell away as he spoke directly to Trella, losing himself in the shift of gray and green in her irises.

When she said, "I do," it reverberated within him, so visceral he knew that he would feel bound by this promise his entire life. She was his responsibility now, but he would have to turn away from her to perform the rest of his obligations. The war of dueling duties already hammered a crack into his psyche, causing a schism that would never heal.

"Do you have the ring?" the bishop asked.

"I'll only have to remove it when I go into the hospital." Trella waved off the case.

It was an unexpected swipe of claws at a part of him Xavier hadn't realized he'd exposed. What did he care that she didn't even glance at the ring he'd spent more than an hour dithering over, wanting it to match her sparkling, multi-faceted personality?

Her mother's tiny sniff broke the silence. Mario smoothly withdrew the ring. The bishop quickly finished the ceremony.

"You may k-kiss the bride…" Everyone had got the memo this was not a conventional marriage.

Her wary gaze grew even more vulnerable.

Should he have forgone this custom? Probably. But he set his hand at her waist and drew her toward him.

She braced her forearm along his and clenched her fist into his jacket sleeve, leaning on him for balance as she offered her mouth.

He brought his hand to the side of her neck, felt the cool tickle of a few strands of hair, and reminded himself not to make a fool of himself. Keep it brief.

He nearly groaned at the onslaught of sensation when his mouth covered hers.

As tenuous as everything else might be, in this second, they were as united as they'd been in Paris. Everything in him wanted to deepen and ravish, requiring all his willpower to keep the kiss short and sweet.

Her mouth moved under his with equal restraint, but he tasted the desire for more in the way her lips clung to his. Paradise hovered like a promise, but he couldn't surrender to whatever this thing was between them. All he could have was this. One kiss.

And it was already over.


"Mario tells me you wish to cancel Australia." The Queen looked up from her breakfast. "Why?"

He *had* cancelled, if Mario had done his job. Xavier filled his plate and gave the butler a nod, sending him from the room so they could speak in private.

"Don't play dumb," he said as the door closed.

"It's an important initiative."

Unlike some of his counterparts, the royals of Elazar took specific, active roles in government. His entire year had been a series of trade talks in various regions. It wasn't appearance for the sake of it, but business meetings and presentations to push for expansion of

existing agreements that would keep his country from going bankrupt.

"She isn't due for weeks," his grandmother continued. "Even when she goes into labor, what help do you think you will be?"

"She's alone in a strange country, stuck in the hospital. I'm not leaving for a month of press interviews where the first question will be, 'Why aren't you with your wife?'"

"Is that why you visit her every day? Because I'm told she keeps herself amused. Drawing. Chatting to family. You wouldn't be missed."

Perhaps not. Even Trella had asked if he was only visiting for appearances' sake.

The press release on their marriage and impending parenthood had been short and vague, playing to concern for a successful pregnancy without going into detail. It had made Xavier sick to hear his team discuss how spinning the pregnancy as a miracle would create a groundswell of support, overcoming judgments about a scandalous, ill-timed affair.

Trella hadn't reacted beyond a remote, "I've played this game a long time. Say whatever you have to."

She had played the isolation game as well and did know how to amuse herself. He wasn't needed and didn't know why he counted down the minutes until he could dodge the paparazzi on the hospital steps and enter the guarded sanctum of her room.

Her prison was as cozy as it could be made. Monitors and equipment feeds were tucked behind panels. The walls were a comfortable mocha, the blankets

printed with Elazar's national pasqueflower—the white buttercup that grew wild in their alpine meadows. Trella even wore regular clothes rather than a functional hospital gown.

But she reclined on the bed twenty-four-seven. Rising to use the toilet or shower was all the activity she was allowed.

Because of potential rupture.

Her doctor had scared the hell out of him when Trella had been admitted, explaining the need for such vigilance.

Trella had been stoic. She had checked into Hospital del Re the night they'd married and, despite only having resided in his apartment for a week, he'd felt her absence. Why? She'd been angry with him, cool when she'd been forced to speak to him, but somehow she had infused a sense of liveliness to the palace. The sound of her laugh in another room, or even just the splash of color from an abandoned scarf, made it less of a museum and more of a... Hell, it had always been his *home*. How could it suddenly feel like one?

He shook off the impression.

"You're very well-informed," he said, realizing the silence was stretching. "Yet you've never once asked *me* how she is."

"How is she?" She used her among-the-people tone of fabricated warmth, smile inching toward supercilious.

*Anxious*, he wanted to say. Trella *was* keeping herself busy, but he read the stress that lingered in the corners of her mouth and the tension between her brows.

"As well as could be expected."

"Then you should be able to leave her."

"I know what you're thinking." He shook his head. "I'm acting like a decent human being, not becoming attached."

Yet he was indulging himself with the visits. She hadn't asked him to come.

*I've done this before*, she'd said of her seclusion, then had revealed her best coping strategy. She was an accomplished sketch artist.

*Practice*, she had dismissed when he went through her book. He'd been taken with each image. Some were graceful gowns, some intricate patterns for beadwork. Some were colored as brightly as a children's book and others were shades of gray.

Then he had found one of their wedding day, copied from a photo her mother had taken. Trella's hint of a smile as she gazed up at him held shy awe. He wouldn't call his expression tender, but there was no hiding that he was absorbed by her doe-eyed stare. The captured moment was uncomfortably revealing, yet honest enough he couldn't be ashamed.

"I meant that for Mama, but I think you should hide it in the palace, to be discovered a hundred years from now. Give the art historians something to get excited about." She tore the page from the book and signed it. Her conspiratorial grin as she rolled it had tugged at him to play along.

It had been the first time she'd warmed up to him since their marriage, eyes sparkling with the vivacity that had first ensnared him in Paris.

He'd accepted the drawing with the strangest tingle of pleasure, liking the idea of her being resurrected generations from now, pulled from the footnotes and celebrated.

For a moment, there'd been nothing between them but this frivolous secret they were planning to keep. Then, as their gazes stayed locked, sexual awareness had crept in. The attraction was still there, ignored and subverted, but in those seconds, he felt the lava churning below the surface, swirling and burning, building with pressure against the cracks.

"Surely you can make arrangements with one of her family members if the round-the-clock care at the hospital isn't sufficient?"

He snapped back to the breakfast room and his grandmother's facetious tone. The heat in him faded.

"I've discussed that with her." He had suspected Trella was homesick after catching her tearily viewing photos of her infant nieces. "Her brother and his wife are tied up with their new twins. Her mother is on hand to help them. Her sister can't leave her new husband." They were trying to get pregnant, if Xavier was reading the subtext correctly. "And something has gone off the rails with the brother who was engaged. She'd rather not speak to him, so…"

"You're being manipulated."

"By whom?" He held her gaze, turning one of her best weapons—barely disguised derision—against her.

"You have obligations," she began in a very quiet voice that held no hint of a tremble. It was the very lack

of emotion, the stamp of inarguable logic, that made her words so powerful.

The splinter he had experienced on his wedding day rent deeper, ringing with agony as he felt himself stretched on the rack of conflicting duties. Wife. Crown. Temporary commitment. Eternal service.

A sharp rap on the door had them turning their attention to Mario as he stepped in without waiting for an invitation.

"Apologies, Your Majesty, but the Prince is requested to go the hospital. Immediately."

"They're prepping her for surgery," he was told when he called from the back of his car. He broke into a sweat and urged his driver to hurry.

He was shown to a lower floor when he arrived. She was in pre-op, flat on her back in a hospital gown, hair covered in a blue cap, lips white, tubes taped to her arm.

"You made it." She held out her free hand.

He grasped her fingers, disturbed to find her grip clammy and weak. "What happened?"

"Pain. Tearing. They scanned and said it has to be now." Her mouth trembled.

Thirty-four weeks. So early.

"Shh." He leaned to shelter her, trying to smooth her tense brow with his thumb, but feeling the trembles coursing through her. "Are you having an attack?"

"No," she choked. "This is real fear, Xavier."

"It will be okay," he insisted, undone because she had every right to be scared and there wasn't a damned

thing he could do. *He* was scared. "I'll come in with you."

*What help do you think you will be?*

"You can't. I asked."

How did that reach inside him and squeeze his lungs dry? Her wanting him with her spun and wrapped and pierced his heart like a barbed hook, deeply uncomfortable, but inexorable, tethering them together. "I'll come in anyway."

"You *can't*, but listen. I asked them to wait until you were here so I could ask... I've texted my family. Tell them how it goes as soon as you can. If I don't make it—"

"Of course you'll make it." He closed his ears against any other outcome.

"*Listen*. If I don't, swear to me you'll give the baby fair time with them. They'll need it." Her eyes filled. "Our baby deserves to know what love is."

Her words punched a hole clear through him, leaving an expanse of emptiness that was replaced with agony. The gentle rebuke in her eyes was another blow, searing and brutal, too painful to withstand, too impactful to avoid.

"You're going to come through this," he managed. What if she didn't? He couldn't even.

"Promise me on everything you hold sacred. Your crown. Everything." Her nails dug into the back of his hand.

"If you need to hear it, yes. I'll take the baby to your family myself." He would promise anything to ease that terror in her eyes. To ease his own sense of failure. Of

being so lacking she had no faith in him to give their child what it needed. Their baby *did* deserve to know what love was. If she wasn't here to offer it...

"Sir, we have to take her now."

"Kiss me goodbye," Trella whispered.

He swooped without hesitation, felt the tremble in her pouted lips, thought he ought to be gentle, but he took. Ravaged. He invaded her mouth with his tongue and drowned in all she was, trying to slake a hunger he feared would last all of eternity. Her lips opened, surrendering, even as she responded, flavoring the kiss with sweetness amid the shared desperation.

He kissed her as though it was the last one they would ever share. He couldn't bear the thought that it might be.

"Sir—"

He straightened abruptly, feeling the loss like he was torn away by a tornado, hating that he was forever doing what *must* be done.

Trella covered her mouth with her wired hand, eyes blinking above her white fingers. She kept her grip on his fingers until she was forced to let go.

"Sir, there's an observation room for students. Let me show you."

A nurse showed him to a small room with a window. Beyond, he saw Trella nod at the anesthesiologist before her face was covered with a mask. Her doctor motioned gloved hands to the team then everyone moved into place so all he saw were backs clad in scrubs.

"It shouldn't take long," the nurse said. "If you feel lightheaded, there's a chair."

He ignored her, all his attention on the surgery.

"They're waiting for confirmation she's out," the nurse said. "There they go."

They began to move in a controlled, efficient way and the nurse was right. In a very short time, the doctor was handing a tiny, naked infant to the nurse standing by with a towel. The nurse angled the baby to the window, showing him it was a boy.

The anguish in the small face at being separated from his mother pierced Xavier unexpectedly. He felt ridiculously helpless, wishing he could comfort the boy.

"We've been preparing for a premature birth. He's small, but that attempt to cry is a good sign. That's the pediatrician who's taking him. He'll run tests and place the Prince in an incubator then come speak to you. You'll probably be able to hold him. Your son, I mean," she said with a wry attempt at humor. "Not the pediatrician."

*Son.* Xavier nodded and texted Trella's family, including his grandmother.

A boy.

It seemed such an inadequate few letters for the magnitude of what was happening to him. He had a child. A son.

His phone buzzed with returned texts from Trella's siblings, congratulating him and asking after her.

He glanced up and something had changed. The team around Trella had snapped into frantic action. The anesthesiologist was clearly alarmed and the sur-

geon's movements became agitated. Through the glass, he heard raised voices issue sharp commands.

"What happened?" Xavier slapped his hand to the window, even as his gaze looked for the door to enter the room.

"Sir, I—" The nurse made as if to close the curtain.

"Find out what's happening."

"Of course." She hurried away.

He pressed his forehead to the cold glass, terror snaking to squeeze his heart. He strangled on the one word he managed to whisper.

*"Bella."*

# CHAPTER EIGHT

TRELLA CAME TO in a blurred awareness of voices and stark white. Even Xavier looked carved from pale marble, his blue eyes translucent as antique glass. Bottle blue, she wanted to call it. She should use that shade in next season's collection.

Why was he leaning over her like that? So close and grim?

"Baby?" She tried to say, but there was no sound. Her voice had evaporated.

"Fine. Really well, considering how small he is." He backed off as a nurse picked up her wrist, but his eyes stayed locked on her.

*He.* "A boy?" That came out in a raspy whisper.

"Yes."

She blinked heavy eyelids and tried to smile. "Sadiq."

"What?"

"He saved me." She was becoming aware that she was stoned. Recreational drugs weren't her thing, but she'd been prescribed so many pharmaceuticals to quell her panic attacks that she knew what this foggy haze was. She hated it and fought to think through it. "I wouldn't be here without him."

"Dr. Lagundo saved you," he snapped.

"Why are you mad?" She frowned, startled to find the nurse was still beside her, fussing with her arm. Whatever she did hurt, but distantly. "Can I see him?"

"Soon." The nurse seemed familiar. Her smile was nice, but Trella couldn't recall her name.

She hated drugs. Hated being dopey and disassociated. She ought to be upset as Xavier's remark belatedly penetrated. "I almost died?"

"There were some tense moments," the nurse said. "Your doctor will tell you more. I'll let her know you're awake."

She left and Xavier came back to her side, mouth pinched.

"Are you angry that I pulled through?"

"What? No! Why would you think that?"

She tried to think through a brain made of cotton balls. "You don't like me. You're mad about the baby."

"None of that is true." He loomed over her again, very intimidating. If she wasn't so spaced-out, she would think he sounded tortured. "You scared the hell out of me."

Was he holding her hand? Something cupped her fingers in warmth. It was nice. She liked the gentle stroke across the back of her hand.

"But it would have been easier for you." She was briefly thankful for the drugs because despair didn't overtake her. "I make things harder. I don't mean to. My family forgives me because... I don't know. They love me, I guess. But you don't, so it's okay if you wish I had died."

"Stop saying that. What would Tyrol do without you?"

"Who's Tyrol?"

"Our son."

She frowned. "I expected a girl."

"I texted you the name a couple days ago." He sounded disgruntled. Maybe self-conscious. "You said you liked it."

"When? I hate drugs. They make me so stupid. Is it Tuesday or Wednesday?"

"Wednesday. I texted on Monday and asked what you thought of Tyrol or Trentino." He seemed to be petting her arm, combing his fingers into the gaps between hers. "They're family names. You said you liked Tyrol. We're *not* naming him Sadiq."

"But picture your grandmother's face if we did."

He choked out a laugh, turning his face away, shoulders shaking. "You're funny when you're high, I'll say that much."

"You should laugh more."

He looked back at her with an expression she couldn't decipher. Regret maybe, but something like appreciation?

She closed her eyes against his sorcery.

"Did you know, *bella*? Is that why you said those things before you went in?"

"I don't get into trouble on purpose," she grumbled, ignoring the number of times Ramon had accused her of doing exactly that. "And I don't apologize when I do. It makes people feel good when they help me. My whole medical team is feeling super heroic right now."

He let out another incredulous laugh. "That is some seriously backward logic. Exactly how ripped are you?"

"Admit it. This morning you were ambivalent about having a son. Now you're grateful. You're welcome for the clarity."

Stunned comprehension seemed to blank his face, but she didn't gloat.

"I want to see him." She weakly squeezed the hand that gripped hers. "Is he beautiful? Does he look like you?"

"He looks mad." His voice wasn't quite steady. More emotion shifted across his profile, things she couldn't interpret. Concern? "He wants you."

*It's the drugs*, she warned herself, even as her heart turned over with sweetness that he might feel something on their son's behalf. *Don't start seeing things that aren't there*.

She didn't doubt he'd been worried on some level when he thought she would *die*. He wasn't a monster, but he had made it abundantly clear that his heart was beyond reach. He was capable of kindness, but that was the limit.

His phone buzzed. "That's your family. I'll let them know you're awake. Smile." He held up his phone to take her photo.

She stuck out her tongue and crossed her eyes. "Tell them we named him Sadiq."

"That's the friend whose wedding you attended earlier this year, isn't it? His wife would object, wouldn't she?" He tapped the screen.

"She would stab me in the eye. That's why it's funny."

"I'll tell them his name is Tyrol." He leaned down to press a kiss between her brows. "I like your eyes the way they are."

"Xavier?" She touched the side of his head, keeping him from straightening. "It's really confusing when you're nice to me."

His thumb traced near the corner of her mouth. "I never said I didn't like you, *bella*. You do make things hard. All of this is hard. But I am grateful for our son."

*And me?*

His eyes were an endless blue that only grew more intense the further she fell into them, but even in her muddy-minded state, she knew better than to ask.

And he didn't say.

# CHAPTER NINE

XAVIER LEFT FOR Australia ten days later.

Trella and Tyrol were released from the hospital and went directly to her family's compound in southern Spain. Her brother was in residence with his four-month-old twin girls. Her mother was there, along with a team of nannies and servants and guards. Xavier could not have arranged better, safer care for either of them.

Trella had bounced back from near-death with startling cheer, pouring such tenderness and joy over their son Xavier almost thought it was fake; it was so far removed from anything he had ever experienced himself. Her words from pre-op kept echoing in his head. *Our child needs to know what love is.*

Did he? Because the limited feelings Xavier had allowed himself to feel toward her had amplified his fear when her surgery had gone sideways. This level of concern for someone wasn't comfortable. Was he a bad parent for setting up his son to love and possibly to lose?

*He* needed distance as a buffer against becoming

more deeply invested in both of them so he went to Australia as scheduled. He hated every single one of the thirty days he was gone, which only underscored why the separation was necessary, he supposed.

It didn't help that things went exactly as he had warned his grandmother they would. He answered the same question so many times he muddled his lines at one point.

"The plan was tripped last year."

The blond newscaster tittered.

"The trip was planned," he corrected, yanking his mind back from Spain to Adelaide and the trade talks he'd been in. "The early birth made it possible for me to travel as scheduled. I was on the brink of canceling, which would have been a shame."

Several handshake deals were already moving toward more formal agreements. His adherence to duty was producing much-needed results.

"But you must miss him!"

"Technology is a wonderful thing. We check in often. He's thriving and Trella is recovering. That's the most important thing." He flicked a glance at one of his handlers, silently conveying that if they didn't swerve back to topic, this interview was over.

The newscaster took the hint. "We wish them well. About your meeting with the state representative today…"

Did he miss his son, Xavier wondered later? If such an emotion had never been acknowledged, internally or externally, did it register with anyone if it somehow manifested today?

How *could* he miss the boy? Tyrol was an infant who wanted to suckle and sleep. Trella was adept at keeping Xavier apprised of their son's progress, such as it was. She texted often, telling him about a gain of an ounce or other small milestones. She sent him photos—probably half a dozen a day. A more pragmatic man would say one was plenty, but Xavier found himself studying each one, fascinated by tiny eyelashes and miniature fingernails. The boy's eyes looked like his own, but his mouth was definitely Trella's.

One grim night, Xavier let himself recall that for a few moments, this boy's resemblance to his mother had been all that might have been left of her. The despondency that had engulfed him at the thought had had him placing a video call to her.

She had been surprised since she usually initiated the calls if she happened to be nursing and the time was right on his end. She had asked him about his day, which he didn't care to talk about, and he had listened to whatever she volunteered, silently mocking himself for being riveted by small talk about her family and a few shower gifts.

There shouldn't have been any holes of curiosity or unmet sense of obligation within him. His wife and child were well. He was getting on with his life exactly as he should.

So why did he nearly go through the roof when he woke to a fresh message from her?

Ramon and Izzy are getting married! The wedding is at the end of the month, in Madrid. We decamp to

the family mansion the day before I'm due to return to Elazar. I'll extend our stay until after the ceremony since it's only an extra weekend.

On the surface, it was a perfectly reasonable assumption. Moving her and Tyrol with the rest of the staff to Elazar for a few days so she could turn around and go back was a needless expense. Royal detractors would have a field day. She was nursing, so she couldn't leave Tyrol in Elazar while she attended the wedding. Xavier had no reasonable basis to refuse her request.

Nevertheless, the only word that came to mind was, *No.* He didn't analyze it, he only knew he would not go back to the palace and wait for her.

As the youngest, Trella sometimes thought she had received all the leftover DNA after her siblings had taken the best of it. Henri had their father's sense and logic. He was stubborn, yes, but *she* was outright obstinate. Ramon had their mother's passion and determination, but Trella was an opinionated hothead. Gili scooped up all the sensitivity and generosity while Trella selfishly stole all the attention with her nervous breakdowns.

None of them were small-minded or jealous, but Trella—the baby who was spoiled and deferred to all the time—was drowning in envy of all of them.

Why couldn't she have a partner in parenting like Henri had with Cinnia? Why couldn't she have a big wedding that had everyone buzzing with excitement, like Ramon was planning with Isidora? Why couldn't

she have a husband who not only couldn't keep his hands off her, like Kasim with Gili, but refused to have any other woman by his side as he took the throne of his country?

Why did she have so much negative self-talk eating away at her self-esteem? *They* didn't. They were all better and smarter than that.

She was the broken one.

With her arms braced on the side of the pool, she gave desultory kicks behind her while watching Cinnia hand off a freshly fed Rosalina to Henri.

"I'll put her down and work through siesta. You'll finish your lunch then rest before we travel?"

"I will," Cinnia promised, smirking at Henri's overprotectiveness before he erased it with a tender kiss. "Thank you, darling." She gave her wrap dress a final straighten and turned back to the salad she'd been picking at while nursing.

Henri glanced at Tyrol, asleep in the cot in the shade. "Do you want me to take him up? You should sleep before we leave, too."

The flight was an hour and Trella was five weeks postpartum, but her scare during delivery had set them all back to watching her like she was made of spun glass.

"I'll take him when Cinnia goes up. The weather won't be as warm in Elazar. I want to enjoy the pool while I can."

"I'm going to miss you when you go back to Elazar," Cinnia said as Henri left.

"I know. This has been really nice."

Quite by accident, Cinnia had been the first to know Trella was pregnant, when she had been hiding her own pregnancy from Henri. They had become very close in those early months and sharing these weeks of new motherhood had deepened their sister-like bond.

"Is it going to be okay living there, do you think?" The simple question was the reason Trella loved Cinnia. Her sister-in-law invited confidence but didn't intrude.

Trella sighed, daunted enough by the future to admit, "I have no idea. I feel good. Physically, I mean. And stable, mentally. But I'm *here*. That always helps."

"At least I knew Henri when I was in your shoes." Cinnia had been Henri's mistress for years before her pregnancy tore them apart and drew them back together. "It must be hard, having a baby and still being at the getting-to-know-you stage. You two haven't had a proper chance, have you?"

"No." Two nights and daily hospital visits that she'd said she didn't need.

She had, though. She'd soaked up his duty visits like sunshine, trying not to read into the kiss they'd shared when they wed. He'd seemed to be pretending it hadn't happened, sticking to chatting very generally about whatever meeting he'd been in or whatever political scandal was trending.

When he'd gone through her sketchbook, she'd felt very vulnerable, especially when he found the one she'd done of them. Why had she thought it was a good idea to give it to him? He'd probably thrown it out, but she

had longed so badly for him to feel *something* about their wedding day.

He'd looked…touched? Whatever the softening in his face had been, it had caused her to moon so obviously, he'd flinched and looked away.

She was such an idiot. He was probably feeling put-upon. When they did connect over the tablet, he had seemed remote. He wasn't impatient, but she had the sense his prevailing mood was resignation.

She was trying to resign herself as well. Years of therapy had taught her to focus on one small piece of the future at a time. When he had crushed her soul with his news that their marriage would be temporary, she hadn't tried to imagine what her life would look like after their divorce. She had focused on making it to term with her pregnancy.

Once Tyrol had arrived, she'd come here, where she'd been able to focus on Tyrol and her recovery. Returning to Elazar and her looming divorce wasn't something she was ready to contemplate. She didn't even know how to handle the two and a half months left in their brief marriage!

Making a concerted effort to include Xavier in Tyrol's progress had seemed like the right thing to do. She told herself it was her way of encouraging a bond between father and son, but she knew there was a part of her that liked having an excuse to reach out to him. She was still trying to push for something that was futile.

But just when his reticence had her convinced he felt nothing, he would surprise her by phoning to ask how things were going. He would linger on a video call

after she'd run out of things to say, seeming content to stare at a sleeping baby over a screen.

Such a confounding man.

She glanced to where Tyrol slept; the one thing in all of this that made her unspeakably proud. If everything she'd been through in her life, all the pain and traumas and anguish had had to happen in order to bring her son into this world, so be it. She accepted all of it.

"Has your doctor really forbidden you to have another?"

"We talked it over several times through the pregnancy. It was my idea that she would tie my tubes during delivery, so I wouldn't need another surgery in the future. She did. I'm not sorry, or even very sad. I resigned myself a long time ago to not being able to get pregnant. He's truly a miracle. The delivery was such a near miss, though. I wouldn't want to push my luck, especially now he's here and needs me."

Cinnia nodded. "What about a surrogate? I'm sorry. Maybe that's not something you'd consider?"

"Gili told me years ago she would be my surrogate, but that was before Kasim." She tucked her chin. "Can you imagine his reaction?"

"He gives her anything she asks for." Cinnia closed her grin on her fork. "His head would literally explode trying to decide whether to be possessive or indulgent."

"Right?" They both chuckled, then Trella sobered. "They would want to secure his heirs before even thinking of it, anyway. I don't see Xavier wanting to wait." *There is a reason for a spare.* "Maybe I'll find a surrogate someday, but I don't think that would change

Xavier's mind about us. It's not just about another baby. We're not you and Henri." Or Gili and Kasim. Or Ramon and Isidora. "He has other considerations."

*He doesn't want me.*

She *had* to accept that.

It made her chest grow tight, though. Her throat ached. She ducked under the water to hide how she was tearing up. She stayed there, diving deep and crawling along the bottom until her lungs were about to burst, only coming to the surface when she reached the stairs.

"Pah!" She stood and wiped the water from her eyes.

Cinnia had come to her feet and was saying hello to someone.

Henri had returned with a striking blond man in tailored dark gray pants and a collared T-shirt that hugged the fit muscles of his shoulders and revealed his tanned gorgeous biceps.

The newcomer glared at her from his familiar, laser blue eyes. "Should you be *swimming?*"

Suddenly dizzy, Trella panted, "*Hola, cariño.* I missed you, too."

Xavier was distantly aware of Henri retreating with his wife, but if the woman had a name, he had already forgotten it. His entire focus was eaten up by the way Trella rose from the water like Venus herself.

Water sluiced down her body, washing away the grinding aggravation that had propelled him here. He had needed to see her without understanding why. He might have labeled it homesickness if that wasn't such

a juvenile emotion and he was in Elazar, not a part of Spain he'd never seen before.

But he'd come here with single-minded determination and when he'd finally clapped eyes on her, she'd been on the *bottom of the pool*, trying to give him a heart attack all over again.

All his concern, pining and every other thought in his head drained away, however, as she walked toward him.

Coming here was a mistake. He saw that as clearly as he saw she wore a red bikini, the triangles of fabric tied off at her hips and between her breasts. She had been quite comely with the weight of a baby distending her middle, always turning herself out stylishly, even when she'd been in the hospital.

Keeping his mind off sex while she'd been in a delicate condition had been, if not easy, at least quickly forestalled by worst-case scenarios. He had told himself any attraction he still felt was a byproduct of his not having had sex since they'd made the baby sleeping in the cot to his left. Maybe the two kisses they'd shared had ambushed his memory when it was least convenient. Definitely, he relived their night in Paris far too often.

It all added up to an obsession he should have put behind him by now.

He hadn't.

Her approach coiled him tight. He hadn't seen her naked since Paris and her hourglass figure was as spectacular as his libido recalled. Better. Glittering droplets sparkled on her golden skin and her breasts were

positively voluptuous, swaying as she padded toward him, bare feet slapping the tile.

His mouth watered. A distinctly male pulse tugged behind the fly of his pants. He had to resist a telltale swallow and consciously regulated his breathing. The animal, that restless beast that had been scratching and digging inside him, howled as she drew near, wanting to leap on her. Reunite.

"What are you—?" She was squeezing water from her hair, but as she met his gaze, her eyes widened in reaction, pupils exploding like fireworks. Her breath caught, expanding her chest and drawing his attention to her nipples, already sharp from the chill, but poking even harder under his gaze.

"Wh-what are you doing here?" Her hand went to a nearby chair back as if she needed to steady herself.

He was acting directly against his responsibilities, despite the rationalizations he'd concocted. Angry with himself for the hunger clawing through him, he searched his brain for the reasons that underpinned his arrival.

"I'm taking you to Madrid. You'll stay with me there."

Her shoulders fell. "You don't trust me?"

That wasn't it, but he didn't want to admit—even to himself—that he hadn't been able to wait three more nights to see them. Not just his son. Her.

He found his gaze straying to the curve of her hips and the dip of her navel and forced his attention to drag across to the infant in a pale green onesie. The strangest yank in his chest had him stooping to pick up the boy.

The sleeping baby gave a small start of surprise, fingers splaying, then relaxed into a warm ball against the hollow of Xavier's shoulder. He felt heavier. Sturdier.

"He's growing."

"He is." She wrapped a towel around her middle, hands shaking. "Xavier, I swear I wasn't trying to avoid coming back. The wedding is a rushed thing. Izzy's father has been ill. It's a big deal for him to be able to walk her down the aisle so they're indulging him. It's also the only chance for the bunch of us to be together for the foreseeable future. That's why I need to be there."

"I'm not saying you shouldn't go. But it's your first public appearance since we married. We should be seen together."

"Well, of course you were invited. I just didn't think…" She was taken aback, which was justified, he supposed. "Doesn't it send the wrong message?"

Because of the way their press release had been worded.

*Given Ms Sauveterre's preference for avoiding the spotlight, the marriage is a formality to ensure the legitimacy of Prince Xavier's heir and won't be continued in the new year.*

"I've spent a month having my devotion to my family questioned. I'd like to change the optics." There. That was the excuse he had given his grandmother and he stood by it. Their countrymen were going mad over the three photos he'd released of the young prince, but

they were questioning why he wasn't spending more time with him.

Trella understood how the PR game was played. She wouldn't fault this move.

The warmth that had pinkened her cheeks drained away, though. Her expression stiffened. "Of course. And we both know how unimpeachable your sense of obligation is. Most of my packing is done. I only have to shower and change. Shall I send a nanny to take him? After you've had time to post some selfies, of course."

He had set himself up for that, but it still landed on target. "I'll keep him," he said in a tone that let her know she was walking a fine line.

She flipped her wet hair and walked away.

Trella fell asleep on the flight so they were in Madrid before she was alone with Xavier again. Physically she was recovered, but Tyrol was so little he needed to feed often, even if that meant waking him. She was up several times a night so tended to nod off midday. But rather than dozing, she would have preferred to spend the time working through Xavier's surprise appearance.

Optics? Really? It was incredibly insulting. Her entire family had been used a million times over to sell magazines and promote products, all without their consent. She was tempted to tell him what she thought of him, but part of her disbelieved him.

For a minute, as they'd stood by the pool, she'd thought—But, no. His carnal look had been gone once he'd picked up Tyrol. She had imagined it. What kind

of wanton did it make her that she had responded to blatant lust, anyway?

She *had* responded, though. She had run to the shower to cool off, slowing the race of her pulse and willing away the thrumming awareness in her loins.

Fat lot of good it did. Flutters of intrigue were still playing like butterflies in her middle, gaze straying to the cut of his pants over his butt and the sculpted muscles beneath his shirt as he paced in front of her. She had missed him!

Tyrol finished nursing and was fast asleep so she unlatched him and handed him off to a nanny, then she struggled to put herself together behind the screen of a receiving blanket that didn't want to stay in place.

Yes, I'm half-naked under here. *Stop staring.*

A flush of heat went through her. It was a lusty re-action that had simmered at merely sensual while she'd been feeling squat, scared and vulnerable in a hospital. Or when he'd been on the other side of the planet.

Now she was more confident on so many levels, but still unsure of herself with her husband. This was as bad as his ambush in Innsbruck when he'd left her with nowhere to hide.

"Ready?" he said, tucking away the phone he'd been tapping while she'd nursed.

"For?"

"I've been waiting to look around. I haven't seen the house, either."

"Oh. Um, sure." The mansion was on a small es-tate in La Moraleja, farther out of the city from the historical home in the Salamanca neighborhood that

had been in her mother's family for generations. This house was built with old-world touches like columns and wrought iron rails, but it was very modern, perhaps only a few years old.

"Did you lease it? Or…?" Surely he hadn't purchased something for a long weekend?

"It belongs to a friend. We studied architecture together. He showed me the plans a few years ago. I'm interested to see how it all came together."

He waved for her to lead him from the lounge to a small dining area that was likely used for intimate lunches. The gallery that overlooked the main door was above them. A row of tall windows afforded a view of the landscaped grounds.

"I didn't know you were interested in architecture." She watched him take in the elevator, set in a convenient location, but made unobtrusive by disguising it with the rise of the stairs. Why did a bit of small talk make her so nervous?

"I'm an architect."

"Really! What have you designed?"

"My chalet." He bypassed the entrance to the kitchen and opened a door to the patio, inviting her to exit ahead of him.

"You did well. I liked it." A wind had come up beneath the overcast skies, making her hug her arms and try to tuck her wayward hair behind her ears as they walked past flower pots that lined the covered pool.

He was looking sideways at her.

"I wasn't trying to escape because I didn't like the floor plan."

He rolled his eyes, which made her smile, but self-consciousness stuck like a burr, prickly and sharp. It was strange to be with him again, in person, alone, without nurses or valets hovering. With sexual awareness sizzling within her.

"I'm serious," she said, trying to hide her nervousness. "I know you don't need my approval, but I thought it felt cozy despite the open plan. You obviously placed the windows very carefully. Each view was a well-framed photograph of the natural world—what?" she demanded as his look grew penetrating. "I'm an artist. I notice when care has been taken for a particular effect. Don't you? Look at these stairs."

She waved at the way they curved down from the upper terrace.

"Most people see convenience, but the placement balances the turret on the other side, which is probably the master bedroom, situated to overlook—" She turned to look across the expanse of grounds, charmed as she noticed the brook and the wooden bridge. "Oh, that's lovely, isn't it?"

"He wanted to put the master bedroom on this end," Xavier said. "At the top of the stairs, closer to the pool. I suggested the turret and told him to curve the stairs."

She pivoted to face him, watching his gaze track the upper terrace, profile dark with critique, but also… envy?

"What else have you designed?"

"Nothing. My attention is needed elsewhere." He said it without emotion, but she felt the pang that he refused to betray.

"You're frustrated."

His lids came down so the heat of his gaze glowed fiercely behind the veil of his spiky lashes. "We're talking about that, are we?" His attention dropped to her mouth.

Suddenly they were poolside again. Such a hard streak of sexual heat shot through her, it physically stung from the base of her throat, behind her breastbone, sank like a hot coal in the pit of her belly and radiated warmth into the juncture of her thighs. Her heart took off at a gallop while birds took flight in her midsection.

"I meant as an artist!" She blushed, embarrassed at how quickly and blatantly she reacted to a simple look.

His mouth deepened at the corners. He pushed his hands into his pockets. "There are many ways to apply form and function to the role I occupy. I don't have to design something."

"It's not the same." She was still flustered, stewing in heat and being confused by it. "I told you about the time I was depressed? It was because the medication made it impossible for me to create. The need was there, but when I sat down to draw or sew, it was like sending a bucket into an empty well. I wasn't having panic attacks, but I didn't see any point in being alive if I couldn't..." She held up her hands.

"I'm not depressed."

"But you're denied."

"So what?"

"It's something you need."

"It's something I *want*. Desire can be ignored in favor of more important things."

"We're not talking about architecture, are we?" She let her hands fall and blinked, eyes watery from the wind. Or so she hoped he believed.

A long silence followed where only a distant wind chime rang.

"Are you really here because of optics?" It made her lungs feel heavy and raw.

He hissed out a long breath. "I came because I wanted to." He set his teeth after he said it, as though absorbing some inner thought that displeased him, then said in a voice rife with subdued turmoil, "But we don't get everything we want, *bella*. You know that as well as I do."

He wasn't mocking her. He was saying it with deep understanding of the things she would never have—a carefree childhood, another pregnancy. She choked up, wanting to ask if he had come because he'd wanted to be with her, but she was too scared of the answer.

So she only said, "Have you forgotten my name? You're calling me *bella*."

"It's not an endearment. It's who you are. It's what you are." The last bit sounded as though it came out against his will.

She wanted to believe him, but her misshapen heart was so very conscious of her flaws. Of the fact he had rebuffed her.

"I've never felt beautiful." She toed a pebble. "I was the messy one, always grass-stained and needing my hair combed. After my kidnapping, the press called

me 'the fat one,' because I comfort-ate. I starved my-self in retaliation and cut my own hair and looked like a Goth for years, dark circles under my eyes, makeup smudged and face pale from not sleeping properly. It took ages after I got my panic attacks under control to look as healthy and happy as my sister."

She squinted as she looked up, startled to find she had his full attention. That wasn't pity in his expres-sion, though. He was engrossed, which made a squig-gling sensation tremble in the pit of her stomach.

"You asked me that night in Paris, remember? You asked if I was as beautiful as my sister. I thought it was funny to say yes because I was impersonating her. The only time I feel beautiful is when I look like her." She knew better intellectually, but deep down, she still had a lot of demons.

"You were stunning when you were pregnant. You're beautiful now. When I saw your sister in Ber-lin, I thought she was beautiful because she looked like you."

She shook her head. "You didn't even know—"

"I *knew*. I could tell the second I saw her. I just didn't believe it. I thought—"

"What?" She held her breath, brimming with dread and hope, not sure what she wanted to hear.

He grimaced. "I thought I'd been a fool. That the way we'd reacted to each other had been a one-off thing."

She swallowed. "It wasn't?"

His gaze slammed into hers, pupils expanding the way a cat's dilated before it pounced. Lines of tension

pulled the rest of his face into the harsh countenance of a barely restrained barbarian. "Clearly."

She stood on a tipping point, vibrating under the strain, drawn, drawn, drawn. The pull in her chest was nearly irresistible. A prickling wash of sensations made her hyper aware of everything around her, the pale heat of the sun, the scent of the grass, the dampness in the air and, most especially, the way he was looking at her mouth. At the way such a tiny expression of interest from this man could send wildfire through her whole body.

She tore her gaze from his, seeing only a blur of green and blue.

"Please be careful, Xavier." She scraped at the hair tickling her cheek, shaken. "My self-esteem is full of holes. Don't give me hope if there is none."

"For what? You don't want to be married to me. You said so."

"I don't want to be married to a man who doesn't want me." She had to press her lips tight so they wouldn't tremble. Meeting his gaze was hard. She couldn't hide the struggle, the longing, that was eating her up. "If you do…"

"I don't *want* to want you," he ground out.

She jerked back as though he'd struck her. He winced.

"I mean I can't *afford* to want you. My father followed where sexual interest led. It was a disaster. I didn't expect this," he grated. "I wouldn't have come."

She breathed through each of the blows, eventually able to ask, "That's all you feel?" The question was too revealing. She regretted it, even before he answered.

He took a long time, then, "Don't hope, *bella*. You know my views on love."

His gentle reply broke her chest open, leaving her heart pulsing like an open wound. *This* was what she had been avoiding accepting. This was why she couldn't bear to look into her future. He was never going to love her.

Engulfed in agony right to the backs of her teeth, she nodded dumbly. "Will you listen for Tyrol when you go in? I want to see the bridge."

She didn't notice the hand he reached out as she walked away.

## CHAPTER TEN

HE HAD HURT HER. He hadn't wanted to. Cruel to be kind, he had thought, and he had regretted it immediately. What could he do, though? Admit that what he felt was not purely sexual. Even if he was capable of love, which he wasn't, they had no future. He couldn't lead her on.

He hated that he'd returned her to that stiff wariness, though. The woman who had texted without hesitation for the weeks they'd been apart suddenly had a full schedule and little to say. By the time they were at a dinner hosted by the bride's parents the next evening, the tension between them was palpable. Her family smiled around it.

Angelique hadn't arrived yet, Henri was there with his wife and twins along with her mother, and Trella spent most of the evening needling Ramon.

Xavier tried to intervene at one point. Ramon wasn't above getting personal in retaliation and neither was Trella. It was escalating, but the bride, Isidora, tugged him aside. She was a stunning woman with auburn hair and a smile that put anyone at ease.

"It's a rookie move to get involved. Better to ignore them. Trust me."

He waited until they had left to ask Trella, "Why were you being so contentious with Ramon?"

"I wasn't. That's how we communicate." The passing streetlights flicked over her stoic expression.

"I thought you might bring on an attack."

"No." She sounded petulant. "We fight like that all the time. It's fine."

"It wasn't because you're angry with me?"

Silence, then, "I'm not angry. I'm hurt."

He should have left it there, but said, "Either way, you should take it out on me, not him." *Punish me.* He couldn't stand the guilt he was carrying.

"I'd rather fight with Ramon." Her hands twisted in her lap. "I know he won't let me win. Any points I score, I've earned. It builds my confidence. And no matter what I say, he'll still love me. I don't have that kind of trust with you."

*Be careful what you wish for,* Xavier thought, flayed to the bone. He didn't speak of it again.

Trella was a dam filled to the brim, gates stuck. When Xavier bowed out of joining Ramon and his racing friends at a sports bar the next evening, the pressure inside her climbed a notch higher.

"The bar isn't Kasim's thing, either. I invited him to come over with Gili for the evening after they see Mama. Cinnia wants to give the girls a quiet night so she's staying in." Trella desperately needed time with her sister. "Do you mind?"

"You're not going clubbing with the bridal party? I'll stay with Tyrol."

"Isidora will have enough paparazzi as it is. If Gili and I went? We're doing her a favor staying away."

"I see. Of course. Invite them. That's fine." They were being exceedingly agreeable and polite since she'd admitted to her hurt feelings last night. It was horrible. She kept wondering how she would endure two more months of this. A lifetime, really. Would it be worse or better when they divorced and lived apart?

She was so caught up in her own turmoil, she completely forgot that Xavier had met Gili before. *Gili* hadn't, the darling. She rushed him when she arrived, taking both his hands to say beseechingly, "I'm so glad we have this chance to clear the air. I can't imagine what you thought of me in Berlin. You must have been so shocked. But I hope we can be friends because I already adore your son."

Her sister's warmth could melt glaciers and Xavier's expression eased in a blink. "It's already forgotten," he assured with his patented charm.

Trella felt a stab of jealousy. Why couldn't she win him over as easily?

Gili turned to her then, concern in her eyes, because of course she had picked up on Trella's distress. At the same time, something glowed from her like a beacon, a happiness so bright, it blinded.

*Oh, Gili.* Anytime Trella thought she couldn't survive whatever anguish was gripping her, her twin found a way to lift her out of it. Smiling tearily, she hugged her pregnant sister tight.

* * *

Xavier was glad to have an evening with the King of Zhamair. Asking Kasim about a complex situation in one of his neighboring countries was a welcome distraction from his struggle between duty and desire. Between wanting to mend fences with Trella and letting her bruised feelings keep her at a distance.

Thirty minutes in, he realized the women hadn't come back from fetching Tyrol. "Did we bore them? I'll find—"

"Please let them be," Kasim said. "She needs time with her sister."

"Which one?" Xavier asked dryly, hoping Trella wasn't shedding tears over him.

"A fair question." Kasim took up his drink. "Their interdependence takes getting used to, doesn't it? But this…" He chucked his chin toward the ceiling, where the women were likely in Trella's room. "She was bursting at the seams."

"Pregnant?" A surprise rush went through Xavier. He was astonished to realize he was pleased for the couple. Why? It had nothing to do with him.

Except that he knew how good it felt to have a child. It struck him then how important Tyrol had become to him. Not because he secured Elazar's future, but because Tyrol was… Tyrol. Not an insurance policy for the future, a relation.

Disconcerted, he had to clear sudden emotion from his throat as he rose to shake Kasim's hand. "Congratulations."

"Thank you." Kasim darkened with a flush of pride

and hitched his pants to sit again. "It's very early days, only confirmed the day before we left Zhamair. Not something we're making public."

Xavier fetched his own drink and offered to tap glasses, experiencing envy as he thought of Kasim sharing the moment of discovery and every single day of the pregnancy, along with the birth. Feeling robbed was not a new sensation for him. He got over it quickly, but he wondered if Kasim realized how lucky he was, able to go through this process as many times as his wife was up for.

He could, too, he supposed, with Patrizia.

His brandy tasted like snake venom. He abandoned it.

"I'd like you to consider something," Kasim said, sounding like someone unused to requesting favors. "Closer to the birth, I'd like Trella to come to Zhamair."

A strange void opened in Xavier. "We won't be married any longer." It took enormous effort to state that with equanimity. "Trella may go where she pleases." The knowledge knotted his gut.

Kasim's smile tightened. "I expect she'll want to bring Tyrol. I know Angelique will want to see him by then."

Which would require Xavier's permission. He instantly rejected the idea. He had sent Trella to Spain while he'd traveled Australia before he'd realized how unbearable it would be. The King of Zhamair was not plotting to steal his son, he was sure, but at least if Tyrol stayed in Elazar, he knew Trella would come back.

He looked away, disturbed by the dependence that train of thought suggested.

"It was very hard on Angelique to be apart from Trella when Tyrol was born." Kasim took a healthy sip of brandy, like he needed it, and hissed out his breath. "She fainted when Trella flatlined. Then your text came through and I realized why. She was hysterical until Trella was revived."

*So was I*, Xavier could have said, but they were already sharing far past his usual level. He loathed thinking about those long terrifying minutes. It put him in a cold sweat.

"I'll see what I can do," he said woodenly, mostly to end the discussion. Doing a favor for one of the most powerful men in the Middle East was a smart move, he reasoned, but was repelled by the idea of using his son for political gain.

*Duty*. It wasn't a double-edged sword. It was two branding irons pressing him front and back, pinning him in place, allowing no escape and only sinking deeper into his flesh when he tried.

Much later, when the couple had left, he was still thinking about where the line was drawn. Would his grandmother say Tyrol was doing *his* duty by going to Zhamair, cultivating warm relations with a foreign entity?

The poor boy didn't even know what he was in for. He lay unswaddled in Trella's lap, gaze wandering the ceiling, arms flailing and fingers catching in the curtains of her loose hair as she looked over him.

"Who gets another cousin?" she asked the boy with soft excitement.

Xavier sat with his feet propped on the ottoman. Her top afforded him a lovely view down her cleavage and her gentle laughter was as erotic as her tickling hair might feel, sweeping across his skin. It was sheer torture to sit here, wanting without having, but far too soon he wouldn't even have this much so he savored the pain.

"Did you know she was pregnant? Before she told you? Kasim made it sound like you have a supernatural link." He was skeptical, but Angelique had called her that time in the car, seeming to know Trella's panic attack was upon her.

"Was he worried I spied on them while they were making that baby?" She lifted her head, so stunning, with amusement curving her lips, that his heart lurched. "No, it's nothing like that. More an emotional thing." Her smile faded. "I should have realized how happy she was, but I've been distracted."

Pensive because of him. Upset. At least she was talking to him again.

"Do you feel it with your brothers?"

"They're too pigheaded, especially Ramon. Isn't he?" she said to Tyrol. "*Tío* Ramon is a *toro*." A bull.

"But you still love them." Xavier was beginning to see how love wasn't just a romantic notion, or even a desire, for her. It was as vital to her as oxygen. It drove the very blood in her veins.

"I love them very much," she agreed, sober and ultra-gentle as she kissed Tyrol's bare feet. "They got

me through my darkest times. I hung on because of them. Pushed through *for* them. Now I have Tyrol." She dipped to nuzzle his tummy, making his little arms jerk.

*You have me*, Xavier thought, but thorns had invaded his windpipe. He was starkly aware he couldn't pledge anything more than the pittance he'd already offered.

"You never wished for brothers or sisters?" Her head came up. "Your mother didn't have more children?"

"My father has a daughter. Maybe three or four years old by now? My mother has two boys. Teenagers, I think."

"You've never met them?"

"There's no place for them in my life." That's what he'd always thought, but he heard how cold it sounded, especially as she looked so askance.

"You could have made one."

"What would I have in common with them?"

"*Parents*?"

"They didn't act like parents." He shook the cubes of ice in his glass, wondering if he could judge when he'd barely grasped the ropes himself. "Neither were a great example of the importance of sibling relationships, either. I was young, but I picked up on jealousy and resentment between my mother and her sister. Because of her marriage into royalty, I suppose. And my father lost his brother."

"It wasn't his fault, was it?" She gathered Tyrol to her shoulder, tucking his blanket around him. "How old was he?"

"He was sixteen, his brother was eighteen. It was just a bad wind that came up while he was sailing. My father didn't talk about him often, but when he did…" Xavier swallowed, still affected by the memory of his father growing teary. "He missed him. Made me think I was better off without that kind of risk."

"But you'll give Tyrol a sibling."

"I have to." It was the stark truth, but again he heard how indifferent it made him sound when really his emotions on the matter were so tangled he couldn't even begin to name them.

Her brows pulled together and her mouth pouted. "I'll do it because I *want* to."

Without his need for biological children, many options were open to her, adoption among them. He suppressed a flinch, surprised how much it hurt to think of her starting a family with another man.

"You should," he made himself say. "You're a natural at motherhood. Family is clearly your source of strength."

She stared at him like he was a dog that had been hit on the highway.

"Are you going up?" he asked, trying to change the subject. "Leave him with me. I'll put him down when he falls asleep."

Her mouth twitched, but if she was surprised at his desire to hold his son, it was quickly blinked away. He let out a breath as she placed the boy's warm weight in his hands, relaxing as he embraced one of the few responsibilities he was pleased to have.

Trella hovered, watching Tyrol rub his fist against

his cheek, chasing it with his mouth. They shared a chuckle at his efforts, but Xavier's was bittersweet.

"My family was not yours, *bella*. The way you are with them is a foreign culture to me. I can't emulate something I never had. But I do want Tyrol to be happy. Happier than I was."

Her hand settled on his shoulder. It was unnerving not only because they hadn't touched since she'd been in the hospital, but because she gathered the torment rippling through him into a hot ball in the corner of his chest, so it pulsed under the feathery weight of her fingers. He held very still, as if her hand was a shy bird and he didn't want to startle her into flitting away.

"I know." Her thumb moved in a brief caress. "And I know you're starting to love him. I'm glad."

His heart swerved as her hand lifted and he watched her retreat.

Trella was trying hard to resign herself to Xavier's limitations. Gili had hugged her and wiped her tears and said, "Give it time." Things had been rough between her and Kasim before they'd married. *She* wasn't ready to give up on Trella finding happiness with Xavier, but that was Gili. She wanted to believe the best of everyone and everything.

Trella wasn't so sure, but she took heart from the way Tyrol had begun prying himself through Xavier's defenses. Xavier took every opportunity to hold his son. Not for optics. No one was seeing him walk down the hall in the middle of the night. He *wanted* to hold him. He expressed concern about a little spit-up, then

worried the damp patch would make Tyrol uncomfortable and changed him. He talked to his son about architecture, for heaven's sake, then broke off when he realized Trella was listening.

Still, when she had accused him of starting to love his son, she suspected he had been more surprised by his capacity to do so than she was.

And therein lay the problem. She had told him she didn't want to be married to a man who didn't want her. She had meant a man who didn't *love* her. If there was a chance he might develop feelings for her, surely she owed it to Tyrol to give their marriage a chance?

Or was that a foolish rationalization because she was smitten?

Either way, she had to keep the struggle off her face and smile for the wedding photos. Ramon and Isidora's marriage should be perfect, even if hers wasn't.

The ceremony was held in a five-hundred-year-old cathedral, conducted by an archbishop, witnessed by royalty, aristocrats, heads of state and celebrities from film, stage and the athletic arena. The route to the hotel, where the reception was held, had been blocked off and was lined ten-people deep with bystanders, photographers and even television cameras. Drones buzzed between the cars and a helicopter pattered overhead.

They hurried from the cavalcade up the red carpet, past the deafening cheer of the throng behind the velvet ropes, through the security checkpoint and into the relative peace of the ballroom where they finally caught their breath.

Mirrored tabletops reflected the lush floral arrangements of orchids and roses. Wisteria dripped from the
ceiling along with crystals that glinted like snowflakes.
A harpist's delicate notes welcomed them along with
uniformed staff carrying trays of gold-rimmed glasses
of champagne.

"That was insane," Xavier said, not dropping his
protective hold across her back.

"Small wonder I've never been on a date before, isn't
it? We're a nightmare to take anywhere."

Surprise loosened his clean-shaven jaw. "You never
dated? *At all?*"

"Well, there was this one stranger I met in Paris."
She gave him a cheeky wink and made a tiny adjust-
ment to his boutonniere. It was a delicate creation of
spotted feather and red-throated orchid with a lacy
fern frond behind it. She deliberately avoided looking
at the red sash that scored his chest, announcing his
station—the role that was more important than she
could ever hope to be.

"Seriously? I'm the only one?"

She shrugged. "One of Ramon's friends recovered
from a crash at Sus Brazos two years ago. I ate dinner with him by the pool a few times. We kissed once,
but it was…"

"What?" His fingers dug into her hip, something
flashing in his eyes as his expression grew unreadable.
She wouldn't let herself believe it was possessiveness.

"Nothing. Over before it started. Like you and me."
Affair, pregnancy, marriage. They were all slipping
like sand through her fingers, refusing to be slowed.

"But thank you for coming with me tonight. I should have said that before. I was dreading coming alone and having to dodge awkward questions about our marriage."

She made herself smile and meet his eyes as she started to step out of his embrace. His arm hardened.

"The things I'm still learning about you," he muttered. The fingers of his free hand looped around her wrist. He looked across the room, expression tight then came back, fierce and hot. "I hate this, *bella*. We had one damned night that was perfect. The only regret I had was that I didn't have more time to get to know you better and now we have time and we're wasting it."

Edginess came off him in waves, rattling whatever defenses she still managed to hold up against him. Her bottom lip grew wobbly and she had to tuck it between her teeth. "I thought you were just putting the time in, waiting for us to be over."

"No." He shook his head, voice deepening. "No, I'm… I'm trying to protect you."

"Oh, Xavier." She sighed. "I'm *tired* of being protected. That's why I slept with you. I wanted to feel what other people feel. The ones who aren't sitting in a vault waiting for their lives to start. I wanted to flirt. Feel pretty. Dance."

"Go on a date?"

"Yes."

His thumb stroked the thin skin inside her wrist. "This is a date."

*Not a real one*, she thought. People who went on dates were hopeful of a future. But beggars couldn't

be choosers. She forced herself to make a face of for-
bearance as she said, "It's not dinner and a movie, but
I suppose it will do."

His expression relaxed, lips twitching. "Too cliché.
I've brought you star gazing." He deliberately let his
attention scan the growing crowd of celebrities.

Relief as much as amusement sent laughter bursting out of her. She slid her arm around him, hugging
herself into him as lightness filled her. "If you promise to have me home by curfew, then yes, I would love
to be your date."

*Over before we started.*

These last few days had given Xavier an unprecedented glimpse into Trella's world. She was right. All
too soon they would be strangers again. He couldn't
countenance it. Like his last night of freedom in Paris,
he was compelled to grasp this chance with her.

Unlike Paris, he couldn't steal her away and it was
delicious torture standing beside her, setting a subtly
possessive touch upon her, but unable to do more. All
the while, he fell under her spell, as did everyone she
spoke to.

It was humbling, in a good way, to be with a woman
whose attention was as valuable as his own. Rather
than having to consciously include her in a conversation, they operated as a unit. One minute she introduced him to a family friend with a pedigree that
matched his own, the next he was catching up with a
diplomat he'd dealt with in the past whose wife was a
client at Maison des Jumeaux.

Then they were interrupted and she threw herself into a man's arms. "Sadiq!"

The man's wife, who happened to be Kasim's sister, Xavier learned, was clearly a close friend, too. They spoke with the couple for a long time, until Xavier couldn't wait to dance with Trella again.

"Explain to me exactly how he saved you?" He prompted when they were on the floor.

"Hacking." She glanced around as she said it. "We're not supposed to talk about it. He still does some high-level work on the side. He found out where I was being held and alerted the police."

"How old was he?"

"Fifteen. Crazy to think of, isn't it? He didn't know us very well, either, just had some classes with the boys. I think it was the challenge of it. He's stubborn that way. It definitely wasn't a desire to be a hero because you can see how self-effacing he is. But he wanted to help and persevered until he had something. Every time I see him, I'm reminded that he gave me this life and I should be grateful for it. Not waste it."

She met his eyes as she echoed what he had said earlier, but he read the deeper question in the longing look she gave him. They'd been engaging in subtle foreplay all night, not pawing each other, but neither shy about taking the other's hand or pressing close. He'd watched her nipples harden and heard her breath catch and felt the goosebumps that rose on her arms under the brush of his hand.

God knew he was aroused just by her nearness, never mind the scent that had hardwired itself into

him or the way watching her quick mouth as she talked and laughed made him want to kiss the hell out of her.

He touched her chin then couldn't resist letting the backs of his fingers slide down the heat of her soft throat. As he let two fingertips rest on her pulse, the one that confirmed she was alive when she might very well have been lost and he never would have known her at all, he wondered how the hell he was ever going to say no to her again.

# CHAPTER ELEVEN

TRELLA CHECKED ON Tyrol as soon as they arrived at the mansion. He was sleeping soundly, completely oblivious to the potential shift in his parents' relationship.

As she stood over him, she thought of all the reasons her marriage was impossible. Progeny, publicity, even Xavier's rejection of love over duty. His refusal to open himself *to* love.

She thought of all the ways she was broken, but miracles happened. This tiny boy, for instance. She owed it to him to try with his father, didn't she? Really try to reach his heart?

Was it a rationalization? Perhaps. She couldn't deny that lust was alive and well inside her, but so was something deeper and more nascent. She didn't want to believe it was love. Not yet. Not when she was about to risk rejection. Not when there was every chance she would have to spend her life yearning for a man who might very well be incapable of the emotion.

"How is he?" Xavier asked in a whisper, coming up behind her.

His need to see his son fed her hope that he was more than capable of deeper feelings.

"Perfect," she answered, watching his profile soften as he looked at Tyrol.

"He is," he agreed, turning up the flame of desire inside her.

She led him from the room, heart hammering, and went to his room, not her own.

*"Bella,"* he protested as he followed, but stayed in the open door, backlit by the light from over the stairs.

"Close the door, please."

He sucked in a long breath, like he needed it to face a Herculean task. "I can't. You know I can't."

"I don't want to make a fool of myself in front of the guard in the hall."

He pushed the door shut and leaned on it, breath hissing out. He was a dark shadow in the unlit room. She saw his fist close against the hardwood next to his thigh.

"Can you even make love?"

"As of midnight, yes," she said ruefully.

His head thumped back against the door. He swore. "You know this is impossible. You know—"

"I do." She went to him and picked up that rock hard fist, gently rubbing his fingers, trying to coax the tension from his hand. "But who else am I going to have sex with? Hmm? Who else do I trust with myself?"

"I still don't understand why you ever did."

She kissed his fingers. "Because no one else makes me feel like this." She set his open hand above her breast, where her heart raced. "If it's not the same for you—"

"It is, damn you." He hooked his hand behind her

neck and dragged her closer, voice growing hoarse. "No one else has *ever*—"

He covered her mouth with his, cutting off whatever he'd been about to say.

She didn't care. All she cared about was being up against his lean, powerful body, feeling him devour her mouth as though it was the only thing he would ever need. It was an onslaught, his hand shifting to her hair to drag her head back. His other arm crushed her into him while his lips ravaged and his tongue invaded.

Her heart knocked into her rib cage, sending sweet pulse beats through her arteries, weakening her limbs. She felt helpless, but not to him. To this yearning. Lethargy stole her strength when she longed to cling to him. All she could manage was to crush the edges of his jacket in her fists and moan into his mouth.

He made a jagged noise and dragged his teeth along her generous lower lip, tugging then releasing. "I'm being too rough."

"I need to know you feel the same. I want you so *bad*. You have no idea."

"I do." Another rough noise scraped from his throat. He dragged up the skirt of her gown, so when he picked her up as he pushed off the door, her legs were free to twine around his waist.

"But it's only lust, *bella*. Tell me you understand that."

She was on the verge of laughing, loving his easy strength. Her self-assurance slipped a notch, but she could feel him hard and straining between her legs. It

was too beguiling to ignore, making her tighten her arms and legs, trying to increase the pressure there. "Whatever it is, I need it."

He walked her unerringly to the bed and came down to settle his weight on her, mouth sealing to hers again. Writhing under him, she tried to touch all of him with her whole body, tried to drag his clothes out of the way while searching for hot naked skin.

"Slow down." He grabbed her hands and pinned them over her head, then dragged his mouth along her jaw, down her throat and bared her breast for his fierce gaze. "This will *not* end before it starts." He used his teeth on the swell of her breast, making her shudder. "I've fantasized about it too many times to rush now that I have you where I want you."

A surge of moisture hit her loins. "I think about us when I'm in the bath."

He lifted his head and with a hiss said, "You witch." He levered up and rolled her over, swept her hair out of the way then slowly tugged open the ties behind her neck. "Tell me exactly what you do when you're in the bath." He set kisses down her spine. "Be specific."

"I could show you." She lifted into his hardness.

He grasped her hip and met her pressure with thrusts of his own, breaths thick and animalistic as he ground his erection into her soft cheeks. Then he slid a hand under her bunched skirt and across her stomach, fingers delving beneath her silk panties as he settled on her again. "Keep moving," he said, gently sawing two fingertips between her damp lips, mouth

planting wet kisses on her nape. "Show me how much you want me."

She did. She rocked herself between his hand and his heavy hips until she was trembling with desire. She stopped, shaking with arousal. "I'm so close. I want to feel you inside me."

"Not yet." He shifted and settled his hand deeper, so his fingers slid inside her, so satisfying yet maddening. "Keep going."

Helpless to her own body, she did, until she was releasing broken cries, fists clenching the blankets, body clasping uncontrollably at his penetration, shivering and completely lost. Utterly his.

"So good," he said, licking between her shoulder blades, still mimicking lovemaking with light thrusts of his hips, drawing out her orgasm as he kept his hand in place. "I want you in a thousand ways. There will never be enough time for how much I want you."

And he called it *only lust*?

She pushed against the mattress, trying to twist beneath him. He withdrew his hand, but hooked his fingers in her panties and pulled them down and off, sitting up on the edge of the bed to throw them away, then he shrugged off his jacket and kicked off his shoes.

She knelt behind him and reached to work down the buttons of his shirt. He turned his head to catch at her mouth with his, easily distracting her. Their tongues met and the heat kept growing, not appeased in the least. She sobbed and he turned to scrape his hands down her shoulders, brushing her gown away so she knelt in a puddle of near-black velvet.

He stood then, chest expanding in deliberate breaths between the edges of his open shirt, as if he strained to keep control of himself. "Don't ever ask me again if you're beautiful. Know it, *bella*. You are the kind of beautiful that could topple a kingdom."

He reached out and wound her hair around his hand then bent to kiss her.

She tried to balance the bitter with sweetness in her own kiss, but her desire was too potent. It was all lust. He pulled back to yank his pants open then stripped, checking for a moment with one hand and reaching toward the night table.

"I can't get pregnant," she reminded.

He snorted and found a condom anyway, tearing it open with his teeth.

It shouldn't have made her want to cry, but it did.

*"Bella,"* he chided as he pressed her flat and used a knee to part her legs, "I'm protecting *you*."

It didn't feel like it. But when he stroked his tip against her, hot and beguiling, he seemed to send electric lines of pleasure radiating through her. She forgot to be outraged or hurt. She set her hands on either side of his head and kissed him. Extravagantly. Invitingly.

And when he sank into her, it was her turn to bite his lip and groan.

"I'm going to make it last," he said into her mouth. "All night."

"Yes, please…"


Mario met them as they entered the palace. He smiled benignly at Tyrol, who was fussy after the travel, and

said to Xavier, "The Queen expects you. She'd like to hear about Australia."

Completely attuned to her husband after their night of lovemaking, Trella felt his surreptitious sigh.

"Of course." He glanced at Trella from eyes bruised by their sleepless night. "Eat. Get some rest."

She nodded and followed his retreat with her gaze, feeling as though he took her heart and spun it out like twine behind him.

All of her felt undone and achy. They'd had one conversation in the dawn light, bodies still damp with exertion, while her nerve endings had still been singing with joy.

"You know this doesn't change what has to happen." His voice had been grave, his body steely against hers.

She had shifted her head on his shoulder. "I know. But I'm not sorry. Are you?"

"I'm trying to be."

She had turned her lips in to his throat and they had started all over again.

"Gerta can take the Prince up to the nursery, Ms. Sauveterre," Mario said as they arrived on the second floor.

*Signora Deunoro*, Trella longed to say, but it had been agreed from the outset that she would not change her name. After Tyrol's christening, she was to receive an honorific title of *Dama*, the lowest of Elazar's ranks. A future monarch could not have a parent who was common.

"I'll keep him. He's having an off day." And she was

feeling neglectful after leaving him in Gerta's care during the wedding last night. "You go settle in," she said, since Gerta hadn't actually seen where she would be living in the palace. "I'll bring him when he's ready for a long nap."

With a curtsy, Gerta followed Mario's direction to the nursery level while Trella turned toward the room she'd occupied before she'd gone into the hospital, the ones adjoined to Xavier's.

Mario cleared his throat. "You're in the dowager's wing now, Ms. Sauveterre."

*This doesn't change what has to happen.*

Speechless, composure fraying, she let Mario escort her across the gallery, through a pair of doors, down a long hall where paintings of Xavier's ancestors watched her progress in silent judgment, and through another set of doors.

The temperature grew cooler as they walked. Tyrol's fussy cries echoed off the high ceiling with the sounds of their footsteps. She didn't try to soothe him, just let him express exactly what she was feeling, and was viciously pleased to see Mario's obsequious expression grow more and more strained.

She understood that the dowager's wing had been deliberately placed to provide as much distance as possible between former queens and new ones. It wasn't a horrible place. It had been prepared for her occupancy with cheerful floral arrangements, a new sofa and her very own lady's maid, Adona, who was eager to prepare her some soup.

Mario offered a quick tour, pointing to a bright,

empty room as a potential studio, if she wanted to provide a list of items she would like placed there.

"A crib and a change table," Trella said, growing as fractious as her son. "Tyrol needs a nursery."

Mario tilted his head in a way that was unbearably condescending. "Royalty inhabits the royal wing."

"I see." She sat on the sofa and dug in her shoulder bag for the receiving blanket she carried. She shook it out with a snap then tucked a corner into her collar as she met Mario's gaze with a challenging one of her own. "And do I go on safari to the nursery to feed him? Or does he exercise his lungs through the palace every two hours as he is brought to me?"

Tyrol was showing off the growing strength of his lungs, recognizing the feeling of the soft flannel against his cheek as she draped it over him and growing frantic for her to open her buttons.

"It was understood the Prince was taking a bottle," Mario said, mouth pinched, gaze averting self-consciously while his whole face went red.

Oh, was he uncomfortable with her breastfeeding? What a shame.

"He'll *need* a bottle, won't he? Or he'll starve to death before we get to each other. Am I even allowed into the palace without an escort? He's *six weeks old*. Still a few days shy of his due date. He's not weaned and won't be for a *year*."

"As I see." Mario cleared his throat and turned to the door. "I'll leave you to it."

"Do."

*This doesn't change what has to happen.* Xavier

should have told her *this* was going to happen. How *dare* he use her up last night, thinking this would be okay.

Trella woke thick-headed from a heavy nap to hear Xavier's hushed voice, "Give him a bottle if he needs it." A door closed.

She jackknifed to sit up and shot a look to the travel cot she'd had Gerta bring down from the nursery. It was empty.

Sucking in enough breath for a scream, she leapt from the bed and stumbled into the lounge, wearing only the oversized T-shirt she'd thrown on for sleep. Xavier was there, but no one else. No Gerta, no Adona, no *Tyrol*.

"Oh, *hell* no," she informed and rushed after her son.

"Trella." He caught her arm and reaction kicked in. She used the momentum to round on him, heel of her hand aimed straight for his nose.

He deflected, tried to catch her into a hold, but she expertly twirled out and broke his grip, the movements ingrained in her muscles from years of practice. Knocking a lamp in his direction to force him to leap back, she backed up too, out of his reach, neatly balancing on the balls of her feet, breathing in hisses as she gauged the distance between him and the door and how she would take him out in order to get there.

"I didn't *know*," he growled, holding himself in ready stance. "*Calm down*."

"Bring him back." She reached for a slender vase

and flicked its three tall irises at his feet, spattering water on the bottoms of his pant legs, then tested the heft of the blown glass as a weapon.

"You're going back to the room you were in, next to mine. I sent him up because he needs a bath. I stayed to tell you that and keep you from throwing a righteous fit when you woke and saw he was gone. Calm the hell down."

"You should have told me last night this could happen. This, by the way, is how you put up a fight." She shook the vase at him, mocking his lame attempt to turn her away last night.

"This was always going to happen!" He pointed at the door. "If not today, soon enough. In a few weeks, you'll move out of the palace and he'll come and go between us. That is reality, Trella. I have damned well made that clear to you. More than once. *You* came to *my* room, last night, knowing that. Don't pretend this is news."

She threw the vase at the fireplace so it shattered and droplets of water made the dancing flames sputter and crackle. Then she stared at the destruction, chest heaving.

"Is this bringing on an attack?"

"Don't pretend you care if it does."

"I *care*," he bit out. "Why the hell do you think I'm here?" He looked positively tortured as the words escaped him. He wiped his expression away with a stroke of his hand, releasing a heavy sigh.

"I've just been raked over the coals for *one* photo." He held up his finger. "And because a debate has

sprung up online. Team Trella or Team Patrizia. My fault." He turned his hand to tattoo his chest with his finger. "I promised to undo all of that, as if it's even possible, and walked back to my room to learn you'd been sent here. Do you know how much furniture *I* wanted to break? Do you understand what I'm doing, taking you back there? It's pure weakness!"

No, it wasn't. That's not what caring was. He wasn't ready to hear or believe it, though, and she was too angry and hurt to explain it.

"Why does she hate me so much? Why—?"

He closed his eyes. "I keep trying to tell you. Emotion has nothing to do with it. It can't. That's the point."

"The crown is all that matters."

"Yes."

"I hate your crown! I hate that our son will be raised with this same hard-hearted attitude."

"Hate away. It changes nothing."

"And you want me to come to your rooms again, anyway."

"Yes."

"Even though it won't change anything, either."

"Yes."

Mouth trembling, she knew that, like him, she didn't have a choice. She would go with him and believe what she believed, that he would change, and one of them was going to lose.

She nodded jerkily, but before she could step forward, he leapt to meet her, not letting her walk through broken glass to get to him. Then he was cupping her cheek, tilting her lips up to the hungry weight of his

own. She moaned, knowing what that taste was now. That narcotic that filled her with hope when he kissed her. *Love.* She was madly, deeply, hopelessly in love with him.

# CHAPTER TWELVE

"You're neglecting your duties. The Australian agreements have completely fallen apart." His grandmother had called him on the carpet before he'd even digested his breakfast.

"Both parliaments have risen for the year. The committees adjourned," he said.

"Yet I am informed the deadline is the end of the year. If it's not finalized, we start over in the new year." She held out a missive.

He took it and quickly gathered how certain opportunistic corporations were manipulating the fine print, trying to push Elazar into a stress position and a renegotiation that would be advantageous to their own interests. She was right. He should have caught on when the meetings had begun experiencing delays two weeks ago.

"This is the first I'm hearing of this," he muttered.

"Because you've been distracted. Dating. *Shopping.*"

He gritted his teeth. Trella was preparing to move her design house's head office to Lirona. The fashion industry was waiting with baited breath for her to

purchase her property. Real estate and tourism would boom the minute the new fashion district was born. Squiring her to potential locations, ensuring the choice worked as well for Elazar as it did for her, fell right into Xavier's trade negotiation bailiwick.

His grandmother ought to be thanking Trella, but she only said, "Mario has set up an emergency meeting of the council. You're expected at ten o'clock. We cannot afford to lose this, Xavier."

*Duty.* It was killing him. Quite literally chipping away at his flesh. His belt had had to go in an extra notch and the scale had him four pounds under his usual weight. He had no appetite. Of course, he was on his wife like a stallion with a mare every chance he got. No wonder he was skin and bones.

Bristling with culpability, he returned to his apartment. He would have to hurry to make the meeting, but he was more aware of the clock ticking down on his marriage.

In a few days it would be Christmas, his one and only with his son's mother. Then their marriage would melt away like snow under rain. Gone, gone, gone.

He nodded at Vincente to leave his jacket on the bed and dismissed him, then he went through to Trella's room, where he slept every night with her naked body resting against his. They tried to keep a low profile but were fooling no one, except possibly themselves. Despite the intensity and excruciating pleasure and profound satisfaction they gave each other, they had to keep rising and moving apart.

Soon that would be permanent.

*Not yet.* His hand closed in a tense fist. He wasn't ready.

"I have to run to a meeting—" he began as he entered.

She sniffed and turned with surprise. She had showered while he'd been to see the Queen and wore only a slip. She was on the phone.

"*Esta bien, Mama. Te amo,*" she finished and signed off, then swiped her cheek.

His heart lurched. "What's wrong?"

"Nothing." She turned away for a tissue. "Ramon and Isidora arrived safely at Sus Brazos. Gili and Kasim will be there tomorrow."

And this was her first year apart from them. She was homesick. She didn't have to say it. He watched her wither daily, saying nothing because they both left many things unsaid, aware their days with each other were numbered. They didn't want to waste them with animosity and problems they couldn't solve.

Guilt assailed him, though. He was *stealing* time with her. Neglecting his duties while he neglected her needs. He pinched the bridge of his nose. "If you want to spend Christmas with them, you should."

"With Tyrol?" She brightened.

"*Bella.*" He hated saying no to her, but it echoed in his voice. "You're upset. You miss them." She was going to need them more than ever soon.

"I can't leave him! He's still feeding in the night. I would miss *him*." She waved in the direction of the nursery, where a nanny took him for a bath every morning while they ate breakfast and started their day.

She softened her tone, her expression so vulnerable she put an ache in his chest. "You could come."

*You're neglecting your duties.*

"No, I can't." This was it, he realized. The fracture that had begun working its way through him on their wedding day began to cleave open, tearing him apart. *But he had no choice.* "The Deunoros spend Christmas here."

"And I'm not a Deunoro. Why should he spend Christmas with her? She hasn't even looked at him since—"

"Leave it."

She buttoned her lip, but the glare she sent dropped the room temperature lower than it had been on the sleeting day of Tyrol's christening.

He couldn't let her bring it up because he was ashamed of his grandmother's behavior. Rather than the traditional pomp of open-topped carriages and a public stroll with the future monarch back to the palace, they'd all traveled by car. His grandmother had come in her own, arriving last and leaving first. Exactly one photo had been taken of Queen Julia standing with her grandson at her side and her great-grandson in his bassinet. Trella had been left out of the picture.

He closed his eyes, afraid he couldn't do this if he looked at her. His voice was hoarse with strain. "You should go see your family and come back to the new house."

He heard her breath suck in, sharp and mortal. "No, Xavier. Not yet."

"I was hoping we could get through Christmas, but we're only putting off the inevitable."

"What about…" Her voice faded. "What about a surrogate?" He had seen her afraid before, but not like this, with her throat exposed while she offered a knife.

He had to consciously remember to breathe. "It's not about another baby, *bella*."

His own composure threatened to crumble as her chin crinkled and her eyes filled. She caught her mouth into a line to hide its tremble, then that glorious Valkyrie in her came forward, steeling her spine and refusing to be cowed.

"I'm not leaving Tyrol. I'll move into your stupid ugly house if you make me, but I'm taking him with me."

That stung more than it should. He hadn't been able to design a home from greenfield for her, which felt like a breach of duty in itself, but he'd personally overseen all the renovations and security upgrades to the one he'd bought. He'd taken the utmost care with every detail.

"Don't make this ugly. The agreement is three and a half days each." That was not renegotiable.

"You're *busy*. Why should someone else feed him a bottle when he could be with me?" Oh, she was fierce when she wanted to be. Flushed, with her eyes glimmering, she threw the forces of nature at him. "At least I *love* him."

"So do I!" It exploded out of him. Within him. *Nothing* would come between him and his son.

She threw her head back, fury fading into sorrow. "But you don't love me. I can live somewhere else."

He jerked his head to the side, slapped by the torment in her voice.

"Say it," she choked. "Tell me these last weeks of…" She waved at the bed where they had writhed with passion. "I have tried *so hard* to show you we could make this work. Every breath I take is carefully measured to make sure I don't impinge on your role in any way. I should bite my tongue right now. You have a meeting to get to, right? I give and give and you can't offer me a crumb? A maybe? A *chance*?"

"You think I like seeing you holding back, afraid to laugh too loud, keeping to these rooms when you should be able to say and do whatever the hell you please? I hate what I'm doing to you. You never wanted this."

"But if you *loved* me—"

"I *can't* love you! I've upended my world as far as I can. Things are tipping off. *This has to end.*"

She rocked as if buffeted by a hurricane wind. He watched her lips go white with the rest of her. Her fingers twitched at her sides and she swayed again then locked her knees.

*"Bella."* He reached out, feeling the chasm in him widen to a canyon, pushing her further and further beyond him.

She drew a jagged breath and leveled her shoulders. "You should go. I don't want to be blamed for you missing your meeting."

Had that really happened?

One minute she had been feeling sorry for herself

over her siblings getting together without her, the next
her tiny nascent family of three had been torn down
to one and a half.

How had she not fought hard enough? Aside from
viewing a few buildings for Maison des Jumeaux, she
had lived as a shut-in again, not wanting to make headlines. As painful as she'd found it when he disappeared
for a few days on palace business, she had never once
complained. Even his grandmother's frosty behavior
at the christening had gone unremarked until today.

All the while, she'd been aware of the days lifting off the calendar like ravens, one by one, swooping
away and forming a black, jeering cloud on the horizon. They'd mocked her for loving him despite his lack
of commitment. For waiting so patiently for words of
love that were never going to come.

Did she regret trying to make their marriage work?
No. But failing despite leaving her heart wide open
was liable to kill her.

Shaking, she pressed a fresh tissue to her closed
eyes, soaking up the leak through her lashes, taking a
slow breath and consciously softening her shoulders.

*Uno naranjo, dos naranjos...*

It struck her what she was doing. *Oh, no.*

She pressed the tissue harder into her eyes, becoming aware of the sensations pinging to life in her. A
roiling stomach, a creep of foreboding down her spine.
Cold specters began to float in her periphery, voicing
the ugliest of thoughts. *Why would he want you? You're
the broken one. You're soiled.*

"No," she whispered, certain that being susceptible

to these attacks *proved* how unworthy she was of love. Was that the ghouls talking? Or the unvarnished truth?

"*Dama*?" Her maid knocked, making her heart leap. Adona entered. "The Private Secretary is here. Her Majesty wishes to see you."

*Not now.* She couldn't. Not with a spell coming on. All of her went rigid while her blood moved like acid in her arteries.

Why did the Queen even want to see her? Her mind raced, trying to think of an excuse, but what could she say?

"Please give me a moment to dress." *Uno naranjo, dos naranjos...*

She chose the dress she'd worn to the christening, since its red and gold were Elazar's national colors and quietly proclaimed her station as the mother of a future monarch. Adona gave her hair a twist while Trella dabbed on light makeup, even though it didn't matter if she put on clown pants or a G-string with water wings. She was going to the guillotine.

As if that were true, the flutters deep in the pit of her belly grew worse. Mario's dour face made his silent escort that much more ominous. Her feet felt like they didn't belong to her. She couldn't make her throat swallow.

The ghouls chuckled as they stuck to her clammy skin, following her into a stately room of powder blue and white striped wallpaper.

The Queen wore a dark green sweater set and a severe expression. She was seated and Trella was not invited to do so.

Trella ordered her fists to loosen and clasped them in front of her. She took measured breaths, nodded in greeting as the door behind her closed, shutting her in with what she had long suspected was an enemy.

"I'm a woman of well-cultivated patience, but mine has run out," Queen Julia stated. "It would benefit all if you went to Spain for Christmas and did not come back."

Her nails dug into her palm beneath the cover of her other hand. "Xavier suggested the same thing."

Surprise flickered in the Queen's face before she blinked it away. She nodded. "Good. He's finally showing sense."

"I said I'd go if Tyrol came with me." She wanted that so badly, she would buckle into the carpet if the Queen agreed.

The older woman hardened before Trella's eyes. "*No*. But allow me to lend my voice to my grandson's. You do more damage than good by lingering."

The words hit so hard, Trella had to press into her toes to stay on her feet. Still, her inherent streak of bellicosity reared its head. Another woman would have taken this chance to make a good impression and reason with the woman. She wouldn't pour gasoline over the one bridge open to her and light a match.

"Is that what you said to *his* mother when you exiled her?"

The Queen's eyes were so much like Xavier's, it was sheer agony to look into the contempt they held.

"I was told you have a predilection for dramatics." She was like a cat that knew its prey's weakest spots,

but took her time piercing them, preferring to terrorize before putting a creature out of its misery. "Xavier's mother has always had access to him. He chose not to pursue a deeper relationship."

"Because you didn't approve of one. Did you? And he couldn't afford to alienate you. He didn't have anyone left." She showed the Queen how she had won more staring contests than she'd lost.

After a moment, the Queen reached very casually to polish her glasses, then perched them back on her nose. "*My* relationship with my grandson is not up for discussion. But if he's asked you to leave, yours with him is clearly over."

*Breathe. Uno naranjo, dos naranjos...*

"Xavier has been conditioned to believe that people who love him leave and don't come back. I plan to show him that's not true." Would it work? She couldn't think about that right now.

"What he *knows* is that a country can't maintain stability when it's ruled by emotion. Scandal and division among its people are poison. How can he be regarded as a man of integrity when he's with a woman who is nothing but racy headlines?"

"I can't control my headlines!"

"No. You can't. That's why removing yourself is the least you can do. If you care anything for him and your son, protect them."

Score one for the Queen. She knew it, too. She didn't move, but her verbal rapier kept whipping the air, cutting into Trella with casual ease as she spoke again.

"You have no idea the strength required to hold this

position. Your weaknesses would become theirs, undermining what has taken five hundred years to build."

"Loving is a weakness?" Where had she heard that before?

The Queen narrowed her eyes. "Your background, your extensive need for therapy and your delicate mental state are weaknesses."

It was as if she saw into Trella's soul where the specters were swirling and cackling, dragging icy fingers over her bones. *She sees you. She knows.*

"The toll of the throne would break someone like you. This is a marathon that lasts a lifetime. What are you going to do when it becomes too much? Retire behind closed doors and burden the palace with making explanations? If that's to be the end result, do it now. Fade into the background before you do any more damage."

"Someone like me," she repeated darkly.

*They won't come for you. They won't want you after this.* It was the oldest, darkest, ugliest voice. The one that made her eyes sting and her heart shrink.

She hadn't come back to her family in pieces because she had passively accepted her situation, though. She had fought with every ounce of will she possessed, from the first moment through all the other struggles to today.

"You know *nothing* about me and what I can endure. Do not confuse my capacity for love as an inability to stand and fight. In fact, love is my *weapon*. You want to go to war with me? Gird your loins. You might rule this country, but I rule the online world. I'm beloved by

*billions*. You want to protect what's taken five hundred years to build? I belong to something that's lasted millennia. *Family*. When you die, do you think *duty* will squeeze a single tear from Xavier's eye?"

The Queen went white. "You're becoming hysterical."

"You unleashed this!" She stabbed the air between them. "Love is the only thing that pulls us through hardship. *I know that*. And your tepid love isn't enough to sustain him. Yes, you love him in your stunted way, but you're afraid to show it. Why? Because you might have to deal with grief again? Is that why you don't even look at Tyrol? You're afraid he'll die and you don't want to be attached? Now who's weak?"

Queen Julia gave her bell a resounding shake.

"What's wrong? This is what someone looks like when they're fighting for the people they love. Still think I'm not tough enough for the job?"

"*Get out*."

"Ms. Sauveterre!" Mario entered. "Please."

She shot him a bitter look on her way past him then ran blindly to her room.

Voices were droning around him, but Xavier wasn't tracking. He was lost in a fog he hadn't experienced since childhood. Twice. The miasma was cold and gray and left him rudderless. His grandmother had been there to lead him along those other two times, but she was the last person he wanted to turn to right now.

Not because he blamed her. No, he blamed himself.

All he could hear was Trella saying, *If you loved me.*

He had said he couldn't love her as if he didn't have the capacity. For a long time, he had believed he didn't. The love he'd once felt for his parents had stagnated under their leaving, stunting him into an inability to feel anything beyond superficial liking.

And yes, Trella had been a distraction lately as they had tried to cram a lifetime into the short marriage they had agreed to, but the fact that their time was finite had put that pressure on them. Hell, he'd called it off and he was still distracted.

*I can live somewhere else.*

The doom he'd felt at that statement couldn't be measured. He tried to picture Patrizia in the room where he'd held Trella and bile rose to the back of his throat.

No, the real problem was that he was afraid to *admit* he loved her. Otherwise, he might feel like this when their marriage ended. But he did feel like this now, which must mean—

"You agree, Your Highness?"

"Pardon?" He sucked in a deep breath, like he was coming out of a coma. What the hell had he done?

"We were discussing where the tax rate should break."

He shook his head, taking in the dozen people slouched over a boardroom table, surrounded by laptops and scratch pads and coffee cups while snow fell beyond the windows.

"Get the Australians on the phone. We'll request an extension into January. We'd rather be with our families through Christmas and I'm sure their people would, too."

*Screw duty.* He had to fix things with the woman he loved.

He rose just as his PA slipped into the room and hurried across with a message that Angelique was trying to reach him.

Frowning, Xavier excused himself and turned on his phone. It lit up with missed calls and texts.

What happened?
Where is she?
Are you with her?

His heart lurched. He hit reply on a video call, moving farther down the hall to an alcove where he had some privacy.

Angelique appeared, her pinched expression deeply anxious. "Are you with her? She keeps texting that she's fine, but she's not fine. I can tell."

"I'm not with her—"

"Damn it, Xavier, you can't leave her alone when she's having an attack!"

Her tone made Xavier's scalp prickle. He only half-believed in the twin connection, but her alarm was genuine enough that he looked for his PA to signal for his car.

"Is there someone who could check on her and get back to us?" Kasim asked.

"She's really scared, Xavier." Angelique sounded half-hysterical herself.

"I'll try her right now. But if you two feed off each other's mood, you should try dialing back your worry

and send her some calming thoughts." It came off the top of his head out of frustration and sounded too metaphysical.

Her wet face went blank with surprise. "I honestly never thought of that. God, I'm such an idiot. Of course. I'll text her that I love her."

His conscience twisted as he thought of his own refusal to say those words this morning. He ended the call and tried Trella. She declined to answer, but texted a moment later to say she was napping.

"Everything all right, sir?" his PA approached to ask.

Xavier held up a staying hand as he reached Vincente. "Have you seen Trella today?"

A brief hesitation, then, "Adona said she locked herself in her room after her audience with the Queen."

"She spoke with my grandmother? The car," Xavier snapped at his PA. "Now."

# CHAPTER THIRTEEN

SHE WAS DOING this for Tyrol, she kept telling herself, as she bit down on one of his teethers and counted her oranges. Some women went through the pains of childbirth. Her lot was to weather waves of terror. The irrational, fearful thoughts would pass. The sweating and sobs of insecurity needed to run their course. She just had to breathe and count her oranges and wait it out.

It was easier when someone she loved and trusted sat with her and told her she was safe. She didn't feel safe right now. She felt very temporary and unwanted. Abandoned. Forsaken.

"Shh," she breathed, pushing those thoughts away. *I am strong. I am loved. I can do this.*

She should have brought her phone in here. All the texting had been breaking her concentration. She had left it on the night table, but now she wished she was reading Gili's comforting words. It was almost as good as having her here.

"Trella!"

Oh, God. What was he doing here? She had locked

up and told Adona not to let anyone in. Now he would see her like this and know how cracked she really was.

His footsteps crossed into her bathroom. There was a systematic banging noise. He was opening all the cupboards beneath the dual sinks, looking for her.

"You're sure she didn't leave?"

He had someone with him? And someone who saw him searching cupboards for her? She pulled her feet in tighter, driving the curve of her spine into the wall behind her.

The closet light flicked on, blindingly bright even against her clenched eyes. She made a noise of protest and ducked her head.

"Are you here?" he demanded.

She plucked the teether from her bite. "I don't want you to see me like this."

"Get out and lock the doors."

"Yes, sir." It was Adona and a moment later, a distant noise of a door closing sounded.

Xavier came to the back of the closet and swept aside the gowns. He swore when he found her huddled in the corner on the floor. He crouched and wiped her wet cheek with his hand, drying it on his thigh. "Why didn't you call me?"

"I have to do this alone."

"No, you don't," he said grimly and started to gather her.

"Don't." She pressed as hard as she could into the corner, holding him off with one shaking arm.

"What did she say to you?"

She didn't know if her mental state made him sound that lethal, or if he really was murderous.

"Nothing I don't say to myself." She clenched her eyes in anguish. "I am a detriment. A hindrance. You shouldn't be here. What are you going to do? Run out of every high-level meeting because I'm having an episode? This can't happen. You can't be here. I *have* to do this *alone*."

"Look at me," he said gently.

"No, *you* look at *me*. Is this a queen? It's *not*. I pretended for a while that we could find a way and you followed me through the looking glass because duty chafes and the sex is great, but we knew it couldn't last. You were right, Xavier. This was always going to happen. *This*—" she pointed at her position on the floor "—will happen when I can least afford it. I wish I wasn't this person, but I am. And if you stay in here and nurse me through this, you're only proving that I'm a burden. *I have to do this alone.* I'm an adult who will be a single mother. *I* have to know I can do it."

The mention of living alone sent a tumble of unvoiced fears through her head. Intruders. Kidnappers. A million bad, horrible, terrifying things.

*"Bella,"* he said gently. "I want to talk to you about that. Come on. Come out of here."

*"No."* She slapped at his reaching hands and said very clearly, "There is no way. None. Just—go look after Tyrol. Please? I can't look after him when I'm like this. If you want to help me, go do that. Please?"

He stared at her, jaw clenched. "I'll bring him to you. Will that help?"

"I can't use him as a crutch. It would turn into me using him all the rest of my life. I won't put that on him. But I'll feel better if I know you're looking after him. Please?" She clutched his wrist. "Will you do that for me?"

"Trella—"

"I'm begging you, Xavier. *Please*."

He left her in the closet like a child hiding from monsters, hating himself for abandoning her, but she'd knocked the wind out of him. Blind shock held him in stasis for long minutes outside her door.

She thought her attack made her unfit to be his wife?

This was his fault. Not just her breakdown, but her belief that she had to be perfect to be his queen. She was already perfect in the way of fierce storms and jagged mountains and a flower blooming on a broken stem. Her perfection was in her resilience. That's what was needed in his partner. He loved her for her strength and her ferocious capacity to love and her ability to move forward despite how many times she'd been knocked down.

With her emotional bravery top of mind, he strode to the nursery where Tyrol had just woken.

"I was about to bring him down for a feed—"

"Warm a bottle. I'll take him." He carried his son through the palace, pushing into his grandmother's parlor where she was meeting with Mario.

"Out," he said to Mario, and gave the door a light kick behind the man.

"Your meeting?" his grandmother prompted.

"My wife was indisposed. Someone upset her. I had to care for our son."

"We pay staff to care for him."

"He shouldn't need his parents because you and I didn't? We'll never know, will we?" He set Tyrol in her arms.

"What—"

"Hold him. Feed him."

"What do you think you're proving?" She lifted her brows and calmly silenced the boy with the nipple.

"What are *you* trying to prove? Look at your great-grandson. Can you honestly say you feel nothing toward him? Because that's certainly how you act."

She looked at the boy. His hand found her thumb and gripped it. A dribble of milk leaked from the corner of his mouth and his eyes were focused on her.

A flinch of anguish crossed her expression before her mouth softened in tenderness. "He looks like your father. Let's hope he doesn't have his temperament. Your father wasn't cut out for the crown. I let him go because I had to, Xavier." Her head came up, blue eyes clouded with sorrow and a pleading for forgiveness. "He wasn't his brother. He wasn't you. He was never going to survive the demands. I let him go and yes, you suffered, but I had already lost both my sons. I couldn't let you go, too."

It was the most sentimental thing he'd ever heard her say. Shaken, he lowered to sit across from her. "I'm a parent now. I do understand," he said at length. "I

can't stomach the idea of his being across the city three and a half days a week, let alone not in my life at all."

"You shouldn't have agreed to share him."

"I intend to renege."

Her head came up, surprise in her lined face.

"They're both staying with me. I'm not asking you. I'm telling. If that means you stay on the throne the rest of your natural life, so be it."

"So she's won you over." She sniffed her disdain.

"No, it's up to me to win her."

Her gaze came up again.

"If I can't give the woman I love what she needs, how the hell can I give our country what it needs? She makes me whole. Stronger. I want to be a better man *for her*. That can only make me a better leader. A better king."

Tyrol finished his bottle. She set it aside and brought him to her shoulder to rub his back, exactly as if she'd been mothering infants all these years.

"After the risks she took bringing him into this world, how can you not want to know her? If you knew the things she's been through…" It was killing him, what she was enduring right now, but she seemed to need to prove something to herself and he had to give her that. "She's stronger and more determined than either of us can conceive."

"Her reputation, Xavier. Patrizia is such a good fit."

"I don't love Patrizia. I love Trella." It was conviction. Will. Fate. But he couldn't help pointing out, "So does everyone else, judging by the online polls. She's the more popular choice by a long shot."

"Don't be vulgar," she said crossly. "What about another baby?"

"We'll find a way. I am going to find a way to make it work. I have to. I can't live without her."

She let out a sigh of defeat. "Some monarchs would rather die than watch the next generation struggle to master the art of ruling. I've always thought I could give up the throne to you quite confidently. You rarely make mistakes. I will trust your judgment holds true in this instance."

He didn't need her approval, but he was glad to have it. Now he only had to convince Trella to stay.

Trella woke to bright light beyond the cracks in her blinds. She squinted gritty eyes at her clock. It was late morning. She had pumped milk a few hours ago when her swollen breasts had woken her, so she wasn't too uncomfortable, but she missed Tyrol enough that her chest hurt just thinking about him. She texted the nursery, then glanced at herself in the bathroom mirror, cringing.

She had done it. She splashed her face, brushed her teeth, then texted her sister.

It's over. I'm okay.

She earned a heart emoji in response.

The residual depression of an attack hovered like a cloud, though, along with profound loss as she accepted she and Xavier would never be. It had been a serious trip to hell and back, but she was *back*. That

was something, she reassured herself. She had proved
to herself she could not only grit her way through an
episode, but that it wouldn't actually kill her.

Where was Tyrol? She checked her phone and saw
Gerta had replied.

The Prince is with the Prince.

Xavier had had more meetings today. Was Tyrol
sick?

She tugged a robe over her nightgown and yanked
open her door—to find Xavier slouched in an armchair,
clothes rumpled, eyelids heavy. Tyrol was fast asleep
on his shoulder. It was such a tender scene, it pushed
tears into the backs of her eyes.

"Is he okay?" She gently gathered the sleeping baby
into her arms.

"Missing you, but otherwise fine. He just ate. That's
purely for show," he added as Tyrol began to stir and
fuss at the sound of her voice.

She sat to feed him, but Xavier was right. Tyrol nodded off before he'd taken more than a few gulps and
she cuddled him instead. Oh, he smelled good and his
skin was so soft. His hair was fine against her lips and
his grip on her finger, endearing.

*I'll always come back to you, my sweet, sweet boy.*
She had thought about him a lot last night. She had
thought about Xavier and how delusional she had been,
ever thinking she could be his queen when she had this
awful shortcoming.

Fresh agony washed over her.

When she couldn't avoid it any longer, she looked at where Xavier hadn't moved.

"Was it a rough night?" she asked.

"For him? Not particularly. For me? Yes."

With a lurch in her heart, she noticed the glass on the table beside him. "Are you hungover?"

"No. I poured it, then thought I'd prefer to be sober if you decided you needed me."

"Were you worried? I'm sorry."

He snorted and reached for the glass. "Now, she's sorry." He made a face at his first sip and clunked the glass back onto the table. "Mostly water now. How was your night?"

"Awful."

He nodded in grim agreement.

"Why are you angry? Xavier—"

"I'm not angry." He shot to his feet, though, and paced a few steps only to turn back abruptly. "I am angry. I respected your wishes because fine, I accept that you had to feel you could get through an attack alone. But I have issues, too. *Because* of you. You ignored my texts for months before you admitted you were pregnant. Then you locked me out of a delivery room while you *flatlined*. We've been apart more than we've been together. You damned well need to stay accessible to me. I need to know you're alive, even if you're not at your best."

That was the problem. Sometimes she was at her absolute *worst*.

And she really wasn't up for a scolding over it. Or facing how she was supposed to be accessible from

across the city. Much as she had given his grandmother a show of bravado, that's all it had been. She couldn't be his wife. She knew that now and it hurt so badly; she had to escape to hide how anguished she was.

"I want to shower. Can you take him and order breakfast?"

He said nothing as she handed him Tyrol again.

Swallowing, heavy with a melancholy that would never lift, she went back to her room and started the shower, blinking hot eyes as she did. She wasn't ready. If she hadn't had that stupid attack, if they hadn't had that big fight yesterday, they could still play alternate universe a few more days. Why had she shortchanged them like that?

She stepped under the spray and turned to see Xavier had come in behind her.

"Where's Tyrol?"

"Nursery." He peeled off his clothes, dropping them to the floor as the glass walls gathered steam.

"What are you doing?"

"What does it look like?" He opened the door and came in, crowding beneath the head that rained from the ceiling.

They'd showered together before, daily, but that was *before*.

"Xavier, I can't." Her heart was too tender, still pulling at all its old fractured lines and itching from fresh stitches.

"What did I just say about locking me out?" He cupped her wet head and planted a single kiss on her mouth, hot and possessive. Oddly tender.

She moaned and ducked her face as soon as he let her, tucking her forehead into his collarbone. Her vision filled with the golden skin she loved, taut and smooth over hard muscles. He was growing aroused, which always excited her.

"You know we're just putting off the inevitable. You were right all along," she muttered.

"You're staying here. We're staying married."

For a couple of heartbeats, she thought she'd imagined it, then she jerked back her head and looked at his implacable expression. The wetness in her clenched eyes wasn't from the water raining on her face.

"The future king decrees it? We both know I'm not a suitable queen."

"You are."

"You saw me last night!"

"And I see you this morning, having survived it. That's who and what you are, *bella*. You survive. You push through hardship to come out the other side, bruised maybe, but you make it. You don't give up on yourself, you would never give up on Tyrol and I won't let you give up on us."

Her mouth trembled. "If you loved me—"

He made a noise of imprecation. "If? *If*?" His hands cupped her face again. "You put a spell on me the first time we met. You gave me a son and helped me kickstart my heart so I could give him the love he deserves. Of course I love you, you infernal woman. How the hell else are we here?"

"You don't have to yell about it. What about Patrizia?"

"Are you seriously worried about a woman you have never met? You've ruined her life, *bella*. Just as you have ruined mine. But you won't feel bad about it because you've saved us both from a terrible mistake."

"Tyrol did. Lay the blame where it belongs."

"I thought I just did. God, I love you." He kissed her and this time he meant it, fusing his mouth to hers and letting her taste his desperation.

She grasped his wrists and pulled away, gasping, trying to speak from soul to soul. "Do you mean it? Because I don't think you understand how much it means to me that you can accept me, with all my breaks and imperfections. Don't say it unless it's true."

"You are flawed. You're unpredictable and defiant and shameless. You're also brave and creative and you love with everything in you. If you can rise out of your past and risk your heart, what kind of coward would I be if I refused to do the same? I'm privileged to be one of the people you love, Trella. I know what an exclusive club it is."

They kissed again and this time they didn't stop. The water rained down, washing away any ghosts that lingered, leaving only the love they had for each other.

Her body melted against his and she found herself pressed into the wall by his flexing muscles.

"Mine," he growled, kissing and licking at her neck and shoulders, across her breasts then between them. "There is no more locking yourself away. Understand? Not from me." The kisses continued, down her arms, across her hips.

She needed this doting attention. This all-consuming passion from him. It soothed and healed and made her feel cherished. By the time he knelt and hitched her thigh onto his shoulder, she was nearly weeping at the sweetness of him pouring such love all over her.

Her stomach jumped in reaction at the way he claimed her. He pleasured her until she was delirious, crying out with abandon. Then he stood and took her where she was, against the hard tiles, naked and slick as he drove into her, hard and deep. It was lust and bonding and naked unabashed love. When the climax came, they were in it together, trying to meld their slippery bodies into one being so they could never be separated again.

Then they leaned there, panting and wrung out, the water cooling, barely able to find the strength to get to the bed. They fell asleep in each other's arms, waking to make love again without the frantic pace driving them.

"We have time, *bella*. All our lives," he murmured, rocking lazily within her.

She released a shaken sigh, combing her fingers through his hair and was astonished at the lightness in her. The breadth of view. Years and years to come of this.

"I love you. You're the only man who could have given me this."

"You're the only woman I want or need. The only woman I could love so much."

Later that evening, he placed his rings on her finger as they dressed for dinner. The Queen wasn't one

for making apologies, either, but she invited them to dine with her and suggested Xavier take his son and wife to Spain the day after Christmas if it was something Trella wanted.

It was, he did and it was wonderful.

# EPILOGUE

*Press release five years later...*

*Inconceivable Twins!*

The Deunoro Palace surprised the world today by announcing that King Xavier and Queen Trella are celebrating the arrival of their daughter, Vivien.

Queen Trella's sister, Queen Angelique of Zhamair, also celebrates with her husband King Kasim the arrival of their third child, and first daughter, Genevieve.

While it was widely reported that Queen Angelique was carrying twins, it has now been revealed that, with the help of the world-renowned fertility clinic in Lirona, Queen Angelique was implanted with one egg from each set of parents.

Mother and babies are in excellent health.

The Queens' brothers, Henri and Ramon Sau-

veterre, were on hand with their own growing families to welcome this latest and most unusual pair of Sauveterre twins.

* * * * *

*If you enjoyed*
*PRINCE'S SON OF SCANDAL*
*why not explore the first three parts of*
*Dani Collins's*
THE SAUVETERRE SIBLINGS *quartet?*

*PURSUED BY THE DESERT PRINCE*
*HIS MISTRESS WITH TWO SECRETS*
*BOUND BY THE MILLIONAIRE'S RING*

*Available now!*